Craving Candy

Rü Finley

Book Cover by Rii Finley
Illustrations by Rii Finley
Proofreading by Stephanie Morales
1st edition 2025

If only the tentacle toy I dreamed up for *that* scene actually existed...

Content Warnings

While the love in this book is not dark, the story contains several dark topics. Please check your triggers prior to reading. In this novel you will find:

Strong language
On-page explicit consensual sex
Talks of drug/alcohol abuse
Brief other woman drama
Implied cheating
Death of a family member
Health crises
Unplanned pregnancy
Discussion of sick animals
BDSM and kinks including:
    Bondage
    Edging
    Degradation
    Dom/Sub dynamics
    Exhibitionism

Playlist

Scan me on Spotify

Lose my Breath – Stray Kids, Charlie Puth
Sweet Caroline – Neil Diamond
Hey Jude – The Beatles
Let it Be – The Beatles
Candy – Doja Cat
Juicy – Doja Cat, Tyga
Too Sweet – Hozier
Heaven – Julia Michaels
My Girl – The Temptations
Iris – The Goo Goo Dolls
Hooked on a Feeling – Blue Swede, Björn Skifs
Waiting for a Girl Like You – Foreigner
Dangerous Woman – Ariana Grande
Drivers License – Olivia Rodrigo

Can't Fight This Feeling – REO Speedwagon
Dangerous – Sleep Token
S&M – Rihanna
Wrecking Ball – Miley Cyrus
Love Story (Taylor's Version) – Taylor Swift
I Don't Want to Miss a Thing – Aerosmith
Brown Eyed Girl – Van Morrison
Faithfully – Journey
All Out of Love – Air Supply
Bubblegum Bitch – MARINA
Cool for the Summer – Demi Lovato
You Love Is My Drug – Kesha
Teenage Dream – Katy Perry

GLOSSARY

Ivan uses Russian terms of endearment throughout this book. Here is a quick guide.

Lyubimaya (lyoo-bee-mah-yah) - Darling/Beloved
Solnyshko (sol-nish-ka) - Sun/Sunshine
Malish (ma-leesh) - Baby
Mladentsy (m-lad-yent-say) - Babies

CHAPTER 1

Caroline – 7 years ago

The air has been stolen from my lungs. My thoughts have come to a screeching halt. Time? Never heard of it. Everything that has happened in my life, prior to this moment, is completely irrelevant.

Where am I again?

Veronica jabs me in the ribs from her seat to my left. "Girl, are you even listening to me?"

"Ouch! What do you want?" I swat blindly at her and hiss, not bothering to spare a glance in her direction.

"Holy shit," she breathes out, "Biology is my new favorite class." Her gaze is now zeroed in on my fixation. "Addie! Future husband at two o'clock," she whispers to Adalina on her other side.

"Oh my God! I think I just spontaneously ovulated," Adalina quietly squeals.

Great, the first guy to ever catch my eye and the vultures are already circling. I adore my friends, really, but they're feral for just about any man who breathes. I've never shared their fascination, but *this* guy has my undivided attention. I'm eternally grateful the only empty seat is next to me.

Cedarwood and spices infiltrate my space as he saunters my way. Espresso colored eyes connect with mine briefly before darting to the floor. His sharp jaw is clenched tight—from nerves or anger? I'm not sure. My hungry eyes are drawn to the glint of silver in his pouty lower lip. Facial piercings are suddenly attractive as hell.

Am I still not breathing?

"Hi there," Veronica sing-songs, wiggling her perfectly manicured, French tipped fingers. Her flirting is already in full swing, and the poor guy *just* sat down. "I'm Veronica. I'm pretty much the smartest person in this class. If you need a private tutor to catch up, I'll *gladly* give you my number," she purrs.

Adalina giggles and waves, not offering to introduce herself further since Veronica has already drawn a line in the sand.

Twisting in my seat, I throw them a vicious scowl over my shoulder. There are approximately fifteen other guys in this class, why can't they leave me to enjoy this new mystery man in peace?

I turn my attention back toward him, rolling my eyes semi-playfully. "Don't mind them, they're shameless. I'm Caroline, and while I'm not the smartest in the class, neither is Vi." My defiance earns a pinch to the forearm but I just shrug her off. She can deal with it. Class will be starting any minute, and I need to know everything I can about him before we commence.

"Like the song?" he asks.

With his attention focused solely on me, my world tips on its axis. He has an unexpectedly rich, soulful voice. Combine it with that intense southern drawl and my heart is toast.

Words, dummy he asked you a question.

"Uh, yeah, maybe. My dad's pretty old. Mom's a wild-card so... it would make sense."

Wow, Caroline, such an intellectual response.

"You don't know?" A slight rise of his dark brow, and quirk of his full lips all but reduce me to a puddle.

Veronica sighs, or maybe it was Addie? I couldn't tell you if I tried.

Damn it, mouth, say something.

"Oh, umm... I never thought to ask. Not really that familiar with the song, to be honest with you," I stutter all over myself.

"You don't know 'Sweet Caroline'?" His face twists in shock, as if I just told him I don't like pizza.

"No. She listens to bubblegum music. You know, lame shit. She's pretty much human candy," Adalina quips.

I whip my head toward her and pour all my energy into the sharpest glare possible.

"I like candy." His words draw my attention back to him. Judging by the flirtatious smirk pulling at the corner of his mouth, his whisper was undoubtedly meant only for me.

I'm not going to survive this man, I can feel it.

"Okay, everyone please settle down. Jude, since you're new here, welcome to Biology 101." Professor Davidson's voice booms, demanding our attention. "Now, please turn to page seventy-two in your textbooks, let's discuss meiosis."

Rustling pages and the thrumming of my racing heart are the backing track of my mind.

Jude. His name is Jude.

We share playful glances throughout the remainder of class, but don't say anything more to one another. I want to wait around for him after dismissal, but Veronica and Adalina drag me to the campus cafe for boba and gossip.

After we place our usual orders we sit at a table and the conversation immediately drifts to Jude.

"Wanna take bets on how long it will take me to get his number?" Veronica rests her chin on the palm of her hand, swirling her cup of matcha tea.

"Oh? Are we down for a friendly competition? Because I want to jump that man's bones sooooo bad. Did you see his jawline?" Adalina sighs.

"Can you not? I swear you two are so boy crazy it isn't even funny." Jealousy prickles the back of my neck. My tone is admittedly sharper than intended.

"Oh shit, does goodie-two-shoes have a crush?" Veronica's head recoils and her face crinkles, as if she's disgusted by the thought.

"No, Vi. It's just exhausting watching you two compete over every attractive guy you see," Shoulders slumped, I huff and stare at the table.

She's never had to worry about me being potential competition before and this new dynamic has her claws out and sharpened.

"Oh! I think you're right, Vi!" Adalina nudges her, while chewing on a boba pearl.

"Guys, seriously. I don't care, okay?" I sip on my strawberry milk tea, hoping they can't read my horrible poker face.

"So you won't care if I fuck him senseless then? He doesn't talk much, it's always the quiet ones that are wild behind closed doors." Veronica wiggles her brows playfully, but the glint of ferocity in her eyes doesn't get past me.

"Incoming." Adalina pushes her shoulder.

In perfect synchronicity, our heads swivel. Sure enough, on the far side of the café, heading straight for us is the object of our collective obsession.

"God he's tall. What do you think? Six foot four maybe?" Veronica whispers.

"Shut up Vi!" I grit back at her.

"What? Isn't your yummy cousin about the same height?" She continues her quiet fawning.

"Do not call Nikolai 'yummy'." I shudder dramatically.

"He *so* is though! All tall and lean, the Clark Kent glasses make his eyes pop. I bet he's packing, too." She flutters her lashes.

"You're sick. He's practically my brother. The last thing I want to think about is his dick," I fire back in response.

Her objectification of him genuinely upsets me. Nikolai's mom died when he was an infant and my parents took him in. He's a few years older than me and has always treated me like an annoying younger sister, but we love each other. Our family is close so we both still live at home, which means he's unfortunately subjected to tolerating my thirsty friends.

"No offense, Chica, but I'm pretty sure the last thing you *ever* think about is dick," Adalina interjects, pulling me from my festering annoyance.

"That's because I have standards," I grumble, swatting to hush them as Jude approaches our table.

"Hey, uh. Can I sit with y'all?" Velvet, his voice is like luxurious velvet.

"Oh, of course. Is that an accent I hear? I'm Veronica, by the way."

"Yeah, you mentioned that earlier," he mumbles back, taking the empty seat next to me.

"Oh, sorry I guess I was distracted." Veronica flutters her lashes across the table from us.

"So, where are you from? Don't often get new classmates mid-term. I'm Addie, by the way. You can call me yours, though." Her full lips pucker as she blows a kiss his way.

"Uh, I'm from Alabama." He squirms in his chair, pulling at the sleeve of his tattered black Metallica hoodie.

"Oh, a proper southern gentleman." Veronica beams

a pearly-white smile his way.

"Sure," he replies dryly.

All three of our eyes bulge as he pulls his hoodie off and the deep blue Nirvana T-shirt underneath rides up with it. A smattering of dark hair trails down the peek of his abs we've been given. The black, beautifully intricate, forest scene tattooed up his left forearm has my hand itching to trace every line.

While I give it my best effort to remain respectful in my admiration, Veronica ogles him, unapologetically and Adalina bites her lip, practically drooling from across the table. Catching a glimpse of their shameless staring, he shoots his gaze to meet mine—face turning cherry red.

I'm sure he's already figured out that he's thrown himself into the lion's den with these two.

"So, I'm a little lost in class, are you available to help me catch up?" he asks.

His full attention is on me again as he unpacks the sad excuse for a sandwich he brought and takes a big bite. Burning glares from my best friends make my skin itch, or maybe it's just his presence.

"Yeah, I can do that. Do you um, want to come over and study tonight? I can see if my cousin will cook dinner. That is if you want to..." I ramble. Why won't my mouth stop? If my confidence could return to this planet, that would be great.

Chewing his lip ring, he glances over toward Veronica and Adalina, then immediately back at me. "I'd like that."

Part of me feels like he wishes we were alone—maybe it's just my own delusion talking—but, sadly, we're very much not. I can *feel* the vibrating energy from across the table as Veronica and Adalina sit slack-jawed watching us.

"I'll write my address down for you. Is six a good time?" I mumble, feeling like I've been transplanted into a nineties rom-com.

Who writes their address down anymore?

I grab a notebook from my bag and scribble it for him as he finishes his sandwich.

"Six is good. I'll be there." He lifts the corner of his mouth slightly before scooting his chair out. I watch silently, burning inside with anticipation, as he cleans up his lunch mess and leaves.

"Well, Addie, I guess it's a party at Caroline's tonight. I might let you have the new guy if her delicious cousin will look my way. Or is he too busy getting richer?" Veronica asks with a challenge in her eye.

"Jesus, I don't know his schedule. You're not exactly his type though, I think he's made that clear," I spit. I hate it when she talks about his money, she reminds me of his current gold digging girlfriend.

"Girl, I'm everyone's type." She winks.

Vi *is* a gorgeous woman. Tall, thin, blonde haired with crystal blue eyes. In the eight months I've known her, she's had no trouble finding men to dote on her. Fortunately, Nikolai seems immune to her flirtation.

"Aye, maybe he needs a little Latina in his life." Adalina wiggles her shoulders.

"No. Neither of you are sleeping with my cousin. Got it?" I pinch my brows with a scowl.

The roll of their eyes and reluctant nods are going to have to be good enough.

The house is silent when I step through the front door, which is uncommon.

My father is a large and imposing Russian man, but on the inside he's quiet and reserved. Mom is a live-wire, blowing through the house like a tornado on an adrenaline high. She's the definition of over the top and loud. Dad probably wishes I shared more of his mannerisms but secretly loves that I'm a lot like her... or at least I used to be.

Nikolai is on the couch with Lilah when I stroll into the living room. They've been together for about a year now, unfortunately. She's a fame chasing phony who's only with Nikolai because of his money. I hate her. My face is incapable of hiding my disapproval, permanently pulling into a sneer in her presence.

Am I a bit childish? Yes, but I don't care.

"Hey there, Parasite, how was class?" Nikolai asks, ignoring the stare off between me and the succubus clung to his side.

"It was fine, Nerd. Where are Mom and Dad? I need

to talk to them."

"They went for a walk in the field. They should be back soon. Auntie T was getting antsy," he replies, shifting awkwardly in his seat.

"Sounds about right." I know that 'antsy' means Mom was annoyed by Lilah and her incessant PDA.

He seems to be the only one who can't see her for what she is.

"What do you need? Anything I can help with?" He leans forward, shrugging off her grimy paws.

"Can you cook dinner tonight? I have some friends coming over."

"Trouble and Chaos I presume?" He tilts his head.

"Their names are Veronica and Adalina." I tap my fingers at my side. "And it's not just them. There's a new guy in my biology class and he needs to catch up on material." I glue my eyes to the floor, dodging his questioning look.

"A guy? Like, a full-on man? How old is he? Are your friends already fighting over him?" He chuckles, knowing that's exactly what's happening.

"I don't know how old he is. I barely even know his name!" I throw my hands up, ready to be done with his interrogation. Jude isn't even here yet and the questions have *already* begun.

"Oh, your dad is going to *hate* this. I can't wait." The sound of his hands clapping together echoes through the room.

"Boo Bear, I thought you were taking me to the fancy

new rooftop bar that just opened?" Lilah pouts.

"But I want to be here for this!" he protests, "I'll make it up to you, I promise." His, normally bright expression drops.

Their dynamic is... uncomfortable. I'm not used to seeing him so subdued. Nikolai was always such a vibrant, fun-loving, over excited guy. Then the soul sucker showed up.

He's a minor celebrity in his own right, having painted murals for the city, and custom portraits for actors and musicians. For a twenty-two-year-old, he's accomplished a lot. Before Lilah, he had a few flings, but never anything serious. Then she sunk her claws in and has been draining him of his love for life ever since.

"Ugh, you're lucky I'm in a good mood." She folds her arms, leaning away from him.

"I'll make stuffed shells and garlic knots, everyone loves Italian food." He jumps up from the couch with excitement shining in his eyes.

"Eww, so many carbs, I'll pass. Call me when you're done." Lilah makes a show of kissing him as sloppily as possible.

Just then, the front door creaks open, "We're back!" my mother chants, announcing their return. When they enter the living room, she glares at Lilah's disgusting display. Dad's face reddens as his blood pressure undoubtedly skyrockets.

"Bye, Boo Bear," Lilah says with an obnoxious attempt at sounding sultry. Her retreat is quick, fortunately for her.

My mother looks to be mere seconds from losing her mind. Folding her arms, she pops her hip out and addresses Nikolai, "Baby Boy, are you ever going to kick that trashy woman to the curb? She can't be that good in the sack."

"Theresa!" Dad sputters.

I snort so hard I cough, glad I'm not on the receiving end of her teasing.

"Ivan, don't be a prude. The kids are grown. Caroline is almost nineteen for goodness' sake." Mom pats his shoulder.

"*Lyubimaya,* that doesn't mean I want any sort of insight on their sex lives." He pinches the bridge of his nose, shaking his head.

"We all know Caroline doesn't have a sex life. My sweet girl, are you ever going to find yourself a man? Surely with those wild friends of yours, and my genes, you've got some fire in your veins by now." She shimmies, bumping shoulders with me playfully.

"I'm too old for this," Dad groans.

"Oh, just wait, Uncle. Caroline is having a boy over for dinner," Nikolai interjects, like the instigator he is.

"What?!" My parents shriek in unison, only my mother's is full of excitement, while my father looks like he's about to pass out.

"It's not like that!" I wail, "He's a mid-term transfer in my bio class. He asked if I could help him catch up."

"So... he's not a potential lover?" The pout on my

mother's face is pitiful.

"No, Mom. Besides, Vi and Addie have already started fighting over who gets first dibs. I can't compete with either of them. So, just forget it."

"Hey now, don't be so hard on yourself, Parasite. I know I make fun of you all the time but don't sell yourself short," Nikolai cuts in.

"Exactly what Nicky said, Lovey. You've got so much to offer to a good man... or woman." My mother looks expectantly at me.

"Mom, I don't like women. I just... I don't really like men either." Despite my dramatic groan, the pitch of my voice lets a bit of truth slip out—unable to fully hide my attraction.

"Caroline, it's completely fine that you're focused on your education and building a future. Don't be like your boy-crazy friends," my father speaks up.

"Thanks, Dad," I say flatly.

If he had it his way I'd live in a bubble, away from 'temptations'. Only giving him grandchildren through immaculate conception.

"Okay, well, I'm going to get started on everything. Try to keep your thirsty friends off my ass tonight, yeah?" Nikolai raises a brow.

"Hah, good luck. The new guy already has Veronica especially keyed up," I fire back.

"Oh, so he's a cutie then? Why didn't you say so, Lovey? Shoo! Go get prettied up for him." Mom nudges me toward the hallway.

"Theresa, our daughter is better than that. We don't even know this boy. What if he's some sort of deviant? Caroline, what *do* you know about him?" Dad grumbles, already deciding he's impressed.

This'll be good.

"Well... he's from Alabama." I bite my lip, staring at a spot on the wall.

"Oooh! A southern boy, how precious." My mother's grin splits her whole face as she clasps her hands over her heart.

"Uh. He's not exactly what you'd imagine. He has a lip piercing, and tattoos," I intentionally mumble.

My father chokes, loudly. Nikolai doubles over with laughter watching my mother pat his back.

"A-and... how o-old is he?" Dad wheezes.

"I don't know, okay! It's just a school thing. I'm not about to marry the guy!" Frustrated, and flushed with a touch of embarrassment, I stomp my feet and storm out of the room.

Maybe I'm not about to marry him. Maybe I'm not a model-esque, blue-eyed blonde like Veronica, or a feisty Latina with big doe eyes and luscious lips like Adalina. But I'm me, and I think I'm cute. I can only hope Jude does too. The way I feel around him makes my entire body tingle in the best way.

For now my main goal is to make it through dinner.

CHAPTER 2

Caroline

A cid churns in my stomach threatening to burn straight through me. Why am I so worked up? Jude likely won't even care that I touched up my makeup and put some fresh perfume on.

Should I have worn a different perfume? Everything I have is sweet and fruity.

Jesus, I really am a lost cause.

"We maaaade it!" Veronica bursts through the front door with Adalina on her heels. "Hottie isn't here yet? Do you think he'll flake?"

"Well, hello to you too. And I told him to come at six, it's only five-thirty. He still has time." I cross my arms and huff, already annoyed. She's normally *not* this excited to be here.

"What do you think he drives? I'm betting on some sort of classic muscle car. Maybe an old pickup truck. He *is* from the south." Veronica rests her chin in her palm as she leans on the counter, staring dreamily into the distance.

"Wow, you weren't kidding. I'm standing *right* here, and she hasn't even tried to hit on me." Nikolai is so shocked his eyebrows are acquainting themselves with his hairline.

Veronica turns her attention to him as he stands at our old gas stove. "Oh, I didn't even see you there, silly me. Are you cooking me dinner? How sweet of you." She bats her eyelashes with too much enthusiasm, as if Jude doesn't even exist now.

Nikolai's mouth is pressed in a firm line as he shakes his head and turns back to the pasta sauce bubbling away in the old stock pot.

"Vivi you're too much." Adalina laughs, pushing her playfully.

"A girl has to keep her options open. Nikolai is kind of rich, after all. I'm always down for a sugar daddy," she presses, her tone even more flirtatious.

"You know I have a girlfriend, sorry," Nikolai grits out with his back to her, wiping down the tiled counter top.

"Don't you dare apologize, Nicky. You'll only enable her delusion," I deadpan as Veronica pins me with a sharp glare.

"I thought I heard commotion. Good evening, ladies, how are we doing?" My mother prances into the room in the light, carefree way of hers, easing the tension.

"We're good, Mama T." Adalina bounces over to her for a hug.

"I hope you're all prepared to study after dinner.

That's the whole meaning of tonight's get together, right?" My father grumbles upon entering the room.

"Yes, Ivan," they both chant in unison.

Nikolai pulls fluffy, golden garlic knots from the oven before washing his hands and removing Mom's frilly apron. "Alright, I owe Lilah a nice dinner. I made enough for everyone but she's going to be upset if I actually cancel. I'll catch you all later."

"Nicky—" Dad starts to oppose.

"Just don't, it's fine. I'll be back later. Enjoy the shells. I made a quick meat sauce and there's fresh parmesan cheese to top it with. Love you!" Before anyone has a chance to protest further, he grabs the keys to our family car and slips out the door.

"Damn, well I guess there goes my plans for the night." Veronica laughs. "I'll win him over eventually."

"Or not. That sounds great," I groan.

At that moment, the unmistakable sound of a motorcycle can be heard pulling up outside. A fast, very non-father-approved, motorcycle. My body buzzes at the thought.

Dad's face contorts as a familiar off-tune jingle resounds through the house.

Oh God, the doorbell. It's him. He's here.

As protective as ever, my father stands tall and answers the door. The sight that awaits Jude as it swings open is sitcom worthy. Dad, with his arms crossed, scowling as this poor guy just stands there unassumingly. Ducking under his elbow to get a better look is my mother. Veronica and Adalina wiggle from excitement against the far wall.

And then there's my awkward self, standing here like a total buffoon, completely frozen in place. Fortunately for me, his view is blocked by the giant Russian wall formerly known as my father.

"Good evenin', Sir. Uh. Is Caroline home? We were fixin' to study biology," he speaks directly to Dad, only wavering slightly.

"Biology huh?" My father puffs up his chest.

"Okay, stop!" I push him out of the way and—holy hotness—the front porch looks great tonight.

Black has never been so appealing. Jude is wearing torn jeans, combat boots and the same tattered hoodie from earlier. Tucked securely under his arm is a matte black motorcycle helmet with a mirror finished visor. His milk chocolate hair is mussed from the ride over.

Stop staring before you start to drool.

"Hi. Sorry about him. Dad, go sit down before you hurt yourself." I glare, pointing to our well-loved dining room table, but he doesn't budge.

"Nice to meet you, Sir. My name is Jude Carlisle." He extends a hand, and with that simple action I'm entirely smitten.

"Jude. Like The Beatles?" Mom speaks up while Dad begrudgingly shakes his hand.

"Yes Ma'am. My mama loves classic rock." The vibrant blush that lights up his face is so precious I want to bury my face against him.

No, bad hormones, go back to the cave you've been hiding in.

"Oh, how amazing is that?! Just like our sweet Caroline." My mother smiles brightly, voice filled with joy.

I tear my attention from Jude and look at her like she has three heads. "How did I not know you named me after a song?!"

"Oh Lovey, your middle name is Diana for a reason, too. 'Endless Love' was our wedding song. Wasn't it, Honey Bunny?" Dad is jolted from his stupor as she wraps him in a tight hug.

"Well, now that we've got that settled, come in. My cousin made dinner, but he had to placate his facehugger." I motion to the spread on the table.

"Facehugger, like from *Alien*?" Jude's head tilts with his question, sending stray locks of hair cascading over his brows.

"Never mind her weird analogies. She's always watching the strangest things with her cousin." Veronica finally speaks up, Adalina snickers behind her.

Jude jerks his head toward them with wide eyes. Apparently just now processing the fact that they're here. "I love *Alien*, I'm a sucker for the classics. I was just surprised you made the reference. So, we don't like your cousin's girlfriend?" He looks directly at me when he speaks, as captivating as ever.

"She's the worst," Adalina confirms.

"Okay, kids. Enough about Nicky's dating life. Let's eat so you all can study and get home before it's too late."

Dad directs us all to sit.

I watch Jude intently as he inspects our modest little home. The fear of not making a good first impression has me sweating. Anyone else would probably be embarrassed by how simply we live. But this house, these chipped dinner plates, the floral curtains, the giant old sauce pots, and rusty tea kettle, they tell our story. There's so much love and warmth in every flaw here.

I'd be content to never leave.

"So, Jude. Tell us about yourself." Dad scoops some gooey cheese filled shells onto his plate.

"He's here to study. Please don't make this awkward." Slumping back in my chair, I rub my temples.

"Oh no, please tell us *all* about you." Veronica perks up, biting her lower lip.

Jude's cheeks redden before he speaks, "Well. I'm twenty-one. I live on campus alone. I was raised on a family farm in Alabama, and I love animals. Studying veterinary medicine seemed like a no-brainer."

"Oh wow, I love that. I'm studying to be a pediatrician, I love kids. Do you?" Veronica leans forward, pressing her breasts together.

I want to push her out of the rickety chair she's dangling off for blatantly flirting with him in *my* home.

Whoa, hello there jealousy.

"Uh. Kids are cool." He shrugs.

"Well, I'm studying to be a cardiologist. My family has a history of heart issues and revolutionizing treatments is my whole goal in life," a proud Adalina interjects.

"Wow. That's impressive. Who knew biology would bring all of you kids together?" My mother says with genuine delight in her voice.

"Mom, I knew Addie and Vi from last semester," I explain like it's not common knowledge.

"Oh honey, I know, but now Jude has the pleasure of knowing all of you, too." She's glowing with pride as she passes the garlic knots around the table.

"What about you, Caroline?" Jude tips his head at me slightly.

My name coming from his lips does funny things to me. Tingly, chest squeezing things. "W-what about me?" My eyebrows pinch together as I try to make words.

"Whatcha studyin'?" The full twang of his accent fills my stomach with flutters.

"Oh. I'm a vet-med student, too." Why are my cheeks suddenly hot? I don't blush.

What is happening?

"So, you're a perfect study buddy then." His statement is innocent enough, the sensations in my belly intensify anyway. He wants to spend more time with me.

He called me perfect.

The context is irrelevant to my delusional brain.

It's funny how some people can read you like a book. Veronica sees the excitement on my face and immediately butts in, "I could help you with *all* sorts of studies."

His blush deepens and my heart cracks at the sight. Clearly her insistent flirting works on him. Like a gentleman he's trying to ignore her, but I know her game.

I've seen her in action far too many times. She'll be on his arm, and in his bed by the end of the night at the rate she's going.

Thankfully, everyone has their food plated up and dives in, so I'm spared from any more embarrassing conversations. As always, the dinner Nikolai prepared is delicious and doesn't take long for any of us to finish.

"I'll clean up. You kids get your studying done." Dad rounds the table, gathering up our dirty plates.

"It's nice outside, we'll be out back if you need us." I lead the way through our living room and out to the enclosed porch.

As we take out seats at the old wooden picnic table, Veronica extends an expectant hand. "We should all exchange numbers! Jude, give me your phone." Timidly, he obliges. With a few swipes she's satisfied. "There. I've made a group chat for all of us."

"Thanks." He nods, pocketing his phone.

"No problem, Hottie." She winks and he blushes in return.

The next hour is filled with a little studying, and a lot of Veronica flirting. Jude is quiet but constantly flushed. It's a nerve frying, and obnoxious, back-and-forth between them. One that is slowly chipping away at my resolve. By the time they pack up to leave, I'm a wreck. I can already tell I have no chance in hell with him.

After I see them off, I head promptly to my room and silently weep into my mountain of pillows.

Sunlight warms my face as I unlock my phone to check the time. Seven a.m. is a terrible hour to be awake on a Saturday.

Rubbing my crusty, sore eyes, I blink away the blurriness and a text notification catches my attention. Jude messaged me, but not in the group chat. My pulse picks up as I tap the notification.

Jude: Hey, sorry if this is weird, but I wanted to thank you for everything. Your parents are really cool and you are too, friends?

There it is.

If he wants *friends*, I'll friend him so hard he won't know what to do without me.

Me: Not weird at all. You're pretty cool too. I guess we can be friends. :)

Jude: Awesome. What do you do for fun around here, anyway? Other than listening to Vi talk about herself.

Me: That's about as entertaining as it gets, sadly. I'm boring. We do like to go to trivia and karaoke nights at the arcade room downtown.

Jude: Karaoke? You sing?

Me: NO. We go to listen. I could never.

Jude: You self-conscious, Candy Girl?

Wait. Did he just give me a nickname?
Swoon.

Me: *Candy Girl huh?*
Jude: *Sorry. I like nicknames.*
Me: *So does my cousin, I feel like you'd get along with him. He's a jerk though and calls me "Parasite"... >:(*
Jude: *You do call his girl a facehugger.*
Me: *You'll understand if you ever meet her. If you're lucky, you won't have the misfortune.*
Jude: *That bad?*
Me: *I'd rather contract the plague. It's crazy how quickly she's dimmed his light.*
Jude: *You're close?*
Me: *Yeah, like siblings.*
Jude: *That's nice. Anyway, I'll see you around, Candy.*
Me: *Later, Big Guy. ;)*
Jude: *;) I like it.*

Holy shit he winked back.

Ear-piercing squeals burst out of me. Nikolai flings my door open, half awake, sporting fresh love bites on his bare chest. Clearly Lilah had her way with him last night.

Gross.

"What?! Is it a spider? Are you hurt? Nobody else is home. Should I call the police?" His hands are buried in his hair as he panics.

"I'm fine. Jude just texted me. We had an actual conversation. It wasn't about studying!" Boundless energy has me bouncing up and down in my bed.

Nikolai stands in my doorway, blank faced. "Who the fuck are you and what happened to my cousin? Caroline doesn't get excited over boys."

"She gets excited over *this* boy... unfortunately." My face falls, remembering how much he blushes over Veronica's flirting. "How do I tell if he's a player?"

"Oh Jesus, I'm *not* equipped for this conversation so early. I had a long night. Can I at least get some coffee first?" He scrubs a hand over his face.

"Whatever, see if I ever ask you for advice again!" With a huff, I storm past him toward the kitchen.

"You know I'm shit at relationships in the first place. Ask one of your friends. I'm sure they have first-hand experience." He trails behind me.

"They're the problem!" Grinding my teeth, I stir a heaping scoop of sugar into my coffee and plop into a chair. "You wouldn't understand."

"No, I guess I wouldn't. But I am sorry you're having boy troubles. It's just... weird." He scratches the back of his neck, sitting across the table from me.

"I know, it's weird for me too, okay? I don't know what it is about him. For once I want someone, and I know I can't have him," I grumble into my mug savoring the sweet roasty goodness.

Stirring his coffee, Nikolai hums inquisitively.

"What the hell is that supposed to mean?" I scrunch up my face.

"Why can't you have him?" He raises a brow clinking

his spoon against the rim of his mug.

"Uh, because the most beautiful girl in the world has almost flirted her way into his pants already. Why else?" Setting my coffee down, I scoff and cross my arms.

"You think a little too highly of Veronica. She's nothing special. Sure, she's pretty enough, but she's also conceited and honestly, vile." He shudders dramatically with a curled lip.

"You're one to talk. Coming home after being mauled by a facehugger with nothing more than her looks going for her." A grimace pulls at my face as I gesture to the constellation of angry red hickeys on his body before picking my cup up.

"Hey! You wanted my advice, I didn't ask you for yours, so hush!" He chuckles. "You're great, and I love you, Parasite. Everything will work out in the end. Just be yourself. If he's a decent guy, he'll see your worth." He tips his chin, and takes a long sip.

"I love you too, Nerd, even if you're a hypocrite." I smile into my mug.

Nikolai rolls his eyes, cleans up after himself and ruffles my hair in passing before leaving the room.

Alone with my own thoughts, my mind flits back to Jude. I wonder what he really thinks. Is he a decent guy? If so, why does he humor Veronica's advances? Does he text her too?

What a mess.

CHAPTER 3

Jude - 2 weeks later

"Jude, you finally remembered to call, huh?" My mother sniffles into the phone, the telltale sound makes my skin itch.

"I didn't forget, just been busy. Figured you'd like to know I'm doin' good." My death grip on the phone says otherwise.

"Real good... fixin' to do somethin' with your life. You havin' fun pretendin' you're not a good for nothin' little shit?" She spews the age-old insult out fluidly. It's well practiced.

"Ma, please—"

"You stayin' clean out there?"

"Yes Mama. Haven't touched a thing." My blood pounds through my veins, knowing she can't say the same.

"When Pa passed, everyone thought he was crazy for leaving everything to you. Be damned sure to make good use of it, boy." Her voice drips with disdain.

"I'm gonna do better here." My nose tingles as I hear her inhale another line.

"Just stay out of trouble. Try to find some good influences." Her sniffs grow louder and I nearly hang up.

"I have a few... friends already." Damn it, I can feel my pulse picking up. This conversation is shit. Why did I do this?

"Are they girls? You swore you'd behave." Her tone only stokes the fire burning in my chest.

"Mama—"

"Don't go breaking any hearts this time around," she cuts in, leaving no room for argument.

"I found a good girl. She's blonde, has big, beautiful eyes that are so kind and expressive. She's funny, sweet, and so smart. I met her in biology class."

"I've never heard you talk about anything more than a woman's body," she says flatly.

"I know you have your doubts about me, but she's different for sure," I spit, forgetting to mind my tone.

"Just take it easy, Jude. Nobody there knows you, or your history. Don't mess it all up for some tail."

I can just picture the white residue on her nose at the sound of her sniffling again.

"Yeah, yeah. I'll text you." I hang up, rolling over in my bed.

She's right, this is my chance to be better.

No more drugs, no more drinking, no more street racing and mindless hookups.

No more being the product of her mess.

My first two weeks of this new adventure have been exhausting. I've been so busy acclimating that I've barely taken time to message the Study Buddy chat Veronica created. That hasn't stopped her from blowing up my phone in private.

Nonstop flirting isn't new to me. I'm six foot two and have my dad's Spanish features—warm brown hair, dark eyes, naturally tanned skin. The girls ate it up back home. Sex quickly became one of my many vices, usually never with the same girl twice, until I ran out of options anyway.

Now, freshly twenty-one, starting at a new school—now that I can afford it—I have the opportunity to make new friends without any biased opinions.

I hadn't planned on meeting the woman of my dreams week one, but I'll be damned if that isn't what happened.

My phone chimes, pulling me from my daydreams, filled with long glimmering blonde hair. I frown at it, disappointed that the notification is just the Study Buddies group.

Vi: Are we going out tonight or what?
Addie: Duhhh.
Candy: What are we thinking?
Vi: I haven't gone to shake my ass at Karaoke night in weeks. We down?
Addie: Yes! We haven't hit the dance floor in so long.
Candy: Yes!
Vi: Jude?? You're coming right?

Me: *Sure.*

Vi: *Hell Yeah! Arm candy. All the other girls are gonna be so jealous.*

Addie: *You're wild, Vivi.*

Me: *Y'all fixin' to drink?*

Vi: *Oh my God I love that I can imagine your voice in my head asking that.*

Addie: *That accent is everything!*

Candy: *Sorry about them. But no, it's an arcade bar, and they ID. I also don't think I'll have a ride.*

Vi: *Boo! I was hoping you'd drive all of us.*

Addie: *Can I ride with you in your Jeep, Vi?*

Vi: *Yeah, Caroline will have to stay in, I guess. Sorry Girl.*

Candy: *It's okay. You guys have fun.*

No way. I don't want to go out with just the two of them. I need Caroline there as a buffer. She's the only one who doesn't constantly come on to me. Her dad fucking terrifies me, but she has to come. I pull her contact up to message her directly.

Me: *Hey, can I come over?*

Candy: *Uhh. Sure.*

Me: *Don't sound so excited.*

Candy: *Sorry, I was just surprised.*

Me: *I'll be there in 15. Get ready.*

Pocketing my phone, I lace up my boots and dig

around in the boxes filling my closet. I really need to finish unpacking someday. Eventually, I find what I'm looking for and head out.

When I make it to Caroline's little brick house, she's already at the door. As I approach, her eyes lock onto my left hand, more specifically the helmet I'm holding.

"Oh, no. Nope. No, sir." Her arms wave in front of her in an "x" motion.

"You don't want a ride?" I raise my visor and lift a brow.

"My dad will kill both of us." Her hands plant firmly on her curvaceous hips. The skintight jeans she's wearing should be illegal.

Stop thinking about how soft she looks.

"I'm a safe driver. I'll go nice and slow, just for you," I drawl, dropping my tone.

She sucks in a sharp breath and I watch intently as her warm, amber eyes scan my bike—and my body—as she weighs her options.

Chewing her lip, she nods slightly. "Okay, but don't complain when I squeeze the shit out of you."

I huff out a laugh and slip my spare helmet over her head, making sure it's secure. Her eyes sparkle with excitement. Even through the visor, I can tell she's got a vibrant smile stretched across her face. Nervous energy radiates off her as she settles in behind me. I reach back, grabbing her firmly by the calves and pulling her flush against me. Her playful squeak goes straight to my dick.

Down boy.

"Do I have to be this close?" She presses up against my back, completely contradicting her question.

I take her hands in mine, wrapping her arms around my upper body. "Yes. Hold on tight, when we stop, hands go on the tank."

The heat burning in my stomach increases as her fingers slide down my abs while she secures her grip. I desperately need to get myself under control before we get to this karaoke spot.

"Like this?" Her voice is laced with an innocence that my body itches to corrupt.

Nodding, I twist the throttle, and she squeals, squeezing me tighter as we pull out of the driveway. She's warm and soft, pressed against me for the entire ride. For a moment I consider getting 'lost' just to keep her this close.

When we arrive at the booming arcade bar, Veronica and Adalina are hopping out of a rag top Wrangler. If looks could kill, Caroline would be a goner.

"What the hell? I would have totally taken the hottie express and let you and Addie take my Jeep. You probably peed a little," Veronica blurts out in a mocking tone as we approach.

"It wasn't that bad. He went slow for me." She slips her helmet off, straightening out her wild hair.

"Well, *I* like it fast. So, if you ever want a proper ride, call me." Veronica's polished nails drag down my chest. I'm glad my helmet is still on, so I don't have to cover up my reaction.

"I'll remember that," I grumble.

She smiles impishly, with a victorious glint in her eye. Fuck, I shouldn't have said anything, Caroline has completely deflated next to me.

Nice going, idiot.

The last thing I need is to cause a rift between them. I'm trying to do better, after all. These three make it hard though. Well, two of them do.

Veronica is the definition of a spoiled rich girl who is used to getting whatever she wants. Her long—obviously fake—blonde hair is never out of place. Sparkly, bright blue eyes with thick—equally fake—lashes and full, glossy lips. She drives a pink soft top Jeep to boot. Girls like her didn't exist back home. Everything about her screams "good time" but that's it.

Adalina is short and spunky. Thick curly hair nicely frames her round face, dyed a deep red. She wears crop tops and painted on jeans almost exclusively. She's a fun flirt and would undoubtedly be a fun fling, if I were even remotely interested in that right now.

Standing in the background is Caroline. Adalina was accurate in her description, she's human candy and even smells like it. Her long, golden-blonde hair is all natural—courtesy of her mother. Shining, expressive honey colored eyes take up way more real estate on her face than you'd think possible. She has pouty, heart shaped lips that I want to bite while she moans for me. Her curves are the landscape of my dreams.

I have no idea what I've stumbled into. It isn't going

to end well though, I'm not a total idiot. There's already tension between them where I'm concerned and I don't like it.

"Okay let's get our grind on. Dibs on the hottie! You two find your own!" Veronica grabs me by the arm and drags me inside, straight to the dance floor.

My pleading eyes scan the room and stare into Caroline's soul as she stands alone in a corner.

"I don't really dance." I try to bail, but my effort is pointless.

Veronica wraps her arms around my shoulders and leans up on her tiptoes. "You don't need to. Just stand there, run your hands all over my body and let me dance on you." She pecks my cheek and turns around, pressing her ass firmly against me as she swivels her hips.

Following her attention to the side of the room, the hurt on Caroline's face is devastating.

Apparently, the nail isn't driven far enough in her coffin, because Veronica grabs my hands and places them on her chest. "Touch me, Jude. Show everyone who you're here with." She spins around as I rip my hands away from her.

"I'm here with all of you, as a friend. This was supposed to be fun," I grit out, scanning the crowd to look for Caroline. Only, she's nowhere to be seen, she reacted exactly how Veronica wanted, I'm sure of it. "I'm not some pawn in your game," I spit and storm off the dance floor, straight out the back door.

On the patio, in the cool night air, Caroline sits alone.

Tears glisten on her face, but she's quick to wipe them away as I approach.

"Oh, hey." Her plump lower lip protrudes from her furious pout.

"Candy, I—"

"No, it's fine. Don't apologize to me, I'm stupid for being upset." The quivering of her chin draws me in. Sitting next to her I wrap her securely in my arms and let her cry.

"S-sorry. I'm just being a big d-dummy," she sputters against my chest.

"No, you're not dumb. Veronica is playin' you like a fiddle."

"What?!" She pulls her head back, looking up at me with mascara streaked down her face.

I furrow my brows. "You don't see it? I just told her off back there. I'm not tryin' to be the reason y'all have drama."

"She's one of my best friends. Don't tell me you hate her too." Her pout returns.

"I don't hate her... I just don't like drama. I got my fill of it back home." I rest my chin on the top of her head and we sit in comfortable silence for a few minutes. I breathe in her sweet perfume and get lost in the moment while she calms down.

"Thank you," she whispers.

"Don't mention it, Candy. Let's get back inside and enjoy the night, okay?" I stand, offering a hand to help her up.

After a short deliberation she takes it and we return inside, only to find Veronica and Adalina long gone. Apparently, I caused drama while trying *not* to cause drama.

Great.

I turn to Caroline. "Well, we can either go dance, or I can take you home. It's your call."

"You'd dance with me? But... I heard you tell Vi you don't dance." Warm, hopeful eyes stare up at me.

"I don't, but for you, I'll make an exception." I take her hand in mine and guide her to the dance floor, drifting through the crowd until we find some privacy in a far corner.

"I don't really dance either, just so you know. Not *with* people anyway," she mumbles shyly as her cheeks flush pink.

"I mean, most of what people call dancing is practically dry humping so..." I shrug.

Her eyes widen. "Did you just ask me to dry hump you?"

"N-no. I was just makin' a comparison. We can just go if you don't want to dance." Ducking my head, I turn away from her.

Much to my surprise, she holds onto my hand tightly and spins me back around. "Let's try... to dance, that is, *not* dry hump." An adorably crooked grin pulls at her lips before she turns away from me.

I huff out a loud, unrestrained laugh—probably my first in months.

We're awkward in the beginning. I don't know where to put my hands and she doesn't know that I'm more than willing to let her grind her round, full ass against me. We tiptoe around the sexual tension until I'm officially over it. When the song changes to romantic ballad I spin her around and pull her against me, resting my hands on her waist.

After her initial shock and disbelief fade, she slides her hands up my arms and links them behind my neck. We begin to move together and she nestles her cheek against my chest.

Feeling braver than I should, I slip my hands into her back pockets, almost pulling away when her breath catches—until she leans into me further. My heart is racing like never before, threatening to beat out of my chest. She smells like cherries and sugar. I've never had much of a sweet tooth, but she's slowly converting me.

"You're so smart and have such a kind soul," I lean down and whisper into her ear. "Stop letting people dull your shine."

A frown pulls at her face as she looks up at me. "But they're right. I'm always the smart one, or the nice one, or the funny one. I'm never the pretty one, or the one people want to take home, not that I've ever really cared. But being the last choice is starting to get old."

"Is that how you feel?" I pull back, looking into her watery eyes as they fill with fresh tears.

"It's the truth, even for you. You're only here with me because *they* left." She turns her head away from me.

Hell no.

In a flash I pull her from the dance floor, out the door, into the dimly lit parking lot.

"Where are we going?" Her words are muffled as I slide the helmet on her head.

"I'm taking you home. Since you're *so* convinced that I don't want to be here with you." I plop onto the seat of my bike. "Hop on."

Gravel crunches under her foot as she digs it into the pavement. "But—"

"Nope. You don't get to fight me on this. If you want to sit around and wallow, go ahead. I would be fuckin' Veronica in the bathroom right now if you were the last choice. Instead, I left her high and dry on the dance floor the second I noticed you were gone. Go on ahead and pretend she's better than you, but I'm not humorin' your pity party. You deserve better than her toxic cattiness."

"You ditched her for me?" Pure disbelief coats her words.

"Yes, because you matter. I don't want to ruin friendships, and I honestly don't want to fuck Veronica."

"Tell *her* that." She scoffs, rolling her eyes.

"I've tried. Now, get on." I slip on my helmet and wait.

With a stomp of her foot and a huff she obeys, sitting too far back for my liking. I grab her with more intensity than I should and pull her against me. I want to speed home, let the adrenaline rush relieve my tension, but I can't do that to her.

I'm not mad at *her*, I'm just mad at this wild situation.

CHAPTER 4

Caroline

Tears stream down my face as I burst through the front door. Of course, everyone is home to see what a giant mess I am. To make it worse, they heard Jude's motorcycle drop me off, then speed away.

Could my life get any more tragic?

"Lovey, are you okay?" Mom's usual boisterousness is gone, buried under layers of concern as she approaches me.

"Were you on that bike?" Dad asks. His protective tone is too much for me to bear right now.

Nikolai says nothing, surprisingly, but I can see questions and worry all over his face.

After kicking my Converse off unceremoniously, I make a beeline for my room and crawl into bed. Hiding under my blankets isn't quite as good as therapy—or screaming out my feelings—but it'll have to do for now.

A soft knock and the creak of my bedroom door alerts me to my mother's entrance. She scoots up next to me as

I silently sob into my fuzzy pink pillow.

"Lovey, please talk to me. I've never seen you so upset." Her voice is soft and warm, exactly what I need.

"Mom. He's m-mad at me and I don't know why!" I shriek, burying my face further into the plush fabric.

"Who's mad? Jude? Is that who you were out with? Talk to me." She rubs my back softly.

"Yes, I was out with Jude and the girls. We went to karaoke. I—He... Ugh!" I stammer, unable to form the right words.

"Breathe, it's alright. Take your time." Her whispers and warmth wrap me up, calming my inner turmoil.

"He was dancing all over Vi. I was... I think I was jealous, Mom. I don't get jealous. I don't care about guys. Or who Vi hooks up with." I sniffle and take a deep breath.

"But Jude is different," she affirms. It's not a question, she can see right through me. "You know, sometimes the things we want the most hurt a bit at first. Until we figure out how to handle them."

"I just feel like he's playing us all. He ditched Vi after I stormed out of the building, then told me he doesn't want to sleep with her. But the way he was letting her grind on him says otherwise." My lower lip wobbles as I turn to face her. "He told me that I'm smart and kind and shouldn't let people dull my shine. Then stomped all over my heart!" My face presses against her shoulder as she pulls me close.

"Maybe he's just not great with words. Maybe his

feelings are twisted up and he's trying to make sense of everything he's just stumbled into." She rubs more soothing circles on my back.

"Whose side are you even on?!" I pull my head away from her shoulder and pin her with a sorrowful scowl.

"Lovey, I'll always be on your side, which is why I also need to give you a little tough love. Give the boy a chance. He's young, too. You don't even know anything about him, really. I'm sure he's got just as many feelings to figure out." She kisses my forehead.

"But he didn't even give me a chance to explain. He just shut down and brought me home." I pinch my brows together, staring down at my lap.

"It's late. Maybe he was just tired and not in the right mindset to handle all of this." She waves her hands around at me.

"Thanks," I deadpan.

"You know what I mean. You can be a lot when you're upset. You get that from me. But don't fret, he'll come around and learn to deal with it if he's meant to. If not, you'll find someone who will. He was right, you know, you shouldn't let others bring down your vibrancy. You've lost your spunk."

"Not this again, Mom. Not you too." I sigh, plopping onto my back dramatically. "Veronica is my *best* friend. I haven't 'lost' myself. I'm just finding a new me."

"Well, the new you that she's brought about is bland and no fun. I hate to see you so... gray. You hardly ever wear sparkles or colorful clothes anymore. You're just not you when you're around her." Her face is soft, but the words are still far more sharp than I expected.

"Maybe I'm just growing up, has anyone ever considered that?" I retort.

"Growing up and giving up aren't synonymous." She pats me on the shoulder before getting up and exiting my room. Leaving me with nothing but more questions and confusion.

Morning light warms my face. My head is pounding from the excessive sobbing last night. I drag myself out of bed and pull open my old oak dresser drawer. As I peruse the stacks of neatly folded shirts, my mother's words float around in my mind.

I know she's right. I don't dress like *me* anymore. The beige, burgundy and gray tones in this drawer are boring—my life is boring. I don't remember the last time I did anything that was actually fun. Karaoke and trivia nights don't count, they're just excuses for Veronica to find hookups.

Impulse—or maybe it's instinct—takes control and I dig into the back of my drawer. An old tie-dye sweater dress I used to wear like a second skin unfurls in my hands. Buttery-soft fabric, so familiar and nostalgic it feels like a lifeline. Once I've slipped it over my head and found a pair of pastel purple leggings to wear with it, I admire myself in the mirror.

Staring at my reflection is invigorating. It's as if a small, previously lost, part of *me* has been re-absorbed into my soul. I feel unstoppable as I march out of my room... until I reach the kitchen.

My mother's ocean blue eyes glitter with excitement and warmth. Dad, on the other hand, is slack-jawed and rightfully confused. The third person has me frozen in place. I had heard my parents talking to someone as I approached, and assumed it was Nikolai.

I was *very* wrong.

Standing in front of me is an awestruck, completely speechless Jude, less than twenty-four hours after making me cry myself to sleep. He's wearing yet another pair of ripped black jeans and a deep blue Foreigner shirt stretching across his broad chest. He's every father's worst nightmare personified. Milk chocolate helmet hair falls over his thick brows, but I can still tell they're glued to the ceiling.

Right, I look like the nineties exploded all over me. He'll never look at me the same after this.

Hello, embarrassment, we meet again.

"Uh, hi," he squeaks out, cheeks flushing with unfamiliar rosiness, unlike the way they redden for Veronica.

"Why are you here?" I snap.

Shit, my tone was too sharp.

Jude visibly winces.

"Now, Caroline. Jude came to apologize. He also assured me that he's *extremely* safe while you're on the bike with him. Right?" My father squeezes him on the shoulder before taking on his signature 'Dad' pose—arms crossed, slightly raised brows, mouth in a straight line. Nothing more than an intimidation tactic.

Oddly, it seems to work on Jude, who nods stiffly as he replies, "Yes, Sir."

"Now Honey Bunny, leave the poor boy to his apology. Caroline, go on and take a walk out back with Jude." An ear-to-ear grin pulls at my mother's face.

"A... walk?" I still can't move—my legs are locked in place. "Why?" My nose crinkles as I scrunch up my face.

"I upset you last night. I didn't really know how to react, but I want to tell you I'm sorry for bein' a dick." My father sputters next to him. "Sorry, Sir." He worries his lip, chewing on the silver hoop looped through it.

"Well let's go then." Slipping on a pair of white flip-flops, I march out the door toward the field behind our house. Angrily trying to stomp away from Jude is of no use. He's nearly a foot taller than me, so his long legs eat up the short distance my efforts put between us.

"Candy, please slow down."

Everything stops as he takes my hand in his. The electricity shooting up my arm sends my heart into overdrive. Flutters, there are *actual* flutters in my stomach.

"I like this." He slides a finger along the cut collar of my sweater dress. "It's cute, has character. You look alive and radiant." His eyes melt into mine, voice earnest and low.

Well, shit.

How am I supposed to stay upset with him now?

Right, I'm upset, completely pissed.

"I thought you were going to apologize?" I fold my arms, shrugging off his touch.

He sighs, scrubbing a hand over his face. "I am sorry. I just... I've been through a lot, and I can have a short fuse. I was in over my head last night. Veronica is relentless and it kills me to see how much her actions hurt you. You just let her make you feel so... beneath her. But you're not." He pulls me down to sit next to him in the grass.

My first instinct is to defend Veronica and tell him he's wrong, but everything that has happened since he came into my life has slowly started to open my eyes—and my mind.

"I'm sorry." I mumble, my damn lip wobbles on its own.

"Hey, no. Please, I can't handle it when you cry." He scoots closer, putting an arm around me.

"Sorry. Everything is just so overwhelming. I'll pull it together."

But I don't.

His warmth is welcoming, and the tears fall on their own when I lean into him.

"Shh. Please you're too beautiful to cry over the likes of Veronica." He wraps his other arm around me, too. I'm securely cocooned in his presence as his large hands rub my back, similar to the way my mother does—only this feels *much* less platonic. The firmness of his chest and strength of his embrace make me tingle all over.

I bury my face in the crook of his neck and inhale. As

familiar cedarwood and spices fill my senses, I let out a shaky sigh.

Am I turned on right now?

Panic floods my system as Jude tenses up. Realizing what I'm doing, and fully aware that there's no way in hell I'm his type, I attempt to pull away. But he doesn't let me. Instead, his arms tighten, holding me securely against him.

"Don't move. Please." His voice sounds oddly husky, strained even.

"I'm sorry. I didn't mean to make it weird." Wiggling in his grasp, I tilt my head up toward him to catch my breath.

Without warning he tips his face down, pressing his lips to mine softly—far more timidly than I would have expected.

Caught off guard, I let out a squeak of surprise. Until now, kissing Jude had been a hopeful fantasy, something I convinced myself was completely unattainable.

Yet here we are.

A low grumble resonates deep in his chest sparking flames under my skin. In a fluid motion, he pulls me onto his lap, settling his grip on my waist.

Holy shit. I'm kissing Jude and straddling him and he's kissing me back.

I gasp from the sensations rushing through me, and he slips his tongue into my open mouth, tangling with mine. They dance together like they were made for each other. His hungry, exploratory hands travel up and down the length of my body, stopping to rest firmly on the curves of my ass.

My own hands finally catch up and move tentatively to his hair. As I lace my fingers into his waves, his grip tightens guiding my hips to grind my aching core against him.

Oh my God he's hard.

I pull my tingly lips from his. Despite the throbbing between my legs, desperately begging for more friction, the feeling of his arousal has pulled me from the moment.

"I'm sorry. God I'm—" I sputter, unsure of how to spill my guts to him.

"It's okay. I'm the one who's sorry, this isn't why I came over. Fuck." He rakes his fingers through his hair as I climb off his lap. He shifts his weight, adjusting the bulge in his jeans.

"I-I've never kissed anyone before. Like *really* kissed them anyway. I wasn't prepared for all of that. Just so you know, I'm not desperate or anything." A vibrant blush burns my cheeks.

"You—" He bites his lip, exhaling through his nose. "That was your first kiss?" Wide eyes search my face, as if they're trying to find a lie buried somewhere.

"Yes, okay? I'm almost nineteen and have never kissed anybody. Honestly, I've never really cared about it befo re... well, you." I stand, dusting myself off.

"Jesus, Candy. Why didn't you say somethin'? I was two seconds from rippin' those leggings apart and fuckin' you in this field," he says, while standing and brushing off his pants.

"Holy shit. Here?!" I spread my arms out, motioning to the grassy expanse surrounding us. "With me? Why?"

"Yes, right here, and you tell me."

"Tell you what?" I tilt my head with a quirked brow.

"You're askin' me why I want you. But the real question is why do *you* want *me*? You don't even know me. Why am I the first person you've ever kissed? It doesn't seem like you didn't want it." His tone isn't judgmental, I can hear the confusion in his words, though.

"You're just, *you*. I don't know what it is, but I just feel little sparks when you're around." My voice trembles as I peel back a small layer of my defenses.

"So, it's okay for you to feel that way about me, but you can't begin to comprehend that maybe I feel like that about you, too?" His rich, deep brown eyes burn with intensity.

"You could have anyone you want," I mumble, intended more for myself than him.

"I don't want anyone but you. I shouldn't even want you, but I do. There are things about me that you need to know before anything else can happen between us. What you learn may just kill those butterflies you're feelin'." He turns and stalks back in the direction of my house, leaving me dumbfounded.

CHAPTER 5

Jude

What a colossal fucking mess. How stupid can I be? The second those soft, sweet lips of hers landed on mine I should have pulled back. I should have broken her heart even further. I should let her leave me behind and never look back. But I just can't let her go.

You're a selfish fucking idiot, Jude.

I'm already slipping. My chest feels tight. I don't want to cut Caroline off, but she needs to know what she's getting herself into. Divulging the deepest, darkest parts of yourself to someone is utterly terrifying. I could use some words of encouragement, but I don't have anyone for that. So, I'll settle for a reminder of what *not* to do.

My hands shake as I pull my phone out and dial my mothers number. She picks up on the third ring.

"Jude. What do you want?" Her voice sounds colder than ever.

"I'm not gonna sugar coat it, I'm struggling." I puff out an exasperated breath.

"Already?"

"It's just... girl problems, and they're makin' me itch," I grumble, preparing for the verbal lashing.

"I guess it could be worse. How many? Nobody is pregnant are they?" The judgment in her tone stings, just enough to slap some sense into me.

"Ma, I haven't slept with anyone."

"What's the problem then? Drama in the friend group? I thought they were *study buddies*." The increased sarcasm in her voice grates on my nerves.

"It's not that—" I lean back against my wall, softly banging my head off it repeatedly.

"Oh! It's *the* girl then?" she cuts in.

I sigh, knowing exactly what she's going to tell me. "Yes, it's Caroline. That's her name."

"Oh. Caroline Carlisle is a bit of a mouthful." She jokes flatly.

"Mama! This is serious. I messed up." I lean back, resting my head against the wall I'm leaning on.

Why did I call her again?

"Not shocked to hear, just grow a pair. Don't be like your daddy." If eye rolls made a sound, hers would be deafening.

"But she's the exact opposite of me. She's a good girl, doesn't drink, and has probably never come close to a drug in her life. Hell, she kissed the shit out of me then blushed and told me she's never kissed anyone before, meaning she's probably a virgin, Ma. What am I supposed to do?" I groan, pushing off the wall.

"Let her live a normal life. Don't you dare hurt her."

"What are you, *her* mom?" From my tone alone I'm sure she can tell how hard I'm scowling.

I'm fairly certain Caroline's mother likes me, unlike the she-devil on the other end of my phone.

"If I was her mama, I'd lock her in a room to keep your grimy hands off of her," she grumbles.

"Good thing her mom is a decent woman." A sneer tugs at my face.

"I've had enough of your attitude, Boy." She hangs up, leaving me to spiral.

I unlatch my futon and toss my phone on the mattress next to me as I flop down onto it. Staring blankly at my ceiling, I contemplate my next moves. If I'm going to do this, I need to slowly show Caroline that I want *her* and only her. Not Veronica, not Adalina, not anyone else. At the same time, my mother's words fester in the wounds she's opened. Deep down, I know Caroline deserves better. If I was a good man I would just cut my losses and let her live a normal life without me.

It's been the longest month ever. Having Caroline *right* there within reach every Wednesday and Friday is torture. She's been putting on a brave face and trying to act like our make-out session in the field meant nothing, but I know better. Not only was it her first, but it was also the kiss of a lifetime.

Nothing in my life has ever lit my soul on fire and felt so right before.

"I still don't know how to feel about all of this." Veronica frowns, motioning to Caroline's outfit as we sit at a table in the campus café.

She has been wearing vibrant colored frilly tops and high waisted pleated skirts that do everything for her curves. I haven't heard one fucking word Professor Davidson has said these last few weeks.

"I've missed color. I don't know why I ever stopped wearing fun clothes." She beams.

Veronica rolls her eyes, visibly unimpressed.

"Chica, it's... *you* that's for sure." Adalina chuckles.

She's definitely the meat in the middle of the strange friendship sandwich these three have going on. Truthfully, I think she just wants to be included—even if that means alienating others.

"I think you're cute."

Shit was that my mouth?

Three shocked faces whirl in my direction.

"You think she's *cute*?" Veronica spits like a threatened cat.

Caroline has a warm, hopeful look on her face, completely contrasting the disbelief all over Veronica's. At this moment I wish I could disappear.

"Y-yes," I stumble over my words, fidgeting with the wrapper of my sandwich. "She is cute, her clothes really show off her sweet personality." I smile softly at Caroline, who is now glowing with a bright blush.

"Oh, I forgot. I've got an appointment and can't do lunch today. See you all later!" Veronica stands and dashes away.

"That was... odd," Adalina speaks up from across the table.

"Tell me about it." Caroline quirks a brow.

"Are you coming to karaoke night tomorrow, Chica? We haven't been since before your birthday." Adalina pops a tater tot into her mouth.

I missed her birthday?

"Oh, yeah, I should be able to make it. Nicky bought himself a little Camry. It's nothing fancy but frees up the family car for me to use more often."

"He's some famous artist, right? How is he still living at your place with nothing to his name?" Another tater tot meets its fate between her molars.

"He's being 'smart' as he says. Something about planning for the future." Caroline shrugs. "I don't mind. We're close and I'd honestly be lost without him. I don't think any of us are ready for him to move out yet anyway."

"What about you, Handsome? You coming out?" Adalina winks at me, wiggling her eyebrows.

"I don't have anything better to do." My eyes meet Caroline's, asking for silent approval.

"It'll be fun." She forces a smile. "My birthday was Monday and I didn't celebrate so we can call it a late party."

Images of our last karaoke night flash through my

mind. Caroline's devastated face haunts my dreams. Veronica isn't going to get the better of me this time. I won't allow her to.

Caroline makes her way out of the café when we've finished our food. I know her classes, like mine, are done for the day.

Hot on her heels, I tap her on the shoulder. "Are you sure karaoke is okay?"

"Yeah. I didn't get the chance to celebrate my birthday with everyone, so it'll be great. I might even try to sing something this time." Another strained smile crosses her face.

"Well, maybe I'll sing you somethin' as a belated birthday present." My voice might just be my secret weapon. She told me she can't sing, but I never told her that *I* can.

"I was only kidding. You don't want to hear me butcher a song you might like." She snorts adorably.

"You know what I want to hear?" I lean toward her, earning me a tentative shudder. "Anything that comes from that sweet mouth of yours."

"Oh." A breathy sigh rushes out of her.

Fiery desire burns in her eyes as she bites her lip. There's no doubt in my mind that she wants me too. I'm doing my best to move slowly, but the opportunity to tease her and build the tension is too good to pass up. An entire month has gone by since I had that taste of her. I'm dying for more. Fuck being the bigger person.

With a satisfied, crooked grin, I break off and head for my bike.

She follows, speed walking to keep up. "What is your deal?" She huffs out of breath.

Grabbing my helmet, I turn to face her. "My deal? What do you mean?"

"You've been acting weird. You never actually apologized to me for being a dick. Then you kiss the hell out of me, only to ignore me ever since. But I feel like you've been undressing me with your eyes every time you see me." A pouty scowl covers her face as she crosses her arms.

"I don't have my spare, here." I hand my helmet to her.

"What is this for?" She squeaks.

"Get on. I need to talk to you, in private."

"I'm in a skirt. I'm *not* showing my goods to the world." Her heels dig into the pavement.

I reach into my bag and pull out a pair of spare sweatpants. "Here, these will work."

"Wow, I'm *so* telling Vi I got in your pants." She chuckles mischievously.

My mind goes straight to the gutter at the thought, paired with the sight of her pulling my pants over her thick, luscious thighs.

"Oh, they're a bit snug." She pulls her lip between her teeth, trying to hide her embarrassment.

"You won't be wearing them for long. It's just to get you back to my place."

She jolts, eyes wide. "Y-your place? What are we going to do there?" I can't tell if she's nervous from discomfort, or excitement.

"I told you. I want to talk. I said there are things you need to know about me, and I think it's time you do." I clench my jaw, biting back my own nerves. I'm either about to scare her off for good, or she's about to make my day. "Just know that I won't blame you if you never talk to me again."

"Jude. Are you a serial killer? Am I about to be a statistic? Will you at least let me tell my parents I love them?"

I know she's joking, but I've also learned that she uses humor to hide her discomfort.

"I'm not going to hurt you, Candy." I offer her my hand.

She slides my helmet on and lets me help her onto my bike, relaxing against me. The ride to my apartment isn't long, but I'm tempted to take a few wrong turns to just enjoy this feeling, in case it's the last time she ever let's me this close. But, this needs to happen, so I make quick work of getting us to my place.

We climb the front steps and I lead her inside.

"I thought you lived in the dorms?" Her eyes travel around my space, undoubtedly taking in the disarray as she kicks her shoes off.

Damn it, I need to finish unpacking.

"Nah, just found this little gem. It works." I grab two bottles of water out of the fridge, make my way over and stretch out on the futon that doubles as my bed. "Come sit." I pat the spot next to me.

She pauses for a moment, before wiggling out of my

pants. Dropping down next to me, she displays some more of her newfound confidence and swings her legs over my lap.

Fuck, why does she have to be so comfortable around me? Why can't I keep my hands from rubbing her feet? Why doesn't she stop me?

Speak, Jude.

"So..." I trail off, tracing a circle around her ankle.

"So..." She raises her brows with a slight tilt of her head, sighing as I massage her calves. "If this is how I die, so be it. Totally worth it."

A laugh bubbles out of me before I can stop it. "You're not going to die. Hell, I'll massage these perfect legs of yours every day if you still want me to after this."

"Jude, we're... friends. I don't know much about you, but how bad can your secrets be?" Her face crinkles playfully.

"I had a rough upbringing." I sigh, working my jaw as I try to remember the plan I had for this conversation.

"Okay. Are you a secret mafia heir or something?" I twist my face, completely caught off guard. "Sorry, I read a lot of romance novels." She snickers.

"No, not a mafia heir. But I, uh—" I gulp down a swig of water. "—I'm not exactly a good guy." She tenses under my palms. "Wait, that came out wrong. I'm not a bad guy either... not really anyway. But I did go to juvie for a few years." I can't look at her, my eyes are glued to a stray freckle on the top of her left foot.

"Juvie? As in prison for minors?" Her voice raises

slightly, but her legs stay in my lap.

I might be able to save this, if my damn mouth would work.

"Yeah… can I explain?" I turn my hopeful eyes to her and she nods faintly.

Thank fuck.

"Mama was sixteen when she had me, Daddy didn't stick around. She did her best to raise me, but that's not sayin' much. I didn't have a good home life." She nods again, listening intently. "She turned eighteen and went to work at a gentleman's club in the next town over and built a reputation for sleepin' around and chasin' her next high. Our small town was… very unkind. My entire life I was nothin' more than the son of a sinner, so I grew up alone with no friends." I gently squeeze her calf and exhale a rough breath.

"Oh, Jude." She places a hand on my arm.

"I fell into the wrong crowd durin' high school. I was just so desperate to fit in. I did a ton of drugs, sold them too… and eventually got caught." My words are less and less audible as shame creeps in.

"Drugs?! Like what?" She practically screams, but still stays put.

Okay, I had expected worse. This is still salvageable.

"A lot of different types, but Coke was my poison of choice, that's what I went away for, but I was also a heavy drinker and had a lot of careless sex… I probably couldn't name most of the girls if I tried." I chew my lip ring and stare at the floor, afraid to look at her.

"So… am I just another nameless conquest?" She asks with a trembling voice.

The painful tone strangles my heart.

"No, I promise you're not. I moved here to start over. I didn't plan on meetin' you and bein' so drawn to you. I don't want to just fuck you and forget you. That's not who I'm tryin' to be anymore." I fire off as fast as possible.

I'm losing her.

"You don't still do drugs, do you?" While her voice is softer, the warning is evident.

"No, I've been clean for eight months. I haven't even slept with anyone in almost a year. You're the first girl I've kissed in just as long." When I look into her watery eyes, her lower lip juts out.

"I-I don't know what to say. What is your play here?"

"Caroline, I like you, a lot. I've never felt such a strong connection before. I might be the polar fuckin' opposite of who you should be with, but if you can find a way to let me, I'd like to call you mine." I'm sure to keep my eyes on hers, gauging her reaction.

"Like, you want to *date* me?" Her mouth falls open with a sharp inhale.

"Only when you're ready, but if you want me to fuck off just tell me." I soften my face as best as I can.

"Can I have some time to think about it? This is a lot to process, but I really appreciate your honesty. I just… don't know how to feel right now." When her legs leave my lap, it feels like part of me goes with them.

"You can have all the time you need, there's no pressure. I've done some shitty things, and can be a bit of an ass, but I promise I'm tryin' to do better." My voice is small, buried under the weight of my regret.

"I just need to try and come to terms with all the information you just shared." She stands, sliding her shoes on. "I'm going to call my parents to come pick me up."

"Okay." I mumble, completely defeated.

"Hey, I'm not running away. I just need some time to think." She leans over and timidly presses her lips to my cheek, leaving me absolutely stunned.

Maybe there's still hope.

CHAPTER 6

Caroline

I intentionally called my mother to pick me up—asking Dad would only lead to questions I'm not ready to answer. My head is pressed against the window as we drive. A dramatic sigh escapes me as my mind spins out of control.

"Lovey, what were you doing there?" Her voice is tense, laced with concern.

"Mom. That was Jude's place... He wanted to talk."

"About what? Is talking code for sex?" Her tone is playful, yet cautious.

"Mom! Oh my God!" I gasp.

"Caroline you're nineteen, and he's a good-looking boy who is completely smitten with you," she presses.

"First of all, he's not smitten." I cross my arms with an incredulous huff. "He also brought me there to talk about his past. One that I don't know if I can accept. Dad won't, that's for sure." I sag in my seat.

"Your father loves you and honestly wouldn't be happy with just about any boy you bring home. He wants only the best for his little girl, but despite all of the theatrics, he likes Jude." She pats my leg softly.

"He wouldn't if he knew his history."

"Does it change the way you feel about him?" She tilts her head slightly, keeping her eyes on the road.

"I don't know. Part of me feels bad for him. I want to understand what he went through, but his life was so much harder than anything I could imagine. I don't know that I'd have done anything different if I was in his shoes. He went to juvie for drugs, Mom, and told me he used to have meaningless sex with tons of girls he can't even remember!" My hands flail wildly as I ramble.

"Oh, that poor lost boy." She pushes out her lower lip.

"See! That's partially how I feel. I want to give him a chance, but I'm scared. What if he breaks my heart?" My chin wobbles as I choke on the words.

"Lovey, he probably will." She sighs softly.

"Wow. Thanks, Mom," I shoot back in a flat tone.

"You didn't let me finish. He probably will, *but* you can't deny yourself experiences because something *might* happen. Even if he does break your heart, enjoy the good times before and after. Your Dad broke my heart once or twice over the years, you know. I broke his once, too" She pats my thigh again.

"There's no way. Your relationship is perfect," I gasp, wide eyed as we pull into our driveway.

"Yes, it is now. But it didn't start that way, and it damn sure didn't get that way without love and dedication. If you care, there's not a lot that can stop you from making things work. Just as long as it's not self-sabotaging. Don't discount the feelings you have for him because you're scared, that's all I'm saying." She shifts the car into park and hops out. "Now, what's your story so I can cover for you?" She whispers, laughing quietly.

"Mom! You're terrible... but I was at Vi's and we got into an argument, so I had you come get me." I chew my lip from the guilt of lying to my dad. It's never something I've had to do before.

He's seated in the recliner when we walk into the living room.

"Hi, Dad. How was your day?" I ask a bit too cheerfully.

Play it cool Caroline.

"It was good. Five-year-olds keep me on my toes." He says gruffly.

I chuckle at the mental image.

If anyone looks at my dad, the last thing they'd ever guess is that he teaches kindergarten. His sternness is all an act though, there's no masking the way his face lights up when his kids are around. Someday I want to give him the football team full of grand babies he yearns for. If only my body would come to an agreement with my heart.

"Are you alright, Solnyshko?" He asks with furrowed brows.

Shit, was I daydreaming?

"Yeah, I'm just tired. Had a fight with Vi. I'm going to

go lay down." I fake a yawn, it doesn't quite sell my story.

"Was it over Jude?" His voice drops in an unfamiliar way. "That girl can't let you have anything, can she?"

His accent is so thick, I know he's upset. But... why he's upset has my head spinning.

"Wait, you're bothered because of the fight? Not because of Jude?" I stumble, caught off guard by the turn of events.

"Solnyshko, that boy looks at you like you're his salvation. I know the look well. I'm not fond of his bike, or his tattoos... or his questionable fashion choices, but we had a decent chat the other morning. I can respect a man with the backbone to realize he's done wrong, and the heart to work toward fixing it."

"You don't hate him?" Maybe this won't be so bad.

"Heavens, no. But if he hurts you, that'll be a different story." He leans back, opening his arms for a hug. I fling myself at him. Dad's hugs are the best, Nikolai's are a close second. The Koval men are just giant teddy bears. "Be careful," he grumbles in my ear.

"What if I told you he might be as bad as he looks?" My voice is muffled by his shoulder.

"I'd rather not know." He pats my back softly before releasing his hold.

I hug my mother and stroll to my room with boosted confidence. As I lay in my bed, my entire body buzzes with renewed energy. Having my parents' support is huge. My mind was half made up already, but their encouragement tipped the scales.

My palms itch under the weight of my phone. With a racing heart I pull up Jude's contact.

Me: *Hi*

Big Guy: *Hey. I'm honestly surprised you're talking to me.*

Me: *I'm sorry for leaving.*

Big Guy: *Don't be. I expected you to storm out and block my number.*

Me: *Give me a little credit. I'm not that shallow.*

Big Guy: *Sorry, I didn't mean it like that. I don't think you're shallow at all.*

Me: *I told my mom.*

He doesn't respond for a few minutes.

Me: *Don't freak out. She likes you and understands.*

Big Guy: *I'm not sure your dad would agree.*

Me: *He said he'd rather not know, but he respects you for having a backbone ha!*

Big Guy: *Oh?*

Me: *Yeah, so don't stress. Okay?*

Big Guy: *But what about you? Your opinion is all that really matters to me.*

A lump catches in my throat. Nobody has ever cared enough about my opinion for it to hold any real weight.

Me: *I don't know what you mean.*

Big Guy: *Do you still want me in your life? If not, I'll leave you alone.*

Me: *Oh. Of course I still want you around. I really want to spend time with you... alone.*

Big Guy: *We can hang out whenever you want, Candy. Just say the word.*

Me: *What would we do?*

Big Guy: *Whatever you want. I'm just happy to be there.*

My chest tightens. He's so lonely, like a lost puppy looking for a home. Except he looks more like an attack dog. But the little pieces I've seen, the real Jude underneath his rough exterior, is caring and kind.

Me: *How about you come pick me up tomorrow and we watch a movie? I can help you unpack the rest of your stuff.*

Big Guy: *Yikes. I was hoping it wasn't that bad. Aren't you going to karaoke tomorrow?*

Shit, I got so distracted by the thought of spending time with him that I forgot about our plans.

Me: *Oh, right. Well maybe Sunday? I don't have class on Monday.*

Big Guy: *If I don't scare you off tomorrow, then definitely Sunday. Sleep well.*

Me: *Good Night.*

"Mom!" I shriek from my bathroom.

In seconds she's swinging the door open, staring at the

catastrophe in front of her. "Lovey, what on Earth are you doing?" She jumps into action, working to untangle my mass of knotted hair from the round brush it's infinitely tangled in.

"I wanted to do my hair differently and now I'm going to have to shave my head!" I wail, throwing arms up.

"It's nothing I can't manage, just sit still." She grabs a comb and gets to work.

It takes about fifteen minutes, but she manages to get me untangled from myself. I finish my makeup and slip on a pink lace cami. I'm not riding on Jude's bike tonight, so I pair it with a lavender and pink plaid skirt.

"Wow, you look like... you," Nikolai blurts out when I enter the living room.

Lilah eyes me, clung to him like the barnacle she is. "Are you trying to seduce someone? You look way sluttier than normal." Her upper lip is furiously curled as she scrutinizes my appearance.

My mouth flies open to offer a rebuttal, but Nikolai speaks up before I have the chance, "She's not slutty, Lilah! It's cute, very... *Caroline*."

"Wow Nicky, you found your balls. Good job." I smile smugly at him.

"Ew, you're so unladylike." Lilah places her hand over her chest as if me saying "balls" is the most atrocious thing she's ever heard.

"I'm just glad he's finally got his *balls* back. You've had them clutched in your talons for far too long." I sneer.

Nikolai snorts, attempting to cover it by fake coughing.

"Boo Bear!" Lilah cries. "You're not going to let her talk to me like that are you?" Her over plucked brows crinkle together as she frowns.

"Eh, it's all in good fun." With a shrug, Nikolai shuts her down.

I'm not sure what's been going on between them recently, but he's far less susceptible to her manipulation.

"Anyway, I'm leaving. It's karaoke night. We haven't been in over a month. I don't know when I'll be home." With a wave, I grab the keys off the table and saunter out the door, feeling confident and empowered.

Jude had better be ready for me.

CHAPTER 7

Jude

My soul lights up when Caroline enters the building. She's as vibrant as ever. The lacy little top she's wearing showcases her curves like nothing I've ever seen. If only Veronica and Adalina would have gotten a flat tire on the way here, so I could have her to myself.

As they break through the crowd, my eyes land on her lower half.

Mother of God. She's in another tiny, pleated skirt, but her signature leggings are nowhere to be found. My eyes devour every silky inch of her exposed legs. I bite my cheek, calming the fire building in my veins. I need to stop openly ogling her. The increased tension between the three of them over the last month is all because of me. There's a competition going on, and I despise it.

Eighteen-year-old me would have just fucked all of them, most likely at the same time, and dipped out. But that's not me now and Caroline isn't the type of girl you just get a taste of and walk away, I know from experience.

One kiss was all it took for every part of me to want so much more with her.

I can almost picture our life together—A bunch of dogs, maybe a few kids. Lots of love and affection. Knowing where I stand and having someone so vibrant and carefree to keep me grounded.

That hope crashes and burns in an instant as the small, logical portion of my conscience wakes up. Immediately I'm reminded that any dreams of a future with her are foolish. She may not have completely freaked out over my past, but she's too pure for someone as tainted as me. In a perfect world, we'd be college sweethearts. She'd be the same smart, driven picture of perfection, and I'd be someone worthy of walking beside her.

Fortunately, the semester is almost over. If this weekend flops, I have a plan to slowly remove myself from her life.

Do I want to do it? No—especially not now.

Seeing her like this is absolute torture. She's all the things I never knew I needed.

The music is almost deafening tonight, so I've found a nice table away from the stage. A drunk man is currently butchering "I Kissed a Girl" but I barely notice. Caroline is all smiles when they make it to where I'm sitting, drawing my full attention.

"Will you sing a duet with me?" Veronica bats her lashes my way as they join me. "I bet that deep, silky voice of yours would sound hot as hell singing 'Your Man'." She fans her face.

Caroline rolls her eyes. "That's so stereotypical, Vi."

"Tell me I'm wrong. Addie, you agree with me, right?" Veronica uses the same coaxing look I've seen a dozen times now.

"Most definitely," Adalina replies with a lackluster nod.

She's taken a back seat to Veronica in the past few weeks. I'm not sure if it's surrender on her part, or if she's started to tire of Veronica's game. Regardless of the reason, she's much more respectful than Veronica and I'm thankful for it.

"I'm not really into country music. I know the song but won't be singin' it. I signed up for a *solo* spot later though. No duets for me." I toss back the last of my beer.

I shouldn't drink, especially since I rode my bike here. But with Veronica's incessant flirting, I'm going to need more where that came from.

"Can you sneak me a drink, Baby?" She brazenly presses her tits together, as if it would make a difference to me.

"Nope, you're only twenty, and I'm no one's *baby*." I shrug her off. My patience for her antics is already paper thin, and they just got here.

"But I'll be twenty-one in a few months." Her lower lip—painted bright red—pops out.

"Then you'll have to wait a few months." I offer a tight smile and make my way to the dance floor. It's not the safest spot, considering Veronica will likely try and steal me away again, but I can't keep sitting here and subjecting myself to this bullshit.

This is only our third outing as a group. The last time was just to watch a movie. I should have sat in the aisle seat and made sure Caroline was next to me, but I didn't. I ended up awkwardly sitting between her and Veronica—who started indiscreetly rubbing my thigh and, naturally, my dick took it upon himself to respond. Even after I removed her hand she leaned into me and grabbed a hold of my hard-on through my jeans. I definitely shoved her away harder than necessary, but fuck it.

Caroline saw everything that happened and called her out on it. The confrontation was surprising to say the least. Call me a cynic, but I had assumed the worst. I thought for sure that Caroline would take Veronica's side and never talk to me again. It's just how life goes.

I'm always disposable.

But my Candy Girl continues to amaze me. Like right now.

Confidence radiates off of her as he struts up to me, swinging her curvaceous hips—with a challenging glint in her eye. All my good intentions crumble when she trails her hands down my chest, twirling around to face away from me. We dance, but it's nothing like the last time we were here. Her body sways seductively, the way she rolls her hips against me is borderline indecent.

I love it.

Grinding against my growing erection, her skirt rides up exposing the faintest bit of her ass. I lean down, inhaling her sweet perfume and press myself harder against her.

"This skirt should be illegal," I murmur into her ear, ghosting my lips over her neck.

"You would know, Big Guy." She smirks back at me.

"Who are you and what have you done with my Candy Girl?" I whisper against the exposed skin of her shoulder.

Thank God we're in a secluded corner of the club, the music is just quiet enough to hear each other and the crowd couldn't care less about what we're doing. After scanning our surroundings, I slip my right hand between us. The soft skin of her ass is warm in my palm as I caress it.

"You're playing a *very* dangerous game." A rumble rolls through my chest.

Biting her lip, she arches her back as we continue to move together, allowing me the smallest amount of contact with her pussy. Too far gone to care, I slide her lacy panties to the side, teasing her with my middle finger.

If she's nervous, there's no sign of it in the way she continues to roll her hips. She's not even bothering to look around. Fortunately, I'm alert and making sure nobody can see what's going on in our little corner of the room.

"Keep it up and I'll make you scream for me in the middle of this club. This is your only warning." I growl into her ear.

"You wouldn't." She breathes out.

I lean into her, and she stills. "Oh, but I would." I slide my free hand up to grip her throat.

The subtle way her breath hitches almost snaps my control. Defiantly, she presses against me, slipping the tip of my finger inside of her. A needy whimper breaks free from her throat, vibrating against my palm. We're going too far and I know it, but I nip at her neck regardless. With a gasp, she rocks back pushing my finger deeper into her warmth.

Fuck, she'll be the end of me in one way or another.

We can't do this here. Our first time—her *first* time–can't happen like this, I won't allow it. But she's also a fucking brat and needs to learn that being a tease comes with consequences.

Pulling my finger out of her, I tighten my grip around her throat and work her clit until she's squirting against me. Tiny gasps and jerks of her hips almost convince me to let her come. But she hasn't earned it yet.

"You're misbehavin' and this is what happens. Be a good girl for the rest of the night and I'll fuck you on *every* surface of my apartment tomorrow." I force through my clenched jaw and release my hold on her.

"Jude. Please," she begs with a breathy whine.

"No, not here. You deserve better than this, better than me. But I'm a greedy bastard and I'll take whatever you're willing to give. Just not like this." As I pull the hem of her skirt back down, she spins around, ready to protest.

Her pout disappears, replaced by pure shock, as I slide

my fingers into my mouth. Tasting her sweetness almost changes my mind.

"Jude!" She pushes at my chest, backing away slightly, finally taking in our surroundings. Worry etches into her expression as her lusty daze breaks.

"Nobody saw a thing, I made sure of it." I smile lazily at her.

"Stop hogging the hottie." Veronica butts in. Her breath reeks of alcohol as she fills the space between us.

What poor asshole was desperate enough to buy her drinks?

She all but pushes Caroline out of the way to press her front to mine. "Oh my. Hello there," she slurs as her wandering hand lands on the bulge in my jeans.

I'm so turned on from Caroline that my hips jerk at the contact before I have a chance to think. The second my mind catches up, I push her away from me.

"If you touch my dick *one more fuckin' time*, I'll break your Goddamned hand beyond the point of repair," I seethe, clenching my fists at my sides.

I can feel the crowd staring, but I don't care. My panicked eyes dart around until they land on Caroline across the room, her face full of hurt. My ice-cold gaze shoots back to Veronica.

"I'm not playin' these games with you," I grumble. Storming away from her, my feet carry me straight out the front door and, if Caroline is smart enough, out of her life. A message lights up my phone as I climb onto my bike.

Candy: *Please come back. :(*

Me: *Not gonna happen. I can't stand this drama. If I go back in there it'll be to drink myself numb and that's not a good idea.*

Candy: *I'm sorry. I shouldn't have been so obvious.*

Me: *What are you sorry for? You're not the problem. Don't you see that? None of this is your fault.*

Candy: *If I come outside, can we sit in my car and talk?*

Me: *Just us?*

Candy: *Yes. Vi is leaving, taking Addie with her.*

Me: *Okay.*

This is a recipe for disaster.

"Hey," she says, her voice barely above a whisper as she approaches.

"Hey," I mumble, "where's your car?"

"This way." She tilts her head, and I follow like a damn lap dog.

She cranks the engine when we're inside and turns to me.

"I'm just taking us down the road to the park, it's far less crowded, especially this late," she explains as my questioning eyes find hers.

Fortunately, the drive is short so I'm spared the awkward silence.

"So," she starts, shifting the car into park and killing the engine. "Vi is upset. I guess she thought you were interested in her." Under the dim light of the streetlamps

I can't quite read the expression on her face.

"'I'm not. Do I need to spell it out for you?" My tone is harsher than I intend, but Caroline is surprisingly unaffected.

"With your tongue?" She says with a coy smile that breaks through the darkness.

Fuck.

"You don't know what you're asking for, Candy." I reply, my voice gravelly.

"Then show me. I'm sick of pretending I don't want you, just to protect myself and my 'friendships' Jude." She huffs out.

"Your friends suck."

"I'm realizing that. I know that a bit of it is pride on Vi's part, though. She's used to men falling at her feet, begging for a chance with her. It's hard for her to think you aren't interested." The frown on her face says exactly what she's thinking—that if I don't want Veronica, there's no way I could want her.

"You're no less worthy than Veronica. I promise it's you and *only* you that I want." I turn my full attention to her, leaning over to brush her hair out of her face.

"Really?" Her eyes brighten, filled with hope.

When I nod, she squirms in her seat.

"Caroline, you're all I can think about. Wantin' you scares the shit out of me. I'm all wrong for you." I grind my teeth forcing out the harsh truth.

Instead of arguing, she stuns me by maneuvering over the center console and straddling me.

"I don't care what you think," she whispers, leaning in and kissing me.

Fire burns in my veins as my hands grip her waist. Quickly, our kiss grows feverish with need. She whimpers, sucking on my lower lip as her hand finds my zipper.

I grab her wrists to stop her and pull my mouth from hers. "Wait. I'm not fuckin' you for the first time in some random parking lot."

"But I'm ready for you." She leans in and nibbles my ear and my arguments almost disappear.

"STOP." Fuck, I said that way too harshly. I can see the cracks in her confidence forming already, so I gently cup her face in my palm. "Hey, I'm sorry. I didn't mean to be a dick about it. I just really want to do right by you. I know it's frustratin' now but just trust me. Can you do that?" I stroke her cheek with my thumb.

With tears welling in her eyes she flicks her gaze away and nods, biting her bottom lip to stop it from trembling. She lifts herself off me and returns to the driver's seat, defeated.

"I'm s-sorry." She swallows a sob.

Shit, I never want to see her cry, I can't handle it. "Hey." I reach out and cradle her jaw in my hand, turning her attention to me. "You're everything." Leaning over, I kiss her in a way I've never kissed anyone.

All of the passion and longing I feel for her ignites between us. My only hope is that she feels exactly how much I want her with each caress of my tongue against hers.

Her swollen lips pull into a content smile when I finally pull away. "Wow. That was amazing." She hums.

"Just wait 'til tomorrow, there's a lot more where that came from."

"I like the sound of that. I'll drive you back to your bike so we can get home." She starts the engine with a sleepy smile.

"Wait. I thought you were the driver for tonight? How did Veronica and Addie leave?" I lift a brow up at her.

She shrugs casually with a mischievous grin. "I may have yelled at Vi and told her to find her own ride home, Addie was just collateral damage."

Holy shit.

A chuckle rolls from deep within my chest. "Look at you standing up to her. Good girl."

"Jude, please don't call me that unless you're going to do something about it." With a whine, she pulls out of the parking lot.

"Praise kink, got it." A smirk pulls at my lips.

"I guess so. You learn something new every day, I suppose." She shrugs, trying to act unbothered but the slight rise in her voice tells me all I need to know.

"So, will I see you tomorrow? You don't have to show up. Just know that if you do, I plan on defiling you over and over again." I'm not being insecure, merely giving her the opportunity to change her mind about all of this. I'm a stubborn asshole who can handle the fallout of her friend group. But can she?

With a chaste kiss on her cheek, I get out of the car fully aware that she didn't answer. The shudder and gasp that snuck out spoke volumes.

CHAPTER 8

Caroline

I f nerves alone could kill, I'd be dead five times over. I'm sure my mother can see how hard I'm trembling from the driver's seat. Today is most likely my last day as a virgin. How does one even prepare?

I snort at the thought.

Surely most people don't know they're about to lose their virginity before it happens. I'm not some sort of puritan who cherishes it or anything like that. I just hadn't ever been interested—until I met Jude.

Attraction isn't even half of the equation. Sure, anyone with eyes can see that he's extremely good-looking, but I'm drawn to his entire existence. It doesn't make any sense to me, but I'm not complaining. There are far worse people I could be into, even though he seems to think he *is* the worst.

"What's going on in that pretty little head?" My mothers voice cuts in.

Startled, I jump and face her. "Shit, I forgot you were

here." The heat spreading across my cheeks is scalding.

"Well, Lovey, the car doesn't drive itself. Sorry for interrupting your daydreams." She chuckles softly. "Will you humor me for a second?"

"Sure..."

Oh no.

"You're freaking out and I can only assume why. I don't need to know, but if my intuition is right, just breathe. If you're ready, don't overthink it, you get that from your father. As long as you're doing it because *you* want to then try and enjoy yourself. It's going to hurt a bit at first, but if he's considerate and truly cares, it'll be worth it. If he's not, don't go back. Life is too short for bad sex with mediocre men." She shrugs, as if she didn't just completely gloss over the fact that she's read my mind.

My jaw hangs wide open, unsure of how to respond.

"Oh don't act so surprised. You're my mini-me. I know what that dreamy, infatuated look means. Just make sure he's good to you. And be safe, please. I'm too young to be a grandmother." She looks over and smiles lovingly.

"Mom! I don't even know where to start."

"Well, hopefully with some kissing, maybe a hand—"

"MOM!" I squawk, almost incoherently, "That's not what I meant!"

"Oh, I know. I'm just enjoying seeing you squirm." She chuckles. "I wouldn't worry about it, Lovey. I'm sure Jude is a good man. He seems genuine and sweet under that rough exterior he uses to protect himself." Warmth radiates from her words, easing some of my worries.

"I really like him, Mom. I don't know what I'll do if he's actually playing me." I fidget with the hem of my skirt.

"Is that why you're nervous?" She tilts her head.

"Yeah. I know it's judgmental of me, but seeing how openly touchy-feely Vi is with him makes me question whether there's something going on between them. She acts like there is, he swears there isn't. I just don't know. Maybe it's her being extra aggressive in an attempt to claim him as her own? Maybe it's just me being insecure? Why would he want me over her?" I lean against the headrest and groan loudly.

"She's always been persistent. Do you not see how she is with Nicky? She'll get all handsy with him right in front of Lilah. Rubbing his arms and back, batting her lashes. She's shameless." A slight curl pulls at her upper lip.

"Yeah, I guess you're not wrong. He did threaten to break her hand at the club last night. Though I doubt he'd actually do it. But it was reassuring enough."

"Well, we're here. You call me if you need anything and I'll be right over."

"Thanks Mom." I wrap my arms around her and squeeze until she grumbles.

I get out of the car and take a deep breath, giving myself a silent pep talk before moving. With each step closer to Jude's front door my knees and self-confidence weaken.

What am I doing? He tells me he's all wrong for me, but his greedy touches and the intensity of his lips on mine feel so right.

I raise my hand to knock, but the door swings open before I have the chance to make contact.

"You're here." Jude beams a genuine, earnest smile at me.

He doesn't grace me with them often, and every single one is an equally precious experience. He's wearing a snug black Aerosmith shirt and gray sweats. Freshly showered, his hair is still damp and his delicious scent wraps around me, drawing me in.

Someone else is in control of my body, that's the only way I can explain how utterly desperate I've become for this man. Rising to my tiptoes, I wrap my arms around his neck. He meets me halfway for a quick, yet passionate kiss—one that reinforces all the promises he made to me last night.

"Hi." His minty breath tickles my lips as he pulls away. A lively glimmer shines in his soulful eyes.

"Hi." I smile up at him. "Can I come in?"

"Oh, right. Sorry." An adorable blush stains his cheeks.

In an unexpected turn, *he's* nervous, which is probably more comforting than it should be.

"Oh." My head swivels, cataloguing his space, which is far less cluttered than the last time I was here. "You unpacked everything."

"Yeah, I've had a little time, and a lot on my mind. I got sick of lookin' at it all piled up." He smiles crookedly.

There are posters on the wall of various rock bands. New dark green curtains line the windows. He has a fruit bowl on the counter of his kitchen area with real apples and oranges in it. The little apartment is cozy and decorated surprisingly well for a twenty-one-year-old man. Sure, he sleeps on a futon, but there's nowhere to put an actual bed so I can't fault him for that. The green shag area rug is soft under my feet as I kick off my Converse. I move timidly and sit on the left side of the futon.

"So, what are we going to watch?" I ask, faking as much confidence as possible.

He circles around to the other side of me and sits close, not touching, but within reach if either of us were to shift slightly.

"Um. Well, I have some DVDs of old nineties comedies. If none of those sound good, we can stream somethin'. What's your favorite movie?"

My heart flutters. Such a simple question shouldn't get to me like this. But the version of Jude I'm being met with now is so different from the one I see around everybody else. His nervousness, and awkwardness, is endearing. Still, I don't want to answer.

"It's okay, you wouldn't watch it." I murmur, shying away from his gaze.

"If you like it, I want to know," he responds, far too sincerely.

Damn him.

I exhale, still avoiding his eyes. "*Legally Blonde.*"

"Haven't seen it. Why do you love it?" There's no judgment in his voice, just genuine curiosity.

"Elle is a lot like me... She's kind of an underdog, but she's smart and a great friend. She also loves pink." My cheeks heat as they flush. "I just relate to her, except she becomes a lawyer, not a vet." I smile shyly.

"Lawyer, veterinarian, close enough." He shrugs with a lighthearted grin. "Let's order some food and I'll see if it's available to stream. Is pizza okay?"

"More than okay. But just know that pineapple is mandatory." I pin him with a serious stare.

"I thought you were perfect before. That just solidified it." He pulls his phone out of his pocket to call in our order, completely unaware of how fuzzy my insides just became.

"We'll start once the food arrives. Can I get you a drink while we wait? I should have asked already, sorry." He winces and makes his way to the fridge. "There's bottled water, soda, I bought some fruit punch, and made sweet tea."

"I know you have the accent, and wear flannels sometimes, but it's almost easy to forget you're from the south. Then, boom! A pitcher of sweet tea." I giggle, standing to join him in the kitchen area.

"It's heaven. Don't hate." He pokes me in the side playfully. "Just for that I'm not givin' you options anymore. You'll drink the tea and love every drop."

Okay, bossy.

With the pitcher in hand, he shuffles to the cabinet and produces a plastic cup. After placing it on the counter he drops in some ice cubes and pours tea up to the brim.

"Really?" I glare at him. "I don't even get a sip to try it first?"

"Nope." He pops the "p", handing me the overflowing cup.

Under the heat of his intense gaze, I sip the smallest bit into my mouth.

"Well?" Anticipation has him practically vibrating in front of me.

"Hmm," I tease, "It'll do." I shrug and round him to return to the futon.

It's actually delicious—nice and sweet, earthy with a slight bitterness—but I can't resist toying with him. When the doorbell rings, he tips the delivery man and dishes out two paper plates full of pepperoni and pineapple pizza. We dig in immediately.

"Not big on dishes huh?" I ask around a mouthful of cheesy goodness.

"No. It's just me, and half the time I don't even eat here. So I never bought plates or nothin'." He kicks his feet up on the coffee table and presses play.

I'm a nervous wreck by the ten-minute mark. We finish our pizza, and Jude throws our used plates away. When he sits back down I inch closer to him. This may be my favorite movie, but I can't focus on a single line being said.

Torture, that's what this is. My body is burning with anticipation.

Our kiss in the field behind my house plays on repeat in my mind. The feeling of his hands on me, and his finger inside me at the club last night only fuel the fire. If I scoot in a tiny bit more, maybe he'll get the hint.

Just a little closer.

Only, instead of discreetly sliding up next to him, he has the same idea, and we simultaneously close the gap between us. In an instant I'm pressed snugly into his side. He's still for a second, then wraps his strong arm around me.

"Hi there." He scrubs his chin against the top of my head.

Feeling increasingly confident, I lay my hand on his thigh and let out an anxiously held breath. The next several minutes are spent in tense silence. With my forefinger I trace mindless patterns on his thigh as my mind whirls, waiting for him to make a move.

A breath later, he leans back, adjusts his hips and pulls me closer, laying a soft kiss against my hair. Every single nerve ending in my body is ablaze from his casual affection. Under the dim light from the TV I'm able to just make out the growing bulge in his sweats. Daring myself to explore him, I drift my fingers a fraction higher on his thigh. His breathing catches under my touch, causing a surge of arousal to shoot through me. Then his hand glides down my arm and settles on my hip.

"Don't you dare touch me until I've made you come at least once," he whispers in my ear, turning toward me.

I don't have a chance to argue before our mouths meet. This kiss is overflowing with his raw desire. Any doubts I've had about his attraction to me instantly fly out the window.

Using our connection to coax me onto my back, he rises above me, eagerly slipping his tongue between my lips. I moan into his mouth, drawing a husky rumble from his chest as my fingers lace through his hair. Arching my back, I squirm underneath him, desperate for more.

"Jude," I plead.

"Shh. I'm right here. You're going to be saying my name a whole lot more over the next few hours." His scorching, full lips move languidly from my mouth and trail down my jaw.

"H-hours?" A breathy gasp rushes out of me as he nibbles on the sensitive spot at the crook of my neck, sliding his hand out of my shirt to find my knee.

"Mmm, yeah. I promised to make you come all over my apartment, didn't I?" Rough fingers glide up my thigh. "Do you have any fuckin' clue how hard these sexy little skirts make me? I'll have to buy you more," he mumbles against my skin, slipping his hand under the hem as his mouth slowly continues its descent down my chest.

Aching for *more* I quickly pull my shirt over my head, breaking our connection. Jude leans back on his heels and drags his gaze all over my body. Exposed like this, I feel insecurity begin to creep in—until I see the heat in his eyes.

"Jesus, Candy look at all of this silky perfection you're gonna let me explore." Leaning forward, he trails his lips across my stomach, leaving goosebumps in their wake. All of my lingering self-consciousness is forgotten.

"Please," I beg as my entire vocabulary is reduced to one word.

A devilish grin splits his face. When he pulls back I want to protest, until he slips his fingers into the waistband of my panties, sliding them off in a slow, smooth motion. I move to pull my skirt off, but he grabs hold of my wrists.

"It stays on, for now. Understood?" His command is hypnotic.

There's a rough, domineering edge to him that breaks through occasionally. My body tingles when he lets it show.

Swallowing hard, I nod, still unable to speak.

"Glad to see you can be a good girl when you're motivated." He lifts one of my feet to his shoulder, kissing my ankle, and my world tips on its axis. I quiver as he continues up my calf, stopping at the bend of my knee. "Good girls get rewarded. So tell me, do you want to come on my face, or fall apart on my fingers first?"

Repositioning himself, he lays between my legs and trails teasing kisses up to the crease of my thigh. He stops to slide my skirt up and glances at me while nibbling at my sensitive skin. As I continue to squirm, he places both hands on my hips, pinning me in place.

"I asked you a question. You won't like what happens if I need to repeat myself." A warning bite pulls a squeal from my throat.

"Taste me," I breathe out, keen for more attention from his mouth.

A loud moan rushes out of me the instant his lips make contact. Mere seconds in and I'm a twisting mess. He's expertly swirling his tongue around my clit, squeezing my ass and thighs with bruising intensity, driving me closer to the brink of climax.

"Fuck you're so delicious. You're gettin' both. I need you ready for me." He growls and pulls back. As a tearing sound echoes through the room. I stare wide eyed at the remains of my skirt fisted in his hand. "This is my reward. Now it's time for yours."

Burying his face between my thighs, his tongue resumes its assault, trailing down to my entrance and back up.

Watching my reactions intently, his eyes don't leave mine as he slides a finger into me. The sight of him rolling his tongue over my tingling clit combined with the pressure of his finger working inside of me is intoxicating.

I gasp, pulling his hair as he inserts a second finger and curls them against a sensitive spot. Heady groans rumble out of him, while I whimper and moan his name as he takes me over the edge.

"Fuck, you're so responsive. Your pussy practically begs to come for me. This is fixin' to be a fun, *long* night." Picking up the fabric I once called a skirt, he uses it to wipe his face.

"Wh-what?" I blink rapidly at him, panting as I recover.

"Don't worry, I'm not gonna break you, no matter how badly I want to. We'll finish the movie, and then you're mine." He extends his hand, helping me sit up next to him.

"But my skirt." My brows pinch together as I frown. "I liked that one."

"I'll replace it. If I had my way you'd be just like this every time you come over here." He leans into me, trailing a finger down my chest, between my bra-clad breasts. "Are you going to be uncomfortable staying like this?" His whisper tickles my ear, prompting a shiver to work its way through my body.

"No. I might get cold though." I flutter my lashes.

Am I teasing him? Yes.

Judging by the fire in his eyes, he's more than willing to keep me warm.

CHAPTER 9

Jude

*K*eep it together, Jude, she's different.

I'm terrified that I've screwed this up.

We haven't come anywhere close to talking about preferences and what she's comfortable with, but the way she melted for me will forever be ingrained in my mind. The look on her face when she came apart on my face was everything.

I've decided that she's mine, whether she likes it or not. Nothing in my life has ever made more sense than us together. Any chance she had of getting away from me is gone now. I want—no, *need*—her, but I have to ease her into it. It's going to end me, but I have to do it right. She has no clue how much I'm going to ruin her when she's ready. There's a little vixen hidden under that candy-coated exterior, I just know it.

And I can't wait to meet her.

Cuddled into my side for warmth, she's still in nothing but a little pink bra. Her touch is tentative, which drives me wild. The faintest sensation of her fingers grazing my cock makes it jump in my sweats. Her breath hitches when I adjust my hips, leaning back to allow her better access.

"Can I touch you now?" She asks in the sweetest tone, eyes glued to the spot where her hand lies.

"You can do anything you want to me, Candy," I rumble, basking in the way she shudders.

Through the barrier between us, I'm still able to feel the warmth of her hand as she wraps it around my shaft. After a few hesitant strokes she stops.

"Can I?" Her polished fingers slip into my waistband as she looks up at me. Even in the near darkness of my apartment her eyes are warm and filled with uncertainty.

"I meant what I said. Just be prepared for what you're gettin' into. You *will* finish what you start." With her jaw in my grasp I catch the challenge in her eyes, setting me ablaze.

That's my girl.

"Don't think I'll let you get away if you try to run when you see my cock. You'll take it and you'll like it. Understood?" With an impossibly hard swallow, she nods as much as my grip will allow. "Good girl, now wrap those pretty little fingers around me." I press a kiss to her lips before releasing my hold. The way she responds to my first commands has me aching. I can't wait to have her tied up, begging for me.

Slowly, she frees me from my sweats and gasps.

"You're—" Her wide eyes travel from the silver glinting at the tip of my cock to my face.

"Yeah, it's called a Prince Albert piercing," I smirk.

"Wow." A breathy whimper rolls out of her as she wraps her hand around my length.

Squeezing me with a glorious amount of pressure, she strokes me from base to tip, admiring the full extent of my hardness. My hips jerk on their own, desperate for more of her touch. Following my lead, she works me for a couple minutes, exploring every inch.

"There's no way this will ever fit inside me." She chews her lip, face full of concern.

"I'm not *that* big. You'll take it just fine when I'm done gettin' you ready." Slipping my hand between her thighs, I begin rubbing small circles around her clit.

Her grip tightens as she opens up for me. When I work two fingers into her, she throws her head back. I don't even care that she's stopped touching me. Just the sounds she's making could get me off.

"I want you so badly," she whimpers, moving to straddle me. "Please?" Her heavily lidded eyes hold me hostage.

Any semblance of self-control I had is gone.

I'm gone.

"Fuck, I don't have a condom." My lusty haze breaks in an instant. I meant to buy some but was so pissed off over the mess we got into last night I forgot. "But I haven't been with anyone in months and I'm clean."

"I'm on the pill. Just fuck me," she demands.

"Yes ma'am, but that's the one and only time you'll get away with that tone." I bring my mouth to hers, aligning myself with her entrance. Hungrily swallowing her needy whines, I ease a few inches into her. My eager hands explore her softness, as if they're trying to memorize all their favorite parts.

She grips my shoulders and slides herself further down onto me, wincing at the pain of her body accommodating my intrusion.

"You're such a good girl. Take a second to adjust, I want this to be good for you." I brush her long, golden hair out of her face so I can admire the blissful expression that's overtaken her features. "That's my girl. Just look at you, takin' all of my cock on the first try. You thought you couldn't do it, but you were made for me." I thrust upward grinding into her. She rolls her hips in tandem, and a wanton moan rushes out of her.

"Jude, can we do this all the time?" She scrapes her nails through my hair and over my scalp as we move together, working at a steady, unhurried pace.

"Any fuckin' time you want." I lift my hips and lean back until I bottom out.

She throws her head back, rolling her hips as I nip at her neck. When she tightens around me, I know I won't last much longer. My thumb finds her swollen clit and she squirms in my lap, squeezing her thighs around me.

Her hands snake under my shirt, nails dragging along my back as our bodies continue to work together.

When I readjust to give her a better angle she screams,

leaning in to kiss me. She increases her pace, grinding herself against me. I drive into her harder, bottoming out over and over again, swallowing her cries of pleasure.

Too soon, a powerful orgasm rips through her and as she falls apart, I'm right there with her. Waves of my cum fill her, pulling more ragged whimpers from her lips. She brushes her hair out of her face, and a small, breathless laugh bubbles out of her.

"Everyone told me my first time would suck. I never cared because I didn't think I'd ever want someone enough to have a first time. This did *not* suck."

A laugh breaks free from me in return. We may be on a creaky futon in my tiny apartment, but with her laying boneless against me, I know this is the closest to heaven I'll ever be.

"Just wait until I have *my* way with you." I kiss her softly.

"So..." She bites her lip as her voice trails off. "Does that mean you want to do this again?" She asks, eyes hooded over dreamily.

My throat is tight from my impending confession. "Of course I do... listen. I don't really date. I mean, I never have. If you want to, I'd love to try. I'll probably be the worst boyfriend ever, just so you know."

Get it together, mouth.

"You... want to date me?" She leans back, giving me her full attention.

"Yes. I know this is an ass-backwards way of goin' about it... and my dick is still inside of you... but would

99

you be my girlfriend?"

She nods with a soft smile. "Yes, Big Guy. I'd love to."

With a quick, tender kiss, I slide out of her and tuck myself back into my sweatpants. "Hold on, I'll be right back with something to clean up with."

I return with a warm cloth and kneel between her legs. There's a slight smear of blood on her inner thighs, and a lot of cum leaking out of her.

My worried eyes dart to her face as she winces. "Are you sore?"

"It's alright, I promise. Your dick is huge, but you didn't split me in two or anything. So don't worry, I see straight through that bad boy exterior." She chuckles.

I can't help but stare. She's the picture of perfection with her wild hair, flushed cheeks and swollen lips.

"I held back on your account. I want to keep you around, can't go scarin' you off already. Now, stand up." A curious expression crosses her face as she rises to her feet. When I release the latch under the seat and lay the futon out into a bed she gasps softly. "There's not enough room to hold you without layin' it down." I pull my shirt over my head and watch her eyes travel the length of my body.

With a coy smile, I grab the blanket and pillows from the small closet. "Come here." I pat the empty spot on the bed after laying down. She stands there, frozen in place. "Don't make me drag you in here." My scowl makes her giggle.

If only she understood how seriously I want to pull

her down against me.

"I've picked up on your bossiness, you know. I like it, but it doesn't really work while begging for cuddles. I can't take you seriously." She bites her lips to suppress her laughter.

"Get in the damned bed," I grumble as my patience teeters on a dangerous ledge.

"Or what?" The glitter on her nails reflects light from the TV as she places her hands on her hips. The rebellious smile on her face goes straight to my dick. "You gonna make me, Big Guy?"

I raise my brows, surprised. "I'm not going to tell you what'll happen if you don't get in here. Don't be a brat. I know that's hard for you," I tease back.

"I think I'll call my mom to come get me. I'm sleeeeeepy." She theatrically stretches her arms out, faking a yawn.

"You gonna have her come pick you up in just your bra? I still have your panties in my pocket." I prop my head up on my hand.

I can see her brain calculating a comeback. The little line between her brows when she's thinking is one of my favorite things about her.

"You could always come get them," I challenge.

"Hmm, this is a nice shirt here." Intentionally facing away from me, she bends over to pick up my discarded shirt, shimmying with her bare ass and pussy on full display.

Seconds. That's all it takes for me to untangle myself

from the blanket and pounce on her. In a swift motion I hoist her over my shoulder and slap her ass, hard.

"Jude!" Pain and pleasure lace the squeal she releases. "Put me down, you'll hurt yourself!" She kicks her legs, trying to free herself from my grasp.

"You're the only one who's going to get hurt, brat. You've earned a punishment."

She stills and a part of me worries I went too far, until she releases a shudder.

"When I ask for a color, you answer. Green is good, yellow means slow down because you're gettin' uncomfortable. Say red and everything stops." I grit into her ear, laying her face down on the futon.

This is probably too soon, but she needs to know what she's getting into, and I need to know if she can handle me.

"Okay." She shivers.

I give her glorious ass a sharp slap and she gasps, letting out a needy moan.

I lean into her, pinning her wrists above her head while I whisper my demands, "Rule number one, you address me as 'Sir', are we clear?"

"Yes."

Considering her inexperience, I wait, giving her the chance to correct herself. She turns her head, exposing a cheeky grin.

Oh, it's on.

"You asked for this. It's only going to get worse the more you defy me."

"Bring it on, *Sir,*" she says in a mischievous tone.

I wasn't expecting tonight to get this far, so my supplies are tucked away in the closet. The drawstring of my sweats will have to do. After sitting her up, I pull it from the waistband and wrap it around her wrists.

"Color?" I grit out, anxious for more.

She's wide eyed and silent, sitting with her hands bound in front of her.

"Candy, what's your color? You need to answer." I bite my lips and hold my breath.

"Green," she breathes out, chewing her lower lip. "Sir." Excitement shines in her eyes.

Fuck yes, she's into this.

I rise to my feet, and she freezes. "Rule number two." my sweatpants slide to the floor. "Until you can behave, I don't give a fuck about what feels good for you. If you really want to be with me this is what you can expect when you act up. Got it?"

Her body trembles and I almost stop, until she glues her lust-blown eyes to me.

"Yes, Sir." Her chest rises and falls on ragged breaths.

All of my reservations dissipate at the sight of her. I haven't felt this alive in a long time, hell maybe ever. I'm going to ruin this girl and let her ruin me in return.

She licks her lips and parts them as I fist her hair and pull her toward me

"Mmm that's more like it. Now, you're going to swallow my cock until you choke. You'll take all my cum and thank me for it." Fortunately, I possess just enough self-control to remember that this is all new to her. "Open up for me. Stick out your tongue." I pause, pressing the tip of my cock against it when she obeys. "You're so fuckin' beautiful like this. Such a good girl for me when you want to be. Do you like how I taste?" I watch her with bated breath as she flicks her tongue against my piercing a few times and hums in approval. "What's rule number one, Candy?"

"Yes, Sir." She bats her eyelashes and my cock twitches.

I inch myself deeper until I reach her throat, then pull away to let her breathe. She coughs around me when I plunge back in.

"Fuck. This sweet little mouth of yours is almost as good as your perfect pussy." A strained groan escapes me as I fight to hold myself together.

With her hair still gripped in my hand, I angle her head back, allowing me deeper access. "Such a needy little slut for me." I force through my clenched jaw.

Her eyes go wide.

Shit, maybe degradation is a hard limit for her. We really should have talked about this.

Pulling back, I brush the hair out of her face to peer into her watery eyes. "Color?"

"*So* green, Sir." She lets out a ragged breath.

"Good girl. Are you ready for your punishment?" I stroke myself, quivering as I await her response. My restraint crumbles when she opens wide. My cock is back in her throat an instant later. "Tap my thigh if I need to stop. Okay?"

She nods and I let her have it.

She writhes and moans as I drive myself into her mouth repeatedly. I wrap her silky hair around my fist, pulling her head back with more force this time around. When I hit the back of her throat, she gags, pushing me closer to the edge.

"Fuck. I'm gonna come so hard. Look at the mess you're makin' filthy girl." I wipe the tears and saliva from her face. "Someone needs to learn her manners. You're goin' to swallow every drop. Got it?"

She hums in agreement, vibrating around me, pushing me over the edge. I drive into her and roar with my release. As my cum shoots down her throat she whimpers around me.

"Not yet. You can breathe in a second. I'm takin' what I want from this tight throat first." With a final thrust I groan and pull back.

She gasps, catching her breath. Her mascara is smeared, streaking down her face from her tears, and it's the most beautiful sight in the world.

"Oh God," she sputters, chest still heaving as I bend down and untie her hands.

"Now, lie down and roll over," I demand.

For a second, I almost think she's going to resist again, but she doesn't. I slide up behind her, wrapping her securely in my arms.

"Did you learn your lesson?" I nuzzle into the sweet-scented mess of her hair in front of me.

"No, I think I'll need lots of punishments in the future." She wiggles her bare ass into me and I'm officially hooked on her.

She's so playful and fun. I didn't expect her to also be so teasing and submissive given her self-proclaimed indifference toward sex. After tonight, there's no doubt in my mind that she's my end game.

"You're mine now, forever," I mumble into her shoulder as I trail my hand down her side. I can't help myself. My fingers find her clit, and she squirms. I press firmly, rubbing slow, calculated circles until she moans. "Tell me who you belong to." I nip at her neck and she arches into my growing hardness.

"H-how are you g-getting hard again?" A needy whimper breaks up her question.

"You, that's how." With a tilt of my hips, my cock nudges her entrance, asking for permission. "Who do you belong to?"

"Y-you, Sir," she shudders, opening herself up for me.

"That's right, Candy. I'm yours, too. Don't forget it."

I can feel the quickness of her pulse against my lips. When I begin sinking into her, she whimpers and clenches around me.

"Jude. I'm actually a little sore. Please be gentle." Despite her request, she sinks onto me further, moaning breathlessly when she's taken all of me.

"Of course, Candy." I kiss her shoulder softly, still circling her clit.

Gently, I pull back and press in deeper, holding her close as we climb slowly to the peak of ecstasy. We move lazily, hips working together in perfect harmony. When she crests the top and falls down the other side, gasping my name like a final prayer, I follow willingly.

Hissing as I slip out of her, she rolls to face me. Droopy-eyed, she lays her head on my chest and glides her finger along the ridges of my abs.

I trail my hand up and down the silky skin of her back, kissing the top of her head.

"You're too good for me, but I'm selfish and want to lock you away in a tower forever," I murmur against her.

"I think people would notice if I went missing." She laughs, tipping her head up toward me.

"Worth the risk." I pull her mouth to mine for a slow, passionate kiss, which she returns in kind.

This has been the best night of my life. No drug has ever given me such a high. I'm officially addicted to Candy.

CHAPTER 10

Caroline

O h no.

Oh no, no, no.

Where is my phone? Dad is going to kill me, and then kill Mom. This is bad. Well, last night was *amazing*, but this morning? This is *very* bad.

In no universe is my father going to let this slide.

Turning to pick my phone up off the coffee table, I suppress a gasp when I look at the time—and the *numerous* missed calls.

"Shh, come back to bed." Deep and raspy with sleep, Jude's voice vibrates against me.

"It's ten in the morning!" I force out of my raw throat. "Can I have some water?"

"Of course." Tossing the blanket aside, he stands up and stretches, gifting me with the sight of his *very* nude body.

The man has no shame—If I looked even half as

sculpted as him, I wouldn't either. Just like that, I'm reminded of my own lack of clothing.

Jude saunters to the fridge for a cool bottle of what may as well be liquid gold at this point. He twists the cap off on his way back to the... bed? Couch? What does one call a futon when it's laid out like this?

"What's that look for?" He tilts his head, causing loose locks of hair to flop over his brows. "Admirin' what's yours?" He leans down, kissing me on the forehead and hands me the goods.

"No. I was just... lost in thought." Memories of last night cause a heated blush to bloom over my cheeks as I bring the bottle to my lips. Waves of soothing water travel down my ragged throat.

"Careful. I might get jealous and kick that bottle's ass for makin' you blush like that." A playful smile crinkles the corners of Jude's eyes.

"Oh, shut up, you're ridiculous." I snort, immediately covering my face to hide my embarrassment. "I can't believe I just did that. We're naked, in bed and I *snorted*!" I groan into my palms.

"Oh, I heard." Chuckling lightheartedly, Jude's arms wrap around me, dragging me into his lap. "It was cute. I love how carefree and silly you are." Light kisses trail down my neck.

"Jude," I plead desperately.

"That's my name, Candy. Wanna moan it again?" My ass is cradled in his large, warm palms. He groans against my neck and squeezes, pressing me against him.

We're still *very* naked, and he's already getting hard.

"You're insatiable, and I really need to get home soon. My dad—"

"Shit, you're right. He's fixin' to whoop my ass for sure," he interrupts, pulling back to look me in the eye. A hint of panic pulls at his features.

"Nah, he'll interrogate *me* and I'll make up some sort of excuse. My mom definitely figured out why I was coming here though. So, at least I'll have her in my corner." My shrug falls short. He can read the worry on my face plain as day.

"I'm sorry. I made it even worse by rippin' your skirt. He's gonna be furious when you show up in a pair of my sweatpants." His face pinches, showing an adorable touch of concern.

"And a hoodie?" I ask coyly, smoothing the crease between his brows.

"As if I could say no to you." With a chaste kiss, he releases me from his grasp.

If Jude takes me home, it would be infinitely worse, so after I get dressed I text my mother to pick me up.

She's here in no time.

Her knowing, playful gaze drifts over my hoodie and sweatpants as I do my first ever walk of shame to the car. Jude insists on accompanying me, which honestly makes me the tiniest bit giddy. When he opens the car door I throw myself into the passenger seat.

"Ma'am." Nodding, he acknowledges my mother—who is smiling widely—then leans in and kisses me softly. "See ya later, Candy."

Blush stains my cheeks from his simple act of affection. My eyes follow his retreating form on their own accord. Each step he takes makes my stomach light up with familiar flutters.

"Oh my. He sure is a sweetheart isn't he."

I think my mother is swooning over my boyfriend?

And, now my face is burning even hotter.

"Lovey, you're the color of a tomato. Your father is going to have *so* many questions if you don't dial it back," she warns with a humorous tone.

"Oh no! I don't think I can face him. Mom, please tell me he's not going to make a big deal out of this?" Pinching the bridge of my nose, I inhale deeply.

"You know he will. I had to hide the car keys to keep him from coming to 'rescue' you last night when our calls went unanswered. He stayed home from work today for goodness' sake." A snicker bubbles out of her. "Do you need anything? Were you safe? Was it everything you'd hoped for?" She shimmies her shoulders, wiggling her brows.

"MOM!" I screech, but it does me no good. Her teasing stare holds strong. "I'm fine. We didn't have condoms, but you know I'm on the pill and he promised he's clean. It's fine." With a roll of my eyes, I turn toward the window, attempting to dodge more questions.

"And? Was he good to you?" A hint of genuine concern shrouds her words.

"Yes, Mom. I had a good time." I bite back a grin.

"Well, that's going to have to do for now then. Just be prepared for the third degree from your father."

"Yeah, nothing could ever prepare me for him. Do you think I can try and lie my way out of it?"

"Lovey, you're wearing Jude's clothes. Don't insult his intelligence by trying to play it off. Where is your skirt anyway?" She asks.

I turn my attention back to her. There's never been a point in my life where I was *so* glad she's driving and can't look me in the eye. The scandalized expression on my face can't be contained.

"He, uh, ripped it off." I teeter as the car swerves.

"Good grief, Caroline. Warn me next time! My heart isn't what it used to be." She fans her face. "So, you're going to need a clothing allowance?" A playful grin pulls at her lips.

"He said he would buy me more clothes." The string of his hoodie twirls around my finger as I mindlessly fidget with it.

We pull up to the house and no part of me is ready for what I'm about to walk into. I make it two steps in the front door and am met with my father, seated at the kitchen table.

"Caroline Diana Koval, what were you thi—" His scolding is interrupted when he takes in my appearance, wide eyed and unblinking.

"Nice clothes, not really your usual style," Nikolai laughs from his seat across the table.

"Shut up, Nerd." I crinkle my nose and attempt a

quick retreat to my room.

"You could have at least called to let us know you weren't coming home. I was worried sick about you, Solnyshko." The intensity of his accent is unsettling, he's definitely more upset than I expected.

"Dad, I'm sorry. I wasn't planning on staying. We ate pizza and watched movies. I was really tired, and time got away from me." My confidence has entered the room, thankfully. I stand tall, straightening my spine. Just enough to see Nikolai behind my father, smiling smugly into his coffee. "Go on, I see the comeback written all over your face, Nicky. Let's just get it all out there."

"Oh, it's nothing, really. I was just wondering if you watched a sad movie and that's why your mascara is smeared down your face." He beams a Cheshire Cat grin at me.

Shit.

There was no time for me to clean myself up before I left, and I never took the time to check my reflection on the way home.

Why didn't anyone say something sooner?

Despite his teasing, Nikolai gave me a coverup story. But I don't know if it's entirely believable.

Just own it, Caroline.

"You've never had a girl choke on your dick, Nicky? Is Lilah too selfish?" I fire back at him.

In another world—one where I wasn't so fed-up with Lilah—I probably wouldn't have come at him so harshly, but he asked for it.

"There goes my appetite." Dad throws his hands up dramatically. "Why are you two like this? You're not *actual* siblings. I can't handle all this depravity so early in the morning. Solnyshko, I'm happy you're alive. Now, if you need me, don't." He pushes his chair out quickly and laces up his shoes. Without another word, he heads out the front door, letting it slam behind him.

"Well, I guess a walk through the field does sound quite nice." My mother follows closely behind him, no doubt to run damage control.

"Sorry, I shouldn't have said anything." Nikolai rubs at the back of his neck, blanching under the weight of my stare. "Are you two dating or do I need to kick his ass for humping and dumping?"

"No, you don't get to act all 'big brother' now," I snap, wincing as I sit in the chair next to him.

"That good huh?" He jokes, earning a pinch to the arm. "Hey! It was a compliment. Good sex is awesome and I'm happy for you. But he'd better treat you right... You also might want to invest in some better make-up. You know, something to cover the bite marks." He vaguely gestures to my throat, and my face flushes. "They also make waterproof mascara. Unless he's into seeing it run, judging by your overall 'I got fucked hard and dirty' aesthetic I bet he does."

"You'd be absolutely right." A coy smile crosses my face.

He extends his fist to me, and I tap my knuckles to his.

This is my favorite thing about Nikolai. While he likes to fill the role of an older sibling, he's also my best friend. We both speak fluent sarcasm and, to the outside world, probably come across as hateful toward each other. In reality our love is unconditional, and he just *gets* me.

"About Lilah, I've been thinking it might be time to reevaluate my relationship with her," He mumbles—definitely on purpose. He isn't confrontational, but his pride is easily bruised. Admitting we're all right about her has to be rough.

"Finally coming to your senses?"

"I just feel like I'm missing out on so much family time because of her. She never wants to be here, and it bothers me. I haven't even met your... what is he? Boyfriend? Lover? Friend with benefits?"

"Boyfriend," I respond with a broad smile and his face lights up with genuine happiness.

"Your boyfriend. Man, I never thought I'd see the day. I'm pretty sure your mom thought you weren't into guys at all." He nudges me with his elbow.

"She wouldn't have been far off. Until now I wasn't into anyone. People were just... *there*. But Jude is different. I'm not sure what it is about him, if I'm being honest."

"Sometimes you just know." He shrugs, pushing his chair out. "I'm going to think some more about my current love life. Because as it stands, I no longer have a fucking clue about anything." With a blank expression he slips out of the kitchen.

If a shower could last forever, I'd will this one to do just that. Relief washes over my sore muscles with each warm drop. Exfoliating my face, deep conditioning my hair, and thoroughly scrubbing every spare inch of my body has never been so enjoyable.

After patting myself dry and lathering on my signature cotton candy lotion, I plop down onto the bed and dissolve into my mattress. My phone vibrates from its spot on the pillow next to me, interrupting my bliss. Annoyed by the intrusion, I pick it up. Any anger I'd felt vanishes at the sight of Jude's name on my screen.

Big Guy: *So, how much trouble did I cause?*
Me: *You, trouble? Never! :)*
Big Guy: *I'm trouble personified. You're just too caught up to see how terrible I am for you.*
Me: *Noooo! Don't talk about yourself like that. You're amazing, Big Guy.*
Big Guy: *As long as you think so, I'll accept it. Your opinion is the only one that matters.*
Me: *Stooooopp! You're too sweet.*
Big Guy: *Only for you.*

The light flutters in my chest are becoming one of my favorite sensations.

Me: *I'm lucky then. You never got to sing me that song, by the way. I'm going to hold you to it.*

Big Guy: *I'll sing you to sleep every night if you'd like. Just call me.*

Me: *Right now?*

Big Guy: *It's the middle of the day... are you going to bed already?*

Me: *Well, a nap counts. Right?*

My phone rings instantly. After hesitating for a second, I accept his call. My nerves in this moment rival the ones from yesterday.

It's just a phone call. Don't overthink it.

"H-hello?" I chew my lower lip.

"Hi there, Gorgeous." The warmth in his voice can only mean he's smiling. Such a special thing only I ever get to see. "Do you have any requests?"

"You pick." My phone is sandwiched between my cheek and the pillow I'm hugging.

He clears his throat. "One second." There's rustling on the other end of the phone. A moment later his voice returns. "Had to get the old girl."

Before I can ask, strumming vibrates my cheek.

"You play guitar?"

"Just a bit. I'm not great, but it'll do." I don't recognize the chords he's playing, but it doesn't matter. "This is my rough version of "Waiting for a Girl Like You" by Foreigner."

When his first note breaks through, I'm smitten—completely lost for words. I've never heard this song before, but it just might be my new favorite. Jude's voice is deep, velvety and soulful. My mind and body completely relax, getting lost in his serenade. When he's done, I can barely keep my eyes open.

"That was beautiful." I sigh.

"You're beautiful, Candy. Next time you're over I'll sing to you for real. Until then, call me any time."

"Promise?" My drowsy voice makes him chuckle.

"I promise, now take that nap. You deserve it."

"Thanks, Big Guy," I mumble half awake.

He doesn't hang up. Instead, he softly sings me another song I don't know.

CHAPTER 11

Caroline

Life is good.

I passed all my finals with flying colors. I've been so busy studying and focusing on my grades that I've barely left my house, or bothered going out. Unlike Veronica and Adalina, Jude has gone out of his way to stay in touch. We text all day, every day—when I'm not nose-deep in text books anyway. Every night he sings me a classic love song before bed.

It sounds crazy, but I think I love him. We've only been dating for a couple weeks but the connection we have is magnetic. Neither of us have said it, but part of me believes he feels it too.

My phone pings on the nightstand and my face lights up at the sight of his name.

Big Guy: *Hey, gorgeous.*
Me: *Hi there :) What are you up to?*

Big Guy: *Well... I was just thinking about you. Come out with me.*

Me: *Hmmm. What's in it for me?*

Big Guy: *About 2 weeks worth of overdue kisses.*

Me: *You drive a hard bargain. Where do you want to go?*

Big Guy: *Anywhere as long as you're there and I get to hold you.*

And just like that, I'm breathless.

Me: *We could do that at home.*

Big Guy: *Even better. I won't have to behave.*

Me: *JUDE!*

Tingles run through my body as memories of his hands trailing over every inch of me flash through my mind.

Big Guy: *Okay, how about we just go to dinner? I'll pick you up.*

Me: *9pm is a bit late to eat, don't you think? I'm exhausted from the week, can we maybe do it tomorrow? That way we can spend the day together. :)*

Big Guy: *You sure you're ready for that? If you're in my space again dressed all fuckin' cute, I'll probably try and keep you.*

Frantic knocking on my bedroom door startles me.

"I was three seconds from falling asleep! Wh—" my screeches get caught in my throat. Nikolai stands in my doorway, completely panicked with tears streaming down his face. "—what's going on?"

"Get dressed, we have to go. Dad's already in the car."

He called my father "Dad"... something is wrong.

Adrenaline jolts through me like electricity, lighting my veins up like live wires. Pulling on Jude's hoodie and a pair of pink sweatpants, I slip on my Converse and bolt to Nikolai's car.

The two of them are already buckled in. Dad is staring at the dash in the passenger seat with an unnerving, vacant expression.

Something is definitely *very* wrong.

"Is anyone going to tell me what's going on?" My voice trembles. "Where's Mom?"

The woeful looks I get in response to my question shatter me.

Oh no.

"There's been an accident. The hospital needs..." Dad's voice stops working, paralyzed by emotions.

Please, no.

"Needs what?!" Stinging tears fight to escape their cages behind my eyes. I don't want to hear his response, but I *need* to. All of my burning suspicions could never prepare me for the pain etched into Nikolai's face as he turns to me.

"They need someone to identify the b-b—" a heaving sob interrupts his words. "—body." He slams his palm against the steering wheel while gritting his teeth.

I've never seen him this worked up over anything in my life. My mother is the only maternal figure he's ever known. If my heart didn't shatter the second he uttered the words, his reaction would have done the job.

"A-are they... sure?" I ask around the tightness in my throat. My chest feels heavy, breathing seems like an impossible task. I can feel myself crumbling apart at the thought of life without her.

"It was our RAV4." Dad chokes out through his clenched jaw.

She's the love of his life. If this is true it's going to destroy him, probably more than any of us.

"No. There must be a mistake. She was such a careful driver." As I wrap my arms around myself in the back seat, Jude's cologne wafts into my nose from his hoodie, providing a small amount of comfort.

"That's why we need to go. To be sure... and say our goodbyes." Nikolai sputters out. His ability to drive while sobbing is a feat.

My mind races with the force of emotions exploding inside of me. Grief, doubt, rage, confusion, all balled into a festering monster. This has to be a nightmare. I'll wake up any minute and everything will be fine.

I know it.

The drive to the hospital is short, but tonight it seems unending. Dread gnaws at my stomach like a caged animal as we park.

Walking through the sliding doors, the hospital lobby is bleak—virtually lifeless. The air is clinically clean, smelling of laundry detergent and disinfectants. This blank purgatory is the last place I want to be on a Friday night.

A dark-haired police officer greets us, his wrinkled face impassive. Nikolai takes my hand, seeking my comfort and lending me some of his.

"Are you the Koval family?" He asks flatly.

"We are," Dad speaks up.

Thankfully one of us has a voice right now, because I couldn't form a word over the gigantic lump in my throat if I tried.

"I'm Deputy Sanders. Right this way, I'll fill you in." His face stays expressionless.

Surely this isn't his first car crash, but it would be nice if he'd show even a fraction of sympathy.

"It seems the other vehicle swerved into her lane. Toxicology will shed some more light on the situation." His words are blunt, impersonal.

A thin, timid man greets us when we arrive. "Koval, I presume?" Dad nods stiffly in response. "Right then. This way." He ushers us to a viewing room. A blanket covers the table in the center. My knees turn to mush and Nikolai holds me up as I fight the urge to collapse on the spot.

"We found a purse in the wreckage. Her driver's license was recovered, but we'd still like a positive I.D. before proceeding with the autopsy. Are you all certain you want to be here?" Deputy Sanders looks me directly in the eye and asks with the same detached tone.

"We're here aren't we?" Nikolai snaps. I squeeze his arm and nod, unable to formulate a response.

Dad strides apprehensively to the table, hands fisted tightly at his sides. His head is bowed, eyes settled on the blanket-covered form before him. "Let us see h-her," his voice cracks.

Nothing could have possibly prepared any of us for this.

Nikolai and I stand just behind him, as he holds me. The instant we're met with my mother's lifeless face, bruised and scraped from the impact, our hearts collectively implode. Heavy, suffocating agony fills the room. My father's knees buckle, bringing him to the floor in a howling frenzy. Nikolai cradles me in his arms as we crumble to the ground with him.

"Lyubimaya. I'm s-sorry I couldn't protect you." He wavers, slamming his palm against the linoleum. "P-please forgive me in our next lifetime. I'll find you again, I swear." Violent sobs shake his body as he takes her hand in his.

"This isn't real," I wail into Nikolai's chest, gripping his shirt. "She can't leave us. Wake me up, Nicky. P-please wake me up!" Hyperventilating, I choke on tears as they gush from my eyes. "M-mom..." My voice fails.

She can't be gone.

Nikolai's chest heaves, trembling as he holds me. "W-we need to leave. Th-they need to p-proceed with the autopsy." Rising onto shaky legs, he extends his hand to help me up.

Righting myself is nearly impossible, but once I'm able to stand we help my father to his feet and the three of us stagger numbly out of the room.

"I'm sorry to ask this of you now, but how shall we proceed with her remains?" the morgue attendant asks timidly, as if he wasn't a witness to our mutual anguish.

Nikolai's glare is fierce as it bores into him. Fortunately, Dad is somehow of sound enough mind to reply,

"She's to be cremated. We'll scatter her ashes in the field behind our cabin. It's what she always wanted. I just didn't think it'd be s-so soon." His voice breaks on the last few syllables.

The drive back to the house is cold and dreary. The world will forever be a darker place without her light. It's one in the morning and I know any chance I had at sleeping is long gone. I try to call Jude when we get home, but he doesn't answer.

I had expected it, I left him on read for the last several hours while part of my heart was ripped out and trampled on. It's honestly for the best that he doesn't see me like this. I don't want to scare him off so early in our relationship. Even if I think he loves me, I'm a blubbering mess and honestly embarrassed to even have my father and Nikolai see me so disheveled. At least they're both going through it with me.

I blink and my phone pings, startling me. Evidently, I was wrong about my inability to fall asleep. Staring at the time on my screen, I can't believe it's eight a.m.

A message from Jude awaits my reply, but I don't know what to say.

Big Guy: *Hey, I saw you called late last night. What's up? Are you okay? You just disappeared on me...*
Me: *No.*
Big Guy: *Care to elaborate?*
Me: *I'm just not okay. I'm sorry. I didn't mean to worry you.*
Big Guy: *Do I need to come over?*
Me: *No, please don't do that. We're going through something right now. I don't want you to see me like this.*
Big Guy: *I don't like this. I want to be there for you.*
Me: *Me either. But please just... Let me have some time to get my thoughts together.*
Big Guy: *Did I do something? Was I too much? Please talk to me. Was 'Hooked on a Feeling' a bad song choice?*

A faint smile teases my lips, only to disappear as quickly as it began.

Me: *No, I loved that. I love your nightly serenades. It's nothing to do with you. There's been a family emergency, I won't be in any shape to come over later. I don't want you to see me like this.*
Big Guy: *Okay.*
Me: *I'll talk to you later. I need to go be with my family right now, okay?*

Big Guy: *Alright. Talk later...*

I should tell him everything, but my family falling apart isn't anything he should need to worry about. In a few days when I'm in a better mental state I'll tell him what happened. For now, my father and Nikolai need me, as much as I need them.

Dad is already making plans for us to travel to the cabin and stay for a week to clear our heads and try to come to terms with life without Mom. There's no cell reception out there, but the disconnect will be refreshing. It's July, so Dad doesn't have work. Nikolai doesn't have a traditional job, and I'm a full-time student on summer vacation. So, a week away sounds like a much needed mental break.

The drive is usually scenic and bright. Mom loved the journey almost as much as the cabin itself. It's never seemed so... gray, muted, completely lackluster before.

Dad has barely said a word since we hit the road two hours ago. Nikolai, uncharacteristically, has been equally silent while he drives.

The buzz of my phone snaps me back to reality.

Big Guy: *I know you said you needed time. But I just need to know that you're okay. Please reply. :(*
Me: *Hey, I'm not okay but I'm working on it. We're*

actually on our way to my family's cabin.

Big Guy: *Oh. When will you be back?*

Me: *We're planning on staying for a week. I don't really get service out there so I'm sorry if I don't respond.*

Big Guy: *I wish you'd talk to me.*

Acid churns in my stomach. I'm not accustomed to having anyone else who cares. His concern is equal parts comforting and terrifying. He deserves answers, but I can't tell him like this, not while I'm still such a mess.

Me: *I don't want to tell you over text, and am in no condition to talk about it in person. I'll tell you when I'm ready.*

Big Guy: *I just want to be there for you... WITH you. You can be your raw, unpolished self with me. I hope you know that. I want every part of you.*

A sob bubbles out of me, catching my father's attention.

"Solnyshko." He swallows hard. "I know it's difficult, but we have each other."

"It's not just that. I feel bad for not telling Jude. He's just being so sweet right now." Tears stream freely down my face.

"You could have asked him to come. I'm not crazy about the boy, but he's mad about you. Right now we all need as much love and support as we can get." His face is soft, filled with compassion and his own pain.

"Nicky didn't invite Lilah. So I didn't think Jude was welcome. I thought this was just for us." I choke out, voice trembling with each word.

"I didn't invite Lilah because, let's be honest, she would have just made things worse," Nikolai says with a surprisingly bitter tone.

"And Dad hates Jude so he would have made it worse too." I frown with a trembling chin.

"I don't hate him. I apologize if my actions have made it appear that way. You're my baby girl and I wanted to make sure his intentions were good. He's a decent man." He reaches back and pats my knee.

"Well, I wish I would have known. I'll apologize when we get back." I smile softly and return my attention to my phone.

Great, no signal.

Welcome to life off the grid.

I'll make it up to Jude as soon as we're back in town. I know I've been vague and he's worried, but it's not every day life flips upside down. Nobody prepares you for it, there's no training or rules for how to grieve such an abrupt loss.

I only hope he will forgive me when I see him again.

CHAPTER 12

Caroline

C risp, fresh air greets us as we step out of the car. Being here without my mother feels wrong, but we *need* this. Aside from the brief conversation about Jude, we were all silent for the rest of the drive, which is unlike us.

The quaint log cabin always feels like a second home. Mom's enjoyment of this little piece of nature was rivaled only by her love for the three of us.

I trail my finger along the worn fence as we climb the front steps. Dad makes his way around the back to check the solar panels. The setup here is actually pretty nice for off-grid living. My parents loved taking long weekends to get away, and invested a lot of their savings into ensuring life out here is as comfortable as possible. A cabin in the mountains might seem like a strange place for a vacation home, but to them it was a perfect fit.

After opening the front door, I falter.

Crossing this threshold is a seemingly impossible task,

as if a barrier forbids me from entering. Nikolai steps up next to me, resting his hand on my shoulder with a consolatory look.

"I'm right here. We can take our time," he murmurs softly with a slight squeeze.

True to his word, he waits several minutes for me to move, and we step inside together. My father—finished with the solar panels—enters behind us and latches the old wooden door closed. Silence swallows the room as we stand in the entryway, too numb to move.

My tears are the first to fall, splattering onto the dusty hardwood floor. Nikolai wraps me in his arms and rests his chin on my head, sniffling as he fights his own emotions. Releasing a shaky breath, my father pulls us both into him.

The past twenty four hours crash down on us with unyielding force. I wail into Nikolai's chest as he sobs against my hair. Tears soak into my shoulder as Dad lets his walls down. Unmoving, the three of us stand and unreservedly weep together.

Out here, we're free to be as broken as we need, that much I'm thankful for.

We eventually find the strength to unpack our bags and wipe down the surfaces. My parents came for a long weekend a couple of months ago, so it wasn't in dire need of a deep clean. Still, there was a thin layer of dust. Mom always liked to come on her birthday weekend. She called it her "reset button" and swore it was the only way to start your next year of life. I'll do my best to keep that in mind as we start this new chapter without her.

None of us make any progress by the end of the fourth day. We barely bother to eat, or shower. Any semblance of joy, or desire to live is lost. Time is only so powerful, and it has become increasingly obvious that one week will not be enough for us. The decision to stay longer is an easy one to make.

Sadly I have no way to let Jude know we're extending our trip, but I know he'll understand. Another week or two won't hurt anything.

For three weeks we wallow as misery threatens to consume us. It still isn't enough time, but life must go on, and I know Mom would hate to see what we've become.

Sure, the time to grieve is needed, but we're all suffocating under the weight of her loss. Well, Nikolai has patched himself together a bit, but that's not a surprise. He's always been the supportive one—somebody you can rely on—who puts everyone else above himself. One day I hope I'm strong enough to be there for him, too.

Dad has made the decision to sell our house. We're packing up as soon as we get home and moving to Seattle. We'll find a nice apartment to rent until someone buys our place. We're going to honor Mom's wishes to have her ashes scattered on the land around the cabin. The plan is to do it on her next birthday. It was her favorite place, after all. I'm sure she would love to spend eternity here.

Once we make it back to civilization, I need to call Jude and let him know. It's not a long drive from Tacoma to Seattle, so I'm sure we can make it work.

The second I have a signal, I dial his number but my call goes straight to voicemail, so I text him instead.

Me: *Hi. I'm so sorry I didn't reach out sooner. Our stay was longer than expected. I missed you like crazy. Call me when you can. <3*

Anxiously, I stare at my phone, waiting for his reply... except it doesn't come.

It's noon, what could he possibly be doing?

Pulling up our girls' chat, I don't even know what to say. We haven't talked much since Jude and I started dating. The time apart and Mom's death have caused the distance between us to grow. I don't know how to bridge the gap—or if I even want to. Still, I have to try.

Me: *Hey, sorry I went radio silent.*
Addie: *Wow! She's alive!*
Vi: *...*
Me: *What?*
Vi: *You've got a lot of nerve SLUT.*

My blood goes cold.

Me: *WHAT?*

Vi: *Don't play stupid, bitch.*

Addie: *I thought you were better than that, Caroline.*

Ouch. "Caroline" not "Chica" has my mind racing, a cold sweat coats my body.

Me: *I don't understand.*

Vi: *Of course you don't. You fuck my man, then run away so you don't have to face the backlash? Some friend you are. Lose my number, homewrecker.*

Addie: *Same, I can't believe you would do this. Jealousy is uglyyyy.*

My phone slips from my hand, landing on the floor of the car with a thud.

Was he really with Veronica?

Was my intuition right this whole time?

All I've wanted the past three weeks was to be wrapped in his arms, laying my head on his chest, falling asleep to the beat of his heart.

Instead, I'm more alone than ever.

It's been two months since my life blew up in my face. We've moved to Seattle and have had to completely start over, Nikolai included.

Lilah made it abundantly clear that she was not a fan of his unplanned "vacation" as she put it. He didn't take kindly to her trying to control how he grieved, so he broke it off. Now we're just three lost souls in a giant city.

Alone.

Veronica and Adalina blocked my number and wouldn't answer their doors when I went to their houses. Adalina's mother cursed me out in Spanish, so I have no idea what she *actually* said, but it sounded harsh.

I dial Jude's number for the thousandth time. It's disconnected now, so I don't know what I expect to happen. The same automated message greets me again.

All I want is answers, but they'll never come.

It's funny. Part of me wants to mourn the loss of my friends, and Jude, but I have no room left in my shattered heart. Every day without my mother reminds me that the worst has already happened to me.

Dad has withered into a husk of a man. I'm an empty shell. Nikolai barely smiles anymore and that's probably the hardest part of this. He has always been the cheerful constant, no matter how dreary our days were. To see him clouded over and bogged down is like a punch to the gut.

"I hope you know how much we miss you," I whisper into the emptiness of my room.

The walls here are blank, devoid of the vibrancy she brought with her. Nikolai hasn't even attempted to paint anything, which feels *wrong*—he paints all his emotions. The lack of new canvases cluttering our space fully showcases how numb he must feel.

When the toxicology report came back and confirmed that the couple who killed my mother were beyond intoxicated, nobody was shocked. It's such a cruel thing—having someone's selfish, careless behavior tear your family to shreds.

Moving here should feel like a new start, but at the moment it feels like the end.

When I drag myself out of my bed, I shuffle to the living room of our apartment. Nikolai is on the couch watching *Cake Wars*. It's his favorite show, but he hasn't watched much TV since we moved here. I smile softly, enjoying this small sense of normalcy.

"Care to join me?" he asks, patting the spot next to him. "I could use some company." His face pulls into a half smile.

I drop down onto the cushion beside him and let out a heavy sigh.

"You wanna talk about it?" His voice is soft, bordering on cautious.

"I just feel so lost without her, Nicky." I sigh. "I know we all do, but still."

"You're right, we do. That doesn't make your feelings less valid. I'm here to talk whenever you need to. I don't care if it's two in the morning and you have to wake me up. Do it. I see how empty you are. I don't like it." He holds his arm up in a silent offer.

I lean into his side and let the tears fall.

"I just don't know who I am anymore." I sniffle. "I want to be there for you and Dad, the same way you have been for me. B-but I'm not strong enough. How do you do it?"

"I cry a lot." He laughs dryly. "Your dad isn't in much

better shape than you, to be fair. He's just a stubborn ass and doesn't let us see it. I worry about him, too."

"It's so unfair!" I wail, as if I haven't screamed it a million times.

Nikolai just pulls me in closer, rubbing my back.

"What are we going to do? I can't keep living like this." I sob against him.

"It'll get easier but there's no timeline on grief. We have each other and soon you'll have classes to help distract you," he whispers. "You have until next semester to get it all out, taking this one off was a smart idea. Your dad should have taken time off, too. He's just pushing his pain down and burying himself in work. It's not healthy."

"I know, I just hope I'll be ready." I huff.

"I'm making lasagna for dinner, will that help?" His voice has a playful tone to it.

"You're cooking? We haven't had real food since we moved." I lean back and tilt my head in question.

"Yeah, I know. I finally feel like it." He pushes out a heavy breath. "My lasagna is your favorite recipe, so I figured it would be a nice first meal to have here. It's already in the oven." He absentmindedly adjusts his glasses.

"That would be amazing. I love you, Nerd." A foreign-feeling smile teases my lips.

"I love you too, Parasite. Now go shower, you smell as bad as you look." He smirks playfully at me.

"Asshole!" I jump up from my spot on the couch and throw a pillow at him. "I took a bubble bath last night."

Nikolai laughs as I leave the room, the first genuine laugh I've heard from him in the last three months.

I may not actually need a shower, but I take a long, refreshing one anyway. By the time I'm done drying my hair the house smells heavenly.

When I stroll into the kitchen, a pan of bubbly lasagna is on the counter. I snag a cheesy, crispy piece of the garlic bread on the plate next to it, humming in appreciation with my first bite.

Nikolai drifts into the room and pins me with a warning glare. "Don't eat it all before your dad gets home. The lasagna is cooling, he'll be here any minute then we can eat."

"Okay, bossy." I stick my tongue out at him and turn my attention to the front door as it swings open.

"What's this?" Dad asks, eyeing the food as he closes the door. "Nicky, you made food?" His eyes soften.

"Yeah, I was hoping we could eat together... at the table." Nikolai's face pulls into a hopeful smile.

We've hardly interacted as a family since the cabin. I know we're all trying to move on and heal however we can, but this distance between us has been painful. When my father slides into his seat at the head of the table I almost fall over from relief.

Stepping up beside him, I place a hand on his shoulder. "Can I get you some water, Dad?" My voice is quiet in an effort to hide the threatening tears.

"That would be lovely, Solnyshko." He nods, smiling warmly at me.

His affectionate gaze is almost my undoing. My hands tremble, struggling to hold the glass still against the lever on the fridge door. I miss my mother, but her absence has turned Dad into such a ghost that I miss him too. Handing him his drink, I lean down and softly kiss his temple. He takes my hand in his and squeezes, not meeting my eye. The unspoken emotions are deafening as Nikolai serves us our food on familiar worn china.

We may eat in silence, but love doesn't need to be loud.

Right now, we're saying all that needs to be said.

We're going to be okay because we have each other.

CHAPTER 13

Jude – Present Day

W hat the fuck am I doing?

The shiny, perfect glass doors of Navy's Place reflect my internal struggle back at me. I've worked so hard to do better, to be better. My funds are running low, though, and I'm *not* about to ask my mother for anything.

Like she'd give it to me anyway.

While they're not even officially open, this place has a sparkling reputation. They almost exclusively employ troubled youth, and people who are down on their luck. Maybe I'm naïve for thinking they'll hire me, but I desperately need *something* to go right in my life.

My janitor position at the grimy, rundown clinic on the other side of Seattle isn't cutting it. They had promised opportunities for advancement once I finished my classes and passed my vet tech certification. It's been months now, and nothing has changed. I'm sick and tired of biding my time.

Most people would tell me I should be grateful they even hired me. To that, I'd tell them to get fucked with a rusty fork. I'm not the type of man to sit back and let shit pass me by. I've had seven years to do that, and I'm over it.

Sure, I've fucked up, but I paid my dues and did my time. I deserve a chance—just like anyone else who's genuinely trying to do better.

I dust myself off and push the door open.

May as well get this over with.

The worst thing that can happen is they turn me away. At this point in my life I'm used to it. Despite my skepticism, I've decided to let myself feel a sliver of hope.

"Hi there! Welcome to Navy's Place. You must be Jude," Charli greets me with a warm smile.

I recognize her from the advertisements. She's the heart of this place. Her energy is... welcoming, reassuring even. I don't sense any judgment from her.

"Yes ma'am. Jude Carlisle, pleased to meet you." I extend a hand to her.

Large hazel eyes glitter brightly back at me. I almost get lost staring into them. Charli is around my age, but I know she's married, so I should look away.

"You're a proper southern boy, aren't you?" Her voice is laced with playful mischief as she shakes my hand. "Come on, this way." She leads me through the double doors of the colorful lobby, back to the kennel area of the rescue. "Right through here." We hang left around a corner and enter a small office.

File cabinets line the walls and her large desk is covered in what I can only define as organized chaos. She takes her seat behind the mountain of papers and motions for me to sit across from her. In the corner of the room, a fawn and white corgi does an exaggerated stretch before trotting over to greet me.

"May I?" I'm already reaching for him as I ask permission to pick him up.

"Of course, Navy is the real boss around here. He'll be very upset if you don't." She chuckles.

"Oh, this is *the* Navy?" He's already in my lap, rolled over on his back as I scratch his belly. One of his little legs kicks in response.

"In the fur." She beams. "He's a tough boss, but you seem to be on his good side already. So, since he approves, I think we can continue." She flips open a folder that I swear appeared out of thin air. "So, Jude. I see you've recently gotten your certification and are eager to start helping animals. Do you have any hands-on experience?" She's so direct, I would probably be intimidated if I didn't find her energy to be so calming.

"Well, I'm currently working at a local clinic. I mainly clean kennels and walk dogs. I do take the time to give them a quick look over when I'm with them. But no, nothing official." My face falls. Having such a lack of experience at my age is always going to hold me back.

Navy rights himself and licks my face, as if he can sense my disappointment.

"That's completely fine. Most of the people working here have no experience coming in, but they have good hearts." She flips to a new page in her folder.

Dread prickles my skin at the sight of my mugshot. Obviously I disclosed my record when I applied, I know this place hires ex-cons so I thought I'd have a shot. Still, my legs twitch, fighting against the urge to bolt.

"Tell me about yourself. Who are you deep down? Why do you want to work here?" Charli closes the folder, watching me expectantly.

My eyes dart from the file under her palm, to her face, down to my lap—where Navy is now fast asleep. "I'm not the guy in that folder, I promise. I just made some dumb choices," I mumble.

"I know. I'm familiar with sinister men, and you're not one of them." She leans back in her chair, relaxing into the leather. "So..." She raises an expectant brow.

"I've had a rough life." I let myself relax as she nods. "I'll spare you the sob story, but just know that I'm determined to not let my past define me. I had more than enough time to reflect, move on, and grow. I'm compassionate and driven. I can't think of anythin' in the world more rewardin' than helpin' animals who have also been dealt a shit hand." I cringe as I cuss. "Sorry, I've got a bit of a mouth on me. That's probably my worst trait... minus the record."

"Just wait til you meet my husband." Charli laughs. "He's going to love you. You seem to be exactly the type of person that we enjoy working with. Welcome aboard, if you're still interested." She slides a new folder toward me.

Seriously, where does she keep these?

Inside is an employment contract, already drafted and filled out with my information. I stare blankly at it. My shocked eyes drift up to meet her wry smile.

"You had this ready?" My voice is rough as I choke down the emotion burning my throat.

"Yes, I just had a feeling about you. Your mugshot sold me, to be honest."

"What the fuck, really?" I must have lost my mind, who the hell talks to their boss like this before they've even signed the paperwork?

"Yes, it's your eyes. You *look* like the type who would be a giant douche bag... no offense." She crinkles her face.

"None taken." I shrug.

"When we looked through your file, I saw the hurt and sadness in your picture. Something told me you were just the type of person we'd love to have here. Meeting you solidified my decision. So, if you're sure you want the job, sign on the dotted line and you can start Monday. You'll be assisting our veterinarian. She doesn't know we're hiring you because she's stubborn and 'can handle it' but she needs an extra pair of hands." She grins.

"I look forward to helping her out." I smile tentatively back at her.

"I just hope you're patient, or maybe not. She could use someone to put her in her place." Judging by the glint in her eye, the innuendo was *not* an accident.

"Oh, uh. That would be unprofessional." I clear my throat.

"Jude, we're not your average employer. As long as it doesn't interfere with work, you're welcome to date, or sleep with whomever you wish... Just not my husband." She playfully quirks a brow at me and stands.

"You won't need to worry about that. Trust me, I'm very much *not* into men." I place Navy back on the floor and get up from my chair.

"That's what they all say." She dramatically rolls her eyes, and leads me out of the room.

"We'll see you Monday, wear scrubs. Or do you need a longer notice for your current job?"

"Nah, Monday is great. Thank you so much for this opportunity." I hold my hand out to shake hers, drawing a chuckle from her.

"Thank you for wanting to be part of our dream." She smiles brightly and shakes my hand.

After making my way down the steps, I close my eyes and let out a relieved breath and hop on my new-to-me Kawasaki Ninja 400. It's matte black, just like my old girl back before everything went to shit. Scoping out the area, it sinks in that the parking lot is empty. My interview was after hours, so the general lack of cars isn't a surprise... but how did Charli get here?

I'm not left wondering for long.

I watch from my bike as a deep blue Corvette rolls up to the front of the building. A man hops out with a wide, smitten grin on his face. Charli bounces down the steps holding Navy close, straight into his eager arms.

Ah, her husband, that makes sense.

He is a good-looking guy. Tall, dark wavy hair, wearing a casual T-shirt and jeans with some black rimmed glasses. He opens the door for her, stealing a kiss before pushing it closed. They speed out of the parking lot an instant later.

Maybe he won't be a bad boss. Especially if we have a mutual appreciation for speed.

I take the long way home to my shit-hole apartment, weaving through traffic a bit more recklessly than I should. It's been tough since I moved to Seattle, but I'm not about to let life win.

My apartment is stale and musty when I get home, but it's a roof over my head. Kicking my boots off, I grab a bottle of water from the fridge and head to my bedroom. I should call my mother and let her know I'm good now—that she won't have to bail me out in a few months and drag me back home.

I had thought she hated me before all this happened, I was proven wrong. She was quick to let me know how much of a waste I am when I got locked up. Told me exactly what I'm worth in her eyes. Not that the opinion of a strung-out stripper means shit to me.

I throw myself down onto my bed and relax into the mattress, pulling up the number of my soon-to-be ex-boss. The phone rings three times before he picks up.

Fuck I was hoping I could leave a voicemail.

"Carlisle, what the hell do you want?" He's at a bar by

the sounds of it. Already slurring his words at—I pull my phone away from my face to check the time—six thirty on a Friday.

This is going to go well.

"I found a better opportunity and won't be comin' back to work." May as well just get it over with.

"You filthy fucking felo—"

I hang up, having no desire to listen to the same shit he spews at me every time I ask for anything.

My palms are clammy. I wish I could go to a bar, get shit-faced, and find some girl with more daddy issues than me to fuck silly. But my parole officer would have a coronary.

Don't even think about it. Just breathe.

Me: *I'm starting a new job as a vet tech for a dog rescue on Monday.*
Mama: *That's nice.*

My chest tightens as I read over her dry response.
I feel so alone.
A solitary tear splatters on my phone screen.

Me: *I hope y'all are good.*
Mama: *Nothing new here.*
Me: *That's good. I guess I'll talk to you later.*
Mama: *Talk later.*

I pocket my phone, chug my water and get up to wrap

my wrists. A quick round with my punching bag before bed should help blow off some steam and get my head in the right place for Monday.

This fresh start is everything I've been needing. Not a damned thing will stop me now.

Standing in the parking lot of Navy's Place, I try to gather my courage.

I spent my weekend studying and trying to overcome the imposter syndrome that is creeping in. I know that I'm qualified for this job, and I know that they're great people to work with based on glowing reviews.

Despite my self encouragement, I can't shake the paranoia itching at the back of my mind. Life has turned me into a cynical pessimist but can you blame a guy? Every good thing I've ever had has blown up in my face. What a cruel joke it is to be named after such an uplifting and motivational song.

After securing my helmet to my bike, I straighten my scrubs, run my hand through my wild hair and climb the front steps—eager to embark on my first official day of work.

I'm early, the receptionist isn't even here yet. I take a moment to admire the murals of the front lobby. They're vibrant and beautiful, like a beacon in the night.

"You like my work, huh?" A deep voice sounds from behind me.

I twist around, caught by surprise. I had been so entranced I didn't even hear footsteps. Wearing a deep blue polo shirt with the corgi butt logo of Navy's Place, Charli's husband stands with his hand extended to me.

"Nikolai. Pleased to meet you."

"Hey, I'm Jude. Nice to meet you too. You painted this?" I shake his hand.

"Yeah, I'm not good for much, but if you need anything painted to look like rainbows and shit exploded all over it, I'm your guy." His grin is infectious. Charli wasn't kidding.

"I can see that." A rare smile pulls at my lips.

"Oh, this is going to be great. You're exactly what we need!" He claps his hands together, motioning for me to follow.

Walking through the doors to the holding area, I'm introduced to a few teenage boys—busy scrubbing kennels. Another man around my age is tossing bags of food onto a pallet. He wipes his brow and waves as we approach.

"Bailey, this is Jude. He's our secret vet tech hire. Look at him, isn't he perfect!" Nikolai pats him on the shoulder with a chuckle.

Bailey's crystal blue eyes crinkle as he beams back at Nikolai. "Doc's gonna lose her shit. You're the yin to her yang for sure. Are we taking bets on how long until they're at each other's throats?" He practically doubles over laughing causing his shaggy blonde hair to fall over his forehead.

"Is she that bad?" My usually stoic face twists. Not that it matters to me, I need this job and nothing can be worse than my last boss.

"She's fine, just a bit dramatic. Don't be too hard on her though. Just remember, I'm the one paying your salary, not her. She'll hate you at first, but you seem like the type who can handle her. You're all tall and broody and she's a walking sparkle." He smirks, guiding me to the back rooms. "Here goes nothing." He pushes the door open. "Oooooh Parasite, I've got a surprise for you."

My stomach hits the floor when I lay my eyes on a ghost from my past... wearing bright pink scrubs.

CHAPTER 14

Caroline

The air has been stolen from my lungs. My thoughts stop dead in their tracks as I'm mentally transported back to the moment I first laid eyes on him.

Jude Carlisle.

This time I'm rendered speechless from a different feeling in my stomach. Where butterflies once swarmed, rage now burns white hot.

"What the hell?!" I shriek out the only words I can manage in this cosmic joke of a moment.

Jaw agape, my scorn filled gaze shifts from my clueless cousin to the deep green scrubs struggling to hold in the *man* that Jude has become.

Stop it. Bad Caroline.

"No. Nope. Why is he here, and in scrubs!?" I'm still yelling and an audience has gathered around us.

Great, everyone is in on this sick joke.

"Wow I knew you'd overreact, but this is excessive. I know you don't want help, but you need it," Nikolai speaks up, completely oblivious.

Next to him, Jude is unnaturally pale. Who knew someone with such naturally tanned skin could look so ghostly?

"We need to talk. Now!" With an iron grip I drag Nikolai to my office.

"What the fuck, Caroline?" he grits out.

"I should be asking you that!" I'm still screeching as my heart twists, thumping wildly. The panic and seething fury flowing through my veins hasn't even begun to settle down.

"I didn't think you were *this* against help. What is wrong with you?" He plants his hands on his hips.

"Jude! That's what! Are you insane? Of all the people you could have hired, Jude fucking Carlisle was the one you decided on?!" My yells are whispers now, but no less sharp.

Nikolai is quiet for a beat. I can see his brain working out how he knows the name. The instant he connects the dots his face contorts.

"Oh fuck. That's *Jude*?" The color drains from his face.

I nod in response, my brows scrunched together in disapproval.

"I had no idea. I never met him before. He's also not your usual type. Scott is the exact opposite of him." He scratches the back of his neck.

"That's the problem! He's *exactly* my type. No other man has ever come close. I tolerate Scott because he leaves me the hell alone and only bugs me occasionally for mediocre sex."

"Gross. At least tolerate someone for good sex. I thought you had better standards." Nikolai grimaces.

"My standards started and stopped with Jude. But you know how that ended. My hope for a life-changing love was born, and died with him." The stinging of my nose warns me of approaching tears. I fan my face, sniffling the emotions away.

"Hey, it's been years. He seems like a decent enough guy with the right values to fit in here. You really do need the help. Can you please try to give him a chance?" Nikolai places a hand on my shoulder, slightly calming my frayed nerves.

"You mean like I did seven years ago?" My lip juts out on its own accord.

"No, I'm not telling you to fall for him again. Keep him at arm's length, but let him lessen your workload. Can you give him a month to prove himself?" His sage green eyes chisel away at my defenses.

"I'll do my best. That's all I can offer at the moment."

Seeing him after all this time is such a shock I lost my cool for a minute. Maybe we can make this work. I really do need help and, until now, it's been nearly impossible to find the *right* person.

"Such a *you* response." He snorts.

"In all honesty, I know we need the help. I just need a minute to breathe before I can look at him and not want to scream... or cry."

"Or jump him?" Nikolai wiggles his brows. I pinch his forearm, making him hiss and swat me away.

My time to breathe is short lived, we have too much to do to get this place ready for our grand opening. I can vent my feelings to the girls after work.

I inhale deeply and tip my head toward the door, giving Nikolai a soft smile.

As we step back into the clinic, Bailey is the only staff member still here. He's chatting quietly with Jude, who has regained some of his color, but he still looks tense.

"Bailey can you make sure the breakfast rounds are on schedule, please? I need to finish Jude's orientation," Nikolai speaks up.

"Sure thing, Nicky. Later Jude! Bye Doc!" He drifts out of the room, with a lightness only Bailey could possess after witnessing the drama that just unfolded.

"Okay, so here's the deal, Jude. Caroline filled me in back there. She agreed to give you a month to see if you guys can make this work. I like you, but I love her. She's the closest thing I have to a sister. You're adults, so I want to believe that this can benefit both of you. Please just try, okay?" He looks between us with his arms folded and eyebrows raised.

"Jesus, just because you're a father now doesn't mean you have to 'dad pose' me." I cross my arms back at him. Jude has the nerve to snort, earning him a fierce glare from me. His cheeks redden as his eyes meet the floor.

"Something funny, Carlisle?" I snap.

He's wide eyed, almost robotic as he shakes his head.

Weird.

"So then, you two start giving general check-ups to the dogs we have ready for adoption. The grand opening is this weekend and I want to make sure everyone is in perfect health," Nikolai says, breaking the awkward tension.

"Yes, Nicky. You know I won't let you down." I roll my eyes.

"Yes, Sir." Jude nods.

My breath catches and I try to cover it up with a cough. Jude chews his lip ring and scans my face with a questioning expression. He's well aware of the images flashing through my mind. I can see the simmering heat in his eyes.

"Don't call me 'Sir'. You're also not in prison anymore, relax a bit." Nikolai pats his shoulder, as if he wasn't watching our whole wordless exchange.

My head whips to Jude, eyes threatening to pop out of my skull. "Prison?!"

How did I not know ?

Right. He abandoned me, destroying the last bits of my heart when it was already a pulverized mess. The shame in his soulful, longing eyes is evident.

Did he not want me to know?

"Caroline, don't act like he's the only felon working here. It's kind of our thing." Nikolai offers me a straight-lined, but otherwise blank face.

"Sorry, I know. I just wasn't expecting it. They let you keep your piercings in prison?" Nikolai's eyebrows knit together at my question.

"They didn't close up, so I just put them back in when I got out," Jude says to the floor.

"Both of them?" My eyes drift on their own to his waist.

Why am I asking?

The twisting of Jude's face tells me he's mulling over the same question. "Y-yes."

"Oh god, please don't fuck on the exam table. I'm leaving." Nikolai turns to us before stepping out of the room. "Seriously though, try to work together civilly."

We nod in unison and watch him stroll away.

"Right then, where should we begin?" I ask with an all too cheery, forced tone.

Jude doesn't have a chance to respond before I anxiously answer myself. "I know, we'll go over to the kennels and see some of the dogs. We have about twenty ready for their new homes, and ten more who will hopefully be good to go by Friday. As long as you and I can get them in ship-shape condition."

If I treat him as a co-worker, and not someone I have a heart-shattering history with, this will work.

It's fine—totally, completely, absolutely, fine.

"Yes ma'am. Just show me what needs to be done." He follows close behind me.

The nostalgic scent of cedarwood and spices sneak their way into my senses. My heart stutters from the devastation flashing into my mind. Long-suppressed memories fight to resurface.

"Sorry, I need to use the restroom. Go find Bailey and Sean, they know the dogs we'll be working with." I ramble out, far too urgently.

"Sure thing." He still hasn't looked me in the eye. I don't blame him. He has some nerve even staying here.

I scramble to the ladies room and pull my phone out of my pocket.

Me: I lied, I don't think I can do this.

Nicky: ...It's been SEVEN minutes since I left you two.

Me: Yeah, the WORST seven minutes of my life.

Li: What? What did I miss? Is she taking it that bad? Jude is great, you'll love him.

Nicky: Sugar, bad choice of words. I'll fill you in. Parasite, suck it up. He's here to stay unless deemed unfit for the role.

Me: But how am I supposed to do this? There's no "How to work closely with the man who destroyed other men for you." handbook!

Li: Oh. Well... have you talked to him about it? Maybe I can get Claire to come in and mediate.

Me: Don't diminish her genius by expecting her to drop everything and be my relationship counselor.

Nicky: It wouldn't hurt to talk to the guy. I saw the way he reacted to you. Your heartbreak may not be as one-sided as you think.

Me: Hah! Right. Jude Carlisle, playboy douche-bag is heartbroken that he ghosted me when I needed him!

Li: Where are you?

Me: *Ladies room. But don't worry about it.*
Li: *Stay there, I'm coming.*

Great. My rambling hurled me into a "mom" talk with Charli. I can just hear her now—she's spent too much time with Claire. It's like having an in-house psychiatrist with her around.

Every issue is met with a, "Claire would say..." this, or a, "Well, I'm sure Claire would tell you..." that. Nobody is allowed to come close to being upset with old mother-hen Charli around. It's even worse when Claire is actually here.

"Caroline, are you okay?" She knocks on the door of the stall I'm huddled up in.

"Yes." The pathetic sound of my voice says otherwise.

"Listen, I don't know Jude, and I only know the brief bit of history you've told me, but he seems sincere. Nikolai filled me in a bit and I just want you to feel safe and comfortable. Do you want him gone?" Oh, Charli. She might be Nikolai's wife, but that woman is my best friend. Even if they were to separate, she'd still be stuck with me.

"No, that's not fair to him. I need to put my big girl panties on and power through the awkwardness." The latch on the stall door clicks as I slide it open.

Charli wraps me in a hug, wiping my tear stains away. "Well, we can't just fire him, I won't do that. He's been through a lot and seems to be really trying to get his life together. Just know that we'll find something else for him to do that will limit his interactions with you, if you wish."

"No, I do actually need the help, I don't think I'll be able to get these last ten dogs treated in five days by myself. A few are pretty sick and the kennel staff likely won't have the knowledge to properly assist," I huff.

Despite my reservations I know it's true. Even if I don't want it to be him, I do need someone. I'm quite burnt out from doing it all by myself the past couple of weeks. We aren't even open yet. I can't even begin to imagine how I'll manage the chaos all by myself when we do.

"Just know that you're family. Your comfort will always come first. But, maybe we should have you two sit down, in a supervised setting, and hash it out. Just think about it and let me know, Claire has the resources. Okay?" Gently, she squeezes my arm before pulling away.

"I hate talking about it, but if you think it'll help, okay." I shrug, defeated.

"Perfect. We'll figure out a time to do it soon. For now, go help get everyone up to speed in the quarantine wing."

"Yes, Boss." I stick my tongue out at her playfully.

With a soft slap to my shoulder she leaves the bathroom.

If Mom was still here, she'd tell me to forgive Jude. She'd probably see the same thing in him that Charli and Nikolai do.

Too bad I'm not her, and she's not here.

My dad is going to lose his mind, though. That much I know for sure.

After touching up my mascara and reapplying my lip gloss, I'm ready for whatever else this day will throw at me.

Jude is intently focused on the kennel in front of him as Bailey does his best to describe Cannoli's condition.

I think I'll give myself just a second to appreciate how taut his scrubs are, stretching over his muscular back. The itchy part of my brain that's responsible for jealousy is thankful that our entire staff consists of men and troubled boys, except for the snarky teenage girl at the front desk. She's too good to talk to anyone, so I've got nothing to worry about there.

I know I don't hold any sort of claim over Jude, but I just might fight any woman who stares at him as long as I have.

CHAPTER 15

Jude

I don't know if Caroline realizes she's staring. I'm not going to let it faze me, even if it's raising alarm bells in my head. She doesn't want me, I know this.

If she did, she wouldn't have pushed me away years ago, tearing my heart to pieces.

"Doc, thank God you're here. I was giving Jude the rundown on the setup, and it was all going well until we made it here to quarantine. I was trying to explain what's going on with Cannoli, but all your medical terms make no damn sense to me." Bailey is my savior for cutting through the awkwardness so effortlessly.

"Ah, my sweet little Cannoli. She's a special case and I'm honestly going to be sad to see her go." She opens the kennel, and the teeny black and tan miniature pinscher puppy lifts its wobbly head to greet her.

"Well visually I can assume she had mange at the very least." Anyone could see that her skin is still pink and irritated in places.

"You would be correct. She had early signs of Demodex mange, which is part of the reason she's back here in the quarantine room. This little fighter is actually recovering from parvovirus. She's not positive anymore, but I still like to keep her close because she was touch-and-go for so long." She scoops Cannoli up and the tiny pup nestles comfortably in the opening of her scrubs

I'm all too familiar with how warm and soft her chest is—or was, anyway. She's filled out even more since I last saw her.

No, Jude. Keep it in your pants, she doesn't want you.

"So is she gonna be up for adoption durin' our grand openin'?" Like a fool I reach over and scratch Cannoli under her chin, unintentionally grazing the top of her breast.

At least, if anyone asks, it was unintentional. I just can't help myself when it comes to her.

Caroline puts on her best poker face, but the pebbling of her skin and the pinkness of her cheeks is unmistakable.

She turns away, placing Cannoli back into the pile of blankets she'd previously been burrowed in. "She won't be ready in time, sadly. But, I'm not completely upset if it gives me a little more time to love on her. She was surrendered by her owner because they weren't prepared to pay for her medical care." As she talks, her eyes shine for that puppy in a familiar way.

So many things have changed. But part of my Candy Girl is still hiding behind the hardened exterior she's built. If I didn't need this job, I'd run. There's no way I'm going to survive this woman a second time. Being her right-hand man is going to kill me.

Once again, I shouldn't want her. But that giant fucking heart and the way she embodies everything pure in this life will be my undoing. The fact that she's even curvier and more confident than before only fuels my long-burning desire. Seven years apart have done nothing except make her more alluring.

I don't know who I'm trying to fool, I've never stopped wanting her. My cold, dead heart is still wrapped in the bright pink ribbon she double knotted around it back then.

Too bad we had our chance, and I fucked it all up by pushing her too hard, too fast, until she ran away. I should have seen the signs; how she never found time to hang out after that night, even though Veronica told me she went out with them every weekend.

I tried to make her see how much I cared—how badly I wanted her love.

But a love like hers is far more than I deserve.

With one last kiss to Cannoli's head, she closes the door to her kennel and strolls to the main clinic. "So, did Bailey give you the tour of the whole place?" She asks, looking over charts.

"Everythin' except the actual veterinary offices." If I keep my answers short and minimize eye contact, I might actually make this work.

"Right, of course. You'll need to know where everything is." She turns on her heel.

"Bailey's a good guy," I say, ensuring my tone stays neutral.

"Yeah, he's been here since the beginning, a real sweetheart. He oversees operations and reports directly to Charli."

"Is he, well—"

"An ex-con? Yes. Most of the adult staff members are. Nicky and his savior complex." She chuckles. "He'll hire anyone who isn't a violent felon really."

"Oh, interesting." The surprise in my voice doesn't go unnoticed.

"Jude... are you a violent felon?!" She whisper-yells at me with a tight expression.

"Technically, no," I mumble.

"What the hell does that mean?!" Her feet stop moving and she whirls around in front of me.

I'm not fast enough to stop myself and crash into her. As we topple to the ground, I cage her in my arms, shielding her head from hitting the floor. For a moment, I allow myself to lay here holding her close to me. Her breathing picks up as our gazes collide, causing my blood to rush to all the wrong places.

"Shit, I'm sorry." Rising to my feet, I reach out a hand to help her up.

"Thank you for breaking my fall at least," she grumbles, straightening her scrubs. "So, what exactly does 'Technically, no' mean?" She stands as tall as she can at five-foot-four with her hands planted on her hips.

Oh, how I've missed her sass, as adorable as ever.

"It means that I was charged with and did time for assault. But it was a misdemeanor. The other charges were the heavy hitters."

"Assault!? Jude! I don't even know who you are," she squeaks.

Is she serious?

"No shit," I retort, voice low but intense just the same, "you never took the time to really know me before fucking destroying me."

"*I* destroyed *you*?! Whatever you say." She stomps away, leaving me completely confused.

We tiptoe around each other for the remainder of the day.

The job itself seems straightforward. My duties mostly include making rounds, checking to make sure the healthy dogs stay healthy and helping Caroline with exams on new arrivals.

Charli and Nikolai are standing at the exit as I go to leave.

Dread squeezes me so tightly I can hardly breathe.

I'm getting fired, I just know it.

"Jude! Fantastic job today. I know my cousin can be a lot to handle, so I just wanted to touch base with you on the way out. Are we going to see you tomorrow?" Nikolai pats me on the shoulder like we're old friends meeting for a drink.

"You want me to come back? Caroline didn't convince you to fire me?" I jerk my head back, bewildered.

"Quite the opposite, Nikolai and I both talked a little sense into her. Right Caroline?" Charli leans around me, addressing the bright pink whirlwind power walking through the lobby.

"Yeah, yeah. He can stay... for now." With a huff she continues past us. "I'm heading to Scott's so if you need me, don't."

"So, if it's four o'clock now, we'll give you twenty minutes for the drive over, then another two for him to disappoint you. You'll be free by four-thirty at the latest. Got it." Nikolai, with his arm leaning on my shoulder, grins impishly at Caroline.

"I should have never said anything to you!" She spins around, rips the door open and leaves without another word.

"Nikolai, don't be so mean." Charli tries and fails to hide her smirk.

"Hey, I'm a realist. She's the one who told me the sex is disappointing. She needs a better fuck buddy." His face pulls tight as my muscles tense. "Shit, do you still have feelings for her?"

"No. It's just a lot to process. I had it bad for her before everythin' happened. But we're not the same people we were back then," I say flatly.

"As long as you two stay civil, that's enough for me," he says, still leaning on me.

An unfamiliar sense of what almost feels like friendship has me smiling back at him. "Thank y'all for givin' me a shot. I'm not used to such a warm and welcoming work environment."

"That's what we do, Jude. This is a family and you're part of it now. Until you get sick of us." He straightens, removing his arm from my shoulder.

"I don't see that happenin' any time soon." My grin reaches my eyes for the first time in years.

"I'm glad to hear it!" Charli claps. "Anyway, we have a grandpa to relieve of his babysitting duties. We'll see you tomorrow."

"Yes ma'am." I nod at her.

We head out of the clinic and part ways. My ride home is a bit of a blur.

Life feels brighter. I've got more energy than I've had in a long time.

Five minutes after I walk through my front door, my phone pings with a text message. The number isn't one I have saved, which strikes me as odd.

Unknown: *Hey man! It's Bailey. I hope you don't mind that Nicky gave me your number.*

Me: *Hey Bailey. What's up?*

Bailey: *Nothing much, I know it's probably weird but, aside from Sean, you're the only guy at work around my age. So I just wanted to ask if you'd like to hang out some time?*

Me: *As friends right? You seem nice and all, but I'm not* *into dudes.*

Bailey: *Hah! Totally platonic, I promise. I just don't have many people I can relate to.*

Man do I understand that. Having a real friend who gets it would be nice.

Me: *Yeah, what do people even do around here when they're out on parole?*

Bailey: *That's the thing. I'm in AA and can't really go to bars. Hence the reason I don't have friends. How do you feel about sports? There's an amateur fight coming up. Nothing fancy but it could be a good time.*

Me: *You're speakin' my language.*

Bailey: *Hell yeah! Are you coming to the pool party Saturday?*

Me: *Pool party?*

Bailey: *Yeah, Nikolai and Charli are hosting, to celebrate the grand opening.*

Me: *I haven't been invited.*

Bailey: *Oh. Awkward. I'm sure they just haven't had the chance, it's only been a day after all. You should totally plan on coming though!*

Me: *If they invite me, I'll come.*

Bailey: *Awesome! See ya tomorrow!*

Me: *Later.*

Going forward I'm determined to make each day an improvement over the last. Even with the drama, today was good. I know tomorrow will be even better. At least this time I know what I'm walking into.

CHAPTER 16

Caroline

Scott rolls off me, panting like he just ran a marathon. It doesn't make any sense how he can get so sweaty after just a couple minutes of erratic thrusting. Sighing dramatically, I pull my scrub pants back on and find my shoes while he disposes of the condom.

Nikolai is right, if I'm going to tolerate someone, I should at least make sure the sex is worth it.

Scott's nice. He's welcoming and always willing to listen to my problems, but I'm just not satisfied with our… situationship. It's not even his fault. As cliché as it sounds, it really is *me.*

"You want food before you go? I have some pizza in the fridge." Scott's eyes twinkle as he asks.

I know he's hopeful I'll actually stay the night. For about the hundredth time since we started hooking up, I find myself questioning why he even keeps coming back for more.

"Nah, I'm heading to see my family. I'm sure Dad's got

something made. I appreciate the offer." My keys jingle when I scoop them up off the counter. I breathe deeply and turn to face him. "Also, I think this will be the last time we do this. I'm just not the romantic type, and you are. It's not fair that I keep stringing you along. Find yourself someone who can love you back." My smile is soft as I watch his face fall.

"Oh. I thought you were starting to really like me." His lips pull into a solemn pout.

God if he cries, I'll lose it.

"I was trying, really. But I've never been the type to have feelings like that for anyone. I know this isn't fair to you, but I've also been honest from the beginning," I say firmly.

He rakes his fingers through his hair and huffs. "I know, but damn. It's been months. I've been trying to be patient in hopes that you would come around. You know I can take care of you."

Ew.

"Scott, I don't want to be taken care of. I don't *need* to be taken care of." I fold my arms over my chest, popping a hip out.

He's in finance and makes decent enough money, but I have no desire to be a trophy wife.

"I'm sure the right woman is out there for you. I'm just not her, and can't keep trying to convince myself that I am." I reach for the door handle.

"Caroline." My name is a desperate plea—one I have no desire to answer.

"No, we're done here, Scott. Thank you for everything." Not that there's much to thank him for. Still, I don't want to absolutely crush him. "You deserve love that I can't give." Surely a more emotionally sound person would have tried to stick around and lessen the blow—but that's not me. I walk swiftly out his door without looking back.

It's five o'clock when I pull into Dad's driveway. I know he had a nice dinner planned for all of us tonight. My dick appointment with Scott was a last-minute decision, but as Nikolai predicted, it didn't make me late.

Seeing Jude today, even after all this time, had me boiling over with reawakened feelings. I had hoped the residual arousal from him accidentally touching my chest—and laying on top of me—would have at least been enough to get me close to an orgasm with Scott.

It was not.

I'm hopeless.

"Aw, damn. My calculations were off." Nikolai laughs as I walk into the house. "Scott must've pulled out some extra moves today." He wiggles his brows.

"CiCi!" Ivy wobbles over to me. She's almost eighteen months old and looks just like Charli, only her soulful green eyes are all Nikolai. Her little black curls bob as she tumbles into my arms.

"Hi there munchkin, how's my favorite girl?" I blow a raspberry against her cheek, and she squeals.

"She was an angel, as always." Dad beams. "I'll be sad when summer is over, and I won't be available to babysit her during the week."

"You could always retire." Nikolai nudges him. "Ivy wouldn't mind at all, and you're old enough now, sixty-six is a respectable age."

"He's right, Dad." I put Ivy down and she scurries over to him.

"Pop." She throws her chubby little hands in the air, and he scoops her up.

"But if I retire, she'll never go to work with you and will miss out on all the doggies." He tickles under her chin and her giggles fill the room.

"Oh, she does love all the dogs." Charli chuckles as Ivy makes a barking noise. "Speaking of which, does your place allow pets, Caroline?"

"Oh, yeah. I just don't have time for all that right now. Maybe when things calm down at work."

"What about Scott? Does he like dogs?" Nikolai raises a single brow, and his face fills in the blanks. He's not asking because he cares, he wants to see how serious I am about keeping Scott around.

Typical annoying older sibling-like behavior.

"I broke it off with him. Okay? You were right," I grit out through my clenched jaw.

His cheeky grin grates on my nerves. "Oh, and absolutely nothing else influenced your decision?" The smug insinuation in his tone has me crinkling my face up at him. "A tall, tan, sexy vet tech maybe? He filled those scrubs out *real* nice."

"Shut up! You've lost your mind," I seethe.

"Could you two please be civil for once?" Dad grunts.

"Tell him to stop, it's all Nicky's fault!" I whine.

"Technically, Charli hired him. I didn't meet him until today. But I see how he looks at you." Nikolai leans back in his chair, folding his arms.

"He doesn't look at me." I scoop a mound of potatoes onto my plate, slathering them with the rich brown gravy Dad whipped up with juices from the pot roast. "This smells so good, I miss living here." I drop into my seat, joining everyone at the table.

"I do miss you, but I enjoy my peace and quiet. Now, tell me about this vet tech." Dad tips his head my way with an inquisitive look.

I tense up, shooting a furious look at Nikolai that says "Look what you've done.".

"Well, Pop. We had a very wonderful candidate submit an application. He was the perfect fit for the job and possessed all the qualities we'd hoped for. So, I hired him." Charli's eyes shine with pride.

"I don't understand the issue then. Is he coming to the pool party? I'd like to meet him. Is he on parole?" Dad rolls out questions faster than my brain can process.

"He is, he's been out for a little over a year now, finished his tech certification and was looking for a place to call home." Nikolai smiles, all too happy with himself.

"That's nice to hear. I do admire what you kids have built. The people you have working there are all such good souls." My father smiles while cutting into his steak.

"Dad. It's Jude," I blurt out, "Jude Carlisle."

He freezes mid-cut, eyes shooting up from his plate, to Nikolai. "Jude Carlisle? Nicky, this must be a joke. In no world should that boy be anywhere near Caroline." The intensity of his accent spells out exactly how upset he is by this news.

"God, Pop. Don't make it sound like he physically hurt her. They were young, shit happened, and hearts got broken. There's no reason they can't have a professional relationship as *adults*." Nikolai curls his lips, directing a serious glare my way.

"He took advantage of her and then left her! Are those really the values you want to be associated with?" Dad seethes.

"I can't help but feel like this is partially my fault. I knew the name sounded familiar, but he seemed so genuine and kind. There's a sadness and loneliness in his eyes that made me want to give him a chance," Charli speaks so kindly about him, I almost feel bad for being upset.

I know she has a huge heart. She was kidnapped, held captive, and assaulted for years. When she got free, she found us, and Nikolai has been utterly devoted to her ever since. She shouldn't have so much compassion for criminals and outcasts, yet here she is. If she sees some good in Jude, maybe it's really there.

A long-suppressed part of my soul wants to trust her intuition. How badly I desire to feel that spark again. The fire I felt for Jude all those years ago is unlike any other connection I've experienced. What he did to me, though... I just don't think I can ever forgive him for. Regardless, I'm stuck working with him now.

"He definitely shows promise and could prove to be a great asset for the rescue. The dogs' health and well-being are far more important than my own personal feelings." Even *I* am shocked by my words.

"Wow. That's probably the most mature and sensible thing I've ever heard you say." Nikolai sits wide eyed across from me.

"Don't get used to it," I snip back at him.

"If you don't feel comfortable just say something and we'll address it, okay?" Charli's thoughtfulness almost makes me tear up.

"I promise. But for now, I just need to get over myself, for the sake of the dogs."

"Well then, that settles it. Just know that if he so much as *thinks* about hurting you again, I'll find him this time." Dad's hands are balled into fists around his utensils.

"Calm down, Pop. There's no need for all that. You'll put too much strain on your heart if you're not careful." Nikolai chuckles.

"I would still like to have a word with him. What he did to you was uncalled for." His face is tight. Knuckles white from his grip on the knife and fork he's holding.

I'm sure it was difficult for him to see me break apart over Jude while simultaneously mourning the loss of my mother. Just like it was hard for me to watch him wither away from her loss.

"I love all of you, but I swear it's fine. I don't want anyone to feel bad or worry." My eyes skim each of their faces, meeting their gazes long enough to convey my honesty.

Whether it's true or not is a great question.

CHAPTER 17

Jude

Of course, my second day on the job and it's pouring outside. I'm usually on top of checking the forecast for rain—living in Seattle means I see a lot of it. I don't exactly want to show up drenched, so I'll have to take an Uber, which means I'll be late.

Awesome.

There's no way this will end well. I should just cut my losses and start looking for a new job.

No, asshole, don't throw away your second chance.

If I just text Nikolai, I'm sure he'll understand.

Me: *Hey, soooooo I only own a bike. Gonna have to find a ride. Might be late. I'm sorry.*

Nikolai: *Shit man, hold on. I'll get you a ride. Don't even worry about it.*

Slack-jawed, I stare at my phone with pinched brows. *Why is he so nice?*

Ten minutes after I send him my address a cherry red Miata swerves wildly into the parking lot of my apartment complex. My stomach flips when I see Caroline behind the wheel.

"Jude." Her eyes are stuck on the dilapidated excuse of a building I unfortunately call home.

"Caroline, thank you for the ride. My bike wasn't going to cut it, and I would have been late if not for you." My knees knock against the dash as I settle into the passenger seat.

"You live here?" She asks, with her face crinkled in a way that almost looks concerned.

"Yup, for a year and a half now."

"Jude, look at this place!" She waves her hands around wildly.

"Yeah, I see it every day," I deadpan.

"I don't understand how you can live here. It's a shit hole." Her face contorts.

"I'm sorry, the gated communities aren't keen on ex-cons. Pretty sure the HOA's would pitch a fit. Why do you care, anyway?" I huff.

This day is already more of a nightmare than yesterday, and it's only seven a.m.

"I know I shouldn't care, but I do," she whispers solemnly, pulling out of the parking lot.

"Now you sound like me." I turn my face to the window, watching the sidewalk as we drive.

"Just forget it, let's get to work. There are a few dogs who have come down with tummy issues. We can't have them going to new homes with diarrhea," she rambles, wiping her nose.

Was she... crying?

"Do you think it might be a food sensitivity? Maybe a probiotic will help." I turn to face her, observing the redness of her eyes.

Yup, definitely crying.

"Yeah, I think that's a good place to start. Good call." She nods, drumming on the steering wheel as she drives.

"This is a nice car, Nikolai must pay you well," I say after an awkward silence.

"He bought me this a few years ago for Christmas, actually. Dad got a new RAV4 that looks like the one we used to have... before the accident." Her voice cracks.

Accident?

The tone coating her words is enveloped in grief. She doesn't give me time to question anything, getting out of the car the second it's parked.

I trail behind her, up the front steps.

Nikolai is in the lobby waiting when we enter. "Ah, just in time! Bailey said there's a few more... eruptions today. He's had the staff hosing down kennels for thirty minutes now. Should we move all the sick ones to quarantine?" His head is tilted, a single eyebrow raised as he regards us.

"That's probably for the best. Nicky, we need to consider delaying the opening if this continues. For now, can we get a load of pumpkin and probiotics?" Caroline asks on the way to the clinic. She's already in problem solving mode and it's captivating. Her quick wit and intelligence will always be two of her most attractive qualities.

"Sure, I'll get Sean to run to the store for pumpkin. Is there anything else?" Nikolai asks with genuine worry in his voice as we walk into the treatment room.

"No, we'll get to examining everyone. I'd recommend enough cans of pure pumpkin for every dog here to have some for the rest of the week." Caroline wipes down the exam table with disinfectant. "For now, Jude and I will run fecal exams on the ones who are presenting symptoms, to rule out a parasite infection."

"Yes ma'am. Four days worth of pumpkin coming right up!" Nikolai dashes out of the room in a frenzy.

"He didn't even panic that much when Ivy was born. This is Charli's dream, and he's determined to have it be as perfect as possible." Caroline's tone is soft, filled with admiration.

"He seems like a great guy." I keep my responses short, since the ice I'm walking on is extremely thin where Caroline is concerned.

"Oh, man. I'm so glad to see both of you," Bailey huffs, pushing the door open with his elbow. Two little mixed-breed dogs are tucked under his arms. "The fluffy one needs a bath." He scrunches up his face.

"He sure does. Jude, you're on butt scrubbing duty." Caroline's smile would seem sweet to anyone else, but I know that cheeky, bratty grin all too well.

Keep it together, Jude.

"You got it." I relieve Bailey of the poop covered puppy and walk quickly to the bathing station.

The pup is absolutely filthy, having clearly decided that his mess doubled as a bed. It takes me a few rounds of lathering and good rinses to get him clean before returning to the main clinic.

"Jude, perfect timing." Caroline ushers me over to the exam table. "They'll need fecal tests. You know how to do that, right?"

"I can scoop shit out of a dog's ass, Candy." I pin her with an intense, unmoving look as I watch her reaction.

As expected, she freezes, her breath catching at the sound of her nickname on my lips. If she wants to play hardball, so be it.

One of us has been to prison and learned to roll with the literal and figurative punches. The other is a brat who is about three more petty tasks from getting pinned up against the wall and taught a lesson.

No, I need this job.

I inhale and remind myself that she won't win. Not this time.

She ruined my life once already. I can't give in and let her do it again.

It should have never happened in the first place.

What a shitty day. In *every* sense of the word.

Nikolai and Charli are at the door again as we're walking out.

"I owe you both so much. Thank you for everything today. Do you need a ride home, Jude? Caroline likes to go to Scott's after work." Nikolai, with a mischievous look, pats me on the shoulder—it's become a habit of his at this point. Strangely enough I find it endearing.

"Actually, I'm going home to shower. I'm disgusting." Caroline waves us off and strides out the door.

Nikolai's face is split by a pearly grin. "She's stubborn, but she'll come around. Let's go, Charli and I drove separately today." He motions to the door, locking it behind us when we exit. He leads me to the parking lot and—oh shit—his Corvette.

My eyes widen with glee. "What's this, a 2018 Z51?"

"A man after my own heart." He beams at me over the top of the car.

Fuck, Charli's warning may have been warranted. I'd consider topping this man right now.

"Get in." He winks before dropping into the driver's seat.

What?

"I smell like dog shit, and I'm not ruining your upholstery. I'll catch a ride some other time." Not only am I half-selling my excuse but my face hurts from the force of the scowl pulling at it.

"Detailing is a wonderful thing. I can always drive my truck or ride with Charli until it's done. No biggie." He shrugs.

The black leather interior feels like butter as I slide into my seat. "I've never been anywhere near a car this

188

nice. Wow." I blow out a whistle of approval.

"I'm thinking about getting a new one. If my portfolio manager is right, I should have a nice investment return coming and can swing it." The casual way he talks about buying a brand-new car like it's a pair of shoes makes me itch with envy. But he's so caring and genuine, it's impossible to even think about hating him.

"Is this custom wrapped? The color is great. It'd be better in green, or black, but this dark blue is clean."

"Hmm. Green, huh? Dark green or lime green?" He quirks his head toward me.

"Dark, definitely dark." I nod.

"Nice. Seems to be your color of choice a lot. Now, are you ready for this?" His foot is on the brake as he hovers a finger over the start button. An excited twinkle glints in his eyes.

"Hell yeah, Boss. Show me what she's got."

When the engine roars to life, we share a look of child-like excitement. The deep rumble as he presses the gas goes through me like a rush of adrenaline... almost exactly like my bike.

"Wanna take the long way home? I know all the best back roads." His right dimple pops from the pull of his lip.

"I'm not going to fuck you for a joy ride, pretty boy," I joke with a soft chuckle.

Nikolai huffs out a laugh straight from his gut. "I have a wife. You may have met her. Five feet nothing, pure firecracker. She owns me, sorry. Besides, if I fucked you,

Caroline would never stand a chance. You seem like a man who likes a bottom."

I gasp, unable to offer a retort from the shock of how easily he's read me.

"Called it!" He throws his head back and cackles.

"Just drive the damn car." My shoulders shake as I laugh.

We drive for a few minutes, enjoying the scenery before Nikolai speaks up. "By the way, we're having a celebratory pool party this weekend. Everyone is welcome. Do you have any food allergies or special requests?"

We're winding down a gorgeous back road, metal music booming through the speakers. For a second I let myself imagine life being this amazing forever.

Right, answer him.

"I don't have any allergies or anythin' and I'm not picky. I'm just thankful to be invited." The lump in my throat makes my words waver slightly, but I mean every one. It's been difficult trying to find a place where I genuinely fit in. This might not be it, but I'm going to enjoy the friendliness while it lasts.

"Awesome! Charli will be ecstatic. I'll send you our address. Bring a change of clothes, we have plenty of spare rooms for people who need to crash." The look on his face makes me feel... seen. Like maybe the offer isn't just in reference to the party.

"Oh, I wouldn't want to impose." My smile is tight, in an effort to conceal my lie.

"You wouldn't be. Bailey and Sean even have their

own room." He laughs.

"Bailey is a good dude." I nod slightly. "I don't know Sean much. He's quiet."

"Yeah, but he's dependable and loyal. We only hire the best." Nikolai tips his chin toward my building as he parks. "Now, get out of my car and go drown in some soap. You reek." He waves a hand in front of his face in an exaggerated fashion.

"I tried to warn you. Thanks for the ride, man." Why is my voice threatening to crack? It's just a courtesy ride. *Get a grip.*

"Any time." His eyes skim the exterior of my apartment building. "I mean it. If you need anything, we're here. Be safe, Jude. And go take a looooong shower." With a playful curl of his lip, and mock shiver, he pulls out of my parking lot. As I watch him drive away, I'm left absolutely mind blown.

CHAPTER 18

Caroline

Today was exhausting, but the grand opening went well. So many dogs got adopted out. Claire came to support us, and brought her husband Theo and their baby boy Henderson. They looked at a few puppies but didn't find one that was quite the right fit. They're busy professionals, so it's understandable. I'm just glad the event went off without a hitch.

I'm also irked beyond belief to admit that Jude played a big part in our success.

Not only was it a stressful week trying to get everything ready, but the Giardia outbreak would have been impossible to manage without him. The icing on my crappy cake is having to acknowledge that he was a lifesaver.

Why does he have to be so good at his job?

After the way he showed up and did everything I asked, there's no point trying to convince Nikolai to let him go. They've already started to develop a bromance anyway, so it would be a fruitless campaign.

Having seen the slum he's living in, I would honestly feel bad if he lost this job. God knows it can't be easy finding work as a felon.

I still can't believe he went to prison.

What was he in for? How much time did he serve? The better question is, why do I care? He played me like the stupid, love-struck girl I was. Love may not be the right word, but it sure felt that way. Losing Jude was almost as devastating as my mother's death. I mourned him—what we had—alongside her.

Now, I lay here staring at my ceiling, wishing the numbness I'd learned to accept would come back. Seven years, a whole lot of loneliness and mountains of resentment still aren't enough to keep my heart from aching for Jude.

I need a friend, which means the only logical choice is reaching out to my two favorite people. That's what best friends are for, after all.

Me: *Trivia night?*

Their responses come immediately.

Charli: *After how great today went? ABSOLUTELY. Nicky and Ivy can go spend some time with Pop.*
Claire: *Only if my guys can hang out with them too.*
Charli: *Of course, Dad has practically adopted Henderson as an official grandson at this point. :)*

Claire: Isn't that the truth. Fortunately, they like Theo, too. :)

Damn it, them gushing over their husbands and babies is not helping the burning in my chest.

Me: Perfect. I'll see you in a little bit!

I freshen up and make quick work of the three-block drive to the local bar hosting tonight's trivia competition. When I step inside Charli waves me down, grinning brightly from ear to ear. No longer in her work uniform, she's wearing a deep blue sundress, her signature look.

"Hey! Thanks for inviting us!" She wraps me in a hug.

"Caroline, you've done a marvelous job in caring for the animals at the rescue. The grand opening was beautiful today," Claire praises, pulling me into her embrace.

She's not the stuffy, cold woman I had once labeled her as. When she was *just* Charli's psychiatrist, I thought her kindness was a charade, some sort of mechanism to help Charli open up. I'm glad I was wrong. She's very proper and put-together, but her heart is pure and I haven't met many other women who are as communicative and supportive. She's in the right field of work, that's for sure.

"How are the hubbies? Did you manage to sneak away without an issue?" I joke.

"Oh, Nicky recruited Theo and Ivan to help get the house ready for tomorrow. So, they'll be making beds and prepping food like the good boys they are." Charli chuckles.

"Surely Theo will be on baby duty. I adore that man, but where he excels in intellect, he's no homemaker. Thank goodness he's a detective and not a trophy husband." Claire beams a perfect, pearly grin. "Shall we register? Triple C as usual?"

Charli and I nod. We dominate these trivia nights, which is a feat considering there are usually a dozen teams or more. Conveniently our names all start with "C", so our team's name was easy enough to come up with.

"Thank you both for coming. I really needed this." I sigh, slumping back in my seat.

"I know that face. What's got you down?" Charli leans my way and takes a sip of her cherry soda.

"You should know," I grumble.

"Come on, Jude has been a great asset." She frowns with a slight huff.

"He has some great assets, too," Claire jokes in a rare display.

I know she's not hitting on him, but familiar jealousy stabs me in the gut. She could almost be Veronica's much smarter—and less conniving—twin.

Breathe, Caroline.

I haven't even thought about that bitch in years. What is Jude doing to me?

"Sorry, that was out of line, especially given your history with him. My apologies." Claire takes my hand in hers, looking me in the eye with genuine remorse.

"It's okay. I'm not with him now, and you're not wrong. He was boyishly handsome back then, but now he's *all* man." I wiggle my brows. "You'd have to be blind to miss how hard his scrubs struggle to contain those glutes." I sip my Shirley Temple and sigh.

"I'm sorry I didn't know who he was before hiring him, but I'm not sorry I did. But, if it's hard on you, we can figure something else out," Charli says, with genuine compassion in every word.

"I love you, but please don't do that to him. He really isn't all that bad and deserves a chance. I just needed some sugary drinks, and to kick ass in trivia. A good old fashioned morale boost. Thank you both for coming out." I smile warmly at them.

Mic feedback echoes through the room as the host announces the starting question. The competition tonight is invigorating, but we're a triple threat. Claire is proficient in science of all sorts and vocabulary. Charli is a master of pop-culture and food knowledge—courtesy of spending every day with Nikolai. I have a love for all things animal related. Put us all together and It's rare for anyone to even make us sweat.

It's a close call tonight, but we come out on top with a near-perfect score.

We collect our complementary drink vouchers on our way out the door. It's not the fanciest prize, but we come here often enough that it does the trick.

With suffocating hugs, we say our goodbyes and go

our separate ways, fully aware that we'll see each other again tomorrow.

Nikolai's backyard is bustling.

Naturally, all the teenagers we employ are too cool to be seen here. Thankfully most of the adult crew came, because there's enough food to feed a small village.

Sean and Bailey are sitting at a picnic table, devouring some of the various snacks and charcuterie spread. A few of the kennel staff are splashing around in the pool. Our crew is under a large umbrella, hanging out in chaise lounges.

Nikolai's phone is making the rounds as people queue up songs for the playlist, while he lazes about with Charli snuggled up in his lap. Theo and Claire are kicked back, sipping fruity mocktails to my right while Dad lies in his chair half asleep. Off to our side, Ivy and Henderson are in a sandbox throwing sand around more than actually playing. Henderson is just a few months younger than Ivy so they're two little peas in a pod.

I lay my head back and close my eyes, soaking up the July warmth.

"Caroline," Nikolai speaks up, drawing my attention to the gate that Jude just stepped through. I lift my sunglasses and scowl at him as he continues, "listen, I told you everyone was invited. I couldn't leave him out." He shrugs.

Jude tentatively strides our way, popping my bubble of enjoyment.

"Hey." He waves, stilling as his eyes lock with my father's.

"Jude. Long time no see. Can't say I missed you." Dad's face pulls into a harsh grimace and he crosses his arms on his chair.

"Pop!" Nikolai gasps.

"No, it's fine. He loves his daughter and she hates me. So, he does too. I get it," Jude says with a pained expression. "Can I still sit with y'all?" He directs his attention to me.

Why does his consideration make me feel tingles?

I can't vocalize a response, so I nod curtly. Jude takes the empty chair next to Nikolai, which was originally intended for Charli, but she won't leave Nikolai's lap unless she has to.

"You're not exactly in swimwear," Charli teases.

"Yeah, I don't have any trunks. Never thought I'd need them." Jude kicks his boots off and leans back.

"I have plenty of spares if you want." Nikolai tips his head toward the house.

Jude looks toward the pool and contemplates for a moment before nodding.

"Hi!" Ivy wobbles over, throwing herself at Jude. He doesn't hesitate to scoop her up. Henderson is close behind, tossing his little arms in the air, silently asking to join her.

"Well hi there." Jude smiles brightly at the toddler duo

curled up on his lap.

"That's new. Usually Ivy takes a minute to warm up to people. She still won't go near Sean." Charli laughs.

"Most people find me unapproachable, even on my best days, but kids and animals love me for some reason." Jude beams back at her.

The knowing grin on Nikolai's face tells me that my own expression isn't even beginning to hide my reaction.

Jude's gaze lands on Nikolai's stomach. "Wow, wicked scar." Wide-eyed, he twirls a lock of Ivy's hair around his finger.

"Yeah, Charli's stalker stabbed me. I shot the crazy bastard in return. Now he's dead as fuck, and I saved my girl," Nikolai boasts with an award winning grin.

"Fuh!" Ivy blurts from Jude's lap, earning Nikolai a playful shove from Charli.

"Words! She's a little parrot right now. You know better," she scolds.

"Sorry, Sugar. I just get all riled up thinking about it." Nikolai pouts, as if she's truly upset.

"Get a room," Dad grumbles, "and you, give me my Mladentsy." He points at Ivy and Henderson, upset at how enchanted they are.

Jude doesn't protest. He stands with a toddler in each arm and passes them to my father. I'm still speechless and losing my internal battle to keep hating this man.

The truth is, I don't think I ever truly hated him to begin with.

CHAPTER 19

Jude

This was a mistake. I'm not wanted here. Nikolai and Charli are doing their best to keep the peace, but I can feel Ivan cursing me out in his head. I don't blame him, I just wish I had some idea of what Caroline's problem with me is. Every time I try to talk to her, something comes up. I'm sure half of the time it's just her avoiding me.

"Come on Jude. I'm positive I have a nice pair of black swim trunks with your name on them." Nikolai shifts Charli off his lap, and motions for me to follow.

"I wasn't plannin' on gettin' in the pool." I shrug.

"Just go, man. He won't give up, I promise you," Theo speaks up with a faint laugh.

He and Claire haven't said much since I arrived. I don't get the impression that they dislike me, they just don't seem to be the chatty type—based on my brief time spent with them.

Surrendering, I follow Nikolai inside, whistling in approval as I get my first true look at how massive this house is. The kitchen alone must be the size of my entire apartment. Obviously Nikolai is well off, he bought his wife a dog rescue for God's sake, but this place is impressive.

"Listen man." He stops in the living room, turning to address me. "Caroline is stubborn, but I want her to be happy." His face is serious, unlike the normal lighthearted grin he wears.

"Do I need to leave?" I ask, fully prepared to tuck my tail and go.

"Fuck no!" He laughs, patting my shoulder. "I want you to do the exact opposite. She's staying here tonight, you do the same."

"W-what?" I stutter, caught off guard by his suggestive tone.

"Stay here, we have plenty of room. Don't let her keep blowing you off. Tie her up if you've got to. I'm sure Charli will let you use her ropes." He smirks, wiggling his eyebrows.

"Charli has ropes?" I jerk my head back in surprise.

"Yeah, they're great." He sighs, with a dreamy look on his face. "Sorry, not the point. Anyway, Caroline is being a brat, which is kind of her thing, but I'm sick of it. What happened between you two was so long ago, and you were young and dumb. She's just holding a grudge for no reason. Talk to her already. I'll wingman as much as I can." He turns and starts down the hall, waving for me to follow.

"I don't even know why she's pissed at me. I should be the one who's upset, but I can't even think about being mad at her right now," I confess.

And it's true.

I've had years of prison fights and lonely nights to forgive her. The anger I felt when we reunited was a secondhand reaction to her own rage.

"I'm not going to play mediator, but I'm giving you the upper hand." He rifles through a dresser drawer in the bedroom we've entered. After finding a pair of swim trunks, with the tag still on, he tosses them my way. "One look at you in these and I'll probably have to shut the party down and give you guys the house to yourselves for a few hours."

I stare blankly at him for a second, allowing my mind to process his words. "Your relationship with her is strange." I shake my head.

"Oh, we're a riot at Christmas, just wait." A hearty laugh bursts out of him. "Now get changed." He turns and leaves the room.

When I walk back out to the yard where everyone is still sitting where I left them, I can feel Caroline's eyes on me through her sunglasses. Ivan's sharp glare is pinned to my chest. He doesn't have to say anything, I know exactly what he's looking at.

"Nice ink," Nikolai says with an impish grin.

I nod and offer a tight-lipped smile in return.

"What on Earth possessed you to tattoo my daughter's name on your skin?" Ivan howls. A vibrant redness overtakes his face, which has absolutely nothing to do with the heat.

I trail my hand over the lettering on my chest. Over my heart is a piece of candy, with flourishes swirling up my neck. The wrapper reads "Sweet Caroline" written in a swirly font I thought she'd love.

"It was part of my forgiveness process," I mutter to the wooden floor of the patio.

Even in his sixties, Ivan still intimidates me and I respect the hell out of him. I wish I had a father that cared half as much as he does. But right now I feel like a kid who got caught sneaking out.

"Your forgiveness process?!" Caroline shrieks, finally breaking her silence. "I need to get some air." She stands and pulls off the pink cover-up she's wearing.

Every thought I had goes straight out the window, all my blood rushes directly to my dick. She's wearing a sexy-as-sin bikini and I've forgotten where I am. Everyone else ceases to exist as I watch her march over to the pool and jump in.

"Ahem." Nikolai stares up at me with shock and humor on his face. Charli, nestled in his lap again, is doing her best to avert her gaze away from my very obvious erection. "Could you sit down so I don't get envious?" He pats the chair next to him. "Good God you could use that thing in the World Series. No wonder Caroline doesn't like sex. You undoubtedly broke her."

Red faced, I quickly sit and adjust myself. Across from me, Ivan is doing deep breathing exercises and counting backward under his breath.

"I'm sorry. I didn't even think about the tattoo. I've had it for a few years," I mumble with my attention returned to the floor.

"Well, I think it's lovely. Very well done... considering," Claire interjects with a hint of awkwardness.

"Not all prison tattoos are bad. Raul was a genius with the resources he had." I smile at her. "I'm sorry for making everyone uncomfortable."

"It's not a big deal, just relax and enjoy the day," Nikolai says in a bright tone.

I fidget with the string on my swim trunks as my eyes drift to the pool. Caroline is laid out on a float, sipping on a glass of punch. Her body is all curves, and I want to relearn every one of them.

"If you keep staring, you might pass out from the blood loss to your brain," Nikolai fake whispers, effectively snapping me out of my daydream.

"Sorry." I chew my lip ring and lean back in my lounge chair.

We sit and talk for a while until the sun begins to set. Everyone leaves except for Caroline and me.

While Charli puts Ivy to bed, the rest of us move inside. Despite the size of this house, the living room is small, cozy, and currently filled with awkward energy.

There's a single sofa. Three cushions, and four of us.

Nikolai sits on one end, Charli curls his lap when she enters the room. Caroline and I are in a stare off over the other seat, determined to not sit in the middle. In the spirit of civility, I move to sit on the floor against the wall, surrendering the spot to her.

"Thank you for today," I say to no one in particular.

"Any time man, I'm glad you came." Nikolai grins my way, briefly flicking his eyes to Caroline.

Her expression is pensive as she stares at the canvas covered wall in front of her. "I'm glad, too," she says after a brief silence.

My eyes find hers, and her gaze immediately darts to her lap. The pain I was able to see there twists my heart.

"You sure about that?" I ask, unable to help myself.

This is the first conversation we've had all night and I'm not even sure where to begin. My tone is colder than intended, but this might be my only chance. So what if she won't look me in the eye? It's a start.

"Jude, you can have our spot, my muse is sleepy and she's extra feisty when she doesn't get her beauty rest." Nikolai stands with Charli in his arms. She's practically snoring already. "Good night you two. Don't be too loud or Navy will bark and wake up Ivy, then she's your problem." He huffs out a laugh and carries Charli down the hall to their room.

I stand up and stretch before slowly sinking into the empty spot on the couch. Caroline sits still, chewing her lip on the other side. This tension between us is too much. I can feel it clawing at my skin, trying to tear me apart.

When she pulls her phone out and starts scrolling through social media, I sigh and pull out my own, itching with anticipation. Nikolai slipped me her number earlier and she has no idea.

Here goes nothing.

Me: *Hi there.*

I watch her brows furrow in confusion as her phone buzzes before typing out a reply.

Candy: *Uh. I think you have the wrong number.*

I silence my phone before she hits send, pretending to mindlessly scroll through my feed. I know I'll be busted if she looks my way. My poker face is non-existent at best.

Me: *I definitely don't.*
Candy: *Oh, but I think you do.*
Me: *Wanna bet?*

Her faint snort draws my attention. She has a playful half-smile on her face and my heart flips.

Candy: *I'm not much of a gambler. What's in it for me if I'm right?*
Me: *Doesn't matter. Name your prize.*
Candy: *I don't know. Maybe it's my romance novel addiction, but accidental texts do make for a fun meet cute.*

Me: *Oh yeah? Do you make a habit of flirting with any random number who texts you?*
Candy: *Four people text me.*
Me: *Five*.*

She laughs under her breath and I bite back the goofy grin on my face.

God I've missed us.

Candy: *So, who do you think I am then? Since you DEFINITELY don't have the wrong number.*
Me: *Let's see... I bet you're blonde.*
Candy: *Technically speaking you had a 1 in 4 chance of being correct. Lucky guess.*
Me: *Your eyes are brown.*
Candy: *Another lucky guess.*

She tucks her legs under herself, readjusting in her seat. Her lower lip is pulled between her teeth as she intently watches her phone.

Me: *What if I told you something personal?*
Candy: *Like what?*
Me: *Like how I'll never forget the first time I saw you. Something in my universe shifted and everything I never knew I wanted became clear as day.*
Candy: *Are you some sort of stalker? I'm not the type of girl people stalk. You really do have the wrong number.*

Shit. I'm losing her.

Me: *I'm not a stalker, I promise.*
Candy: *Funny, that's exactly what a stalker would say. I'll have you know, I think my dad might be part of the Russian mob.*
Me: *Honestly, he's terrifying. I wouldn't be surprised. What if I tell you something else?*
Candy: *Let's see what you got.*
Me: *Your lips taste as sweet as they look.*
Candy: *You could say that about anyone.*
Me: *You could say they're as sweet as CANDY.*

That does the trick.

She gasps and whips her head in my direction.

"Jude? What the hell? How did you—Nikolai," she answers herself, "Were you having fun tormenting me?"

"I wasn't tormenting you."

"What do you call that little flirty text exchange then?" She wants to yell but is forced to keep her voice hushed to avoid waking the house.

"I don't know. You were ignoring me, again, and I just wanted to talk to you!" I fire my own hushed replies back at her.

"What could you possibly want to talk about?" She folds her arms. If we were standing, I just know her hip would be popped out, and there'd be definite foot tapping.

Damn it, I'm still gone for this woman.

"Don't look at me like that!" She shrieks louder than intended and storms off to her room.

A smarter man would leave her be, but I'm a fucking fool for her. So, naturally, I follow.

CHAPTER 20

Caroline

What the hell? I feel like an idiot. How many times am I going to let this man make a fool out of me? The tattoo on his chest made me feel fuzzy inside and I don't like it, his secret text flirting only amplified my frustrations.

I storm into my designated room in Nikolai's "guest wing". In reality it's a fancy extension they built onto the house to act as a pseudo-hotel for anyone who needs a place to crash.

I throw open the door of the bathroom and aggressively twist the knobs on the large round tub. I unwrap a cherry vanilla bath bomb and toss it into the rising water, shedding my cover-up.

"Ca—" Jude stops in the doorway, skimming his eyes over my bikini clad body.

"Get out!" I shriek.

Luckily, this part of the house is far enough from the main bedrooms nobody can hear me. Annoyingly, he does the exact opposite and closes the door behind him.

"Turn the water off and talk to me." His voice lowers to a desperate whisper.

"Or what?" I puff out my chest and tip my head up to stare him in the eye.

"Don't avoid me... please." His fisted hands unfold and slip into his pockets. With slumped shoulders and anguish in his eyes, he sinks to the floor.

"What are you doing? Is this a hostage situation now?" I turn the water off and stare down at him.

"I... I'm sorry for whatever I did. Candy—"

"You don't get to call me that anymore," I seethe.

"—I... What happened between us?" His deep brown eyes glisten with forming tears.

"What happened?!" I wail, "My mom died and you—"

"Your mom died?!" he cuts in, "I thought she was just busy and couldn't make it today. God what—" His lower lip pops out as a tear breaks free. "—It was the accident you mentioned, wasn't it?"

"Yes. Not that you care," I snap as my pulse hammers in my ears.

"Of course I care!" he roars, raking his hand through his shaggy hair. "She was amazing. Always so supportive and had such a big heart. I only met her a few times but she was full of life. What happened?"

"She was in a crash, drunk driver." My lips pull into a half-frown while I fight the wobble of my chin.

"I'm so sorry. I didn't know. When did it happen?"

The sympathy in his eyes makes my knees weak.

He really has no idea. Have I been wrong about him this whole time?

"Jude." I drop to the floor in front of him. "It was right after finals. When I told you something happened and I was going through stuff. That's what it was."

"You mean... when you disappeared?" The residual anger in his voice has vanished, leaving confusion in its wake.

"We went to our family cabin. It was only supposed to be for a week, but it turned into three." My heart somehow manages to beat even faster. "When we got back, I tried to call you."

"But I had already been arrested." He looks at me with devastation clouding his face.

"What?" I gasp.

"Ver—" He starts, but I cut him off with a sneer and scoff.

"You mean your girlfriend that you lied to me about?" I jeer, curling my upper lip.

"What the fuck? No! She told me you were ghostin' me, hopin' I'd give up and move on. I thought I lost you. I went to your house a few times, and you weren't there."

"What?" My throat tightens, stomach knotting.

"I spent years in prison thinkin' I fucked up somehow. I didn't understand what I did wrong." Tears stream freely down his face. "I'm sorry I..." He swallows hard. "I got shit-faced one night during the second week. Woke up naked in bed with Ver—"

"Don't finish that sentence, Jude. I... I can't think about that. You and her..." I pinch my eyes shut, holding in stinging tears.

"I don't know if anything happened. She said it did. I felt so fuckin' bad. In my head we were still together even though you left me." He sniffles and chokes around a sob.

"I didn't leave you!" I snap.

"But you did!" he wails back. "You were the love of my life and ripped the last bit of my heart to shreds!"

"I was broken! Imagine my surprise when I get back in town after wishing for weeks that I could be in your arms. Only for my best friend to disown me because I slept with *her* boyfriend!" I shout, waving my arms around.

"I was *your* boyfriend. She was a jealous, conniving bitch who played you!" he bellows back at me.

"I'm not the one who cheated on the so-called 'love of my life' with her!" My own tears splatter on the floor.

"I didn't cheat on you! W-we weren't together." His voice breaks, shoulders drop. "You... left me."

"She lied, Jude... and you believed her!" I tremble under the weight of our combined emotions as the air goes thin.

"So did you." His blood-shot eyes stare straight through me. "I tried to be good to you, as much as I knew how anyway. But you still thought I was lyin' and believed her words over my actions." His chest deflates, chipping away at my defenses.

214

"Jude, I-I don't know what to say. I was in a bad place. That's not an excuse, I know, but I lost everything." I stare blankly at the ceramic tiles under me.

"At least you kept your freedom. I threw that away too. Losin' you was too much to bear and I spiraled." His voice catches when I look up at him.

"You went to prison b-because of me?" My eyes widen, burning from all the tears I've shed.

"Yes. I thought you were it for me. Everythin' with you just made sense and felt too good to be true. Guess it was." His jaw works, tightening as he grits his teeth. "I regretted that night with Veronica so bad I started usin' again. It didn't take long for me to fuck up. One bar fight and an 8-ball of coke and it was over. The Judge took one look at my record and threw the book at me." He lifts a leg to his chest, resting his arm on his knee.

"Oh, Jude," I breathe out. My body aches to crawl across the bathroom and comfort him.

"I'm sorry. I just... I loved you and thought you loved me too. When she told me you were throwin' me out like the trash I believed I was, it pushed me over the edge." He stares past me at a random spot on the wall.

"Oh, Big Guy." I watch closely as he inhales a jagged breath. "I loved you so much back then. I was young and naïve and didn't know what I was feeling. It was all so new to me, but that's what it was." I scoot between his legs, making the smallest amount of contact—neither of us looking at each other. My body vibrates from his closeness in a way I've never experienced with another man.

He moves slowly, brushing the tips of his fingers against my thigh. "I never thought I'd see you again."

I slide the faintest bit closer, eager for more. Is it absurd to want his hands on me? Probably, but I do. Jude's touch has always made me... *feel*.

Scooting in even further, I look up at him through my damp lashes. His eyes are soft, filled with curiosity and apprehension.

"I'm sorry. Forgive me for being a dummy? Can we start over?" I ask, more pitifully than intended.

Putting his leg down, he leans forward, wraps his arms around me and sobs into my shoulder. "I don't want to start over. I just want my Candy Girl. You're all I've ever needed and I'm so sorry I wasn't enough for you before."

Oh, sweet Jude.

Under the chiseled, hard exterior is such a fragile, tender man.

I lean back and cup his face in my hands staring into his pained, soulful eyes. Something about a man who can share so much of his passion this freely is beautiful. The pull between us is strong as ever, urging me closer until our lips meet. There's no hesitation, he groans into me and every question I've had about him is answered.

Immediately, he grabs hold of my ass, directing me to slide forward, closing the final gap between us. I settle comfortably in his lap, hissing at the intensity of his grip as he pulls me against him. He's everywhere all at once. Tongue in my mouth, hands roaming my body, lacing through my hair.

"Candy," he whispers roughly when I grind against his hardness, "I haven't been with anyone else."

His admission gives me pause.

"You haven't?" I falter, blinking wildly.

"No. Not that I had a lot of options in prison." His cheeks flush. "But nobody has interested me since I've been out." His nose falls to my neck, inhaling. "Just the smell of you is enough to make my heart race."

"I've tried to date," I admit. A strange guilty feeling gnaws at me. "I couldn't find anyone that made me feel anything, just meaningless sex that was lackluster at best. So, I mostly stuck to romance novels and my... toy collection." I worry my lip, oddly embarrassed.

Jude's eyes flash with raw hunger. His erection twitching below me. "You have toys?" He grinds up into me with a bruising grip on my hips.

"Yes," I squeak, face heating.

"What's your favorite?" He nibbles my shoulder, pressing against me once more.

How badly I wish these layers weren't between us. I'm a writhing heap of need for this man—skin pebbled, breaths shallow as he bites down with more intensity.

"I have a tentacle, it vibrates and the tip rotates, the suction cup at the base works my clit better than any man." I whimper when he pulls his mouth from my neck.

"Any man?" Before the words fully leave his mouth, he's pushed my bikini bottom to the side. "Even me?"

He finds my clit and traces slow, firm circles right where I need them.

"No," I moan loudly into his shoulder.

"I'm gonna fuck this sweet little pussy with that tentacle someday, don't worry." He rasps into my ear, working his fingers as I grind against him. "But for now, I want you on my cock. I've dreamed about this for years. The one night you let me experience your perfection wasn't enough." He removes his hand as I'm on the precipice of an orgasm, making me groan with frustration. "Don't pout. I have what you really want." He pulls the waist of his trunks down and nudges my entrance with the tip of his cock. "I'm clean, obviously. Do we need a condom?"

"No, I'm clean, too, I just need you." Eagerly, I slide down onto him, wincing as I stretch to accommodate his thickness.

"Easy, Candy." He sucks in a breath. "Take it nice and slow at first, so you don't hurt yourself. Then, once you're ready, you're mine to fuck exactly how I want." He circles my clit, feathering kisses down my throat until I whine and slide him deeper.

With a jerk of his hips, he's fully seated inside of me and I'm too overwhelmed by the fullness to move. My nails dig into his back as he grips my ass. He bites at my neck, continuously lifting me up, just a few inches, then slamming me back down roughly.

"Goddammit. You fuckin' ruined me." He growls against my shoulder, forcefully driving in deeper. "Look what you've done to me." He grunts, pulling my hair. "Look what you do to me." His grip tightens more aggressively than before. Our bodies slam together as he forces me down onto him over and over. His sudden intensity shoots fire through my veins.

This is what I've been longing for.

He pulls my hair harder and resumes a continuous onslaught of bites to my neck. My knees knock against the bathroom floor while he claims me—roughly, passionately. As the pain turns to pleasure, all I can do is scream and moan wildly while he releases years of pent-up tension and frustration.

"Fuck," he hisses, growing impossibly hard inside of me, "I'm not pullin' out."

"Please don't," I mumble into his shoulder. I should make him, but he wouldn't listen, not when he's this far gone.

"Mine. All. Mine." He groans before slamming our mouths together, expertly working my clit until I see stars. Wailing from the force of my orgasm I'm faintly aware of his shudders. The warmth of his cum floods into me as he presses himself as deep as possible, biting my lower lip until it stings.

"Jude." I pant, collapsing against him, whimpering as I float down from the waves of ecstasy.

"Shit. Did I hurt you?" He tucks my hair behind my ear, scanning my face.

"I loved every second of it." I offer him a sex-drunk smile and lean into his chest. "Take me to bed and hold me, please."

His chest vibrates from silent laughter. "Sure thing, Candy." With a kiss to my hair, he slides me off him and cradles me in his arms.

I faintly register being wrapped in familiar warmth over the emotions racing through me.

What did we just do?

CHAPTER 21

Jude

I fucked up. God what was I thinking? I didn't want to do that to her. She didn't deserve all my anger being unleashed on her like that... not that she seemed to mind.

No. There's no justifying my actions.

She's been curled into my side all night, occasionally nuzzling closer. My heart is at war with my head. While I'd like to think one mutual emotional breakdown turned aggressive, dirty fuck would fix everything, I'm not dumb.

I'm still no good for her, more so than before.

The door creeps open and I roll my head to see Nikolai grinning from ear to ear with a wooden breakfast tray in his hands. "Morning, champ. You guys sure had a *rough* night." He sets the tray on the nightstand and the smell of food awakens my senses.

"Shit, did you hear us?" I grab a piece of bacon—crispy, just how I like it—and pop it into my mouth.

"Yeah, kind of hard not to. Looks like you guys ended on a good note. Do you need some Neosporin or something for your back?" He pulls his lips into a knowing smirk.

"Uh, maybe," I mumble, "I think I'll be alright though. Sorry if we woke you."

"I'm just glad you guys got it all out, but you two might want to get up soon. Pop will be here in an hour or so for our usual Sunday adventures." He tips his head and closes the door as he leaves.

"He's so loud," Caroline groans, rubbing her eyes.

"Hey," I whisper, running my fingers through her hair.

The warm smile she aims my way could thaw even the coldest of hearts. Laying tangled up with her like this feels like a dream. One I never thought I'd get to experience again.

"Is that bacon I smell?" Her voice is hoarse and I'm fairly certain it's not from sleep alone.

"Yeah, he brought a full breakfast."

"God that's *so* on brand." She laughs roughly. "Is there something to drink?"

"Orange juice... and strawberry milk for some reason."

I'm only confused for a second until her face lights up with vibrant excitement.

"This is why I love him." She sits up, unashamedly naked, and grabs the glass of strawberry milk. A satisfied sigh rushes out of her at the first taste.

"That good, huh?" I titter.

"The only thing better than strawberry milk is strawberry boba." She takes another sip and hums with a blissful smile.

"He said your dad was coming over soon." My face, like my chest, is tight at the thought.

How is he going to feel about this?

"Oh, yeah. We go out as a family on Sundays, usually to the park and then Nicky buys us lunch. He used to make us dinner once a week, but now we're all busier and it's easier to just go out and spend a few hours together." Her grin is infectious, drawing an identical one across my face.

"That's nice. I wish my family was half as close." My smile falls, pulling into a tight frown.

"Do you want to talk about it?" She tilts her head. "We've never really talked about your family much."

"I only want to do one thing with you naked in the same bed as me, but you need to get ready for your father... and maybe put some of the cream Nikolai mentioned on my back." I wince at the stinging as I shift.

"Oh god, let me see!" She leaps to her feet, coming around to look at the damage. "Jude! Oh no. Oh Jesus. I can't believe I did this to you!"

"I should be the one apologizing." I scrub my hand over the stubble on my jaw. "I was way too rough with you. Just look at your knees."

She takes in the bruised and battered skin. "Eh." She shrugs.

"No, not 'Eh' I-I'm sorry I hurt you. I shouldn't have come at you like that. I didn't mean to lose my cool." I deflate where I sit.

"Hey." She cups my jaw, directing my gaze to meet hers. "I like it when you're rough with me," she asserts with a playful leer, "a lot."

Fuck.

I'm supposed to let her go. I can't be greedy and hoard her forever.

"Uh oh," she says with a tinge of warning, "you've got that look on your face like you don't feel good enough. Don't even go there. I'm going to take the bath you denied me last night, and when I'm done, we're going to talk. Don't you dare leave. Got it?"

"Yes ma'am."

"Good." Turning on her heel, she struts to the attached bathroom and starts filling the tub. I follow and watch as she tosses a bath bomb into the water and gets in.

"Can I come sit with you? We can talk while you soak." I sound pathetic, but I don't care.

"You can get in the bath with me if you want." She smiles brightly.

I've never been a bath man. I guess that changes today.

As I sink into the tub, I hiss from the sting of hot water on my tattered back.

"Sorry, Big Guy." Caroline winces, but her cheeky grin says otherwise.

"Are you sore?" I ask as she turns and nestles herself

against me.

"Yeah, but in the best way, I haven't had life altering sex like that in... well, seven years." She giggles, soaping up her chest.

"Is that so?" I tease as I lather shampoo into her hair.

The sarcasm in my voice makes her laugh even harder.

"Don't try to flirt your way out of this conversation." Her tone takes on a sharp edge. "We can't just brush past everything that went unsaid last night. I know we can't recount seven years of our lives in one morning, but I plan on talking about everything with you eventually." She passes me the soapy loofah.

"I know. There's not a lot to talk about on my side though. I went to prison, now I'm out and trying to be better."

"We're definitely talking about your self-deprecating thoughts." My body tenses and she takes immediate notice. "Exactly. I know that distant look you get. Your eyes glaze over, and I can't tell exactly where your mind wanders off to, but it's not a good place. You always come back upset. So, talk to me. I want to be here for you now, since I didn't get the chance before." She leans into me as I rinse her hair.

"It depends." I let out a strangled breath. "A lot of the time it's me trying to talk myself out of a relapse when I feel down." I swallow harshly as her breath catches. "I haven't used since I went away. I don't plan on ever doin' it again, but the urge still slithers its way into my subconscious when times get hard." I pull her closer to me, delighting in her softness.

"You still feel like you don't deserve me, don't you?" She turns her head up, looking me directly in the eyes.

"Yes, because it's true." My eyes dance across her face.

"It's not, stop thinking that way."

"Candy, I hurt you for Christ's sake. I literally lost control and fucked you on this bathroom floor 'til your knees were busted open. H-how do I deserve you?" My voice cracks as my frustration builds.

"Please." She scoffs. "Have you seen your back? It's way worse than my knees. I definitely wasn't complaining when I was waking half the house up screaming for you. The Jude I knew seven years ago would *tell* me how much I loved it. He'd probably have me pinned against the edge of this tub right now fucking my throat for back-talking him." Her eyebrows rise in challenge.

She's so perfect.

I swallow hard again. Long bottled up emotions threaten to overflow.

"Don't worry, you're not going to hurt me. I welcome you to try, just not right now. Dad will be here shortly." She releases the drain and stands.

"So... we're okay?" I ask hesitantly.

"I'm not *entirely* okay with everything, but I'm not going to deny my feelings. Life's too short." She tosses a towel to me. "You're not perfect, but neither am I and I've had a lot of time to deal with everything. It also helps that I spend a lot of time with a psychiatrist." She snorts while drying herself off.

"I guess I need to thank Claire for you being willing to forgive me." I smile lazily at her.

"She and Charli both practically demanded that I hear you out, so..." She lifts a shoulder in a playful half shrug and steps out of the bathroom.

I wrap myself in the towel and follow her to the bedroom. She's sitting at the vanity in the corner. Her hair is tossed in a messy bun atop her head while she massages lotion on her arms.

"Need a hand?" Not waiting for an answer, I squeeze some into my palm and rub it into her shoulders.

She melts into my touch, groaning as I work knots out of her tense muscles. "I'll let you be as rough as you want with me every day if it means you treat me like this as repayment."

"This isn't repayment, I just like having my hands on all this silky perfection whenever, and however I can." I lean over and press my lips to her temple.

"Speaking of which, Nikolai snuck in while we were in the bath. He dropped off the ointment, along with your clothes. He's already washed them." She tips her head toward the dresser on the far wall.

"Oh good, you can rub me down next." I chuckle. "But not until I put some bandages on your knees."

"You got it, Big Guy."

We take our time tending to each other's scrapes and bruises and finish getting ready to go. I watch closely as Caroline glosses her lips with glittery pink, cherry flavored goodness. A few flicks of her eyeliner and swipes of mascara and she's satisfied with her makeup.

Slipping on a pink striped sweater and cut-off shorts, she's adorably gorgeous. I look like a storm cloud next to her. My black torn jeans and Fleetwood Mac shirt are the shadows to her light.

My life is definitely brighter with her back in it.

I can't believe I'm going to a family day with them. I wasn't formally invited, but they've just included me in all of their plans. So, here goes nothing.

CHAPTER 22

Jude

Ivan's folded arms and furrowed brows greet us as we enter the kitchen. Passing questioning glances back and forth between Caroline and me, his silent judgment is obvious. When his attention lands on her knees a blazing fury overtakes his expression.

"Solnyshko. What is all this?" He waves his hand frantically between us. "Are you two an item again?"

Caroline stiffens, radiating nervous energy.

"Uh, well... w-we," I stutter, despite my best efforts. I'm almost thirty years old, why does he make me feel like an awkward teenager?

"We're... working on our issues," Caroline responds for me, standing tall as she addresses him.

"It sure sounded like your issues got worked out *real* well last night," Nikolai says with a *clearly* fake yawn as he trails into the kitchen.

Charli, close behind him—with Ivy on her hip—smacks his shoulder. "It's too early for your jokes...

229

because *someone* has a set of lungs on her." She snickers playfully.

Ivan scoffs. "I can't believe this. How on Earth am I supposed to just forget what he did? How can *you?*" His eyes don't stray from Caroline.

I've seen angry Ivan, but this isn't anger. He's hurt, confused... disappointed, even.

"Dad, I can explain. We talked—"

"It sure doesn't look like you *only* talked," he interrupts, scowling at the bruises blooming on her knees.

"Pop, I—" I start, only for him to cut me off too.

"Don't you dare 'Pop' me, that's a name reserved only for my family." He gruffs.

"S-sorry," I choke out around the lump in my throat.

"Come on, cut him some slack. It was a long time ago," Nikolai cuts in.

"It may have been years ago, but he wasn't here to see how devastated Caroline was over his betrayal," Ivan snips, directing a sharp glare my way.

"Okay, can we shelve this for another time and try to have a good day?" Charli pleads, patting down Ivy's wild hair.

"Fine. But only because I love *most* of you." Ivan side-eyes me, as if I need a reminder that I'm the odd man out.

"Jude and I will take my car, since the Tahoe won't seat all of us." Caroline grabs her keys off the counter and slips her shoes on.

"Or he could drive himself," Ivan grumbles.

"No, Dad. Please at least try to be more understanding about this." Caroline lets out a frustrated sigh.

"It's okay, he's had a lot of time to hate me." I brush my hand down her back before lacing up my boots.

Ivan watches with a sneer as I follow her out to her car.

"We'll see you guys at the park!" Nikolai calls out from the doorway.

I already regret agreeing to tag along. I've never cared about being liked, but this is different. I need to figure out how to win Ivan over, but there's a lot Caroline and I need to talk about first.

"So..." I start, unsure of how to open the door for this conversation. "Let me have it. Whatever leftover anger and hate you have. Please just let it all out." I lean back against the headrest in preparation.

"I... I don't have anything. I thought I was going to. But, knowing what I do now, and seeing how you faced my father... that was everything I needed to know that you're serious about us." She chews her lower lip. "Do, uh, do *you* want to yell at *me*?"

"Candy, I could never yell at you. That's... not how it works." I reach over and squeeze her thigh. "I'm not that kind of guy. Sure, I have a temper but I'm not violent unless I'm high. Which, obviously, I don't plan on ever bein' again. Now, I won't lie, for the first few years I was pissed at you." I trace around a bruise on her knee. "But, I came to peace with that as best as I could. Now I understand that none of what happened was your fault. For years I hated you because I thought you abandoned me. But we were both young, going through shit, and let our emotions get the better of us." I exhale a heavy breath. "I don't expect everythin' to be the same as it was before, but I'd love the chance to try and make it good again."

Wiping a stray tear away as her chin quivers, she turns her attention to me for just a second. "I missed you, Big Guy. Please just promise you won't leave me, and I'll promise the same. I'll do my best to never keep things from you again." The anguish and sincerity in her voice nearly breaks me.

"I'm not goin' anywhere. No matter how many times my brain tells my heart that you deserve better." I offer her a rueful smile.

She reaches down and places her hand on top of mine and we enjoy comfortable silence for the rest of the drive.

Nikolai and Charli are already unloading their car by the time we arrive. I've never been to this park before, but it looks nice. Lots of shaded places to sit. The wispy layer of clouds overhead acts as a buffer for the July sun. About a dozen kids of various ages are running around having the time of their lives on the large playground.

As we help to unload blankets and coolers, a familiar SUV pulls in next to us. Apparently Claire, Theo, and little Henderson have decided to join us. Charli waves them over as she lets Navy out of his carrier. He immediately heads off to run and play with the kids skipping around the park.

Claire's eyes widen as they land on Caroline's knees.

"Oh my. Are you alright?"

"I'm more than alright." She chuckles and leans into me.

Claire and Theo share a knowing look. Unable to resist, Theo lets out a hearty laugh. "You guys good then?"

I wrap my arm around Caroline's shoulders, pulling her closer into me and nod. "Yeah, it's a work in progress, but we're good."

"Wonderful!" Claire says cheerfully with a bright smile. "Let's peruse today's food options." She takes Theo's arm and strolls away with Henderson on her hip.

I force out a held breath.

Caroline wraps her arm around me and squeezes. "See, this is fine. It'll take some time but we'll be fine." Her perfect smile eases my nerves.

As we approach the food stalls at the small market, Charli grabs her by the arm and drags her to the bubble tea stand.

Nikolai comes to my side laughing at their giddiness. "Some things will never change. Those two are fiends for strawberry boba."

"Caroline always did love it. Every time we were at the café she'd get one, and nothing else." I laugh wistfully at the memories.

"You genuinely loved her, didn't you?" He asks, guiding me to the pizza stall.

"Yeah, I did." My face falls slightly, thinking about all of the time we lost. "If I could go back—"

"Hush, none of that," Nikolai cuts me off. "You're

here now, look at you guys. She hasn't been this happy in the last seven years."

"You think so?" I jerk my head back, brows pinched.

"Yeah, I'm going to help you really win her over, but it'll take a little bit of work on your part. If you're up for it." He winks conspiratorially.

I nod, like the idiot I am. Anything he has planned is likely to be ridiculous and completely out of my comfort zone. But he knows her better than anyone, and I want her more than anything.

After everyone has their food we gather under a white pergola. Vines have crept up the sides and merged across the top to create a natural canopy. There are a few more just like it around the park. Wrought iron chairs and tables are positioned beneath each one.

When we take our seats, Ivan scoops both toddlers into his lap and pinches their rosy cheeks. His smile is bright and loving, until he catches me looking. That warmth fades instantly, replaced by a new expression that isn't hard to read—blank, yet irritated. His face transforms into a fierce scowl as his attention drifts to my hand resting on Caroline's thigh. I didn't even realize had I put it there. She doesn't seem to mind, so I don't remove it. Instead, I give it a gentle squeeze. She's engrossed in some story with Charli and Claire that I can't hear over the silent battle I'm engaged in with her father.

He knows that I'm intimidated by him, but I know all of the animosity toward me stems from his protective nature.

He's a great dad, I can't fault him for that. Hell, if anything I love him for it. Caroline is my first priority, but once I've proven myself to her, I'll win that stubborn old man over too.

I'm no stranger to working hard for what I want. Nor am I afraid of some pain and suffering, if it means I get to claim my prize. In this case, a real family.

Nikolai is open and friendly to everyone, and Charli is warm and compassionate. But I'm not foolish enough to expect everyone to welcome me with open arms and an open mind. Still, Claire and Theo have been accepting enough. To my face anyway.

"You lost in your head over there?" Caroline nudges me with her knee.

"Sorry, I definitely was." I smile at her.

"Well, I was asking if we want to take this back to the house and I can set up the home theater. You want to watch a movie with us?" Nikolai asks.

"Home theater?" I tilt my head.

"Oh, it's lovely," Claire speaks up with a dreamy sigh.

"Yeah, the kids have a little play area where they can occupy themselves, and there's extra wide recliners so we can curl up together. Claire falls asleep every time." Theo wraps an arm around her and kisses her temple.

"There's a whole theater in your house?" I ask, bewildered.

"It's not a literal theater, he just likes to call it that," Caroline says playfully.

"Hey! There's a projector screen, and a popcorn ma-

235

chine. It counts!" Nikolai huffs in defense.

"Okay, a movie sounds fun. If you'll have me," I answer cautiously.

"Jude, dear, he wouldn't have asked otherwise," Claire replies with a gentle tone.

I nod with a tight smile, holding back the overwhelming emotions. They're doing so much to show me that I'm wanted, but I don't quite know how to let myself accept it.

Theo is a detective, Claire is a psychiatrist. How the hell could either of them want to be associated with *me*? Nikolai saved Charli's life, is a millionaire—at the very least—and way too kind. Charli, god, she's the last person who should want me anywhere near her. After the nightmare she lived through, there's no reason she should be so understanding.

I'm fairly certain Ivan is the only one acting logically. As much as it pains me to think about it, he has every right to despise me.

Even if I didn't have the history with Caroline that I do, my record alone would make any father disapprove of his daughter going anywhere near me.

"Hey." Caroline places a hand on my knee and skims her eyes over my face. "You're doing it again. Don't."

"Sorry," I mumble, dropping my gaze to the ground.

"What's up man?" Nikolai asks.

"Nothing, don't worry about it." I offer my best smile to the group. "What movie are we watching when we get back?"

"Oh! Can we watch a Marvel movie?" Charli's eyes glitter with excitement.

"We sure can, Sugar." Nikolai leans over in his chair and kisses her forehead. Charli smiles at him with so much love and adoration, my chest aches.

"I'll take my Mladentsy so you all can relax," Ivan suggests.

"Oh, that would be lovely. Hennie has a change of clothes and whatnot in the car." Claire beams.

"Thank you, Ivan. It's been a while since we've had a nice couples' night," Theo agrees.

"Now, Son, I've told you to call me 'Pop'. You're *family*." Ivan says in a loving, sincere tone. There's a faint squint of his eyes as they dart briefly to meet mine.

Coffin, meet nail.

I abruptly rise to my feet, startling Caroline, and walk away. "Dad!" she wails as I retreat, before following me to the edge of the park, huffing to keep up. "Jude," she says softly, "I'm sorry about him. He's just protective." She takes my hand in hers.

I lean against the tree we've stopped under, resting my head against the trunk. "No, I'm sorry. He just struck a nerve and I needed to step away. I'm tryin' to keep my emotions under control. It's just been a crazy week." I force out a sharp breath.

"I know. He'll come around. But it's going to take him a little while to warm up to the idea. Believe it or not he really did like you before." She chuckles.

"Really?" I look down at her with a raised brow.

"Yeah, it actually upset him quite a bit that you ghosted me. I think he was hopeful you were 'the one'. He's a big romantic at heart." Her eyes shine with familial love.

"I thought I was too... I-I still want to be." I bite my cheeks to stop the tears threatening to form.

"I want that too." She rubs my forearm. "I just have old wounds that haven't quite healed yet." She frowns with a tremble of her lower lip, shying away from my gaze.

"I'll be here until they do, Candy. You're mine, and I'm not losin' you again. Nothin', and no one, is gonna come between us this time." I cup her jaw and tilt her face toward mine. "Understood?" I brush my thumb over her lower lip.

"Promise?" She lifts her hand with a raised pinky finger.

She's so precious.

"I swear." Linking my pinky with hers, I lean down and kiss her softly.

She smiles brightly before leading me to her car by our still-linked hands. I can only hope we're on our way to forever.

CHAPTER 23

Caroline

The buttery scent of fresh popcorn floats through the air of the theater room as Jude and I enter. He hasn't said much since we left the park, but he's still here and that's huge. I know what Dad is doing, and I'm not impressed.

Our relationship is fragile enough without his interference. I want to spend time with Jude and get to know him again. That can't happen if he's upset and shutting down on me. Even now, as he stands here, staring wide-eyed at Nikolai's candy selection, I'm afraid he'll run.

I can't begin to imagine how it must have been for him—locked away, angry, heartbroken, alone. I think that's the worst. He's always felt so alone. I could see it in his eyes all those years ago. I sensed his fears and abandoned him anyway, because I was too caught up in my own feelings to consider his.

I want to give him a chance, but I don't know if *I*

239

deserve it at this point. I'm scared to love him and ruin it, and him, all over again.

"You two okay?" Theo asks as I step up next to him at the popcorn machine.

"Yeah. Dad just got under his skin." I nudge Jude playfully, trying to lighten the mood.

"Ah, I see." Theo nods and scoops himself a bucket of golden popped goodness. "Don't worry about Ivan, he'll see how happy you are and come around." He grins.

"Thank you," Jude murmurs, smiling halfheartedly back at him.

"I'll get us some popcorn. Could you go grab some drinks and claim a seat?" I hook my thumb over my shoulder towards the mini fridge. "Ginger ale would be great."

He nods and strolls away. Theo follows to grab sodas for him and Claire.

"I thought Pop scared him off back there," Nikolai grumbles as he steps up next to me and starts filling his own bucket with popcorn.

"Me too." I sigh, glancing over at Jude and Theo. "Everyone likes him, right? I'm not just imagining it."

"No, you're not. He's a good dude. Sure, he can be a little hot and cold, but his heart is in the right place." He lifts the corner of his mouth into a warm half-smile.

"Yeah, there's a little Jekyll and Hyde situation going on but I think it's just him feeling like he's not worthy of our time. Even before he seemed to struggle with feeling inferior or unwanted." I huff out a frustrated sigh.

"Eh, give it time. He's had a lot to process recently." Nikolai turns and heads to the recliner Charli is curled up in with her blanket and drink.

Theo joins Claire in the seat she claimed at the front of the room. I stroll as casually as possible to the chair Jude is sitting in. Familiar nerves have my knees weak as I get closer to him. This is my first movie night with a partner and I suddenly don't know what to do with my hands.

Why can't I breathe?

He watches me approach, raising his brows at my visible discomfort. When I slowly lower myself and lean against the opposite arm from him, he doesn't move. My pulse is deafening as it hammers in my ears. I pivot my head and take in our surroundings. Everyone else is snuggled up under their blankets, mindlessly watching the opening credits. We're in the seat furthest back in the room and I wonder if he chose this one on purpose.

Get a grip, Caroline.

"Do you want to come closer?" Jude asks in a hushed tone.

I jolt slightly, not expecting his breath on my cheek.

"Sorry." He frowns, face full of hurt.

"No!" I squeak louder than I intend. "Sorry, I do. It's just..." I chew my lip. "I've never done this before." I motion to the room around us.

"You've never... watched a movie?" He crinkles his face in confusion.

"Not *with* someone," I hiss. "Of course I've watched a

movie! *We* watched a movie together once, remember?"

Jude blows out an exasperated breath. "Just get your ass over here and let me hold you."

His dark eyes lure me in and I slide over, pressing against his side. He brushes his chin against the top of my head and pulls me even closer.

"Good girl," he whispers into my ear, sending shivers through my body.

I glide my hand under the bottom of his shirt and trace along the edges of his defined abs. Apparently he spent a lot of time working out in prison. Muscular doesn't seem like a strong enough word to describe his physique. While my hand freely travels across his skin, he trails his fingertips up and down my side in return.

As the opening credits end, we both shift our attention to the screen. I'm not the biggest fan of superhero movies, so it doesn't take long for me to lose interest, but Jude is completely captivated. I tilt my head up and admire the way he absentmindedly chews his lip ring while giving his undivided attention to the show. He's so at ease right now, like his self-deprecating thoughts have stopped.

The hand he's resting on my hip tightens as his eyes shift to mine. When I smile up at him, he leans down and kisses me softly.

"Are you alright?" He whispers against my lips.

"Yeah, I was just enjoying the view." I sit up, adjusting in the seat. "Do you, uh, want to recline and snuggle, too?" I tilt my head toward the others, laid back in their respective chairs.

"I'd love to." He nods, shifting to help me lean our seat back. "Wow, this is practically a bed, are you sure you're okay with this?"

"Just lay down and hold me." I roll my eyes and push at his shoulder.

The heat that flashes in his gaze makes my pulse race.

His arms wrap around me, pulling me flush against him as he covers us with our blanket. His hand trails up my body and stops at my throat. Long, rough fingers grip my jaw as he captures my mouth in a fiery kiss. As soon as he starts, though, he stops. When he pulls away, I want to pout, but I realize that he's scanning the room. The movie is loud, the lights are low, I'm sure he's drawn the same conclusion I have.

My hand trails down to find the button on his jeans, but he grabs my wrist, drawing my attention to his hardened eyes. All I can focus on is how steadily his chest rises and falls against me.

"Can you be quiet?" He asks, nibbling at my neck.

"The movie will cover up any sounds, we're far enough away from the others. I'm also pretty sure Charli has been edging Nicky for most of the movie anyway. What do you think the blankets are for?" I chuckle softly.

"Y'all are such a weird family." He laughs quietly back at me. "In that case, be a good girl and take my cock out." Releasing my wrist, he bites at my neck before trailing kisses up my jaw.

This is the Jude I remember, intense and demanding.

I want him to take everything I have to give, and then some. When he takes control like this, it's better than anything another man has ever done. Something in the way his energy engulfs mine is erotic on an inexplicable level.

I want to tease him until he hates me and punishes me for it.

This isn't the place though.

He works his hand into my waistband and turns his hips away from me slightly as I free him. Eager to please, I stroke slowly from base to tip, relishing in how thick and heavy he is. My curiosity takes over and I play with the ring that goes through the base of his head. He bites my lower lip as his hips jerk from the sensation.

"Fuck, Candy you're such a good girl. Keep doing it just like that and open up for me." He groans into my shoulder before kissing me roughly.

I gasp into his mouth when he slips his hand between my thighs and slides two fingers into me. My thoughts stop when he bites my lip. Working intently, he applies pressure against the sensitive spot inside of me while grinding his palm against my clit. In just a few minutes he's greedily swallowing my sounds as I topple over the edge, much faster than I've ever experienced.

His cock throbs as I grip him tighter. Rolling his hips, he steadily fucks my hand while our tongues dance together in a slow, sensual rhythm. Before long, I feel him pulse, growing closer to his release.

In a moment of clarity, I realize It's about to get very

messy. Pulling my lips from his, I bend down to take him in my mouth. As I prop myself up onto my knees, granting him access, he slips his hand back between us.

A few flicks of my tongue over his piercing and he shudders, faintly grunting as he fills my mouth with cum. I swallow it all down as he circles his thumb over my clit, bringing me to the peak of another climax. Staying mindful of our surroundings, I whimper around him as quietly as possible.

After tucking him back into his jeans, I curl up against his side with a sated grin.

"Naughty girl," he rasps, licking his fingers clean.

"Look who's talking." I sigh, laying my head on his chest.

He briefly shifts his attention to the other side of the room, then places a soft kiss against the top of my head. "They haven't moved at all," he says against my hair. "You're also right about Charli and Nicky. He looks absolutely tortured."

"He loves it. Their dynamic is... something else." I quietly giggle.

"For the record, I don't like being teased, don't plan on me ever allowing that," he says sternly.

"Oh, I know." I smirk. "But you like it when I play with your piercing huh?"

"Candy, I came instantly. You tell me." He deadpans. *Noted.*

I snuggle closer to him and fall into a blissful slumber as the movie continues.

It's dark and I don't know where I am, but the warmth surrounding me is nice.

Wait.

I trail my hand up the wall of muscle I'm pressed against.

"Oh God." I gasp. "What time is it? We have to work in the morning!" I struggle, trying to free myself from his hold.

"Shh, it's only nine or so," he grumbles, "Claire and Theo left right after the movie, Charli dragged Nikolai out of the room a couple of hours ago. Haven't seen them since."

"You could have woken me up." I yawn.

"Why would I do that?" He stares down at me. "You were sleeping so beautifully, I didn't want to disturb you. Then I fell asleep, too." He runs his fingers through my hair. "Call me greedy, but I wanted to steal a bit more of your time."

"You're not greedy. Nobody else is vying for my time."

"What about that Scott guy?" He asks flatly.

"We weren't even really dating. Just sleeping together. And that's absolutely done and over," I explain flatly.

"Sooooo... what about us then?"

"What about us?" I pinch my brows together.

"Am I just a fuck buddy you're gonna drop when you get bored?"

Hello insecure Jude, I haven't missed you.

I pin him with a serious look. "We're not anything until *you* decide what you're worthy of. You're giving me whiplash with all this back and forth. All over me one minute and questioning my feelings the next. Please, just accept the fact that I want you." I sit up and cross my arms.

"I just..." He inhales deeply. "I'm no good for you. I never was."

"Then leave," I spit out, "break my heart again, go on." I throw my hand toward the door.

"I don't want to!" He howls, throwing his head back. "Can't you see how fuckin' conflicted I am?" Leaning forward, he threads his fingers through his hair and rests his head in his hands. "I'm too weak to resist you."

"You make it sound like being with me is a bad thing." The hurt in my voice draws his gaze up to meet my watery eyes.

"No, being with *me* is. I should leave, should let you find a good man. Let you have a good life with a nice house and a couple kids." He turns his face away from me.

I shift closer to him, and pull his attention back to me. "What did you tell me earlier? You *promised* you wouldn't run. Please don't actually break my heart again. I..." My voice trembles. "I never really stopped loving you, Jude. I just pushed my feelings down. They never went away."

It's not the same as saying the words. But based on the

light that has returned to his eyes, it may as well be.

"I never stopped lovin' you, either. Even when I was blamin' you for all of my shitty choices. Even when I wanted to find a fix and chase a high, you were the thing that kept me straight. I'm sorry for thinkin' it was one-sided." He wraps me up in a tight embrace, heart beating rapidly against me.

"For the record, I think we'd make some cute babies." I beam as he pulls back with a shocked expression on his face.

"Uh, well... how about you let me call you my girl-friend for a little bit first?" He stammers.

"Only if I can call you my boyfriend."

"Deal." He kisses me tenderly, pulling me into his lap. Straddling him, I wrap my arms around his neck and take in the moment, savoring all of his attention—the way his hands trail up my spine, how electrifying the pressure of his hardness against my core feels. I have to resist the urge to grind against him and get lost in a sea of ecstasy again. At this rate we'll never sleep.

"Okay, if we keep this up, we're going to be in trouble. We have work in the morning." I pull away, playing with the hair at the nape of his neck.

"Yeah, my boss is a real hard-ass." He laughs silently and kisses me quickly. "Let's get out of here."

We clean up our mess and make our way out of the house, hand-in-hand. Jude walks me to my car and opens the door, stealing a final kiss before getting on his bike.

"Hey," I call over to him, "it's supposed to rain tomorrow. Can I drive you?"

"I'd like that." His grin shines under the outdoor lights before he slips his helmet on. "Good night, Candy Girl. I'll see you in the morning." As his bike roars to life, my stomach flips.

A lot has happened this week. I can't wait to see what the next one holds.

CHAPTER 24

Caroline

The weather has been strange. Sure, it normally rains a lot here, but July is generally dry. Not this year. As Jude strolls to my car, splashing through puddles, I'm thankful for the rain.

"Need a ride, stranger?" I ask playfully as he slides into the passenger seat.

"The damn bottom fell out." He runs his fingers through his hair as it drips.

"The bottom did what now?" I quirk a brow up at him.

"You know, the rain, it's comin' down in buckets." He gestures out the windshield, as if he's speaking plain English.

"Your Alabama is showing." I chuckle.

"I'm... sorry?" He tips his head and buckles his seatbelt.

"Don't be, it's cute." I smile impishly as I pull out of the driveway.

"Nothin' about me is *cute*," he grumbles.

"You can't try to argue while *actin'* even cuter." I joke back at him with an admittedly horrible attempt at a southern drawl.

"Keep messin' around and I'm gonna jump outta this car at the next light. " He folds his arms and slouches in his seat, knees pressed against the dash.

"Someone's a grumpy boy in the morning. What's wrong? Did somebody keep you out after your bed time, Old Man?" I reach over to poke his leg, but he grabs my hand.

"If you weren't drivin' us to work right now..." He warns, voice thick like honey.

I shudder, imagining all the ways he'd 'punish' me for picking on him.

Game on.

"I think the Giardia outbreak has passed. But you'd better give *every* dog we have a fecal test today. Just to be sure." I shrug slightly with a sly smirk on my face.

"Go on. Fuck around and see what happens. I'm a patient man." He adjusts himself in the seat next to me.

"Are you sure about that? You're squirming around over there."

"Keep your eyes on the road, Candy." He tries to sound annoyed, but I see the corner of his mouth lift slightly.

"Yes, *Sir*." I bite my lips to hide my smile as he fights a groan. I have the upper hand here, if only for a moment.

His jaw ticks, but out of the corner of my eye I can see

the amusement on his face.

"I'm only a couple years older than you. So I guess you're old, too… Granny." He huffs out a faint laugh as I gasp.

"Take that back! I am *not* old!" I squeal, turning to face him as we stop at a red light.

"Nope. If I'm an old man, you're an old bat." He cocks his head, raising his eyebrows in challenge.

"An old bat?! No! That's too far." I fake whimper, forcing my lower lip out while I pull into a parking spot.

"Hey, wait. I'm sorry. I was just messin' around." He reaches over and rubs my shoulder. "I didn't mean it, please don't cry, Sweetness."

And, just like that, my heart is jelly.

"Sweetness?" I turn to face him, swallowing my reaction.

"Yeah, you're my sweet Candy Girl."

"You're adorable, I love it." I beam at him. "Now, we really do need to do some fecal tests today, but I'll help. Let's go."

He grumbles and trudges along behind me.

When we enter the lobby, Nikolai is there to greet us. "Good news! No shit storm!" He grins from ear to ear.

"Thank God." Jude sighs, relieved. "Last week was quite the welcome party."

"You did well, and didn't back down. So thank you!" Nikolai claps him on the shoulder as we pass by. "I'll be out here manning the front if you guys need me!" he calls after us as we pass through the doors to the kennel rooms.

When we enter the clinic, my first stop, as always, is to check on my sweet little Cannoli. She perks up the instant I come into view. Her big brown eyes get more vibrant by the day. Sadly, I don't know how much longer I can convince Nikolai that she's still too sick to adopt out.

"There's my favorite little baby," Jude says in the most adorable voice I've ever heard. I have to brace myself against the kennels to stay upright.

"Y-your favorite?" I stammer as my cheeks heat.

Oh God am I blushing?

Jude reaches out and gently pets Cannoli, scratching behind her little ear. His hand engulfs her head, but he's so gentle and careful with her. The delusional part of my brain imagines him with an actual baby. *Our* actual baby.

No. Stop it.

"Stop what?" Jude pulls back, perplexed.

Wait. Did I say that out loud?

"Uh, sorry. I um. I was afraid you'd crush her with your giant man hands." I feign concern, taking Cannoli from him and turning her—myself—away from his questioning gaze.

"Are you okay?" He places the aforementioned giant hand on my shoulder. "I would never hurt her." His voice wavers, filled with hurt.

"Wait, no. I'm sorry." I spin around, meeting his soft eyes. "I didn't mean it like that. I know you wouldn't."

"But you said—"

"I know," I huff, cutting him off. "I didn't mean to *say* 'Stop it.' I was *thinking* it. Yelling at myself to stop the thoughts racing through my mind." I tuck Cannoli back into her blanket nest and secure the latch on her kennel.

"What thoughts?" He stares into my soul. Those deep pools of espresso swirl with even more questions.

Too bad I'm not ready to answer them. He'll have to exercise some of that patience he claims to possess.

I slip around him and head straight to the kennels housing our patients that had previously tested positive for Giardia. Opening the first kennel to a fluffy little poodle mix, I hand her to Jude. "You test Pickle, I'll go get Cookie. Bagel and Waffle are next."

"Who the hell named all of these dogs?" He scrunches his brows and takes Pickle from me, curling her into his arms.

"Well, we all like food, so it's just a universal thing." I shrug, unlatching Cookie's kennel. The little pug nibbles at my hair as we make our way to the general exam room.

"So, did *you* name Cannoli?" Jude asks while preparing Pickle's test.

"I did. It was a tossup between Cannoli and Strawberry." I chuckle quietly, setting Cookie down on my exam table.

"Damn, you must really love cannolis then," he says casually, as if we're not simultaneously spooning fecal matter.

"You have *no* idea. Ooh! Do you think they make

strawberry cannolis?" I perk up, adding flotation solution to my sample cup.

"I'm sure they do, Sweetness." He smiles over at me from across the room and places a slide on top of his floated sample.

I swallow hard. Candy is a cute playful name, but I never imagined hearing him drawl out 'Sweetness' in my direction. Now that I have—twice in the same day nonetheless—I'm filled with a burning need to hear it while he ties me down and tells me I'm *his*.

"You good?" he asks with a knowing glimmer in his eye.

"Yup!" I squeak, scooping Cookie up and shuffling to her kennel.

Jude puts Pickle back and moves on to Waffle, wasting no time.

Our flirtation continues for the rest of the day. While a few of the dogs we test are still positive, the majority of them are going back to the general kennels with clean bills of health, ready for new homes.

"You two are the backbone of this place, I swear." Nikolai wraps me in a hug as soon as I cross into the lobby.

"Were you up here all day?" I ask with a tilt of my head.

"Yeah, our receptionist didn't show, but it's fine." He shrugs.

"Well, I'm going to take Jude home then go relax. It was a busy day."

"Actually, I wanted to talk to Jude about something.

Mind if he catches a ride with me?" Nikolai raises an eyebrow on our way out the door, expression showing a hint of mischief.

What are they up to?

"Sure, have fun boys," I say as brightly as possible.

"Later, Parasite!" Nikolai waves on the way to his car.

Jude walks with me to say goodbye. "I'll text you, okay?" He leans in and kisses me softly.

I melt against him momentarily as my heart flutters. He pulls me into him, engulfing me as I wrap my arms around his torso and hum in contentment.

"Can we get together soon?" I press my chin to his chest and meet his adoring gaze.

"Your place or mine?" he asks, pressing his lips against my forehead.

My body floods with warmth. "Mine, please. I have no desire to go anywhere near your place." I laugh into his chest.

"Deal, we can go for a ride and get dinner." He traces small circles on my back.

A ride. It's been so long. A sense of giddiness fills me as memories flash through my mind. Being pressed up against him, snaking my hands around his body. I was timid and unsure before. That was the old Caroline. Now, I want to do filthy things to this muscular wall of pure *man* as he weaves us through back alleys and long winding coastal roads. I have a sneaking suspicion he'd love it.

"Get a room already!" Nikolai shouts from the driver's

seat of his car. We rip apart like kids whose parents just caught them making out.

"Shut up, Nerd. You could just let me have him and you wouldn't need to complain!" I snap back playfully.

"No can do. Loverboy and I have plans. You're not invited," he retorts.

"You're really going with *him*?" I tease, quirking a brow at Jude.

"Yeah, we uh, we have something to discuss." He looks everywhere but my face.

That's not suspicious at all.

"Fine, be safe." I pout.

"Always, Candy Girl." A playful half-smirk tugs at his lips.

I'm done for.

Last week was amazing. This one has been no different. Every day follows the same routine. Checking dogs for Giardia, sanitizing kennels, and mercilessly flirting with one another. Thankfully, everyone is all clear now and good to go to new homes.

The worst part of my Friday is happening right now. I've dreaded this day for weeks. My sweet little Cannoli is undeniably better. I know I can't keep putting off her green light for adoption. Still, I'm an emotional mess as we leave for the day.

The weather has been sunny and beautiful, so Jude

has ridden his bike every day since last Monday. While I'm glad for him, I'm sad for me. We've barely spent any real time together, and I need more. I may be a little co-dependent already, but I can't help it. Sure, we see each other at work every day and he's slept at my place most nights the past two weeks. But that's not the same as quality time. I want dates and memories.

He's is supposed to go out with Bailey tonight. They've mentioned it a few times this week and I know they're excited. I hope the it goes well, honestly. Jude needs some good friends aside from Nikolai and Theo. Not that they aren't amazing, but Jude can relate to Bailey, which is hopefully a good thing. He's an awesome guy, so my fingers are tightly crossed.

I'm a giant ball of nausea, surely from the nerves. So, instead of our girls' night out, Charli, Claire and I have opted for an at-home spa night at Charli's place.

Nikolai is here, for the sake of keeping Ivy occupied. He also baked cookies, made a charcuterie board, fruit-infused water, and some herbal tea.

As we lay back on the couch with face masks on, feet soaking in warm baths, and some of Claire's relaxation blend in the diffuser, everything feels *right* in my life. Tranquility envelops me. I'm unnaturally exhausted, but I guess that's the power of lavender and chamomile.

"This is amazing. One of these days I'll convince Nicky to let me hire a masseuse." Charli sighs.

"That would be fantastic, you could convert one of the spare rooms to a legitimate spa room," Claire agrees.

I sigh, sipping on more tea.

"So, Caroline, I must ask. How are things with you and Jude?" Claire tips her head to the side, measuring my response.

"Well, Doc," I joke, earning a playful swat. "They're... good." I shrug.

"Just *good*?" Charli speaks up, "You two have been flirting adorably at work for the past two weeks. Every time I stopped by to check in, I wanted to stand and watch so I could swoon."

"You swoon?" I snort. "I've never seen you come close to swooning."

"I swoon for Nikolai all the time. Have you seen him with Ivy? I want a dozen more babies just from watching him with her." A blissful smile pulls at her lips.

"I stand corrected." I push her softly.

"You're deflecting," Claire says playfully.

"I am not! We're just good. There hasn't been much opportunity to really hang out with so much going on. I've been tired the last few days. Hell, even now I'm exhausted. I don't know how I'm going to survive tomorrow." My shoulders droop.

"I'm sure he won't be upset if you ask to stay in. Especially if you tell him you're not feeling well." Claire places her hand on mine.

"It's our first official date. I want it to be perfect." I frown.

"Oh, I'm sure it will." Charli wiggles her eyebrows suggestively. "Do you need some knee pads?"

"Oh my God! You've been around Nicky way too much. He's rubbing off on you." I wail, smacking her with a throw pillow.

We erupt into a chorus of giggles, until my phone pings on the coffee table and I'm all too quick to reach for it.

Big Guy: *Just leaving, I'll text you when I get there.*
Me: *Okay <3 Be safe.*

"Oh it's got to be him," Claire remarks. "Look at that grin."

"She's gonna marry that man, that's the face of a woman in love," Charli responds, faking a whisper.

"Shut it! He's just letting me know that he's getting ready to head over to meet the guys." I squeal, but the burning of my cheeks betrays my attempted argument.

"It's okay, we're not here to judge you. I love the fact that you've finally found happiness. Just over two weeks with Jude in your life and it's like you're a whole new person." Charli beams.

"Exactly. He appears to be a good man. I adore the way you soften for him. It's refreshing to see." Claire nods with a soft smile.

"Thank you. But let's not throw the 'L' word around. Got it?" I pinch my brows together in an attempt to look serious.

They nod in unison with matching sly expressions. I can only hope Jude gets it just as bad from Bailey.

261

CHAPTER 25

Jude

B ailey mentioned this place was a hole in the wall.
I'll be damned if he wasn't spot on. Sure, there are
dozens of cars lining the street and a packed parking lot,
but on any ordinary night you'd never guess this was
some sort of fight club.

A burly guy, slightly bigger than me, blocks the doorway. He couldn't look more like a stereotypical bouncer
if he tried. I step toward him, admittedly puffing my
chest out.

He sizes me up with a faint curl of his lip. "You fighting or watching?"

"Meetin' some buddies to watch," I answer firmly. A
good fight could be nice, but I'm not entirely sure this
place is legal. My freedom is worth more than a little
thrill.

"Shame, you look like you can handle yourself." He
opens the door and tips his head toward the entrance as
I pay my cover charge.

Stepping inside, I'm met with a surprisingly legitimate looking ring. The seats around it are fairly filled already. If this place is illegal, they're doing a shit job at keeping it a secret.

My eyes find Bailey and Sean in the crowd. I didn't know Sean was coming, not that I mind, he's a decent guy. They seem to be good friends, I just wouldn't have guessed he'd be into this.

Bailey beams his boy-next-door smile when he notices me. Sean, far more introverted, tosses an easy nod my way. His unruly dark hair is pulled back for a change.

"Jude! You made it." Bailey claps me on the shoulder. "Welcome to SCUBA."

"SCUBA?" I tilt my head in question.

"Seattle's Collective Underground Boxing Association. But that's way too much to say. So, SCUBA for short," Sean explains, uttering the longest string of words I've heard from him.

"Is this legal? I could get in trouble by bein' here." I ask, preparing to leave if I need to.

"Of course it's legal. Just low budget, there's no fluff or branding... yet. But they're growing quickly," Bailey says as he leads us through the crowd to a few empty chairs. "I glove up occasionally, so we get good seats." His blinding smile grows impossibly wider.

"Can anyone sign up?" I ask, intrigued by the opportunity to have a legitimate outlet.

"Oh boy," Sean huffs, rolling his eyes. "Not you too."

"He hates that I love it here. I tell him every time that

he doesn't have to come. He could easily stay home with our dogs." As soon as the words fall out of his mouth, both of them stiffen and go quiet.

"Wait," I say wide-eyed, "you two—"

"If it's a problem, say so now," Sean cuts in, shoulders raising defensively.

"What? No!" I shake my head. "I just wouldn't have guessed. Y'all are so... low-key."

"Sean doesn't like attention, but everyone at work knows. We don't wave our sexuality around on the job." Bailey shrugs.

"I don't know how you do it. The discretion that is, not the gay thing." I clamp my mouth shut as a blush burns my cheeks.

Bailey snorts and Sean cracks a faint smile—the first of his I've seen.

"Sorry. I'm a bit out of my element. It's cool that y'all are happy. I could use some tips on how to not be a love-struck fool at work." I scrub my hand over my face.

"So, you and the Doc are a thing then? She's a cutie." Bailey wiggles his brows.

"We have history... and I'm a fuckin' goner for her. Always have been."

"Would you take her last name?" Sean asks in a no-bullshit tone, hazel eyes burrowing into mine.

I'm stunned for a second, but once I blink away the initial shock my answer is immediate. "Yes. I'd marry the fuck outta her and take the Koval name in a heartbeat."

"Good, she's a big fan of her last name." He nods once

and turns his focus to the ring.

"He's not much for sugar coatin' stuff huh?" I ask Bailey, raising a single brow

"Nah, I'm sweet enough for the both of us." He nudges me with his elbow, smirking playfully.

The screech of mic feedback silences the crowd. A booming voice fills the space, announcing the fighters for the first round. Two beefy guys with ice-cold eyes saunter to the ring. My heart is in overdrive when the bell rings. I watch with unyielding attention. Each jab and uppercut shoots electric waves through my veins.

God, if just watching makes me feel like this, how exhilarating would it be to actually spar with someone? My beat up old punching bag doesn't hit back—doesn't duck or dodge.

I don't even realize my hands are tightly fisted until Bailey nudges me. "Wanna have a go after this?" His face is alight with excitement.

"With you?" I blink rapidly at him.

"Hell yeah. You're bigger than me, but I'm nimble. They don't have many guys booked tonight. You in?" His enthusiasm is contagious.

Either I'm about to put him on his ass, or he's about to kick mine. Regardless, my answer is a resounding, "Hell yes!"

Sean gives us both a look that loosely translates to 'You've got to be kidding me' as he rubs his temples and grumbles to himself.

When the last round is almost over, Bailey stands up

and blows a kiss to Sean. I chuckle quietly as he pretends to catch it and tucks it in his pocket.

We weave through the rows of people and find the sign-up board. Bailey wasn't lying, there are three un-filled blocks. He shows me to the weigh-in station and helps me fill out the paperwork and sign the liability waiver. Before I know it, we're digging through the pairs of loaner gloves.

"Jude Carlisle?"

A chill shoots down my spine. I go pin straight and school my expression. Her voice is rough, like life has been brutal. When I turn to face her, Veronica looks as ragged as she sounds.

"Holy shit, you managed to get even hotter. The years have treated you well." She struts up to me with a sala-cious look in her eyes. Her cheeks are gaunt, the signs of bad Botox are evident in her asymmetrical smile. She also seems to have been the recipient of a very cheap boob job.

"It appears you've aged like milk." I scowl. Taking in her bikini top and cut-off shorts, it clicks a second later. "You're a ring girl?"

"Yeah. Being a doctor didn't really pan out. Too much studying." She reaches toward me and Bailey steps be-tween us.

"How about you keep your slimy hands to yourself." He crosses his arms, shutting down her advances. "I see you leave here with a different guy every time. He's tak-en. Even if he wasn't, I wouldn't be a very good friend if

I sat back and watched him sink to your level."

"Fine!" She huffs. "Not like he could get it up when shit got real anyway. Whatever I saw in him before is a mystery to me." She starts to turn away, but I reach around Bailey and grab her by the wrist.

"What do you mean I couldn't get it up?" I pin her with a piercing stare.

"You heard me. Drunk off your ass and still wouldn't shut up about *her*. She didn't even have the guts to break up with you face-to-face and you still wouldn't fuck me!" She sneers, stomping off as I release my hold on her.

"You know her?" Bailey stands mouth agape, and stares at me.

"Unfortunately. But the good news is, I never slept with her." My face lights up with glee. I can't wait to tell Caroline.

"Did she look like *that*?" He tips his head toward Veronica, who is now flirting with a group of rough-looking men.

"No, she used to be fake pretty, which was never my type, but she had potential. Kinda sad to see her like this... but she had it comin'. Her lies and manipulation were the catalyst for my spiral back in the day, but it's fine." I lift a shoulder, brushing off the interaction. I don't need any more closure than the knowledge she just gave me.

"Well, luckily she's not *our* ring girl, let's get ready." Bailey pats my arm and we head to the locker room.

Once we're in the ring, the moment feels surreal. Bailey flashes a blue smile my way, courtesy of his mouth guard. We tap gloves and the bell sounds. Bailey is first to swing with a quick jab to my ribs. His satisfied grin is short-lived as I dodge his right hook, throwing a hard counter strike to his abdomen. He grunts, puffs out a small laugh and bounces back on his toes, creating space between us.

I'm in my element, moving fluidly around him. His surprise is evident, clearly caught off guard by my agility. He lands a clean shot to my jaw, causing me to stumble slightly. In a flash, he unleashes a flurry of blows to my torso, leaving his own face unguarded. I square my hips, bob to dodge his next hit and land a strong uppercut to his chin. He stumbles and loses his footing for a second.

I'm overzealous and let my perceived size advantage cloud my judgment. He *is* fast, and before I know it, he thrusts a strong blow to my left eye. The hit is dizzying, giving him the chance to bombard me with follow-ups. At this point I know he's got me. These are single round fights, so I have no chance at redemption.

It doesn't matter to me either way. We're not actually competing for the sake of the win. This is what friendship feels like, and I couldn't be happier to lose. I'm going to enjoy every agonizing moment. I manage to land a few more solid hits, but ultimately his speed proves victorious.

We clean ourselves up and regroup with Sean ringside. He looks at Bailey with admiration.

"Y'all wanna get out of here and grab a bite to eat?" I

nod toward the door.

"Yes! Victory meal! Loser pays!" Bailey bellows.

"Deal." I smile back at him.

We meet at a local diner and grab a booth at the back. Bailey and I look like we got the shit beat out of us, earning some questioning looks. With them sitting across from me, in a much more intimate setting, I take note of their closeness, wishing Caroline was here. Double dates with these two would be a riot, I'm sure of it.

"You thinking about her?" Sean asks, as he leans into Bailey.

"Am I that obvious?" I sigh, knowing damn well that I am.

"Oh yeah, you can't hide those hearts in your eyes." Bailey rests his head on Sean's shoulder. "We ordered ahead, where is our food?" he grumbles.

"It's coming. Patience, my love," Sean assures him.

Our burgers arrive on cue, as if Bailey summoned them. We silently devour the juicy, greasy goodness like it's our last meal.

When we part ways I leave feeling one step closer to being whole.

I call Caroline, ensuring I keep up our nightly routine. Just like when we were younger, I sing her a classic love song before bed every night, whether I'm there or not. Sometimes she stays awake through the whole thing, but oftentimes I'm serenaded in return by her soft snores. Just like tonight.

My eye hurts and my head is throbbing, but I push that all aside and head to Caroline's place. She let me know when she woke up this morning and I've been waiting for the green light to head her way. The ride over is the longest ten minutes of my life.

When I knock on her door, she's quick to answer. Her eyes grow wide instantly.

"Jude! What happened? You were supposed to go out with the guys," she asks, reaching up to touch my swollen eye.

"Bailey is a better fighter than me." I chuckle, taking her hand in mine. I turn my head and kiss her palm.

"Bailey? He-what?" She stumbles over her words.

"We signed up to fight, and he surprised me. I got a few good hits in, though." I smile down at her. "Think I can come in?" I shift my gaze over her head, into the adorably decorated room behind her.

"Oh, yeah, of course. Sorry, I wasn't expecting you to show up like this." She gestures loosely to my face before turning to lead me inside.

Her apartment is actually a small house. The decorations are so *her*, it's endearing. Her couch has pink, fluffy pillows and the kitchen is decorated with frilly curtains, covered in tiny strawberries. Anything that can be pink is.

There's a hallway with a couple doors off the living room, leading to the bathroom and single bedroom.

I kick off my boots and walk over to the living room, dropping down onto the couch.

I hear her in the kitchen rustling around for a moment. When she sits next to me she hands me an ice pack.

"Here, this will help with the swelling."

"Thank you, Doc" My lips pull into a languid smile.

"So... what do you want to do today?" Her eyes have *many* more unasked questions in them.

"Well, it's early. We can go for a ride, then grab some food. Or, if you wanna stay in and watch movies I'm game. As long as I get to spend time with you, I'm a happy man."

"Won't you get bored?" She chews her lip.

I pull her legs up into my lap and smile at her glittery toes. She hums while I work my knuckles against the arch of her foot.

"Nothin' will ever bore me when you're around."

"I want to do something fun, but I've been so sleepy recently. Can we just nap for a little bit?" She yawns and stretches.

"That sounds amazing, as long as I get to hold you." I shift her legs off my lap and stand up.

Her mouth opens slightly as I bend down and scoop her up bridal-style. "Careful, Big Guy. I'm not exactly a size two." She wraps her arms around my shoulders.

"I'm well aware. I can't get enough of these curves." I kiss her forehead and carry her to the bedroom.

After I lay her down on the plush pink comforter, I shed my shirt and jeans and curl up behind her. She fits so perfectly against me I can't imagine anyone else in her place.

Who needs fancy dates when I have all this perfection to admire right here?

CHAPTER 26

Caroline

D o I have to move? My content heart says no, but my full bladder is screaming yes. I peek my head out from under the blanket and peer out the window. The sun is high, so we couldn't have napped for too long. Honestly, no amount of time curled up like this would be enough for me. Laying in Jude's arms makes everything feel better, it's the only time my brain shuts off. Nothing would make me happier than spending the day in bed, but the bathroom calls to me, and I can't ignore it anymore.

Little puffs of his breath tickle the back of my neck and I let out a small giggle. Gently untangling myself I get up slowly, shivering from the loss of his warmth. I hurry to finish my duties and freshen up—just in case.

When I return he's still fast asleep. Flutters fill my stomach as I stand at the edge of my bed and take a minute to admire how serene he looks. Carefully, I slide back into his embrace, chest-to-chest. When I trail my fingers lightly across the tattoo over his heart he inhales deeply and peels one eye open.

His exhale is accompanied by a low, dreamy rumble. "You feelin' better?" he asks, voice raspy.

"Yeah, I just wasn't ready to be awake yet, I guess," I say into his chest and continue to trace the decorative font on the candy wrapper.

"Do you like it?" Leisurely, he slides his hand up my side, then back down to rest on the curve of my hip, his touch soft and loving.

My eyes trail up to meet his. "Yes, it's beautiful. I love it." I press my lips against the intricate ink and his breath catches.

"Candy," he rumbles, "as much as I'd love another taste of you, I want to spend some real time together. You're making it difficult to do that." He kisses the top of my head and rolls away from me.

"But—"

"Nope. I'll fuck you the way you deserve later. For now, we've got years' worth of dates and quality time to make up for." He slides his pants on—much to my disappointment.

With a scowl on my face, I sit up, grumbling to myself. Jude laughs softly before leaning down and taking my jaw in his hand. "I don't know what kind of men you've been with, but I'm not them. You're not gonna get your way by poutin', Sweetness." He kisses my cheek and releases his hold, leaving me aching for more.

"Pleeeeaaaase?" I push my lower lip out and flutter my

lashes.

"You're adorable when you beg, I'll remember that for later. Now, get dressed." He pulls his shirt over his head and struts out of my room.

I groan loudly, the kind of exaggerated sound that begs for attention. He gives me nothing in return. With a final dramatic huff, I pull on a pair of leggings and a cropped sweater.

Jude is already leaning against the front door by the time I shuffle over to put my shoes on.

"Still a Converse kinda girl huh?"

"Yup," I reply with a slight edge as I stand to face him.

He pushes off the door and stalks toward me. Blood rushes through my veins like lava under the intensity of his gaze as he places a hand on my hip and presses me against the wall, planting his other hand above my head. When he leans in, ghosting his lips over my ear, I let out a low whimper.

"Do you need a lesson in manners before we leave?" He rasps, dragging his lips down my neck.

"N-no. I'll behave," I breathe out, holding back the intense need to push him further.

"That's what I like to hear. It'd be a shame to send you out in public with smeared makeup." He kisses behind my ear, sending sparks straight to my core. "Now, let's go. I have something special planned for us." He takes me by the hand and grabs his keys from the counter, leading me out the door.

When we make it to his bike my throat tightens as I

notice a glaringly obvious new detail. Hanging from the handlebars is a helmet. Not just *any* helmet... a bright pink one, with a rainbow, mirror-finished visor.

Smiling confidently, Jude unclasps the buckles, slides it over my head, and gives me a soft pat before slipping his matte black helmet on. Neon green striping follows the curves and border of his visor.

"Can you hear me?" His voice unexpectedly filters through the speakers at my ears as he swings his leg over the seat.

"You... bought me a helmet," I murmur softly, my nose tingling with emotion.

"Of course, gotta take care of my girl. Let me help you on." He tilts his head my way and holds his hand out.

With his assistance, I slide up behind him and shudder as long-suppressed memories flood back. His hands find my thighs and he pulls me closer, exactly where he wants me. My grip settles on his abs and, for a moment, neither of us move.

I don't need to ask what he's feeling, because I feel it too. Under my touch, his muscles flex, firm and defined. Trailing lower, my fingers meet the waistband of his jeans and he shifts in his seat.

"Candy," he warns.

Deciding to behave—for now—I move my hand back to his stomach and press myself against him. Excitement floods through me as his bike roars to life, I never realized how much I missed the exhilaration until this moment.

We ride for a while and I almost ask where he's taking

us, but I don't. For once, I'm not concerned with the outcome, which is honestly equal parts freeing and terrifying. I'm a planner to a fault, but life loves throwing me curve balls.

Maybe that's what makes Jude so perfect. He takes control, commanding and unwavering, his presence is impossible to ignore. When I'm with him like this I feel weightless, unbothered by the noise that normally plagues my mind. I don't worry about where we're going, because he's got me and that's all that matters.

"You doin' alright?" His voice cuts in. "We're almost there."

The coast line comes into view moments later, and I realize exactly where we are.

"Jude!" I gasp, squeezing him tightly. "Are you for real?"

His lighthearted chuckle echoes through my helmet as we pull into a parking spot. I hop off the bike, vibrating with excitement. When he takes his helmet off, a blinding smile stretches across his face. I pull my own helmet off and jump into him.

He catches me and laughs. "Look who suddenly has all the energy in the world." After a quick squeeze, he plants me back on my feet.

"Jude." My voice cracks. "I-I've always wanted to see real, live orcas! I've lived here all my life and have never had the time or money... or anyone to go with. Pleeeeaaase tell me we're going on a whale watching tour!"

"Of course we are. I'm glad I booked the afternoon cruise, seein' as our nap took up the mornin'. Just means we had to skip lunch, but we'll get food after." He takes me by the hand and leads me toward the tour boat as we talk.

"How late will that be?" I ask as he pulls his phone out to show the attendant our tickets.

"Well, this tour runs into the evenin'. So by the time we're done it'll be time for dinner. They do have snacks on board, though." He winks and leads me to the top deck to find a seat near the front.

When he pulls me onto his lap I curl into his chest, which is quickly becoming my favorite place.

"I'm not bein' too much am I?" He murmurs quietly against my hair, placing soft kisses on the top of my head.

"No, I love your touch, your attention... your everything, I promise." I nuzzle impossibly closer, turning to face him.

"I just..." He trails off, mulling over his next words. "I want to be good for you. I don't want you to question where I stand. I damn sure don't want you thinkin' this is just about sex for me. That's all we've really been doin'." His face pulls tight.

"Jude, I don't feel that way at all. Okay?" I place my hand against his cheek and he leans into it. "You don't have to go all out like this for me. I'm content with a night at home on the couch."

"Liar." He chuckles. "You should have seen your face when you read the sign on the pier. You're not foolin' me." His face softens, voice low and warm.

"Okay, every now and then, nice things are great. But that's not my point." Leaning up, I press a kiss to his cheek. "You're enough." I'm sure to keep my attention solely on him.

The rise and fall of his chest increases. His grip on me tightens ever so slightly, like I might fade away if he doesn't hold on. Unspoken words float between us as our gazes linger. By the look in his eyes, I know he wants to kiss the hell out of me, but other passengers have begun filling seats around us.

I take my spot next to him as the tour guide—clad in his comically cliché sailor suit—greets us and introduces himself. After a brief history of the Puget Sound we embark on the tour.

Jude watches me, captivated by my amazement when a blue whale crests the surface. Cool sea water mists my face as it splashes back into the depths. The sight is beyond beautiful, unlike anything I've ever experienced. My face hurts from the smile that has taken up residence on it.

The tour goes on for another thirty minutes with no more notable sightings. As the guide finishes his stories and educational tidbits, we're given free reign to spectate as we please.

Standing at the railing, Jude wraps his arms around me from behind, resting his chin on my shoulder. I lean into his embrace as a particularly large orca breeches in front of us. Fortunately, there aren't a lot of people on this tour, so we've been able to claim a front corner as our own. I know I'm being loud and far more giddy than an adult woman should. But Jude? He just shakes his head and pulls me closer with every gasp and excited squeal that escapes me.

We drift along for another hour and I'm getting tired again. The sun is slowly descending over the water as we near the end of the tour. I lean on the railing, watching streaks of color fill the sky above, dancing on the waves along the horizon. Jude still has me cocooned securely in his arms and I inhale, fighting the tears threatening to break free.

"I love you." The words fall from my lips so naturally, I don't have time to stop them. Panicked, I gasp, afraid my mouth has ruined the moment.

Jude sucks in a breath, grabs my hips and spins me around. "Say it again. Look me in the eye and say it again."

"I-I love you," I repeat with as much conviction as I can muster, looking directly into his expectant eyes.

Pressing me into the railing, he cups my face in his palms and claims my lips with his. I melt into him, savoring the raw passion of his kiss.

Suddenly remembering where we are, he pulls away and runs his thumb over my lower lip. "I love you too, Candy Girl. So fuckin' much. I have for seven years. Nothin's ever gonna change that." He leans in, pressing his forehead against mine. "I didn't think I'd ever hear you say it, and didn't want to scare you off by blurtin' it out before you were ready."

"I know, and it's crazy because we barely know each other, but I don't care. In my twenty-six years of life, nobody has made me feel like this. I'm *so* beyond fighting it. I *love* you, Jude. I'm still not good at it, but if you keep being patient with me, I'll keep doing the same for you." My chest heaves from the weight of my words.

"We're not goin' out to dinner. I'll order delivery," he declares, voice coated with arousal.

"I thought this wasn't about sex for you?" I tease.

"Oh, don't even act like you don't want it." He slides his finger down to the collar of my shirt.

"I don't know. I'm pretty tired." A devilish grin tugs at my lips as my knees wobble.

"I'll help put you to bed," he whispers, pressing his erection against me as he traces along my cleavage.

We're pulled from our haze by the tour guide's voice blaring through the speakers, thanking everyone for coming and bidding us farewell.

When did we get back?

Jude slips his arm around me as we walk back to his bike and hurry to put our helmets on. All too eagerly I prop myself up behind him and hold tight. He takes a quick second to order us Chinese food and starts the engine. As we pull away from the pier, I slide my hand down and casually trace the outline of his hardness. This time, he doesn't argue, or try to stop me. Faint grunts through the Bluetooth connection in our helmets only encourage my boldness. I grip him and stroke as best as

I can manage in this position.

"Candy, fuck," he hisses, raw desire dripping from his voice.

"That's the goal, Big Guy." I hum with a half moan, continuing to lazily, teasingly, work him over through his jeans.

Wasting no time, he takes the most direct route to my place, arriving just as the delivery driver does. He tips him and follows me up the steps, through the front door, immediately placing the bag on the counter.

"Here," he says, holding a container of lo mein out to me.

"But—"

"No, you need to eat. It doesn't need to be a lot, but you'll need the energy." His eyes flash with heated promises, dropping to my chest then shifting back to my face.

"I'm not hungry." I fold my arms.

"Too bad." He pops the top off of his own container.

Frustrated, but also admittedly starving, I make quick work of a few hearty bites.

Watching intently, Jude waits for me to finish. When he washes his hands and rounds the counter, I quiver at the powerful energy radiating off of him. Scooping me up, his palms curl around my ass, holding me like I belong nowhere else. Our mouths collide and I lose myself in him. I don't even realize he's carried me to my bedroom until I'm tossed onto the mattress.

"Before we do this, I need to tell you something." He

sits down next to me.

"Wow. Way to kill the mood," I joke, his face stays flat and I immediately prepare to be crushed.

"Don't look at me like that. It's actually good news. I never slept with Veronica," He blurts out.

I recoil as the words hit me. "What?!" I shriek.

"I know you don't want to hear about her, and I'm probably cockblockin' myself right now, but it's true. I ran into her last night, she looks like shit by the way. She tried comin' onto me but I shut her down. Then Bailey stepped in, and she spouted off some mess about me bein' too hung up on you to get it up before," he rambles on.

I can't form words, I'm too shocked, too relieved. It shouldn't matter whether he slept with her or not, but it does. I don't even care that she tried to throw herself at him again.

He never slept with her.

My blood is on fire. Something inside me snaps into place and I launch myself at him, kissing him like never before. Grunting from the surprise, he eagerly kisses me back, gasping as I grip him through his jeans.

"So, you're not mad?" He breathes, a moan breaking through his words.

"Fuck me... right now. I need you to show me how much you love me," I beg, breathless and desperate.

Panting, with lust-blown pupils, he breaks our kiss, and leaves the room. I whine in protest, but he quickly returns with his overnight bag. He puts it on the floor and directs his full attention to me

"I brought some of my toys, but I want to start with yours. Tell me where you keep them." Eyes, hooded and heavy, his heated gaze drags unhurriedly over every inch of my body.

I'm about to boil over as he undoes the button at his waist, slowly working to remove his pants. My mouth falls open as he stands before me, hard and perfect, concealed only by the thin fabric of his boxers. When he grips himself and groans, the devilish grin on his face sends waves of excitement to my core. Every inch of my body is covered in goosebumps as I realize I'm a moth, and he's a raging fire.

Based on the promises burning in his eyes, I'm in for a *very* long night.

CHAPTER 27

Caroline

I slide the drawer of my nightstand open, pulling out the bag I keep my *collection* in. Peeking inside, the smile that splits Jude's face is filled with devilish glee. My body quivers with anticipation. We've slept together several times, but it's been tame, after work romps. This? This is going to be a wild time and I'm beyond ready.

"Mmmm. Quite the selection you've got here, Candy." He bites his lip, pulling the tentacle out of the bag. "I promised to fuck you with this. It's quite impressive."

"Y-yeah. It uh... does a good job."

What? Where are my words?

"I can't wait to watch you squirm." He guides me onto my back, kissing me slow and hard. "You're gonna come on my face, then this toy, and finally I'll bury my cock inside you and fuck you until you beg me to stop," he growls in my ear before sitting up to slide my leggings and panties off, far slower than I'd like.

Frustrated, I yank my sweater off with a huff.

Jude leans over me, pressed between my legs, and pins my arms above my head. "Now, now, be patient for me. I'm tryin' to make up for lost time. Understood?" He rasps, scraping his teeth against my neck.

"Yes." I breathe out.

Staring into his eyes, I wait for a reaction. Sparks of arousal shoot through me when his gaze hardens.

"It's been a while, so I'm going to let that one slide. Do you need to be reminded of the rules?" He presses his hardness against me, the friction from his boxers on my bare skin is delicious torture.

"No, Sir." I breathe out on a feverish moan.

"That's right. Such a good girl, aren't you?" He whispers against me, trailing soft kisses down my neck before stopping suddenly.

Shit. He's waiting.

"Y-yes, Sir." I'm already a puddle for this man and he's barely touched me.

He unclasps my bra and tosses it to the side, then closes his lips around a hardened nipple, sucking it into his mouth and moaning with satisfaction. He spends a few long, torturous minutes savoring my breasts, teasing them until I'm breathless before traveling lower.

At the throbbing heat between my thighs, he slowly slides his tongue through my gathered wetness and groans. "Fuck, you're so delicious. Are you going to behave and let me eat my fill?" He watches me intently, kissing just above my clit while he glides a finger around it.

"Y-yes, Sir."

My body betrays me, immediately grinding against him as his mouth makes contact. I gasp when he thrusts two fingers deep inside me, working rhythmically. On the brink of lustful insanity, I wrap my legs around his shoulders as he sucks on my aching clit. As I roll my hips, he pulls back, dragging his thumb through my arousal. When he glides lower and presses it against my ass, my muscles tense.

"You ever tried this?" he asks, kissing my inner thigh.

"N-no, Sir." I whimper.

"Wanna give it a shot? Remember, red means stop, yellow means slow down and green means you're enjoyin' yourself." He locks eyes with me.

"Okay." I nod.

"Fuck, you're such a good little slut, just for me." He licks from my entrance to my clit and circles it while his thumb breaches my back entrance. Taking my moans as approval, he pushes in further, applying delicious pressure to my clit with his tongue and groaning against me.

"Yes!" I cry out, "FUCK." Writhing against him, I lace my fingers through his hair and hold tight as I ride out a powerful orgasm.

He continues to work his thumb inside my ass, pressing deeper while I convulse. "That's it. You're going to come again aren't you, Candy Girl?" He buries his face back into my pussy and moans as I fall apart a second time. Hell, maybe it's an extension of the first but it doesn't even matter, I'm lost in ecstasy.

"God, I fuckin' love you." He pants, pulling his face from me. "But you're not gettin' away with actin' up like that for the next one."

Standing from the bed, he steps around to where our bags sit. The sound of the zipper is almost ominous. I have no clue what his toys are, but I'm anxious to find out.

He pulls his shirt over his head and drops his boxers to the ground. My eyes drop to his extremely hard cock, dripping with precum and I lick my lips. Dragging my attention back up, I stop at the ropes in his hand.

"You're going to tie me up?" A gasp rushes out of me as my eyes widen.

"That depends, what color are you?" He stalks my way, twirling the ropes around his fist.

"So fucking green." I breathe out.

Tilting his head, he lifts a brow.

Shit.

"...Sir." I chew my lower lip with a pleading look, silently begging for forgiveness.

"Lay back, spread wide for me like a good little fuck toy," he commands and takes my left hand, pressing his lips against my palm.

When he has my wrist secured to the bed post he checks the tension. Satisfied with his handiwork, he prowls slowly to the other side of my bed and grabs hold of my right hand, softly kissing my thrumming pulse before binding it in place. "Still green?"

"Y-yes, Sir." I pant, voice unnaturally husky.

Taking his time, he ties my ankles to their respective bed posts and steps back, lazily stroking his cock as he admires the sight of me splayed out for him.

"Fuck I can't wait to hear you scream for me." He walks over to my bag and grabs the infamous tentacle. "This is gonna be a lot of fun." His chuckle is breathy, rich with desire.

Watching him try out a few of the settings before kneeling between my legs, I can feel my core tightening in preparation. At no point would I have thought a partner would be using this with me. Now that it's about to become reality, I'm soaked.

After finding a vibration level that suits him, he wastes no time pressing the tip into me. It's already twisting and I squeal from the sensation. My hips lift, aching for more. He slides another delicious inch of the toy into me as I moan loudly, struggling against my restraints.

"You're not gettin' free, just gonna have to let me play," he says, pumping into me, pulling another moan from my lips. "Such a naughty girl. Goddamn. Look at you fixin' to come all over this tentacle. Let me hear it."

He drives it into me until the suction cup finds my clit. Holding the pressure, he clicks the button on the end that makes the tip wiggle inside me, hitting just the right spot. I cry out his name on the peak of ecstasy, drawing wild groans from him.

Tossing the toy aside, he leans down and runs his tongue through my juices, savoring the last waves of my climax. His chest heaves as he stands and makes his rounds, untying my wrists and ankles. Taking a moment, he massages each one as he releases it.

"Beautiful," he says, climbing over me, "you're so beautiful like this, my sweet Caroline." His breath ghosts over my neck and my heart nearly explodes.

Tender kisses pepper my shoulder as he settles between my thighs. Slowly, he pushes himself inside me, savoring every second until the space between us ceases to exist.

"Jude," I gasp, wrapping my arms around him as he bites down on my shoulder, kissing the mark he leaves behind.

"You're mine," he murmurs against the skin of my neck, "forever. I won't let you leave me again." He thrusts steadily, deep and purposeful. "Say it," he demands against my burning skin.

"I love you, Jude. I'm not going anywhere, ever again." I pull his face to mine and kiss him with everything I have—a passionate claim, sealing a promise I fully intend to keep.

He adjusts his hips, lifting me up to meet him thrust for thrust. Steadily, his hands trail along the length of my body, taking in every curve.

Rolling my hips in sync with him, I whimper into his mouth. He slips his tongue between my lips and our kiss becomes frantic as the pressure in my core builds. Sensing my approaching release, he increases his pace, thrusting harder. My nails find purchase in his back as he sinks his teeth into my shoulder once more.

I whimper his name like a plea, careening over the edge as the warmth of his release fills me. My love-drunk heart pounds wildly in my chest, making no effort to slow. Jude pants above me, supporting most of his weight on his elbows. Puffs of his warm breath land against my feverish skin as he rests his forehead against my shoulder. He hums softly as my fingertips trace the muscular planes of his back.

"How are you even real?" I whisper, breathless and half awake.

"That's rich comin' from you." He chuckles softly.

"No one has ever made me feel the way you do. *Ever*. It's terrifying and beautiful." I swallow hard.

"It doesn't have to be scary. We're both stumblin' into uncharted territory, but it's worth it." He kisses my cheek and pulls away. "I'll be right back, don't move."

My body is weightless, drifting between consciousness and blissful sleep. I'm faintly aware of him re-entering the room, warm cloth in hand. He smiles affectionately and kisses my forehead before cleaning up the mess he's made. After tossing the washcloth in my laundry basket, he slides up next to me and pulls the covers over us.

"Sleep well, Candy Girl. I'll be right here," he murmurs softly.

Still completely naked and carefree, I drift off to sleep wrapped in his warmth.

Clanking sounds from the other side of my apartment wake me up. Jude isn't here and I'm instantly on edge.

What time is it?

The light coming through my window means it must be morning. As my senses wake up, I'm caught off guard by the smell of... bacon?

What the hell?

Wincing at the tenderness between my legs, I drag myself from the warmth of my bed. Jude's shirt is still on the floor where he tossed it last night, so I pull it on. It smells like him, and falls just at the top of my thighs. An inch longer and I could call it a dress.

Jude is a mess, just like my kitchen. The floors, cupboards, counter, every surface has been marked in some way. Leaning as seductively as I can manage against the doorframe, I silently wait for him to notice me. I should probably be upset over the disaster I'm watching unfold, but nothing could dampen how lucky I feel looking at it. He's adorably sexy. Shirtless, covered in a dusting of flour, tongue sticking out the corner of his mouth as he stirs... some sort of concoction. My heart swells watching him. He's no Nikolai in the kitchen, but I'd let him butter my biscuit any day.

"Shit!" He jumps, flinging a bit of the mystery mixture across the room. "You're part cat, I swear. How'd you sleep?" A sheepish smile pulls at his face.

"Like I had four orgasms." I shrug, biting my lip to fight the smile forming. "Whatcha making?"

He pauses, staring at the way his t-shirt wraps my

body. "Uh-I..." He shakes his head. "Sorry, you're just the most beautiful woman I've ever seen, and you're in my shirt." He licks his lips. "Ahem, I'm makin' breakfast." He motions to the chaos surrounding us and winces, like it's the first time he's noticed. "I'll clean up, I promise."

"I hope you clean better than you cook." I dust off a spot on the counter next to him and lift myself up to sit on it. "You made waffles?" I tilt my head, inspecting the container next to me on the counter. They're stacked up high and surprisingly golden and delicious looking.

"Yeah, and bacon... I just need to scramble the eggs and we're all set." He leans over and kisses me quickly, then pours whisked eggs into the pan.

I snag a piece of crispy bacon and pause. "Wait. I didn't even have bacon... or eggs... or things to make waffles."

"I ordered groceries," he replies simply, like it's no big deal. As if he didn't just make my stomach do a dozen back flips and pinch itself. "What?" He furrows his brows.

"Huh?" I blink.

Shit. Was I gawking?

"You just gave me a look." He turns the stove off and plates up our breakfast.

"Sorry, I didn't mean to. You just caught me by surprise," I say, opening my mouth for the bite of waffle he offers me. "WOW! These are delicious, Nicky might have some competition." I moan, licking syrup off my lips.

"Well, it's his recipe. So I guess he knows what he's talkin' about." A cheeky expression dances across his features.

"His recipe?" My face twists in confusion.

"Yeah. Remember when he insisted that he drive me home last Monday?"

"Nooooo! He didn't. That sneaky little shit." I gasp, feigning betrayal.

I'm not actually upset, and definitely had it coming. I still like to take credit for his relationship with Charli working out so smoothly. It's only fitting that he tries to weasel his way into helping Jude win me over... as if he needed a wing-man.

"Well I'm gonna tell him you liked mine better. Just to fuck with him." Jude laughs, feeding me another bite.

The food is delicious, and definitely worth the clean-up. We take our time scrubbing everything down, stealing quick kisses as we go. This is what love is supposed to feel like. My heart aches, remembering how my parents used to act just like this. My poor father hasn't even tried to put himself out there, but he's got plenty to love with Ivy and Henderson.

We're heading to Nikolai's house later, and while I feel a bit under the weather, most likely from the long night, I'm excited to spend the day with my family, now that it feels whole.

CHAPTER 28

Caroline

Everyone is acting weird, like they know something I don't. Jude made me drive, which was my first clue that there's a secret I'm not privy to. Nikolai is jittery, excited for some reason. Charli is focusing on Ivy, and won't even look at me. She's worse at hiding her emotions than Nikolai, so I *know* they're all up to something. I stand in the doorway, hands planted on my hips, and huff.

"Sir," Jude says, tipping his head to greet my father, who is sitting at the table with an unimpressed look on his face.

Whatever is going on, he knows about it too, and doesn't share in the enthusiasm humming through the room. "Jude," he gruffs with a cold stare, "surprised you haven't run off yet."

"I'm not goin' anywhere, I swear," Jude replies sincerely, wrapping his arm around my waist. He doesn't break eye contact with my father, but his face is soft when I look up at him. He's not putting on a display or trying to bullshit.

"What happens when times get tough? Are you pre-pared to be there when she needs you this time?" My father tilts his head, maintaining their stare-off

"DAD!" I shout, "Jude isn't going anywhere. Please believe that. I'm *so* done with this pissing contest!"

"Solnyshko, I—" He starts, but I cut him off.

"No. Just let me be happy. Please?" Tears pool in my eyes as my voice wavers.

"I-I'm sorry, I just don't want to see you get hurt again," he murmurs, dropping his gaze to the floor.

"Sir, I'm not the boy I used to be. Caroline and I have talked about what happened between us, and we both agree that we were young and dumb. It won't happen again. I—" He swallows hard and looks at me silently asking for permission to continue. I nod up at him with a soft smile. "—I *love* her. I did back then but was too hard-headed, and honestly terrified, to say it."

"Before you have a chance to say anything," I interject, "I love him, too. I've never loved anyone who wasn't family. Jude's my person, Dad. I know you hate him, but please, just give him a chance." Tears break free, streaking my cheeks.

"I-I don't *hate* him. I just..." He sighs, taking a mo-ment to decide on the right words. "You deserve the world, and if he's the one you want it from, I just want to know he's willing to put in the work with you to make it happen. Love isn't always easy, but it's worth it."

"I know and she's worth every back-breaking minute," Jude says, kissing the top of my head.

"So is he," I agree, leaning into his side. "*We* are worth it. Life is too short and we've been given a second chance to finally be happy, Dad."

The longest minutes of my life pass as I watch my father. His face stays flat, until he finally speaks.

"Well then, I suppose Nicky has something for you," he announces with a hint of unexpected excitement.

I follow his gaze to the doorway where Nikolai stands. In the midst of our heart-to-heart, I didn't even realize he left the room. Jude places his hands on my shoulders and turns me—and my full attention—to my cousin, who is holding the cutest thing I've ever seen. My heart stutters.

"Cannoli?!" I exclaim, slack-jawed.

She's squirming to get to me, wearing a cute little pink dress with a strawberry on the back. Nikolai walks toward me grinning from ear to ear. I'm frozen in place until Jude gently squeezes my shoulders.

"What is she doing here? This dress is *so* cute." I sniffle, blinking to make sure this is real.

"Well..." Jude leans down, wrapping us in a hug from behind. "She's all yours," he whispers in my ear, resting his chin in the crook of my neck.

"What? I-I can't." My breath catches as Nikolai hands her to me. She immediately settles down and curls into me. "I don't have time. I—"

Jude kisses my cheek. "But *we* do." He looks around the room.

"What? We?" My eyes grow painfully wide.

"You see, Caroline," Charli breaks her silence. "She can come to work with you."

"And on the days you're all too busy, I can watch her with Navy," my father affirms.

"You were in on this too?" My jaw drops, hanging open from shock.

"I asked if he'd be willing to expand his daycare," Nikolai chuckles.

My throat tightens around the sob I'm fighting. Jude rubs his hands up and down my arms, comforting me as I struggle to keep it together.

"She's your little strawberry cannoli." He gently strokes the top of her head as she snuggles against my chest.

"Th-thank you." I let the sob break free, momentarily disturbing Cannoli. "Sorry, I don't know why I'm so emotional." I kiss her little forehead and tuck her closer into my chest. "I don't know how to ever thank you guys."

"Thank Jude, it was his master plan," Nikolai replies, with a roguish grin.

"Yeah, I'm sure it was *all* his idea. Just like the waffle explosion in my kitchen this morning. His were better by the way." I stick my tongue out.

Nikolai gasps and grabs his chest with an over-exaggerated insulted expression.

Jude bursts out laughing behind me. "That was my line, you little thief."

"Well then, you can make dinner, Loverboy." Nikolai folds his arms and smirks with a playful challenge in his eyes.

"Trust me, you don't want that," Jude laughs, eyes crinkling at the edges.

Nikolai opens the fridge and pulls out trays with hot-dogs and hamburgers and moves through the kitchen to the back patio. The rest of us follow and sit in the lounge chairs as he starts the grill. We talk while he cooks, watching Navy and Cannoli bounce around in the yard. My father still isn't what I would describe as overjoyed about Jude being here, but he's noticeably more relaxed. It's a start, and I'm hopeful time will only improve their relationship.

After finishing dinner, we load our dishes into the dishwasher and return to the patio. The late July heat is forgiving today, so we're taking full advantage of the fresh air. Charli is curled up in Nikolai's lap—her unofficial assigned seat—and Ivy is snoozing away in Dad's arms.

Today has been a whirlwind and I'm tired. Stiffly and awkwardly, I stand from my seat and shuffle over to Jude, who is sitting in the chair next to Nikolai and Charli, across from my father. Sensing my intentions, his face lights up. When he holds his arms out, I carefully climb into his lap, settling in against him. Tension hardens his body when his gaze locks with my father's, but he just pulls me closer, tucking my head under his chin. Flutters fill my stomach, and I immediately understand why

Charli loves being held like this. The security I feel being wrapped up in Jude's embrace is calming and serene. Before I know it, I'm crying... *again*.

"What's wrong?" Jude asks softly.

"I just love all of you!" I choke out, "So freaking much. I-I don't know why I'm crying about it. I just am." Blubbering, I bury my face against his chest.

"She's always been a softie, " Nikolai jokes, "but we love you too, that's why we're *all* here." He turns his attention to my father.

"I hate to see you cry, but happy tears are allowed." Dad nods with a soft smile pulling at his face.

"I-I just haven't been this happy since b-before Mom..." I can't even say it, but I don't need to.

Jude somehow finds a way to pull me even closer. Our atoms are going to fuse together any second at this rate, and there's no place I'd rather be. If I never leave this spot—this moment—I'll be perfectly content.

The next two weeks go by in a flash.

Cannoli has adapted to her new life beautifully. I still can't believe she's mine, I cry at least once a day just looking at her, all tiny and adorable.

Jude and I spend almost all of our free time together now, but tonight's fight night. While he's out with Bailey and Sean, I'm having the girls over for movie night. Charli is the first to arrive and wastes no time making herself at home, sprawling out on my couch while I prepare a giant bowl of popcorn.

When Claire knocks on my door, I laugh. She's been here a dozen times since I moved in, but insists on formalities.

"Come in, Silly," I call out.

She steps inside and scrunches her face playfully.

"Claire! Come sit, we're in charge of picking the movie." Charli pats a the spot next to her. They scroll through a few streaming apps while I finish up in the kitchen. Ultimately, *Mean Girls* is a fan favorite, so we put it on to serve as background noise while we catch up.

Charli looks around my living room with a teasing smile.

"What?" I ask.

"Oh nothing. There's just definitely a man living here now." She chuckles.

"He's not *living* here. He just stays over... a lot." I feel my cheeks grow warm.

"And just how often is 'a lot' exactly?" Her perfectly shaped brow raises teasingly.

"Uh. Wellll... every night." My jaw drops open. "Oh my gosh! I didn't even realize how much time he spends here. Half of his clothes are in my dresser! He's practically moved in over the last two weeks."

Holy shit I'm oblivious.

"Are you... upset?" Claire asks cautiously.

"What? NO!" I squeak. "I just feel dumb for not noticing. I've been so caught up in enjoying all the time we've been spending together."

"Well, I'm ecstatic for you, and Charli didn't mean anything negative by it. There's just a t-shirt on the loveseat, and a faint smell of his cologne in the air."

"Oh, that makes sense." I nudge the popcorn bowl, sliding it away from myself with a grimace.

"Are you okay?" Charli asks, taking the buttery offender away from me.

My stomach churns from the smell alone. "Yeah, I just think I have a stomach bug or something. I've been sick off and on all week."

"Interesting," Claire hums.

"Very." Charli passes her a knowing look.

"What?!" I spit, annoyed by their secrecy.

"When was your last cycle?" Claire asks, clinically.

"M-my what?" I freeze.

"Your period," Charli clarifies, like I'm twelve.

"I know what she meant!" I snap back. "I just, I don't know. I'm irregular, so it's hard to keep track. Probably a month or two."

"Road trip!" Charli squeals, jumping up from the couch and grabbing her keys. Claire follows her to the door, giggling. "Are you coming?"

"Uh... sure?" My response is more of a question.

As if I have a choice...

We make the three-minute drive to the drugstore in silence. I sit in the backseat, bewildered, as they exchange conspiratorial looks. After parking, they drag me inside to the back of the store. My eyes almost jump out of their sockets when we come to a stop.

"Pregnancy tests?!" I whisper-yell at them.

Their shit-eating grins mirror each other. Charli nods rapidly, bouncing on her toes with excitement.

"Trust us." Claire nods too.

Grumbling, I grab a random box and trudge to the self-checkout.

When we get back to my apartment, I immediately go to the bathroom.

The minutes may as well be years as we gather around, staring a hole into my kitchen counter where the little plastic test lays. When the timer on my phone goes off, my heart stops. As I look at the result, Charli and Claire grab hold of each other and erupt into a chorus of squeals. I'm numb to the chaos around me as I stare at the two unmistakable pink lines. My blood feels like it's frozen in place, yet somehow my pulse is louder than it's ever been in my life. Gripping the edge of my counter, I wobble as my knees nearly buckle under weight of my new reality. There's a vice around my chest. No matter how desperately I try, my lungs won't work.

Oh God, how is Jude going to react?

"Hey," Claire says, stepping up to my right. "Breathe with me." She inhales deeply, through her nose. Charli stands at my other side and rubs my back as I copy Claire.

Swallowing down my initial panic, I turn around and face my best friends. "What do I do? I-I can't lose Jude. But I'm keeping this baby. I want to be a mom so bad."

"Well, you have to tell him. Sooner, rather than later,"

Claire states in a matter-of-fact tone.

"She's right." Charli nods.

"Well, he'll be back soon. If you guys don't hear from me ever again, I probably ran away and assumed a new identity."

"Hey, now." Charli's mouth forms a firm line. "If he's not happy about this, so be it. But don't psych yourself out. Give him a chance."

I nod slightly. "You're right. I-I need to get myself ready. You two go on."

"We're just a call away, if you need anything don't hesitate." Claire wraps me in a warm hug, when Charli joins in I nearly lose my composure. As soon as the door clicks behind them, I collapse onto the kitchen floor and start to sob.

Careless. I'm stupid and careless.

It's not that I'm upset about the result itself. Hell, I've had baby fever since Charli told me she was pregnant with Ivy. But Jude and I have just fallen into a comfortable rhythm. We haven't even officially moved in together, let alone talked about kids.

I rise to my feet when the door opens. He's home sooner than I was prepared for and I haven't even started figuring out how to tell him. At the sight of my disheveled appearance, he rushes over and wraps me in a hug.

"What's wrong, Candy?" His voice is soft, filled with worry.

"Hey, I n-need to tell you s-something." I stammer,

fidgeting with the sleeves of my sweater as he pulls back.

His muscles tense as he goes eerily still. "Caroline." My name is a mere breath as it leaves his mouth. He leans away from me, chest heaving. "Is that what I think it is?"

Shit. I left the test on the counter.

His widened eyes roam over my face, begging for answers. My gaze falls to the floor unable to say the words he desperately awaits. Dread sends shivers down my spine, preparing for heartbreak. I let out a surprised squeak as Jude drops to his knees in front of me.

He lifts the hem of my shirt, placing his hands on my exposed stomach. "You're havin' my baby?" He leans down and presses his lips against my midriff. Giving his full attention to me, he blinks away tears. "We're gonna be a family?"

Awestruck and speechless, I can only offer a trembling nod in return.

"I love you." He stands and peppers my face with kisses. "Fuck. I-I need you." His feverish lips trail down my neck. "Let me properly thank you for such an amazing gift."

As he lifts me into his arms, a small laugh of disbelief bubbles out of me. "You're not mad?" My lip wobbles, still warring with uncertainty.

"Mad? We'd have about fifteen babies already if we hadn't missed out on so much time."

"That's *waaay* too many." I giggle as he gently lays me on the bed.

"Well, we'll start with this one, and get to work practicin' for number two... right now." He leans over me and nibbles my neck, dragging his nose along my heated skin. "If you're up for it."

"Always." I pull my shirt over my head and lace my hands through his hair. Slowly, his mouth begins its descent, pausing at my navel. He spends a moment there, trailing featherlight kisses around my belly.

His excitement has quieted my internal screams, and it's about to fill our night with actual lust filled ones. At this rate, we'll have to move because the neighbors are bound to complain. Let them.

Tonight, we're celebrating.

CHAPTER 29

Jude

The blaring of Caroline's ringtone startles me. Shit, we were up so late, I know she must be exhausted. Slowly, so I don't disturb her, I grab the phone off the nightstand and answer it.

"Mornin'," I croak.

"Hi there! Glad to hear you stuck around," Charli's warm voice filters through the speaker. "She was panicking when we left last night. I just wanted to make sure everything was alright."

"Oh yeah, we'll be over later and tell everyone the news. I can't wait for Ivan to kick my ass." A rough laugh fights it's way out of my dry throat.

"He likes you more than he lets on. He also loves his grand babies and this might win you some brownie points." I can hear her grin, she's obviously excited which calms some of my nerves.

"You reckon so?"

"Yeah, you'll be fine. We'll see you guys in a little bit."

The line cuts off as she hangs up.

Hopefully she's right about Ivan. I guess we'll find out soon enough.

Caroline stirs next to me, and I pull her against my chest. She's warm and soft and *mine*. To think that this gorgeous, sassy, brilliant woman is in love with *me* still blows my mind—and soon we'll have our own little family. While I should probably be freaking out, I'm more at peace than I can ever remember.

I rub my chin against the top of her head as she nuzzles into me. I may not have much to offer her, or our unborn baby, but I have plenty of love to go around—which is more than I can say for my own upbringing. Even now, my mother has taken to fully ignoring me.

"Good morning," Caroline rumbles and lays a kiss on my bare chest. "Did I dream that my phone was ringing?"

"No, it did. I answered... hope that's okay?."

"Yeah, of course." She tilts her head up and kisses me softly.

"It was just Charli, checking in to make sure you were good. I told her we would be over in a bit to tell everyone the news." I chew my lip ring, which catches her attention.

"Hey, it'll be okay." She puts her hand on my cheek. "Nicky loves you, and Dad... well, he's not so bad. I promise."

"I know, I just don't like doin' it all backwards." I blow out an anxious breath. "I know he's fixin' to give me hell for knockin' you up before gettin' married and all that mess. Not that I don't wanna make an honest woman outta you." I dart my gaze around the room, looking at anything but her.

"Jude, it's fine. He'll be fine. Most importantly, *we'll* be fine. I don't even care about getting married." She brushes her thumb against my lower lip.

I look directly at her. "Because you don't want to change your name?"

Her breath catches. This time it's her attention that shifts away. "I... it's dumb, I know it is. But my last name is just—"

"Hey." Cutting off her rambling, I grab her chin and turn her face to mine, pulling her in for a tender kiss. "Wanna know a secret?" I ask against her lips. Swallowing hard, she nods. "Sean asked me at our first fight night if I would take your last name. At first I thought he was bein' silly, but it didn't change my answer."

She sucks in a sharp breath and blinks rapidly. "Wh-what did you say?"

"I said yes, without a doubt. So when I eventually get the balls to ask, I hope you'll take that into consideration before you answer." After another quick kiss, I roll out of bed. "Let's get ready. The sooner we get this over with, the better."

"Ugh, five more minutes? You tired me out last night." She groans, rolling over and sprawling out.

Of course I'm going to let her rest, she needs it. So, when her eyes drift closed, I busy myself with cleaning up the mess from her movie night. She never had the chance to do it once I got my hands on her. When I enter the kitchen I come to an abrupt stop. The pregnancy test still sits undisturbed on the counter, like a precious artifact on display. With a lump in my throat I pick it up and fight back my tears. Holding it in my hand makes this all *feel* real. I need to frame it and find the perfect spot on the wall, where I can see it every day—a permanent reminder. For the time being, I slip it securely into the top drawer of the nightstand on—what has become—my side of the bed.

Heading across the hall to start the shower, I pull out a comfy outfit I know my Candy Girl will love. Once the room is steamy, I enter the bedroom and scoop her up. I nearly melt on the spot when her sleepy face breaks into a precious smile. I carry her to the shower, gently setting her down. Fortunately—even if we don't start that way—we end up naked most nights, so sweet little moments like this are easy to accommodate. I lather up a loofah and scrub her body down, letting my hands wander and get lost in her curves. I showed my appreciation to *all* of her last night, and she enjoyed *every* inch of me. But now, I'm fighting the burning desire to press her into the wall and have my way with her.

I'll never get tired of the way she feels, or how beautifully she breaks for me.

While I resist the urge to make a mess of her, I do give in to my need to kiss her silly. As our mouths explore each other, I wrap my arms around her and slip my soapy hands down her back, grabbing hold of her ass as she presses into me. Her fingers trail down my front and grip my throbbing cock. She glides her thumb across the tip and flicks my piercing, knowing exactly how to drive me to the brink of insanity.

She can't get enough of me, either.

She trembles when I slip two fingers inside her as she strokes me with the most delicious grip. We've learned each other's bodies so well that we're masters at these quick sessions. In mere minutes we can get each other off, but that doesn't decrease the satisfaction either of us feel. I savored her for hours last night, so this isn't about time, it's about a bone-deep need we share for each other.

Encouraged by her moans, and the feel of her orgasm gripping my fingers, I hiss with my release. My cum lands on her stomach, hand, and the shower floor before washing away an instant later. She lets out a naughty giggle and kisses me before turning the water off. We help each other dry off and head back to the bedroom to get dressed.

Her pink sweat pants and my AC/DC hoodie have never looked so good. She's absolutely radiant. I know they say pregnant women glow, and man does she ever. I just found out about this pregnancy and it's defied rationality, having somehow made me love her even more. White-hot desire surges through me at the thought of her cradling our child while heavily pregnant with another.

Hello breeding kink, nice to meet you.

I shake it off and pick Cannoli up. "Shall we?" I ask, motioning to the door.

She follows me outside, and frowns at my bike. "I guess I can't really ride with you for the next... eight or so months." An adorable pout overtakes her face.

"We can still go on slow rides for a bit, until our little bean gets too big. Besides, we have Cannoli with us today, and she can't ride on the bike. We'll get us a little family SUV or somethin'."

"Juuuuuuude," she whines, "you can't say cute things like that and expect me not to break down in tears." Her eyes glisten.

"I'm sorry. I can be an ass if you'd prefer?" I tease playfully.

"Just get in the damn car, I'm also forbidding you from spending any more time with Nicky. Smart ass." She rolls her eyes and slides into the driver's seat.

Laughing at her adorable temper tantrum, I squeeze into the passenger seat. With Cannoli in my lap, I buckle in, reaching over to lay my hand on her thigh. The tiniest lift of her mouth gives her away. She can't stay upset with me, and I know it.

Our drive is short, but my nerves multiply by the minute. I'm a tightly wound ball by the time we pull up at Nikolai's house. Everyone is already here, and I mean *everyone*. Ivan, Claire and Theo—even Bailey and Sean's vehicle is parked out front.

"Huh, I guess Charli was in charge of invites today."

Caroline shrugs.

My stomach is filled with lead. I know Nikolai will be excited, he already feels like a brother to me. Charli is a giant sweetheart and obviously already knows, same with Claire. Theo is generally easy going and non-confrontational, so I'm sure he'll be as neutral as ever. I'm not so confident about the others, the anticipation has me shaking in my boots, quite literally.

"Ahhhh! There they are, and they brought Cannoli!" Charli beams as she greets us, a bit too enthusiastically.

"Hi," I grit out through clenched teeth as we step through the front door.

"Hey everyone!" Caroline says brightly, "before we head to the restaurant, Jude and I have something to tell you." She takes my hand and I nearly faint.

Man up, Jude.

Taking a deep breath, I lift my chin and steady myself. "We're pregnant." I lock eyes with Ivan and suffocate on the three syllables.

My heart almost stops as the room falls to silence, but It doesn't take long until Nikolai claps, shattering the uncertain tension. Claire and Charli join him—as if they didn't already know. Bailey and Sean are all grins, and Theo's face is soft, filled with warmth.

And then there's the storm cloud brewing in the corner.

Ivan is silent, his face gives nothing away. He stands, slowly and makes his way over to us. "Jude, would you please come with me for a moment?" He asks, tone flat and unreadable.

Nodding, I release my crushing grip on Caroline's hand and follow him to the backyard, nearly pissing myself with every agonizing step.

"Have a seat." He gestures to the umbrella covered picnic table.

Nodding, I slowly sit on the bench staring at the wooden boards of the tabletop as he takes the spot across from me. Silently, I wait as he drums his fingers on the tabletop and stares off into the distance.

Several minutes pass until he finally speaks up. "You planning on sticking around, or are you going to make a fool of my Solnyshko?" He works his jaw, piercing me with a stern look.

"Sir, I know you don't like me, and you have every—"

"Enough of that." He waves his hand, silencing me. "I like you fine enough. Won't lie and say I'm thrilled about how quickly this has happened, but you're here regardless and I can respect that. Don't make me regret this."

"I'm not plannin' on goin' anywhere. I really do love her. Always have." I subconsciously rub the spot on my chest where her name lives.

"I believe you. Your eyes don't lie. The way you look at her like she's the only woman in the universe is pure and true. You had that same love-struck look all those years ago. It's a shame what life has done to the two of you... Just don't let her down, fate has done enough of that." Standing from his seat, he steps up to me and opens his arms. My brain misfires as he wraps me in a hug. "You're stuck with us now, Boy. No more of this 'Sir' nonsense, Pop will do just fine. Good habit for when my sweet Malish comes." He pulls back with a rare smile on his face and walks back into the house, leaving me flabbergasted. While I doubt he'll ever exude fatherly affection toward me, I decide to take this win and call today a humongous success.

Once I gather myself and head back inside we all load up and head to the restaurant Nikolai chose.

Five minutes into the drive Caroline takes my hand in hers. "Are you okay? He didn't scare you off, I hope." She asks, shooting a quick glance my way.

"No... he... hugged me and told me I'm stuck with y'all." I let out a relieved sigh.

"What?! That's... wow. Not what I expected." She snorts. "He's still got some surprises up his sleeve. Welcome to the family, Big Guy." The warmth of her voice eases my residual nerves.

When we arrive at the family-style Italian restaurant, the staff makes quick work of sliding tables together to accommodate our large party. We effortlessly fall into a natural seating arrangement.

Ivan is seated at the head of the table, between the two toddlers in their highchairs. Charli and Claire—across from each other—are in the end seats so they can tend to their babies. Nikolai and Theo sit next to their wives. Caroline takes a seat next to Nikolai, I'm rounding out the far end next to her with Bailey across from me and

Sean sandwiched between him and Theo.

I expected some chaos trying to figure it out but there wasn't even a conversation needed. Everyone just seems to know where they fit. For the first time, I feel like I *belong*. Hope is a dangerous, foolish thing, but right now, I'm letting it flow through me freely.

Our waitress makes her rounds and takes everyone's drink order before excusing herself. When she returns, we make quick work of ordering half the menu.

We're still savoring the garlicky goodness of complimentary breadsticks when our platters arrive. Spaghetti and meatballs, lasagna, chicken parmesan, the spread is glorious. I'm practically salivating, fork in hand, as Nikolai raises his lemonade.

"To family." He looks around the table, as we all raise our glasses in return. "I love all of you, and I'm so excited to be an uncle again." He smiles brightly at Caroline, then at me.

"To family." We echo in unison.

Dishes are passed around the table as we serve ourselves. Caroline stares down at her plate, frustration flickering across her face.

"Nausea?" I ask, wrapping my arm around her.

"It looks so good but just thinking about it makes me feel sick." She huffs.

"I wish I could say it gets better," Claire grumbles.

"I'm just glad I know *why* I've been so sick recently. But that doesn't make it suck any less." She continues to glare at her food.

"Solnyshko, your mother had horrible morning sickness with you too," Ivan says as he cuts up one of his meatballs and slips a bite to Henderson. "Sweets were the only thing she could tolerate for the first couple of months."

"So she had a sweet tooth from conception." Bailey laughs from across the table.

"Her sweet tooth is still doin' just fine. She devoured her waffles yesterday without a second thought." I lean over and kiss her temple.

"Have you moved in, then?" Ivan asks, raising an eyebrow.

"Uh, well... not officially," I stumble over my words. "We haven't really... talked about that yet."

"Well, surely you two should be living together by the time my Malish arrives." He slips a bit of meatball to Ivy.

"Dad, there are a lot of things we still need to figure out. That's one of them, but we literally found out less than twenty-four hours ago. Can we have a little time?" Caroline snaps.

"He's not wrong though." Nikolai pats her leg. "You two know if you need *anything,* just ask. We're all here for you. Everyone at this table, except Bailey and Sean, has been through this. Sorry guys." He shrugs.

"All good." Bailey chuckles.

Sean's shoulders shake with his silent laughter as he sucks in a spaghetti noodle.

"You'll also need... appropriate transportation." Ivan's mouth pulls into a flat line.

"We know, Dad." Caroline rolls her eyes. "We're not kids. Sure, this wasn't planned, but we're both elated and excited about this little surprise." She lays her hand on her stomach and smiles softly.

"Oh, I can't wait!" Charli wiggles in her seat. "I get to love on another baby that I don't have to birth."

"I don't know, we've been doing a lot of... practicing lately. If I had it my way you'd be Caroline's pregnancy buddy." Nikolai leans in and playfully bites at her neck.

"You're relentless!" Charli slaps at his arm while fighting a giggle.

"Goodness, I'm fine just having Henderson," Claire says, looking at Theo.

"I'd love another, but my Darling makes the rules." Theo chuckles. "But you two made an absolutely precious baby girl. I'm sure any future Koval babies will be just as adorable."

"Speaking of Koval babies." I clear my throat and straighten in my seat as everyone's attention shifts to me. "Our little one's last name will be Koval, not Carlisle. No hyphenation. None of that nonsense."

Caroline turns toward me. Her chin quivers, and she swallows a sob as tears trail down her cheeks. "Jude, we... I-I don't know what to say."

"You don't have to say a thing, Candy." I cup her face in my hand. "This is your family. My mom doesn't even answer my calls or texts anymore. I tried to call her earlier and she sent me straight to voicemail." I kiss her forehead and she nods against my lips.

"Well, fuck your mom," Nikolai spits.

Ivan sputters and covers Ivy's ears. "Words, Nicky!"

"Sorry, but seriously, this is *your* family now too, Loverboy. You signed an eighteen-year contract with your dick." He laughs.

"Gross. You're ridiculous." Caroline elbows him playfully.

The rest of the table sounds off in a chorus of laughs.

I let myself enjoy their company, unfiltered and free. It feels almost unreal, but for the first time I can breathe, and truly feel their overflowing love.

CHAPTER 30

Jude

What a whirlwind the last few weeks have been. Caroline and I found a surprisingly affordable house to rent and have spent all of our free time packing. Despite her general exhaustion, she's vibrant and happier than I've ever seen her.

We're sitting in the waiting room at the OBGYN's office. She's leaning against me, phone in hand, scrolling through an online baby boutique while I play with her hair. It's our first appointment, our first chance to see baby K. To say that we're excited would be an understatement.

"First one?" The heavily pregnant woman sitting across from us asks.

"Oh, yeah. We're excited." Caroline smiles brightly at her.

"You're lucky your husband actually shows up. Mine's probably out playing golf with his buddies," she responds bitterly.

"Oh... uh. Thank you?" Caroline replies, her brows knitting in confusion.

I don't miss the fact that she didn't correct her. "Husband" sounds so natural, like the title belongs to me. Some day I'll earn it.

"Koval?" A woman around our age appears in the doorway and asks.

We stand and follow her back to an exam room. She helps Caroline get situated on the table and does a quick check-in before leaving.

When the doctor enters the room and starts setting up, excitement buzzes through me. Caroline takes my hand and squeezes as the gel is spread across her stomach. The screen changes as the doctor zeroes in on a tiny little figure breaking through the darkness. She smiles softly at us and clicks through the measurements she needs to take.

"Congratulations, baby looks to be measuring around eight weeks. Everything seems to be going well so far. Would you like to hear the heartbeat?" She asks, as if anyone would ever say no.

We nod and she presses a button on the machine. As a steady thump filters through the room, I fight to hold back tears. Caroline peels her attention from the screen and looks at me with pure love in her eyes, squeezing my hand tighter.

"Jude." Her chin trembles. "That's our baby. Listen." Tears slip down her cheeks.

"I hear it, Sweetness." My own tears win the battle and

break free.

We watch the screen together intently as the doctor continues her measurements. I pull Caroline's hand to my face and gently kiss her palm as we silently weep together. Forget the pregnancy test. *This* is what makes reality hit me like a runaway train.

I'm going to be a father... one who stays.

Our baby will be here in late April—almost seven months to go. I know they're going to fly by once we get settled into our new home. We're handed a folder with the ultrasound pictures and schedule our next appointment on our way out of the office.

"Can you believe there's a life growing in here?" Caroline says from the driver's seat, one hand rubbing her belly as she fastens her seatbelt.

"I know, you're extraordinary and I love you so much." I lean over and kiss her cheek before buckling myself in. "Are we going to show everyone? Or do you need some rest first?"

"I'm way too excited to relax. We'll head home to get Cannoli, then go show everyone, but thank you for looking out for me."

"Well then, let's head to Nicky's. I'll let everyone know." I pull out my phone and fire off a few texts to our family chat to let them know we're on our way.

It still gives me pause. I'm surrounded by people who love me, and I honestly love each of them just as much. There are no conditions, except treating the goddess to my left like the gift she is. Needless to say, I'm more than willing to hold up my end of the deal.

The best part about our family is that most of us have been through hell, and we hold each other even closer because of it.

By the time we make it to Nikolai's house, everyone else is already here. Most of them are legitimately one or two nights away from being official residents anyway. Honestly, Nikolai and Charli wouldn't have it any other way.

"Pictures! Show me!!" Charli bombards us as we walk through the front door. Ear-piercing squeals of joy rush out of her when she opens the folder. Waving the sonogram printout like a winning lottery ticket, she bounces over to the others. "Look at my little niece or nephew!"

"Let me see my Malish." Ivan takes the picture and examines it. The softness of his face is the sweetest sight.

A foolish part of me was afraid that he'd have some sort of resentment toward our baby. The love in his trembling smile squashes that fear on the spot

Caroline flashes a vibrant grin at him. "We've been calling them 'Baby K' until we know whether we're having a boy or girl."

"Sweet Malish," he says with a warm tone, running a finger over the silhouette. "I'm the luckiest Pop. May I keep this?" Blinking back tears, he holds the print to his chest. "I can put it next to Ivy's in my album."

"Of course, we had a copy made for everyone," I respond with a nod.

"I hope you're going to hang one at work!" Bailey

speaks up, peeking over Charli's shoulder to get a better look. Sean shakes his head with a smile.

"Hennie is going to have another built-in best friend!" Claire's eyes glitter with excitement.

We gather around and mingle for a while until it gets late.

Everyone but us heads home, so we move to the living room. Nikolai has finally bought a bigger couch. It may take up most of the free space, but the sectional easily seats six people, which is a vast improvement over his previous sofa. Ivan props himself up in the—also new—recliner, kitty-corner from us, with Ivy in his lap. She's his own personal piece of Velcro and someday, very soon, a little part of our love will be nestled in his lap beside her.

Caroline sets herself up on the end of the couch, leaning against the arm as she lays her legs across my lap. My hands move instinctively, already kneading her calves. She's been a rock star lately, juggling all the packing and everything we've encountered at work. I'm just glad she loves being pampered because I'll take any opportunity I can to spoil her. When I notice Ivan watching, I pull my hands from her legs.

"Relax. You already got her pregnant. You think I'm going to yell at you for showing her affection? Go on." He lets out a soft laugh, waving a hand.

My cheeks heat and I nod, returning my hands to her calves.

"Have you guys talked about names yet?" Charli asks.

She's almost as excited as we are and it's adorable.

"Oh, we have!" Caroline perks up. "I really want to name him Oscar *so* bad if he's a boy!"

I laugh and shake my head. "Only if I can call him Ozzy as a nickname."

"Ugh, the compromise." She playfully rolls her eyes.

"And what if you give me a granddaughter?" Ivan asks, eyes glittering with emotion.

"Jude wants to name her Iris, I think it's cute. Ivy and Iris sound like perfect partners in crime." Caroline tips her head toward me with a warm smile.

"They'd definitely get up to some shenanigans. Pop would have his hands full with babysitting duties." Nikolai laughs.

"I'll never tire of my Mladentsy. The four legged ones included." Ivan's eyes crinkle from the grin stretched across his face.

"The song 'Iris' means a lot to me. I think it would make me love her even more, as if that's even possible." I place my hand on Caroline's stomach and she lays hers over it.

"I'm just excited to have more little monsters running around. I might mess around and build a playroom. Everybody loves a ball pit!" Nikolai lets out a hearty chuckle.

"The dogs would lose their minds." Charli giggles.

Caroline yawns and repositions herself, turning to lay against me. My heart rate kicks into overdrive with her head against my chest.

Feeling my muscles tense, she tilts her head up to look at me. "What's wrong? Did I do something?" Her face taut with worry.

"Heavens, Boy. Just relax already," Ivan grumbles.

"I'm sorry. I didn't grow up in such an affectionate family. I love how open y'all are, it's just takin' some gettin' used to, that's all." I look around at each of them, how easily they fall into one another. Even Navy and Cannoli are curled up together on the little bed in the corner.

Get out of your head, Jude.

Looking into Caroline's warm, welcoming eyes, I pull her into me and kiss her tenderly. "I love you," I tell her proudly.

"I love you, too, Big Guy." As she nuzzles her cheek against my chest, I meet Ivan's gaze again.

What I find in his expression is comforting. He may still have some residual anger. But he loves how happy Caroline is with me, that's easy to see.

"Are you guys staying here tonight? You're more than welcome to," Nikolai asks with a yawn, "I'll make breakfast in the morning, but I need my beauty sleep."

"I think we will," Caroline mutters sleepily against me.

"Why not? I miss you kids," Ivan says from his spot in the recliner, "I'll put the munchkin to bed. You all go on."

Nikolai and Charli waste no time heading to their room. I take a minute to slip out from under Caroline and take Cannoli outside for a potty break.

When I return, she's fast asleep, already drooling on the couch. I don't hesitate to scoop her up, kissing her cheek.

"You're good to her, I'm sorry for not seeing it sooner," Ivan murmurs from his recliner, "she deserves all the love you have to give. And *you* deserve hers in return, whether you believe it or not."

"Th-thank you... Pop." A lightness washes over my body as he gives me a soft smile.

We're all gathered around the table as Nikolai cooks the fillings for breakfast burritos. Ivy stands at his side watching intently. He stops occasionally and hands her a bit of scrambled egg, which she devours instantly. Eventually, she's had her fill and wobbles her way over to us.

"Sing!" She throws her arms up at me, asking to be held.

She's heard me serenading Caroline—and Baby K—a time or two, and has started demanding that I sing to her, too. It's precious and I wouldn't dream of denying her.

Propping her up on my knee, I clear my throat and start on the words to "Let it Be" by The Beatles. She flashes a gleeful grin my way, her dimples—courtesy of Nikolai's genes—popping into view. We sway back and forth in the chair.

"Bet beeee," she babbles along and my heart swells.

When we've concluded our breakfast concert, I look over at Caroline and see that she's crying next to me. I put Ivy down and take her hand in mine.

"What's wrong?" My voice is soft, filled with concern. I'm not sure what has her so upset and I need to fix it.

"You're going t-to be s-such a great d-daaaaad." She sobs, turning my way to bury her face in my shoulder.

"Oh. I thought I did something wrong."

"NO! You're s-so amazing. My s-stupid hormones can't handle it!" Her voice gets caught in her throat.

I just hold her while she cries through it. Nikolai has a shit-eating grin on his face, one that says he knows exactly what I'm going through. Charli, on the other hand, has a humorous expression on hers. She's well aware of the ups and downs of pregnancy hormones, and is trying to hide how much enjoyment she's getting out of seeing Caroline fall to pieces.

Ivan's face is filled with sympathy, but I'm not sure which one of us he actually feels sorry for.

A few muffled whimpers signal the end of her mini-breakdown, and she leans away. I kiss her softly. "You're so adorable."

She folds her arms and huffs. "You know I have a weak spot for your singing. Pairing it with my niece fawning over you and expecting me to keep it together? That's unrealistic... and rude!"

"Hey now, Ivy loves it, I can't tell her no."

"Don't you dare!" Ivan says with a small laugh.

"Dad! I liked it better when you hated Jude!" Caroline

groans. "Whose side are you on?"

"Well, he can sing quite well, and it makes my two favorite girls happy. So..."

"Unbelievable. Jude, we're going to have to set some ground rules. At least until I stop crying over *everything*." She throws her head back and slouches in her seat.

"I'm not sure that'll ever happen, sadly. I was a mess my whole pregnancy," Charli adds.

"Great!" Caroline throws her hands up dramatically.

"She was so precious. I loved holding her all day while she sobbed over little things," Nikolai confirms. "The cutest was one time Navy went into the nursery and curled up next to the crib, and she completely lost it. Said he knew his new sissy would be here soon. Immediate waterworks."

"It was cute, okay?" Charli grumbles.

"And so were you, my Muse. I love you," he responds, winking her way.

"I love you too, Killer. But don't push your luck." She scowls back at him.

Nikolai finishes making the burritos and serves us all a plate of hash browns to go with them. We eat and enjoy lighthearted conversation. When we've had our fill, we move to the living room and Nikolai puts a movie on the TV.

Our Saturday is spent together, as a family.

CHAPTER 31

Caroline

Pregnancy is for the birds. Everything I've read told me the symptoms get better after the first trimester. Wrong. They're all liars. Filthy, good-for-nothing liars. I've been a miserable, cranky mess for months. Jude deserves a vacation—and a medal—at this point.

Shit. I'm going to cry again just thinking about how great he is.

No. Hold it together.

My stomach is in knots as we pull up to Nikolai's house. Naturally, he and Charli opted to throw us a baby shower. We had the OBGYN seal the folder and only Charli knows Baby K's gender. I worked with Nikolai to plan her shower for Ivy, so she's been over the moon with excitement planning mine.

Breathe, don't cry.

"You doin' alright, Candy?" Jude squeezes my thigh from the passenger seat.

"No," I choke out around the lump in my throat.

"We can take a minute, give you some time to catch your breath and mentally prepare." His thumb traces circles on my leg. "Nobody here is gonna be upset with you for gettin' emotional. We all love you."

"Stoooooop," I wail, "don't be so amazing. I need you to be... less nice."

"Come on then. It's rude to keep people waiting." Unbuckling his seatbelt, he hops out of the car and makes his way around to open my door. My heart still does a little swoop every time.

Taking his hand, I hoist myself out of the car. At almost thirty weeks pregnant, I feel like I've doubled in size. The cold winter air nips at my cheeks on the way to the house. Smoke billowing out of the chimney fills the air with a nostalgic scent that reminds me of trips to the cabin. It's almost like having Mom here to celebrate with us. Baby K is due in April, right around her birthday. Sadly, that means we won't be making our annual trip to stay there. We haven't missed a year since she passed. This is probably the best reason, but it still hurts my heart.

"You're absolutely radiant!" Charli says cheerfully as we enter the house. "Everyone is placing their bets now, come on!" She leads us through the kitchen and into the living room.

Beautiful balloon displays line the walls. A banner draped above the recliner reads "Hello cu-tea" with little smiling boba cups on it. The snack table has cookies that say "boba girl" and "boba boy" I'm sure she had them custom made. If this isn't the most thoughtful baby shower ever, I don't know what is. She even got blue and pink chocolate-covered strawberries and I want to cry just looking at them.

Nikolai is manning the "betting box" taking everyone's guesses with a giant grin on his face. Next to him is a gift table piled high with bags and boxes. We didn't make a large registry, because there's not much we *need*. Jude and I went to work buying most of what we wanted as soon as we got moved into our new place. We have a beautiful nursery set and an entire closet full of goodies already. Our family came through and overdid it anyway, unsurprisingly.

"This is for you!" Claire comes up to us, holding a bag. "It's a shirt for the shower, go change!"

Theo has a playful smirk on his face. Great, If *he* thinks it's funny, I can only imagine what's on this shirt.

I waddle down the hall to the bathroom to get changed.

When I pull the shirt out of the bag a snort escapes me. There's a boba cup on the front, right over my bump, and the text on top says, "boba on board".

I shuffle back to the living room and everyone whoops in excitement. Charli ushers me to the recliner and Jude stands at my side.

Nikolai cups his hands around his mouth to broadcast his voice through the room at an unnecessary volume calling out, "Okay, everyone, It's gift time. Then what we really came for. Get your bets in before the reveal for a chance to win!"

"I'll go first," My father declares, lifting three bags off the table. "I got you each something, and then a gift for my sweet Malish."

I pull the tissue paper out of my bag and giggle. Next to me, Jude does the same. We exchange a look and pull out matching "date night" coupon books. Each one says, "Good for one sleepover with Pop."

"I know how tiring it can be, so don't ever be afraid to cash those in. Now, open the real gift." He nudges the large bag at my feet. When I peer inside I immediately burst into tears. My watery eyes glide up to his face.

"D-dad. How?" I pull the familiar quilt out of the bag and press it to my cheek.

"Your mother kept that at the cabin, I maaaaay have made a special trip out there after you announced your pregnancy. I know how much it means to you, so I had it dry-cleaned and now you can pass it on. It was hand-made by your grandmother for you. No matter how sad you were, it always dried your tears. I only hope its magic still holds true." His voice cracks.

I launch myself—as fast as currently possible—at him for the biggest hug. He chuckles tearily against my shoulder. "I love you, Solnyshko."

"I love you so much, Dad. Thank you for always being there for me, through everything." I sob into his chest.

"Well that's going to be hard to top," Bailey jokes from his seat on the couch.

"Yeah, who wants to follow *that*?" Theo agrees with an adoring warmth to his voice.

"Well," Charli interjects, "I planned the shower, bu-uuut I also pulled some strings and got this super famous, very handsome artist to paint a piece for the nursery." She winks at Nikolai, who blows her a kiss. "I also *definitely* bought a bunch of cute little jammies." She hands me a large bag stuffed to the brim.

"Thank you so much, Girlie. For everything." I smile warmly, pulling her into a crushing hug.

"Okay, well that's more like it." Bailey laughs before standing to grab a large box from the table.

Sean comes to his side, a large smile pulling at his face. "This is from both of us."

Jude places his hand on my shoulder as I tear at the beautifully wrapped box. A gasp escapes me as I admire the beautiful bassinet. "Guys! This is the one I wanted. I didn't even put it on the registry because it's expensive."

"We're just good like that." Bailey shrugs, pulling Sean into him and kissing his cheek. Their adoring smiles make my chin wobble.

Damn it, stop crying already!

"I suppose that leaves us," Claire says as she stands, making her way to the table with Theo close behind. "I hope you find this helpful. I sure wish I'd had one."

The bag is small and practical, much like Claire and Theo. Inside is a single envelope with a coupon for a prenatal massage. My body tingles at the thought. Every muscle is already so sore *all* the time. Getting a great massage geared toward pregnancy-specific aches and pains sounds heavenly.

"This is amazing! I can feel the peace and relaxation already. Thank you guys!" I stand and wrap them in a hug.

We sit and talk for a while, snacking on cookies and finger sandwiches. Ivy and Henderson are making their rounds getting attention—and nibbles of food—from everyone. The love in the air is palpable.

These are my people and I couldn't imagine a more perfect time.

I'm leaning back in the recliner with Jude sitting at my feet, rubbing my legs, when Charli enters the room.

"Okay, it's time! Has everyone placed their bet?" She looks around and takes note of everyone nodding. "Perfect! So, who's ready to find out if it's a boba boy or a boba girl?" She chuckles and begins passing plastic cups around the room. "One of these cups of bubble tea is dyed pink or blue. We'll go around the room taking sips until someone gets the lucky cup!"

"Me first!" Bailey wiggles excitedly. He punctures the seal with his clear straw and sips. White. His boba is plain white. He pouts, as if he'd expected to get it straight away.

One by one, everybody takes their turn.

Claire's eyes cross as she watches the tea ascend in her straw. White.

Sean grabs a cup, impatiently jabbing the lid and sipping. White.

Theo makes a show of shaking his first, as if it makes a difference. White.

"Oh man, no luck. Let me try!" Nikolai takes a cup from Charli, sipping his—also white—tea. "At least it tastes good." He shrugs, drinking more.

"My heavens, how many are left?" Dad asks. "Let me see one." He punctures the plastic top and inhales, pulling the *white* liquid up the straw.

Okay, I'm onto Charli at this point. She's being way too nonchalant. I won't ruin the fun though. She's put so much love into this.

"Looks like there are only two to go! Would the expecting parents please drink them together?" Jude and I stand as she hands us each a cup.

He's finally caught on. I can see the knowing twinkle in his eye.

We stand facing each other. "On three?" I ask and he nods in agreement.

"One... twooooo..." I yawn, drawing out frustrated groans from our captivated audience. "Sorry, so tired." I flash a coy grin at them before turning back to Jude with a slight tip of my chin. "Three!" I shout and we stick our straws into our cups and suck up the tea inside. The room erupts in cheers immediately. I'm so shocked that it takes a minute for the pink liquid in our straws to register.

"A girl! My Iris." Jude wraps me in an exuberant hug and buries his face in the crook of my neck. His heart thumps wildly in his chest as we share a tear-filled embrace.

Through the chaos and excitement, Nikolai manages

to break off, leaving the room.

Odd.

Nobody else seems to notice, not even Charli. At least, if she does, she doesn't let on.

"Congratulations! She's going to be a precious little angel. I just know it." Claire beams.

"Henderson is going to have his hands full with these two as his best friends." Theo laughs.

"I can already picture all the cute outfits you're going to dress her in," Bailey adds.

Sean leans into him, smiling brightly. "All the bows and glitter. I can't wait to let her and Ivy paint my nails."

"Will everyone come with me please?" Charli interrupts.

We shrug and follow her through the kitchen to meet Nikolai at the garage door.

Nooo.

"So, I know you guys have been saving your asses off to get everything and buy a nice little used SUV." His cheeks heat as he guides us into the garage. "Well, we can't have that. I was going to buy a new car anyway... just didn't think it would be for someone else." He dangles a keyring in front of me, but I'm frozen. Time stands still as I take in the new car behind him.

Not just *any* new car. It's the exact Mazda CX-50 I was fawning over a few weeks ago. We were out at dinner and I was wistfully scrolling through local dealership postings. I loved the style of this one, and Jude loved the forest green paint color. We went and test drove it that afternoon and had our hearts set on it.

Until now, it was a pipe dream. We knew there was no way we could come up with the money in such a short amount of time. But here it is. Shiny and... ours.

"No," I say breathlessly.

"Yuuuup," Nikolai responds. "You need it. I don't *need* a new Corvette. I can buy one next year."

"Nicky." I breathe, still in shock.

"We... we can't," Jude says, swallowing his emotions.

"Shut up, take it you shitheads. I love you and it's honestly not even that expensive. Besides, if Jude has to crawl in and out of that Miata one more time he's going to get stuck in that position." He laughs.

"I love you too," I say, wrapping my arms around him.

He grunts and hugs me in return. With no hesitation, Jude joins in.

"Way to one up everyone, Nikolai." Bailey does his best to sound annoyed, but the admiration in his voice is too loud to hide.

"This is the best family ever." My father's tear-filled voice filters through the room.

When we pull away from our group hug, Jude places his hand on Nikolai's shoulder, their gazes locked on to one another. "I-I don't know how to thank you enough." He chews his lip ring, eyes full of emotion. "You're like a brother to me, man. I've never had someone just *be there*."

"Good. Now it's your turn to give her your gift. Just like we planned. I just threw you a curveball." Nikolai pats him on the back and guides our group back to the living room.

"Your gift?" I tilt my head in question.

"Yeah, before I give it to you, just know that I feel terrible about lyin' to you. Nikolai has been helpin' me the last couple months... with budgeting... by holdin' part of my salary." His eyes dart around, avoiding my crinkled face.

"What? Why did you need to budget? How much money are we talking about? Jude, what's going on?" I question.

"Hey, Parasite. Do me a favor, okay?" Nikolai speaks up behind me, drawing my attention to him. "Don't pee on my floor when you turn around."

I narrow my eyes at him before turning back to Jude. Suddenly, I'm glad Nikolai is behind me. He nearly has to catch me when my knees give out.

"Caroline Diana Koval," Jude starts, looking up at me from where he's knelt. "I really love your last name... will you please share it with me?" The velvet box in his hand holds a gorgeous princess-cut solitaire diamond set on a rose gold band. I couldn't have designed a more perfect ring.

With my hands clasped over my mouth, my gaze drifts to every vibrantly smiling face behind him.

Answer already.

I can't find the words. So, with tear-filled eyes, I nod frantically and extend my hand toward him.

With a sigh of relief, he slips the ring onto my finger

and wraps me in a loving hug. Peppering kisses all over my face, his eyes glimmer with joy.

"You had me worried for a second there," he murmurs against my cheek with a soft chuckle.

"Jude, it's beautiful. I-I love you." I kiss him fiercely, and we melt into one another.

I'm overwhelmed, but so content and thankful for every person here.

But how the hell am I going to manage planning a wedding now too? Time will tell, I suppose.

CHAPTER 32

Jude

Caroline moans loudly, breaking the evening silence in our bedroom. I smile up at her from my seat at the end of our bed. The warming massage oil always gets her. Especially when I really get into the arches of her swollen feet.

"God those big hands are soooooo nice," she breathes out.

"Trust me, I know exactly how much you love them," I purr, kissing her calf before sliding my oiled hands upward. I can practically hear her eyes rolling back as I work her tense muscles.

I'm walking a thin line, and I know it. I do this for her every day, and each time, I'm hard as steel. Her little moans and whimpers aren't inherently sexual, but I'm just a man who loves his woman. She's due in about a month, so our sex life has evolved into a lot of hand jobs and solo sessions. I don't mind though, she's so gorgeous like this.

Crawling up the bed to lay beside her, my hand finds her stomach where—by the feel of it—Iris is practicing her Olympic gymnastics routine.

"She's active tonight." I smile before leaning in for a tender kiss. "I'll fix it."

I slide down the bed, gently pressing my lips against Caroline's belly. When I pull away, I start to sing Iris's song. Like her mother, she seems to love my serenades. The kicks and movements still as I drift into the chorus. Caroline's fingers comb through my hair, scraping gently against my scalp. When I finish the last note and move back up to my pillow, she kisses me hard.

The press of her lips reignites the fire in my veins. "Candy," I warn.

"Yes, Sir?" She breathes against my mouth.

"Keep it up, I dare you." A growl rumbles through me as I nip at her lower lip.

"Or what?" She pulls back and flutters her lashes innocently.

Oh, it's on.

"I just got our daughter to sleep, remember that." I slip my hand between her legs and find her dripping for me. "Well, now... What's all this?" My finger slides through her wetness, slipping into her with ease.

"You're just so sexy when you're being sweet." She moans against my neck.

"Yeah? You like it when I take care of my girls?" I press a second finger into her and start working them steadily.

"Yes." She reaches out, arching into me as much as

possible. "Please I-I need you."

Oh.

"Are you sure that's a good idea? You had contractions last time." My fingers stop as I look into her eyes.

"They were just Braxton Hicks, it's fine." She kisses my chest and slips her hand into my waistband. "I *need* you." She whimpers, playing with the ring at the tip of my aching cock.

"Fuck," I groan, "you're going to ride me, got it? That way if it's too much you can stop." My hips jerk toward her.

In a flash she sits up and discards her—my—shirt.

I sit up, backed against the headboard, and shed my boxers. "Turn around. Ride me in reverse just like this. That way your belly has room to breathe."

She turns to face away from me and takes my cock in her hand. Once we're lined up, she sinks slowly onto me, hissing at the stretch. "Oh God, it's only been a few weeks. How did I forget how amazing this is?" She slides down the last few inches until she's fully seated.

Hungry to feel all of her, my hands slide up and down her body. She doesn't move, but that's fine. I tip my hips and give myself the perfect angle to thrust ever so slightly. She whimpers with each movement and grinds her hips against me. I cup one of her beautifully full breasts and groan at the weight of it, thrusting harder into her. She quivers under my touch and picks up her pace. Eventually, my hands find purchase on her hips, pulling her into me harder with each slam of her ass against me.

We work together, pushing each other closer to the edge until I feel the first flutters of her impending orgasm.

"Fuck, I love you. Lean forward," I demand. "I want to watch your greedy little pussy squeeze my cock while I give you what you want." I pant, holding my orgasm back as she props herself up on her elbows.

She rolls her hips, giving me exactly what I commanded of her. I watch as every inch of my cock slides out of her only to slip back in like it belongs there.

"God, what a magnificent view." I slide my hands over the fullness of her ass, gripping as I thrust into her. "This pussy is mine, made just for me." I spank her and she begins to tremble. "You're gonna come all over my cock aren't you, greedy girl? You want my cum don't you?"

"Yes, Sir, please." Ragged moans tear out of her throat as she shatters.

The feeling, the sight, the sounds, it's all too much. I can't hold back the ferocity as I bury myself deep inside her and erupt. My hands tremble as I grip her hips, unmoving.

She's collapsed in front of me, panting heavily. "God, I've missed that." A small giggle escapes her and I huff out a laugh in return.

"You know we can't be doin' this after Iris is here. Six to eight weeks with no sex til you heal. We gotta do better about fuckin' like rabbits." I shift, helping her off me. "Stay there, I'll be right back." I head to the bathroom and clean myself up, wetting a warm cloth for her.

By the time I return to the bedroom, she's already snoring. With a soft smile on my face I carefully clean her up. She doesn't move a muscle.

Scooting up behind her, I pull the covers over us and bask in her perfection. My hand spreads out over her belly and I feel Iris shifting under my touch. I drift off to sleep with a smile on my face.

I wake up to a cold bed.

Strange.

There are not a lot of situations that have Caroline awake before me these days. Usually it's a quick trip to the bathroom and she curls back into bed. The fact that the mattress next to me has had time to lose her warmth is... weirdly unsettling.

I pad to the kitchen, bare feet dragging against the floor. She's not here either. I scrub my hand down my face and take in the darkness around me.

What time is it?

Blinking away the exhaustion, I focus on the numbers lighting up the screen on our stove.

"Three in the morning," I grumble to the void around me, suddenly aware that Cannoli isn't here either, otherwise she'd be at my feet already.

Don't panic. Maybe they're in the bathroom.

The entire house is dark and quiet, every step feels

like I'm falling into a pit as my stomach churns. Thoughts run rampant through my mind, imagining every worst-case scenario.

I stumble back to the bedroom and grab my phone from the nightstand.

The message notification gives me hope.

She didn't just leave. Everything is okay.

Except the second I read the message, I realize how wrong I am.

Candy: *I tried to wake you, but you were out cold and there wasn't time. I packed up Cannoli, and Claire took her to for the night so she doesn't mess in the house while we're gone. You NEED to come to the ER the SECOND you get this please. My phone is almost dead so I won't be able to answer. Just... please come soon. I need you here with me.*

Fuck, she sent that an hour ago. God... how tired was I? I've been running myself ragged with all of the last-minute preparations. Iris isn't due for a few more weeks but it feels like there's not enough time.

Oh no.

Dark thoughts punch me in the gut.

Did I do this?

I should have been gentler with her last night. If I hurt her, or Iris, I don't think I'll ever forgive myself.

Trembling, choking on my nerves, I make the fifteen-minute drive to the hospital in ten. Let a cop try and stop me from making it to my girls, it'd be his funeral.

I look like a mad man as I burst through the emergency room doors. The receptionist takes in my disheveled appearance and flinches as I slap my hands onto the counter.

"Sir, are you okay?" The older woman's voice is calm, despite the absolute horror on her face.

"K-Koval." I sputter. "I need to see her!"

"Sir, Mister Koval has been admitted to the ICU."

Mister?

"Where? Show me." I grit out.

She points toward the wing to my left, giving me quick directions. I can't hear the rest of her explanation over the pounding blood in my ears as I take off. When I reach the ICU another receptionist greets me there. My wild eyes and bedhead—only made worse from pulling on it—give her pause.

"Uh—"

"Koval," I bark, disinterested in her concerned looks.

"Oh." She nods in understanding, rising to her feet. "Let me show you the way." She hurries around her desk, leading me down the hall. "You must be his son-in-law. They told me to expect you."

What?

Rounding a final corner she stops at a closed door. "You're free to enter, since you're family."

As if she would be able to stop me.

I knock softly before swinging the door open. My heart drops into my stomach the second my vision focuses.

No.

In the bed, unconscious, with an endless array of machines and tubes connected to him, lies Ivan. All of the comments make sense now. My blood freezes and I choke on a gasp.

"Jude!" Caroline cries out, moving to stand from her seat at his bedside.

I rush to her side, stopping her. "Candy." I kneel in front of her. "I-I was so worried, what happened?" I pull her against me and turn to address Nikolai and Charli, who are sitting on the far side of the bed.

"Heart attack," Nikolai says with a raw voice, "he... uh. He felt weird, called an ambulance, and they were able to catch it fairly early. It was s-still a pretty b-bad one." He stammers. Charli is silent next to him with her knees tucked under her chin.

"I... fuck." I blow out a breath. "I thought you left me. Then I saw your message and I thought I hurt you, or Iris and I was going to come in here and get the worst news." I swallow hard, sniffling around my tears. "I never considered this. I-is he going to be okay?"

"W-we don't know." Nikolai's voice, lifeless and empty, makes my heart ache.

"Jude, I'm... well, not okay. But I'm not hurt, physically anyway, and Iris is fine." Caroline lays her hand on my cheek, bloodshot eyes as warm and reassuring as she can manage.

My breath catches. "I'm s-sorry for thinkin' so poorly

of you. You're here cryin' and hurt and I let my panic get the better of me."

"Oh, Jude. I'm not ever leaving you again. But please don't leave me either. I need you right now."

I stand and scoop her up, turning to sit in the armchair next to Nikolai. She settles into my lap as her scalding tears soak my chest.

"They resuscitated him and sent him here. It's been almost two hours and we haven't even seen a doctor. But he's stable, just comatose." Nikolai informs me over Caroline's sobs.

"H-he has t-to be o-okayyyy." She wails in my arms.

My own tears drop into her golden hair as I press my cheek against the top of her head. "He will be, Candy. It's three in the morning, and they seem really under-staffed. I saw maybe four nurses total. I imagine doctors are just as scarce."

"B-but he's important!" Her chest heaves as she breathes between sobs.

"I know he is." I sniffle.

"Iris needs her Pop..." her voice trails off.

My heart crumbles at her words as the reality of Iris losing out on his love crashes down on me. My mother wants nothing to do with me anymore, so he's her only grandparent. My Pa was my hero... Iris needs a hero, too.

I tilt my head to the ceiling and let out a strangled cry. Caroline fists the front of my shirt and sobs harder.

We silently let our tears fall, holding each other for a while. Charli and Nikolai have dozed off in the chair across from us, and I can feel the crushing exhaustion trying to pull me under, too.

"Wait, where's Ivy?" I ask.

"With Claire and Theo. They're on standby at Nicky's house with the dogs and babies," Caroline explains around a yawn.

I lean back and pull her close. "Get comfortable, they'll wake us up when the doctor arrives."

She nuzzles into me, sighing softly.

I'm about to finally succumb as I hear a knock on the door.

"Hello, I'm Doctor Cordova with the cardiology team." She introduces herself.

My ears tingle at the sound of her voice. Barely conscious, my mind implodes when she comes into focus.

"Addie?"

CHAPTER 33

Caroline

Jude's muscles tense underneath me. In my exhausted haze, I'm almost sure I heard him talking to... Adalina?

There's no way.

"You.. moved to Seattle, too?" he asks, voice filled with shock.

"Yeah, way better hospitals," the familiar voice replies.

Oh my God. It's her. She still sounds the same.

I need to fake a coma of my own.

Nikolai yawns *loudly*. He was most definitely eavesdropping too. Now that the tension has been broken, I stretch in Jude's lap and roll over. Damn it, she looks good. The petty part of my brain wanted her to also be a heap of failure like *Veronica*. Every bit of her appearance broadcasts success.

Good for her, I guess.

While she greets Nikolai and introduces herself to Charli, I sit up straight. Well, I have to lean back a bit to accommodate the blimp attached to my front, but I'm otherwise upright.

Nikolai and Charli move to join Jude and me on the far side of Dad's bed. When Adalina's eyes land on my stomach, a brief moment of surprise flashes across her face.

That's right, he's mine.

"Hello, everyone. I'm part of the cardiology team. I'm assigned to help monitor Ivan. He had a pretty bad heart attack, and we're not sure when he'll wake up. The ER did run an EKG, MRI, and a cardiac CT and there was no sign of serious damage, so we're effectively in a waiting period right now," she explains.

"And we're supposed to trust you?" I snap.

"Caroline, calm down." Nikolai shoots me a serious look. "I'm sorry about her, as you can imagine her hormones are... worse than usual," he grumble, "We're all very exhausted and fucking distraught on top of it."

"It's okay, I understand. If you'd like, I can have a different member of the team assigned to his care instead." She frowns with pinched brows.

"No. You were always smart and passionate and I know he'll be in great hands," Nikolai reassures her.

I know he's right, and I obviously want my father to get the best care. Guess I'm going to have to swallow my pride.

"He's not wrong," I grunt out.

"You're adorable, do you know that?" Jude leans over and kisses me tenderly on the cheek.

"I'll be by periodically to check on him... but, would it be acceptable to stop by when I'm off the clock too? Just to be here... I-I know how important he is to you..." Averting her eyes, she scrubs her hands together.

Huh, maybe she has a heart hiding somewhere in there.

Nikolai looks at me with a silent question in his teary eyes. With my mouth pulled into a straight line, I nod.

"Yes, you can come whenever you want," I mumble, just clear enough for her to hear.

"Thank you. I'll see you guys in about an hour to check in, that'll be my last round for the day. Try to get some sleep. I won't wake you unless something changes." She gives us a curt nod and turns on her heel, clicking the door shut behind her.

"Well, that wasn't fucking awkward at all," Nikolai groans, collapsing back in his seat.

"Sooooo," Charli says, looking between all of us, "who's going to tell me what *that* was all about?"

"She was one of my so-called friends who disowned me when Mom died." I huff.

"Oooh. That explains *so* much. I've never seen you so blatantly hostile with anyone... well, except Jude." She lets out a snort.

I smirk at his unimpressed face. "Someone is a grumpy boy when he doesn't get enough sleep."

"Which is every damned day." He sighs. "You're lucky I love you, little brat. It was cute seeing you get all possessive though."

"Did not!" I squeak.

"Oh yeah, you were." Charli chuckles. "Even *I* was intimidated by the evil glare you threw at her."

"Well, I'm not sorry about it." I cross my arms. "She should be ashamed of the way she treated me back then. How the hell did they *both* end up in Seattle anyway?"

"Veronica moved here to pursue... *modeling*." Jude shudders. "She cornered me again at fight night, and I interrogated her before telling her I'd rather stick my dick in a meat grinder than go anywhere near her."

"Wow. I am *so* in love with you." I sigh with a dreamy smile.

Charli giggles, half asleep, leaning into Nikolai as his snores echo through the room.

"You're insane, and I love you too." Jude pulls me into his lap and lies sideways in the armchair in an attempt to get comfortable. We're curled into one another, quite precariously.

"If I can get enough sleep, I'll go to the store and get us sleeping bags or something tomorrow. The floor has to be better than... whatever this position is." I laugh softly against his chest.

"As long as I can hold you, so I know you're okay," he mumbles while fighting to stay awake.

"You're here. Of course I'll be okay." I look over at my father lying in the bed, taking in all the tubes and wires. "No matter what happens, we're a family." My tears soak into his shirt as I close my eyes.

My eyes sting. With every ounce of strength I possess I peel them open, blinking until they adjust to the brightness. Jude, Charli, and Nikolai are all fast asleep in positions that would make a professional contortionist envious.

Carefully, I slip off Jude's lap and stretch my cramped muscles. My toes tingle as circulation returns to them.

"Good morning."

I jolt at the sound of Adalina's voice. Whipping around to face her, I inspect her outfit. She's not in her scrubs, so it's been more than an hour. I don't feel any more rested, regardless of how long I slept.

"You guys need to stay in shifts or something, especially you. Sleeping here like this—all the stress—you're going to send yourself into early labor." Her voice is soft—genuine, even.

"How about you pull some strings and get us a bed in here that we can take turns sleeping in?" I sneer at her.

"Best I can do is get you some blankets, unfortunately."

"Then you can shove your concern up your ass," I snap.

"Listen, I-I know we left off on a sour note, and I was too proud back then to admit that Veronica played me." She scrubs her hand over her face. "But I'm sorry. She was very convincing, and I should have never believed her over you."

"You think?" My voice is sharp, but the softness in her face soothes a small part of my burning resentment.

"I'm happy you and Jude worked through it. His love for you was so obvious back then—that's what tipped me off to Veronica's deception." She smiles, looking at my belly. "Is this your first? I have two myself."

My heart tightens at her attempted kindness.

Maybe she's not so bad.

"Yes... and I'm terrified. Not because of Jude—he's literal perfection. I'm just afraid I'll mess it up." I sigh as fresh tears form in my eyes.

How can I cry more?

"Chica, we all mess up. It's how you put it back together that counts."

Oh Addie.

She was always such a bright light. Someone you could count on to talk you into, or out of, anything you needed. I never really considered how much I miss her.

Damn these hormones.

"I'm going to the store to buy sleeping bags. Do... you want to come?" I ask, chewing my lower lip. "I could just use someone to make sure I stay awake behind the wheel. Jude and Nicky are way too tall to sleep in these chairs." I wipe my damp cheeks.

Her face pulls into a grimace. "Actually, I sort of broke the rules letting you all stay here last night. Technically, policy allows *one* immediate family member—so you'd be the only one eligible to stay the night. We don't allow outside bedding of any sort, either."

"So what you're telling me is that we're all supposed to go home, sit around and *wait*?!" My voice rises for a second, until I remember where I am.

"I'm sorry, but yes. I can get in serious trouble if I let it happen again. Since it was a midnight emergency, I was able to convince them that none of you were in the proper condition to drive. That's not going to work now." Her shoulders drop.

"Stupid policies!" I shriek, too upset to care about the others sleeping around us. "What happens if we're not here and... a-and..." I can't say the words, speaking them means admitting the possibility.

"Your mom could stay here all day with him. We allow spouses unlimited visits for elderly patients."

She doesn't know.

"That's not p-possible," I croak, "remember when I disappeared back in the day? There was a car accident..." I don't need to say more. The pain in her expression lets me know she put the pieces together.

"Oh Dios mío. You—and then... Veronica... oh, I'm so sorry. Please can I hug you?" Her arms are spread open, waiting for me to make a move.

I plaster myself against her and sob. She holds me tightly, sniffling and swallowing her own cries.

"I'm glad you two are making up, but could you do it more quietly? Fuck, my *everything* hurts," Nikolai grumbles, awkwardly curled into the fetal position between the wooden arms of the chair he's in.

"You can tell they don't want long-term visitors. These things are barely better than concrete." Charli stands and stretches with a twist.

"Yeah, and you'd know." Nikolai huffs a small laugh, earning a playful swat from Charli.

Addie scrunches her face up, confused.

"I lived in a basement for five years and slept on a concrete floor. Please don't look at me like that, I don't need pity," Charli says, going through the usual speech any time she has to explain her history. "It was a few years ago now, and I don't even think about it anymore. I have so much good in my life." She looks lovingly at Nikolai, then her face falls as her gaze drifts to my father. Her lip wobbles and she curls into Nikolai.

"Well, I'm glad you found such a great family. They've always been full of love and acceptance. Ivan is in great hands here. I know it's not that helpful, but try to think positively." Adalina gives her a small smile.

Rustling behind me catches my attention. Unfolding himself, Jude groans and stands up from the chair.

"Any of y'all ever heard of peace and quiet?" He rubs his eyes.

"Sorry, Big Guy. We gotta get out of here though, visiting hours are apparently over." I turn and softly kiss his cheek.

"I don't like it but I need you to drive, I'm not in any shape." He yawns.

He's obsessed with our SUV and I haven't driven myself anywhere since we got it.

"You're in pretty good shape from where I stand." I nudge him playfully, trying to lighten the mood.

A crooked, half-awake smile pulls at his face.

"Well, Theo sent me a text and everything went smoothly last night. You guys can come over and crash if you want." Nikolai makes a point of looking at each of us, Adalina included. "I feel like there's some catching up that needs to happen."

She freezes for a second, then nods. "I can follow. I'll be the first to receive any update, so if I'm there it'll cut out the middle man."

"But what about your kids?" I ask.

"It's their father's week. He gets one a month. The useless prick." She grumbles.

Touchy subject, got it.

"How old?" Charli's face lights up.

"Excuse my wife's obsession with babies." Nikolai wraps his arm around her and kisses the top of her head with a smile on his face.

"Oh, Mateo is almost two, and Andrea is only nine months. I hate being away from them, but he's not a *bad* dad. He just wasn't a good boyfriend to me, so I ended it." She shrugs.

"Oh my! Did you guys hear that! Ivy and Henderson can have a new bestie!" Charli claps, unnaturally energized.

"You'll have to excuse Charli, she's determined to collect as many kids as possible for their future gang," I joke, "Iris is already VP, and she's not even born yet." I rub my belly with a playful smirk.

"Oh, you're having a little girl? Adorable. I see you're sticking with musically inspired names." Addie chuckles.

"It was Jude's idea. I thought the name sounded cute with Ivy, so it all works out."

"For the record," Jude says, wrapping his arms around me, "I have musically themed names picked out for the next... hmm seven or so."

"Oh *hell* no. I'm with Claire on the 'one and done' train." I shake my head. "This little runt has put me through the wringer."

"But you're so beautiful like this." He pouts, rubbing my belly softly. "I understand, though. It's been hard watching you go through everything."

"How about we give this one a little time, like Charli and Nicky?" I smile up at him.

"Not my choice either, Loverboy," Nikolai says flatl y.,"but the ladies run the show around here. No babies without their go-ahead."

"So unfair," I deadpan.

"Right? How dare we want a breather." Charli laughs humorlessly.

"I can confirm that a year in between babies is not enough." Adalina huffs out an exhausted breath.

"Great, now we're outnumbered." Nikolai turns to my father. "If you can hear me, you'd better wake up and help us convince these two, and Claire, that more babies are needed in the very near future." He squeezes Dad's hand.

For a second I almost forgot why we're here. My throat feels tight again when I look at how lifeless he is.

"He'll be fine for a few hours. Let's go get some real sleep. I'm fucking beat." Leave it up to Nikolai to bring a bit of humor to our darkest days.

I kiss my father on the cheek, and Jude squeezes his shoulder before we leave.

Everything in me is worried sick, but the people by my side have me, and I know it.

No matter what happens, I'm not alone this time.

CHAPTER 34

Caroline

We slept hard. Adalina stuck around for a little bit but had to go back to work. It's lunch time now, so the guys are making food for everyone. I'll give it to Jude, he's come a long way in the kitchen with Nikolai's guidance. It's amazing having men around who cook, even if they're currently using it as a distraction.

The homemade sauce they've whipped up smells divine, but I won't be able to eat it. For once, it has nothing to do with Iris and her hatred for anything delicious. Still, I sit at the kitchen island, watching two of my three favorite men work.

A timer dings, and Jude pulls a tray of cheesy garlic bread from the oven.

Dad loves garlic bread.

Burying my face in my hands, I let the tears flow freely. Silent sobs shake my body. Jude, attentive as ever, drops what he's doing and comes to comfort me. Wrapped in his arms, I wail, releasing a fresh wave of emotions.

"Hey, now. I've got you," he murmurs softly against me.

Melting into him, I continue to cry. "I-I just want him to be here." My hands clutch at his shirt

"I know. Just try to breathe for me, okay? The stress isn't good for anyone, especially you. Can you imagine the lecture he's going to give you if you worry yourself sick and put Iris in danger?" He presses a soft kiss to the top of my head.

"How am I the only one upset about this?!" I shriek. "You're all so... so calm!"

"You think I'm calm?!" Nikolai snaps, his voice sharp with pain, "I'm barely holding on to my fucking sanity. You're not the only one who loves him, you know. Claire and Theo are wrecked, Bailey and Sean haven't stopped checking in. I'm the middle man for EVERYONE and I'm about to lose my fucking mind." His chest rises and falls rapidly as he vents. "You think I'm *calm*? Fuck no! I'm falling apart at the seams and hoping some off-brand duct tape will hold me together." He blows out a harsh breath. "I love you, and I'm sorry you think I don't care, but I do. I care so fucking much I'm pushing my own hurt down into the abyss just so I can *be here* for everyone else." He tosses a dirty saucepan in the sink with more force than necessary.

"Nicky. I-I'm sorry," I rasp out, "I didn't mean it like that. I know this is hard on you too. You're always the anchor, the rock, the pillar of love and support." I slip off the stool and round the corner to where he's standing.

"Come here, let it out." I hold my arms out and he crumbles into me. Charli, drawn in by the commotion, joins our embrace, wrapping herself around us. Jude rounds out our huddle and pulls the three of us close in his arms. Together, we slip to the floor in a mess of limbs as Nikolai sobs.

I don't think I've seen him this upset since Mom died. The four of us stay tangled on the kitchen floor, letting Nikolai be as broken as he needs. Minutes pass as his body shudders. Jude and Charli cry silently beside us, but I can't hold back my own pain. Together, we soak each other's shoulders with molten tears.

"We-we can't lose him," Nikolai chokes out.

"We won't. He's too stubborn to let that happen," Jude says gently.

"He's stable and in great hands, Addie is back on shift and promised to let us know the instant anything changes," Charli adds, rubbing my back.

Nikolai swallows, trying to calm his rapid breaths. "I gave her my number. She'll keep me posted." He pulls away from my embrace, staring at the floor. "S-sorry for blowing up like that."

"You need time to... process too." My voice wavers. "I was being selfish. You don't need to apologize. I love you."

He smiles softly at me. "I love you too, Parasite."

And just like that, he's back.

"I hate that we can't be there," I mumble, fidgeting with the hem of my shirt.

"We can go back later when it's visitin' hours," Jude says, brushing the hair out of my face as I turn to look at him.

"P-promise?" My lip quivers.

"Of course. Til then, you gotta try and eat somethin', alright? Can you do that for me?" His warm hands frame my face.

"I can try."

We pull ourselves together and return to lunch preparations. Jude takes over a lot of the remaining cooking duties so Nikolai can take a breather.

He sits beside me at the counter, mindlessly scrolling through his phone while Jude tosses fresh noodles into a pot of boiling water, humming to himself. I recognize the tune as "Let it Be" and hum along. His mouth curls into a warm smile as Nikolai and Charli join in. Before we know it, we've burst into a full chorus, singing loudly and off-key. None of us care in the slightest how terrible we sound. The moment is exactly what our troubled souls need.

Tears trail down my face as we belt the final note together. Nikolai wraps his arms around my shoulder, pulling me close while I cry it out. These tears carry the faintest trace of hope.

Jude dishes out four plates of spaghetti and meat sauce, sliding them across the island to us. He takes the empty seat next to me and kisses my cheek before swirling saucy pasta around his fork.

I move my food around the plate while they all dig in.

My stomach churns and lurches at the thought of eating any of it. I promised I'd try, but I don't know if I can. Lifting a forkful to my mouth, I inhale and stare at it, building my nerve.

Jude rubs my back, watching me intently. "Just a few bites. You can do it. Gotta make sure my girls are taken care of."

With a gentle nudge from him, I take a small nibble—and immediately groan.

Damn, that's good.

The next bite comes easier, as does each one after. The warm smile on Jude's face is a sweet reward.

"I'll clean up, you all go get a bit more sleep, we've got a bit before visiting hours start." Nikolai gathers our plates and begins wiping the counter down.

"You sure? I can help," Jude says, rising from his stool.

"I'm fine, you guys rest up. Especially you, Caroline." He pins me with a stern look.

"Yes, Bossy," I say, rolling my eyes with a soft laugh.

Charli follows us down the hall toward the bedrooms. "Sleep well. I'll make sure he's okay." She hugs me tightly.

She's been quiet, but I'm fairly sure it's just her way of coping with all of the chaos. Either way, I'm thoroughly exhausted and don't need to be told twice that a nap is overdue. Curling into Jude once we lie down, I let his warmth envelop me and, for a terrifying moment, relax.

The hospital feels lifeless and cold. Not in temperature, but the air feels heavy. Each breath is a struggle as we draw closer to Dad's room. The nurse rambles on about something I don't understand, but Nikolai nods along as if he does.

The four of us enter the room and, as expected, are met with nothing more than the faint hum of machines and periodic beeps of monitors. I hate the thought of him waking up alone in this blank, sterile space. Stupid visitation policies. He needs someone here—all the time.

What kind of heartless creature makes such dumb rules?

"Ah, you all made it!" Adalina beams as she enters the room. "I have good news. It seems his heart attack was not as severe as we initially suspected. While he's still comatose, I'm fairly confident it's temporary. We're monitoring him very closely. I've asked the nurses to increase the frequency of their check-ins, in case he wakes up soon. All of his test results have been great. Waking up is likely to be the hardest part of his recovery."

"So, you really think he's going to make it?" Nikolai asks, tentative excitement creeping into his voice.

"Yes. He's not completely out of the woods yet, and anything could still happen, but based on his latest scans he's going to be fine." She nods, and continues, "You're welcome to stay through visiting hours. If Caroline—being his only immediate family member—would like to stay the night, we can allow it." Her expression is tight.

"Hell no," Jude says firmly.

"I second that," Nikolai agrees, "she's not about to stay here alone. Not when she could literally go into labor at any moment."

"I still have over three weeks left," I grumble, narrowing my eyes at him.

"Candy, you need your rest. The hospital staff will be here. Please." Jude's face falls.

"But... Dad needs me." My nose stings as tears begin to gather behind my eyes.

"Do you think he'd be happy knowing you're putting yourself and his grand baby through hell?" Folding his arms, Nikolai raises a brow at me.

"N-no," I mumble, eyes fixed on the floor, as I wipe the moisture from my face.

"Caroline, I know it's hard, but think about the big picture. The doctor said he's going to be okay, and putting yourself through this isn't helping anyone." Charli turns to face me, gently rubbing my shoulders. "We all love him, and would gladly stay if we could. But at the end of the day, he'd want us together."

"You're right." I chew my lip and glance at him, still and silent. "We'll just be here for him while we can."

"Trust me, everything will be fine. Enjoy your visit." Adalina nods and excuses herself.

I sit in the chair closest to the bed and take my father's hand in mine. For several minutes, we sit in solemn silence. Nobody moves. We barely even breathe.

I swear, that mechanical buzzing is the soundtrack to

purgatory. I sigh and squeeze Dad's hand, wishing for any sign of life. Nothing happens, but his hand is warm in mine, which is enough—for now.

"Remember that time at the cabin when I got that horrible splinter?" Nikolai asks.

"Yeah, you cried and Dad held you. Gosh. What were you, twelve? That was so long ago." I let out a small laugh. "You were a little dramatic, but he didn't judge you. Just let you cry it out."

"So he's always been a softie, huh?" Charli elbows him gently.

"The biggest. Dad was always supportive of us, no matter how silly we were. Hell, until Jude came along, my parents thought I was a lesbian." I belly laugh. "There was never an official conversation, but they definitely dropped plenty of hints."

"I remember the day I talked to them after I made you cry. I came over to apologize to you, and he pulled me aside. I was shittin' myself, thinkin' he was gonna kick my ass. You know what actually happened?" Jude sucks in a breath. "We sat on the back porch and he let me talk about my feelin's. Nobody had ever just... listened to me before. I must've said somethin' right, because he hugged me and told me he was proud of me—for bein' man enough to apologize." A tear rolls down his cheek.

"Oh, Jude. I'm so sorry for making him despise you." I squeeze his knee gently.

"Nah, he's a good father. I'd do the same. He's a fan of mine again, so we're fine." Jude reaches out and pats

Dad's leg softly.

We sit in silence for quite a while, drifting in and out of light slumber. Every one of us is exhausted—mentally and physically.

I'm almost completely asleep against Jude by the time Nikolai speaks up. "Well, unfortunately, visiting hours are over. So we need to go. You guys coming back over tonight? I've got people running the rescue, if there are any medical emergencies they can take them to the local clinic. Claire and Theo are watching Ivy and the dogs for the night again, just in case. I owe them a trip to Paris or something for being such dependable friends." He laughs as much as he can manage.

"Of course we're sleeping over. I'm not taking any chances," I say quickly.

After parting kisses and hand-squeezes, we head straight to Nikolai and Charli's house.

We make our way to the living room and all settle in on the couch. My legs rest in Jude's lap as he massages my feet. A random true crime show is playing on the TV and none of us need to say a word. This is family. I try to stay awake, but it's a losing battle.

I'm jostled, faintly aware of Jude carrying me to bed and wrapping us up. I'm not sure what time it is, but every hour is one closer to... whatever happens.

We sleep for a while, though it feels like only seconds before a frantic knock snaps me out of my dreams.

"Guys, get up," Nikolai calls out, his voice frantic, "he's awake."

CHAPTER 35

Jude

Anxious energy fills the car as we drive to the hospital. I still can't believe he's awake. Adalina didn't give Nikolai much information, just that he's alert and grumpy. I can't help but laugh to myself at the thought.

I can already picture Ivan waking up, scowling at the tubes and wires, probably making a big fuss about it. If his bed is anything like those God-awful chairs, he's bound to be extra cranky.

Nikolai's thumbs drum on the steering wheel as we wait for the light to turn green. He's uncharacteristically quiet, but I've chalked it up to nerves. We're all feeling them right now—of that I'm sure.

I may not be as emotionally invested as everyone else, but Ivan is still family. He's also a huge part of all of our lives, so I get it. If he's not okay, it's going to be heartbreaking. *Awake* isn't always a good thing. What if he has lasting effects? What if he can't be there for his babies the way he loves to be? He'll never be happy if he has to take a step back from the little ones.

Caroline worries her lower lip beside me. I take her hand in mine and squeeze gently. The strain on her face pulls at my heartstrings. God, if he's not okay, it's going to destroy her. I need to prepare myself for the potential storm heading our way.

"What the fuck is taking so long?" Nikolai curses at the light.

"Calm down, Killer. It's been red for two minutes," Charli says, rubbing his leg.

"Two minutes too long," he grumbles.

Caroline's silence speaks volumes. She's usually quick on the draw with a quip back at him. All I can do is be here and hope it's enough. I hate every excruciating second of this.

When we arrive at the hospital, everything moves in slow motion. We march with purpose to the reception desk, where Adalina is already waiting for us. She starts explaining a bunch of medical jargon as we practically sprint down the hall. I don't have the faintest idea what any of it means, except he's awake and seems normal.

The last few steps to his room feel endless. Our stomachs are in one giant collective knot as Adalina opens the door. Her voice sounds far away as she reminds us to approach carefully and not overwhelm him. Caroline completely ignores her and all but sprints to his bedside.

Under the fluorescent lights, he looks... normal. If it weren't for the machines and wires, you'd never know he was in a coma for almost forty-eight hours.

His face lights up when Caroline wraps herself around him. There's no sign of pain in his expression and he's smiling, genuinely smiling.

Huh. A near-death experience seems to have lifted his mood.

"Dad, I was so worried. Don't you ever do that to me again," Caroline sputters through her tears.

"I wouldn't dream of it, Solnyshko. Please don't worry. It's not good for little Iris."

Awake for less than an hour and already back to himself. I can't help but smile.

"You scared us there, Old Man," Nikolai says, stepping up to his other side and placing a hand on his shoulder.

"Needed to add a little excitement to our *very* boring lives." Ivan smirks.

"Pop," Charli scolds gently, "we were worried sick." She steps beside Nikolai and takes his hand.

Tears are already streaming down their faces.

I tuck my hands in my pockets and watch from the corner, afraid to intrude on their moment. Ivan's face is unnaturally kind when he looks at me. Unable to read his expression, my pulse spikes, neck tingling as my hairs rise.

"Jude, my boy." He pats the side of his mattress next to Caroline and I damn near fall apart from the warmth in his voice. "Come here."

Holding my breath, I sit carefully and wrap my arm

around her waist.

"Listen, Son," he says.

That does it—the dam breaks and my tears fall freely as I brace myself on the edge of the bed.

"I know I've been a right asshole. But you're a wonderful man. I'm so happy my daughter found you—and gave you the chance to make things right. You're going to be an amazing father, and the perfect husband for my Solnyshko." He takes my hand and smiles at me.

Good thing we're already in the hospital, because I might be having a stroke.

Say something.

"I love this family. Every single member, blood or not. Seein' how close y'all are, I don't blame you for bein' hard on me. But I'm glad to finally be out of the dog house."

"I love the way you love my family, Jude. It's made me love you too." He gives my fingers a gentle squeeze.

Get a crash cart. We've got a code blue.

Caroline sputters beside me, reminding me that we're not alone. She's trying to hold back her emotions, letting me have the moment. I pull her close, still looking at Ivan. "I love you—and this family—very much." I rest my cheek against Caroline's head.

"Okay," Adalina speaks up as she steps back into the room. "I have a few questions I need to ask, and then we need to run some tests. But first—Ivan how are you feeling?"

"Like I can't wait to be back in my own bed... it feels like I've been sleeping on a bag of bricks," he gruffs.

"I'm sorry to hear that. The good news is, as long as your tests look good, you should be in the clear to go home after another day or two. I just want to be sure there are no complications."

"That sounds amazing. Thank you, Dear. You were always a sweet girl. I'm glad to see you're doing what you love." He nods at her.

"Oh. Well, thank you. I'll leave you guys to it. I'll wait until you leave to come back. Then we can run those tests and discuss your recovery process." She tips her head and steps back out of the room.

"We love you, Pop. We'll be back tomorrow and see if Ivy can tag along. She misses you terribly." Nikolai pats his shoulder. "For now, we gotta love you and leave you."

We say our goodbyes and head back to the house.

Caroline and I are staying at our place tonight, since he's alive, awake, and completely unfazed. We can go visit on our own time, now that our fears have been eased.

"That was a lot. How are you feeling?" Caroline asks as we curl up in bed.

"Well, the last few days have been a blur. I don't know which way is up, and your dad told me he loves me today. All in all, I'm fuckin' fantastic." I press my lips to her forehead, and she giggles.

"That's all that matters... will you sing to us?" She rubs her belly with a pleading look in her eyes.

"Of course," I softly say, sliding down to face her

bump. Clearing my throat, I sing about four lines of "My Girl" before she's snoring softly.

With a content smile on my face, I pull her into me and close my eyes.

"Pop! Pop! Pop!" Ivy chants as she bounces around the living room. She has been his biggest fan since he got home—as if she wasn't before. The last couple of weeks have flown by. We're finally back on track with everything, and today is our first family dinner since Ivan's heart attack. Nikolai insisted we have a huge feast in, since it may very well be our last one before Iris arrives.

Her due date is next week, but who knows when she'll make her entrance into the world. She is her mother's daughter, so I wouldn't be surprised if she's a little late to the party. I'm growing more impatient by the day. So is her Pop.

Ivy and Henderson have been glued to him all day, and he's on cloud nine—but one more would make his heart feel even more full. He tells us so every chance he gets.

Technically, he says, "The more the merrier." But who's counting?

I think Nikolai may have actually talked Charli into baby number two, so Ivan might just get his soccer team yet.

"Jude, could you sous chef for me?" Nikolai calls from the kitchen.

Grinning brightly, I stroll into the room and don my emerald green apron—yes, I have my own now.

"What can I do for you, Chef?" I ask jokingly.

"God, I love it when you call me that." He elbows me gently.

"Shut up and tell me what you need."

"Cut these veggies in a nice julienne." He slides peppers and carrots my way. "We're making stir fry and dumplings. The wives will love it."

"They love anything you cook, to be fair." I shake my head and chuckle.

"Well, yeah... but still." He shrugs. "Never stop trying to impress them."

We work together like a well-oiled machine at this point. Cooking with Nikolai has become one of my favorite things to do. Fight night once a month with Bailey and Sean is great—don't get me wrong—but this is calming. The way our girls' faces light up when they take that first bite is the best reward. Maybe Nikolai's service kink is contagious.

I'll admit that delicate work like filling and folding the dumpling seams are not my strong suit. My big, clunky hands are *not* meant for intricate work—but that's where Nikolai comes in.

"It smells heavenly in here," Charli comments as she watches him fold the little wrappers with precision and bites her lip.

Neither of us heard her enter the room—who knows how long she's been standing there. We've been in the zone and completely engrossed in dinner duties. I'm fairly certain the hunger in her eyes has very little to do with the dumplings. He doesn't miss a beat, but the pinkness staining his cheeks means he's well aware of her ogling.

"I think I've seen you do enough of them, I can finish the rest." A knowing smirk tugs at my lips.

"That would be amazing." Charli smiles, rounding the corner to fist Nikolai's apron. "I'm going to need to borrow my husband for a little bit." She leads him out of the kitchen.

As they reach the doorway, Nikolai throws me a wink and mouths "Thank you." I laugh, tipping my head at him.

"Looks like you could use a hand." Theo strolls into the room and rounds the counter. "I'm no Nicky, but I can sauté with the best of them."

"Oh, thanks, man. I could definitely use the extra hands." My shoulders tense slightly.

Theo and I don't spend a lot of one-on-one time together. In the nearly nine months I've known him, we've yet to have any real conversations that aren't centered around the family. I don't think he dislikes me—he's just reserved. He's also cut from a different cloth and fits the "well-off suburban dad" mold perfectly.

"I think Caroline's nesting has given Charli a change of heart," he says with a playful tone.

"Yeah." I tip my head. "I reckon you're right. She's been all over Nicky this past week." Shaking my head, I attempt to pleat the dumpling in my hand like Nikolai had been doing.

"Maybe Pop being home and doing so well has played a part too." He tosses a few of the already made dumplings into a lightly oiled pan. "Claire actually sat me down and discussed trying for a second."

"No shit, that's huge." I drop the dumpling and turn to him. "She was so against having another."

"Yeah, but I'm pretty sure once Iris shows her pretty little face, it'll be a done deal. You two are also the cutest couple. The way Caroline lights up when she sees you—that's what love is supposed to look like."

Swallowing roughly, my words fail. All I can manage is a nod.

"You've had a pretty tough time, but we're your people now, Jude. Every single one of us has seen your heart and at your core, you're just as good as any one of us." He flashes a bright smile at me.

Several minutes—and many ugly dumplings—later, we throw the stir fry together and call everyone to the backyard. Setting the platters on the picnic table, I inhale the early April air. It's cool but fresh, and smells floral from the early blooms of tulips, daffodils, and hydrangeas planted around the house.

We're all sitting around the table, filling our plates, as Charli and a very rumpled-looking Nikolai emerge and join us. He adjusts his glasses and smooths his shirt before plating up a serving for Charli and handing it to her with a love-drunk grin. There's definitely another

Koval on the horizon.

A faint trickling sound breaks through the silence. "Uh, guys... " Caroline's voice beside me is laced with panic. Our eyes all snap to her pale face. "M-my water just broke."

CHAPTER 36

Caroline

Pain. That's all I can focus on as another contraction hits. I'm curled up in the back seat of Nikolai's Tahoe, cursing Jude's name with every fiber of my being as he holds me. My entire posse is following close behind in their cars.

I feel like a celebrity with this massive entourage. As soon as I announced Iris's impending arrival, everyone sprung into action like a well-rehearsed evacuation plan. Fortunately, I've been keeping my go-bag on hand, and our car seat stays in the Mazda, waiting to be needed. We've prepared for this. I just wasn't prepared for *this*. Braxton Hicks contractions were child's play compared to the real deal.

Doubling over in Jude's lap, I scream as another contraction tries to tear my body in half. "Your dick is the devil." I fist his shirt and clench my jaw.

Based on the tight smirk he's fighting, Jude wants to laugh but knows better. Instead, he lays a cold compress on the back of my neck and massages my scalp.

"Shit, they're already four minutes apart. Traffic needs to get the fuck out of my way," Nikolai grumbles from the driver's seat.

"Nicky, please stay calm for Caroline's sake." Charli's voice is soft and soothing.

The drive isn't long and Jude already called to let my doctor know it's about to be a long night. But the sooner I can get an epidural, the better.

Jude carries me into the hospital, straight to the front desk. I've never appreciated his strength so much before this moment. The receptionist's face flashes with shock until she takes in the sight. She moves quickly, getting a wheelchair and leading us to the labor and delivery wing. Jude is the only one allowed in the room with me, but I know the rest of my family is as close by as possible.

"Well, Miss Koval, you're five centimeters dilated already. It appears you're in for a fast delivery. In just a moment we'll administer the epidural and get you started on an IV for fluids." My doctor skims through my birth plan and leaves the room.

Jude sits at the side of my bed, holding my hand through the next contraction and accompanying string of curses. Before I know it, a sweet anesthesiologist enters the room and outlines the risks and process of the epidural, giving me a final chance to change my mind.

Hell no. Gimme the magic.

Jude steadies me, tracing reassuring circles on my hand with his thumb as I hold my breath. The pain of the needle isn't even in the same universe as my contractions.

Relief comes almost immediately. Sighing, I lay back in the bed and squeeze Jude's hand. His face is soft but edged with worry. He's been quiet throughout the process so far, watching intently as the nurses strapped monitors to me and my belly. Curiosity dances across his face as he watches the little heart rate on the screen.

"I love you. Sorry if I said anything too nasty." I squeeze his hand.

"I mean, in the midst of everything, I'm inclined to agree that I am a giant asshole with an evil dick." He laughs. "I love you, too... insults included."

"I did *not* say that! Did I?" My mouth gapes as the monitors beep, signaling a contraction. "Oh gosh, they're getting closer together... I didn't even feel it though. When should we start to worry?"

"We don't need to worry. The monitors will alert your doctor when it's time. Until then, just breathe, Sweetness. You're doin' amazing." His grip on my hand tightens reassuringly.

Tears pool in my eyes. "There's nobody else I'd rather do this with," my voice trembles. "You're not an asshole... and I love your dick."

He lets out a boisterous laugh. "We'll see if that changes after Iris is here."

God, I love hearing him say her name. The way his eyes sparkle when he talks about her makes all of this worth it. Sure, the pregnancy was horrible and the pain made me want to die, but his excitement makes my heart flutter with pure love. This little girl is going to own him, and I can't wait to see it unfold.

Exhausted and finally comfortable, I sigh and relax back into my pillow. Faint pressure is all I feel when my contractions come. Jude runs his fingers through my hair and sings until I can't feel anything but his love for me.

"Rise and shine." His voice breaks the silence. "The doctor is here, your contractions are saying it might be time."

"Wh-what?" I croak. "How long was I asleep?"

"Maybe four hours, off and on," Jude answers.

"WHAT?! How? You were just talking to me." My eyes bulge.

"You were exhausted, so I let you sleep while I kept watch."

"It's got to be so late. Have you checked on the others?"

"Sweetness, they're fine. I've been talkin' to them in the group chat. Your dad is having a meltdown right now, can't say I blame him."

"Wait, what? What's wrong with Dad?"

"It's eleven fifty-eight..." The way his voice trails off makes my mind race.

When the realization hits me, I break out into a heavy sob. "I wasn't even thinking about the date. She wasn't due for another week."

"Well, based on your dilation, she'll be here very soon," the doctor—who I had completely forgotten about—chimes in.

My heart squeezes, maybe it's a contraction, I don't know.

Everything happens in a blur, the next two hours are a flurry of pushing and breathing exercises. Finally, after I bear down with all my remaining strength, Jude gasps and releases a sob as Iris lets out her first cry. Tears blur my vision as they lay her on my chest. Jude peppers my forehead with kisses, only stopping to cut the umbilical cord. He wipes both of our tears, laying his eyes on the golden-haired angel wailing between us.

"She's perfect. You're perfect," he chokes out between tears. "I-I need to let the family know." He pulls his phone out and fires off a message to everyone.

The medical team makes quick work of the necessary exams and treatments, finally taking her to be weighed. The three of us are given I.D. bracelets and whisked away to our postpartum recovery room.

My father, Nikolai and Charli are our first visitors once we're settled.

"What a gift you are." Dad wipes his tears while cooing over Iris. "You two made a precious little angel. Hair just like her mama and Mimi. She would have loved to share her birthday with you sweet one."

The air in the room gets thin as we all fully process the information. As if him saying it made it real.

"We're proud of you." Nikolai kisses my forehead softly.

"She's the cutest little thing. Oh my goodness," Charli wails, with tears running down her face, "She looks just like a perfect little blend of you two. Jude's deep, soulful eyes and olive complexion, a full head of Caroline's hair, and those rosy little cheeks. Look at herrrrr."

I'm half awake when everyone else makes their rounds, but I faintly hear each of them come in, share their adoration and congratulations, then go.

Peeking my eyes open after Bailey and Sean leave, I was planning to ask Jude what he's going to do while I sleep. Instead, I'm given a front row seat to his first real chance at bonding with Iris. Everything has been so hectic the past few hours, he's just now able to hold her.

He's not aware that I'm awake and is sitting in the rocking chair with Iris tucked securely against his bare chest, swaying gently. Love radiates off of him as he softly begins to sing her song. I close my eyes, letting his voice lull me to sleep.

Our first few weeks at home have been an adjustment. I couldn't even fathom doing this without Jude. The fact that Nikolai has forbidden either of us from even thinking about work helps.

We've settled into a nice routine, and Iris is much nicer now that she's outside of my body. She sleeps so much and hardly ever fusses. When she does, just a few soothing coos from Jude and she settles down immediately.

Same, Princess. Same.

We're on our way to Nikolai and Charli's house for an official welcome-home celebration. It's going to be the first time we'll all be together again and I can't wait to see my family all in one place. Everyone has stopped by randomly since we've been home, but that's not the same.

When we pull up the driveway, Nikolai flings the front door open and waves from the porch.

"Someone's a little excited." Jude chuckles as he parks the car and hops out. He comes around and opens my door first, kissing my cheek as he helps me to my feet. Cannoli hops out when he opens the back door, running into the house—to find Navy, no doubt. Jude hands me the diaper bag to carry. After he unloads Iris, we make our way inside.

There is an entire buffet spread out across Nikolai's kitchen: a taco bar, pizzas, cupcakes, muffins, a build-your-own burger table. The chocolate fountain and fruit catch my eye. I haven't had much chocolate in the last few weeks and that flowing goodness is calling my name. As much as I want to indulge, I know the living room needs to be our first stop. There's a bunch of eager aunties and uncles waiting to fawn over our princess.

"There they are!" Charli jumps up from her spot on the couch. "Look at this precious girl! I'll never get over how much hair she has."

"Same. I can practically put it in pigtails already." Jude beams.

"How are you two holding up?" Claire asks, stepping next to Charli.

"We're great. I would be a mess if not for Jude, he's amazing." I lean against him and he kisses the top of my head.

"Okay, okay, let me through." Dad pushes his way between them, and I watch as his face turns to mush. "My sweet Malish." He bends down and carefully scoops her out of the car seat in Jude's hand. Shuffling slowly to the recliner in the corner, he sits and curls her into his chest.

"Come sit, Jude." Theo pats the spot next to him on the couch. "Tell me about your adventures in fatherhood."

He squeezes my shoulder and I leave him to it, wandering back to the kitchen. Charli and Claire follow close behind.

"His world revolves around her already, huh?" Charli asks.

"Oh yeah." I sigh with a smile. "It's *so* sexy. Something about him treating her like the most precious thing ever makes me melt."

"Are you being taken care of too?" Claire quirks a brow.

"Oh yeah. *Very* well." A coy grin pulls at my lips.

"Girl! You're supposed to give it time to heal." Charli covers her mouth and laughs.

I swirl a strawberry through the melted chocolate and

take a bite, groaning as my taste buds light up. "We're not having actual sex... yet. But when I see him doting on her—and my gosh when he sings to her—I get all flustered. He's attentive and makes sure *all* of my needs are met, too."

Claire sighs, fanning her face. "Stop. You'll remind me of how great Theo was with baby Hennie and I might be tempted to revisit that."

Charli dips her own strawberry and shrugs. "I'm fairly certain I might be pregnant as we speak."

"What?!" Claire and I squeal in unison.

"Girlie, you can *not* just gloss over that." My jaw hangs open.

"I don't know for sure, but I've been all over Nikolai for the past couple of months and my cycle is a few days late. I'm going to wait and test in a week, just to be sure."

"Oh my, Nikolai is going to go ballistic. That man loves kids." Claire pops a melon ball into her mouth.

"It's genetics, have you *seen* my father?" I laugh.

"All of our men do, to be fair. Theo is conservative with his affection, but don't let him fool you, that man is a giant softie. He's just not big on PDA." Claire smiles.

"Well, I'll stand here and eat all this chocolate if we don't get a move on. Let's rejoin the crew." I nod toward the living room and lead the way.

My father has managed to relinquish his claim on Iris and has now wrangled Henderson and Ivy in her place. Sean hands Iris to Theo and his normally flat face comes to life with her in his arms.

Claire swoons next to me. "Lord help me," she mumbles under her breath.

I round the couch to sit next to Jude, who pulls me into his side. Charli finds her spot on Nikolai's lap. Claire claims her seat next to Theo and smiles warmly at Iris.

A lone tear trails down my face as I take in the love surrounding me.

I close my eyes and tip my head back imagining my mother's smiling face as she watches over us.

EPILOGUE

Jude – 6 Months Later

My palms are itchy. I'm sweating bullets. The gnats are going to eat me alive if I don't calm down. But how am I supposed to keep my cool in a moment like this? Our friends are all seated in front of me, watching my every move. I might actually pass out.

Breathe. In and out. Nice and steady. You can do this.

I stand beneath the flower-covered arch in the field behind the family cabin—the same field Caroline's mother had her ashes scattered in. It's the closest we could get to having her here with us.

When the violin cover of "I Don't Want to Miss a Thing" begins to play, my stomach threatens to escape through my throat.

Nikolai and Charli lead the way as best man and maid of honor. Charli's dress barely contains her growing belly. Their son is due in just a couple of months. She's radiant in a deep green gown as Nikolai—in matching slacks, a white shirt, and a pink bow-tie—guides her gently down the aisle.

Theo, who has become one of my closest friends, follows in a blush pink suit, walking arm-in-arm with Claire. Her matching gown nearly conceals her own baby bump. Apparently seeing Theo with Iris really did her in. They're keeping baby number two's gender a surprise, which is surprising in itself, considering their mutual love for order and structure.

Bailey, in dark green pants, struts down the aisle, arm linked with Sean, who's wearing baby pink slacks. Their white shirts are paired with simple black ties. Bailey takes his place on my side of the arch, while Sean takes his place alongside Claire.

The music shifts again, and a soft orchestral cover of "Brown Eyed Girl" filters through the air and the officiant invites our guests to stand. My knees almost fail me as Ivan steps into view. His suit—nearly identical to mine—is black with an emerald undershirt and pink tie.

And then I see her.

My soon-to-be wife. Her long white dress, adorned with pink beading, flows loosely with an ethereal grace. We had it altered to accommodate the few inches our baby boy required. She's a little over four months along, and this pregnancy has been much easier on her. We plan to announce the gender tonight. Ivan is going to be thrilled to have so many little ones around. He officially retired after his heart attack, but at the rate we're going, he won't notice the difference.

He and Caroline share a loving hug at the far end of the aisle before beginning their march toward me—toward our future.

Nikolai sniffles behind me, and I close my eyes for a moment to compose myself. Our gazes lock as they grow closer. The adoration alight in her golden stare just about seals my fate. When they reach us, Ivan kisses her cheek and shakes my hand.

"Hi," she whispers breathlessly from across the arch.

We link our fingers together, and I know she can feel how hard I'm trembling.

"H-hi." I swallow hard, and a single tear escapes. "You're perfect."

A tear filled laugh bubbles out of her and she sniffles to keep her emotions in check.

After the officiant speaks, he asks us to exchange vows. Caroline chooses to go first, and I instantly wish I had.

"Jude," she says, locking eyes with me. "There was a time in my life when nothing made sense and then you showed up. Everything clicked, and my soul lit on fire. I used to wish our love was something out of a fairytale, so we could've had our happily-ever-after right away but that's not how it happened. The truth is, we're two imperfect people who are perfect for each other, and I'm thankful for everything we had to overcome to get here. Nothing worth having comes easy, and we're worth every bit of work it took." She almost stumbles over the last few words, struggling to hold back tears.

I gently wipe beneath her eyes, careful not to smudge her makeup.

Clearing my throat, I inhale deeply and return my gaze

to hers. "Caroline, I knew you were it for me the second your warm, honey-colored eyes locked on to mine. I felt it in the very fabric of my being. I'd always been lost and alone, driftin' through life on a prayer, but in that moment, I knew you were the answer. Even durin' the years we were apart, all I could do was think about you. No matter how bad things got, just the thought of you helped keep me goin'. You're my everything. The love of my life. The mother of my children." I place my hand over her belly. "And now, you're about to be my wife. I can't wait to share your last name. I'm yours. Forever. You're my home."

"By the power vested in me, I now pronounce you husband and wife. You may kiss your bride." The officiant barely finishes before I wrap my arms around Caroline and dip her into a passionate kiss. She lets out a surprised squeak, giggling against my lips as our friends and family erupt into cheers.

"Ladies and gentlemen, may I be the first to introduce Mr. and Mrs. Koval!"

I lift *my wife* into my arms and carry her down the aisle as our adoring loved ones wipe their tears.

This beautifully unorthodox group of people—with all their quirks and differences—fits so perfectly together it could only *ever* be called one thing: family. And I'm so thankful they're mine.

About the Author

Rii Finley is a coffee-drinking, music-loving introvert. She finds joy in all kinds of creative outlets from painting and sculpting to writing (obviously). She loves animals and has two rambunctious boxer dogs. The Spotify team is probably concerned by how much of her listening time is consumed by Sleep Token.

Romance novels are her escape—her happy place—she's usually reading one on her phone in her down time.

If you love good banter and lighthearted humor in the midst of chaos, and prefer your books spicy and heartfelt with a splash of darkness, you've found your new favorite author!

Acknowledgements

To John, again. Thank you for believing in me and only picking on my smut scenes a LOT... You're lucky I love you.

To My amazing Alpha and Beta readers: I wouldn't have been able to contain this chaos without you! Thank each and every one of you for laughing, crying, and swooning with me along the ride. Every draft was special and your continued love and support made this possible.

Honorable mentions

Lexi for once again feeding my delusion through all of this.

Kimberly for helping with clarification and wording choices.

Cerys for being amazing and giving grammar feedback along the way.

Keep up wtih Rii

Hi there! If you've made it this far, I must have done something right! If you want to stay up-to-date on my current and future projects. **RiiFinley.com** has all my relevant links!

Thanks for reading!

www.ingramcontent.com/pod-product-compliance
Lightning Source LLC
Chambersburg PA
CBHW020010120726
47903CB00004B/1220